ALL OUR YESTERDAYS

KENNETH N. PRICE

Published in Australia by Sid Harta Books & Print Pty Ltd,
ABN: 34632585293
23 Stirling Crescent, Glen Waverley, Victoria 3150 Australia
Telephone: +61 3 9560 9920, Facsimile: +61 3 9545 1742
E-mail: author@sidharta.com.au

First published in Australia 2024
This edition published 2024
Copyright © Kenneth N. Price 2024
Cover design, typesetting: WorkingType (www.workingtype.com.au)

ISBN: 978-1-922958-84-6

ACKNOWLEDGEMENTS

The photo on the cover of this book was taken by my wife, Luzvisminda, who has a keen eye for unusual angles and inspirational imagery. I was her hand model for this photo.

On summer evenings, we often take walks on Urangan Pier, where we can enjoy a cool breeze rising from the calm waters of Hervey Bay and the magical moment of a glowing sun as it sets behind Point Vernon.

The helicopter image was inserted into the photo by the creative effort of Luke Harris, a print designer who creates covers for Sid Harta Publishers. Many thanks, Luke, for creating meaningful images for all my books.

My thanks also to Kerry Collison who agreed to publish my three books, especially my third book, *All Our Yesterdays*, a book expressing ideas that I carried with me all my life, and whose publication means so much to me.

May I also thank my editor, Susan NicholsonPierotti, whose sound advice and expert editing was much appreciated.

*This book is dedicated to all those
who served in Vietnam.*

CONTENTS

PREFACE

This photograph was taken of me in the front yard of my parent's home just prior to my leaving for Vietnam. Although this work is written in the first person, it is not an autobiography. Jason's story is not my story. However, I have drawn heavily on my experience for many of the scenes in this book. I chose the first person because I am hopeful that it will help my readers better appreciate the personal anguish that many Vietnam veterans went through at this time.

My purpose was to create characters who best illustrate the struggle that individuals of my generation had to contend with while trying to accommodate the extensive social, economic and political forces of change shaping their lives. I have tried to be objective by presenting as many sides as possible of the arguments that I can remember that Australians made about the Vietnam War. If I have overlooked any viewpoints, please forgive my human imperfections; it was not done intentionally. The Vietnam War was a war that divided our nation and left many with lasting scars, both physical and mental, and introduced cultural changes that are still with us today.

Special note: I know that national servicemen from Australian states other than New South Wales and Queensland did their recruit training at Puckapunyal and not Kapooka, so David would have done his recruit training at Puckapunyal. However, for the purpose of my narrative, I had to place him in Kapooka, where he would meet Jason, Nick and Toby.

Also, I recognise there is no casualty clearing station (CCS) in Melbourne, but I had to locate Jason and Toby in Melbourne for the purpose of my narrative. My unit posting was to 3CCS at Wacol Army Camp between Brisbane and Ipswich, so I wanted to draw on my experience at a CCS for my story.

Furthermore, I felt it necessary to locate my narrative in Melbourne, since that was the centre of the protest movement against the Vietnam War. For those purists, please forgive my use of poetic license.

And all our yesterdays have lighted fools

The way to dusty death. Out, out, brief candle!

William Shakespeare, Macbeth.

HISTORICAL BACKGROUND

On 1 October 1949, mainland China fell to Mao Zedong and the Chinese Communist Party (CCP). Chiang Kai-Shek and his Kuomintang (nationalist) forces fled to Formosa (now Taiwan). The new Chinese government became known as the People's Republic of China (PRC) while the new government of Formosa called itself the Republic of Formosa (now Taiwan).

What occurred on mainland China, after the Kuomintang withdrawal, was capital and land confiscation, along with local denunciations, persecutions and executions of Christians and the Chinese middle class, as China went through its own reign of terror. Many who feared persecution fled to Vietnam, where they sought protection from the communists by the French colonial government. However, the French were themselves fighting a guerrilla war against the communists (known then as the Viet Minh) led by Ho Chi Minh.

On 7 May 1954, the battle of Dien Bien Phu ended in the humiliating defeat of the French. Following this, the French negotiated a peace treaty and fled Vietnam. The peace treaty established the 17th Parallel as a temporary demarcation of Vietnam into North and South. The North became known as the Democratic Republic of Vietnam, the capital of which was in Hanoi where the communists took control. In the south, the state of South Vietnam was established, the capital of which was in Saigon and was led by the former Vietnamese emperor,

Bao Dai. (This state would later evolve into the Republic of Vietnam led by President Ngo Dinh Diem.)

Most of the Chinese who had fled communist China along with Christians and those Vietnamese who did not wish to live under communism now fled North Vietnam for the south. Most of the communists who resided in the south never left for the north.

What followed was a titanic struggle, involving the bloodletting of millions (number taken from the *British Medical Journal*) over the spread of communism in South-east Asia and the American foreign policy of containment. Essentially, the conflict involved the communists of the north (North Vietnamese army, NVA) and the communists in the South (Viet Cong), who were backed by Russia and wanted a united Vietnam controlled by a single communist regime modelled on the Soviet system, and the south who wanted to maintain a free, democratic government in the south modelled on the American system. Some argue this point, however, claiming that South Vietnam was never really free or democratic and never sought the reunification of Vietnam. Unfortunately, what followed for the men and women of both North and South Vietnam and their allies was a war that tore apart the lives of so many.

Australia's commitment to the Vietnam War lasted from 1962 to 1973 and involved more than 60,000 Australians servicemen and women. In 1964, a scheme of selective conscription was introduced in Australia, which created a standing army of 40,000 full-time soldiers. During the war, 521 Australians were killed and over 3,000 wounded. After the war, alcohol and/or drug addiction, anxiety, depression and suicide became endemic among the Vietnam veteran community.

PROLOGUE

When I was young and eager for the world, my father told me,
'Son, you can become anything you want, because you live in
a free country. The only limit you have is the limit you place
on yourself.'

And my mother said, 'Jason, whatever you do in life, know
that we will always love you. Just do your best and try to be a
good person, and remember we will stand by you, no matter
what.'

They said it truly, and I believed them.

CHAPTER 1

Something different

Morning came slowly the day my journey began. Delayed by a broken line of cloud clustered on the horizon, the new light struggled before bursting forth over the hidden shadows of a now fading night. The prospect of a trip into a big city had kept me awake into the early hours, so I awoke tired and gazed passively out the train window at the flickering landscape.

This journey was the beginning of a major change in my life and I contemplated it with mixed feelings. I had been conscripted into the Australian army at a time when many people were beginning to doubt the legitimacy of the war in Vietnam and the ethics of selective conscription, but my feeling was that the part I would play would be something completely different from anything I had come to expect in my life. The exciting prospect of travel and adventure had built an eagerness in me to get started. I also believed I was following in the footsteps of my ancestors, who had never hesitated to defend the freedom of their country and the freedom of others overseas who were prepared to fight for theirs.

I also had a sense of being part of something larger than myself; something directing the lives of many people that would create something momentous in my generation. However small my role in this adventure would be, I had to let it happen and see it for myself. I settled back into the large, old leather seat I was sitting on and closed my eyes, letting the gentle rocking motion sooth me into a shallow slumber.

The train stopped with a jolt. We were at a railroad station and were given a few minutes for refreshments. I yawned, stretched and rubbed my eyes and casually made my way to the dining room.

The usual railroad station rush was on. The clink and clatter of white porcelain. The urgent rattling of cutlery. Raised eyebrows and hands trying to catch a waitress's attention. I was next. No. Can't you see me? I'm next. All said without a spoken word. I waited until the crowd had thinned before I ordered white tea without sugar and a buttered scone. The waitress asked for fifteen cents. I gave her the correct change, then retired to a quiet corner.

Railway dining rooms have always held a fascination for me. They are big with high ceilings and large windows and doors. They have wooden floors and timber walls and brass and clay pots which are always clean and well-polished. They have palms and hanging ferns, which are always bright, green and healthy. But, most of all, they always have travellers who generate excitement; excitement about the travel itself or the mystery of the unexpected.

My tea was hot, the scone was fresh and the breeze from the ceiling fan was soft and refreshing, its blades moving in a slow, relaxed rhythm. The waitress who had served me came out with a damp cloth and wiped a few tables. When she reached my table, she stopped and caught my attention.

'Whaddya think about the dollars and cents?' she asked, holding up a ten-cent coin.

Her question puzzled me, because the arguments about the

currency change had so many dimensions to it. I noticed she was pretty with blonde hair pulled up at the back, a few loose strands falling loosely into her eyes.

'I ... don't know,' I said, my attention riveted on the ten-cent coin. 'I haven't really thought much about it,' I hurried to add and felt my cheeks begin to burn.

'Yeah. Well, we all thought it was gunna cause a lot of trouble, but it didn't. Been pretty simple really with the ten cents being the same as a shillin' and the twenty cents the same as two bob, ya know?'

'Yes. I see.'

I really didn't know what to say after that. She stood there for a while but neither of us said anything.

'Yeah. Well, see ya,' she finally said.

'Yes. Goodbye.'

She walked away and for the first time I noticed the curves of her body. She looked strong and athletic with smooth, narrow hips.

I took another mouthful of tea. What could I have said about the currency change? I suppose the real uncertainty about change happens before it actually takes place. Once the change has occurred, we accommodate it and then wonder what it was like before. I suppose that was happening now; people were already nostalgic about the old sterling currency instead of uncertain about the new dollars and cents.

I wonder if our leaders, who introduce new ideas, give much thought to the everyday implications of the decisions they make, or if they only consider their perception of the national interest. Undoubtedly, the currency change was beneficial and in the national interest, but it did create uncertainty.

I remembered I had had to take my bankbook into the bank

and get it changed over to dollars and cents. That had worried me until it was done. Once I accepted the new money, I didn't worry about it anymore. Mum said some of the shops used the changeover to put their prices up. With twelve pence being squeezed into ten cents, I guess they could have done that.

Mum was philosophical about it. She's that way about most things, really. When she saw me off this morning, for instance, she wouldn't come on to the station platform. She cried and hugged me on the footpath outside.

'I'll say my goodbyes here, Jason,' she said. 'If I go in there, I'll think they are taking you away from me. I've known all along that I'd have to give you up someday, but I want to feel like I'm doing the giving and not someone else doing the taking.'

I'm not sure I understood, but I said I did, and that seemed to make her happy. I remember thinking Mum was a funny one, because when I went in for my medical tests, she said they had better not say anything was wrong with me. Dad went with me and waited anxiously outside the doctor's room like a defence lawyer waiting for the jury's decision.

When it became clear that I would enter the army, Dad took me into the back yard where we sat in the warm afternoon sunshine. He gave me a beer, which made me feel grown up, and told me I was now a man. 'I know you can't legally drink until you're twenty-one, but you'll do plenty of drinking in the army, so you may as well start now with me,' he said. He then recalled some of his experiences during the war against Japan, laughing and chuckling between long periods of earnest concern and sorrow.

Then he turned serious. He drew my attention to some palm trees in the garden. 'These are a very ancient form of life,' he said, while I nodded. 'They hold a secret for survival that few people realise. See the parts that are dead and decaying while new growth pushes up enlarged and enriched by the old?' I nodded again. 'That's the secret of survival in this life, son. You've got to keep regenerating, growing, casting off the old and pushing on to the new. Never be afraid to let go while reaching out for something new. It's those who try to resist renewal, those who try to keep things exactly as they are, who become bitter and stale, fossilised in a life that eventually entombs them. Right now, you work for someone else, and you have no other responsibilities for anyone other than yourself, but you will want to get married soon and start a family, so you'll take on responsibilities that you don't have now. Don't be afraid of these changes in your life. Embrace them, son.'

He looked at me and smiled. 'Listen to me,' he said, 'pretending I know what I'm talking about. All I can say is I've been reasonably happy, and I've never resisted life. Some of it was good, some bad, but I've never tried to hide from it. Let it happen, son, and when it does, keep growing with it.'

This made me think back over my life. I had been an only child. Mum and Dad had tried for others, but, for some reason, conception was either difficult or the pregnancy would not hold. This made them very protective of me, always trying to give me what they had wanted for themselves.

Mother was religious. Whenever I asked her about her faith, she said simply that she loved Jesus and tried to follow his teachings. She would never go beyond this and, if I questioned the motives of some Christians, she would explain that we are all responsible for our own salvation and what others do should not affect what we do. I never really understood her religious commitment. For me, church going was a selfish pursuit; I always felt like a fringe dweller whenever I attended.

She also played the piano and liked classical music. Brahms and Handel were her favourites, and Sundays she would usually play Handel's *Messiah* before leaving for church. She had me take piano lessons, but I never went beyond the easier pieces, my teenage years being more responsive to modern rhythm and blues than to the classical masters. I preferred the Animals and Percy Sledge to Brahms or Handel. Mother's disappointment was apparent, but she tried not to show it.

At high school, History and English had been my favourite subjects and, since graduation, I had continued to read. English, American and Australian history and literature were my favourites, and this had made me something of an amateur in these areas. I had found work in a local music store, which carried a reasonable range of instruments and sheet music; the bulk of our sales, however, came from popular records, guitars and amplifiers. Music in the sixties, with the rise of rock 'n' roll, rhythm and blues and soul had become the domain of youth, and I got to know the young musicians in our city.

When my call-up eventually came, there was some talk among my friends about trying for an exemption because I was an only child. I was also worried that two years in the army would ruin my chances of opening my own business, but Dad would have none of this. 'Other boys are going. You take your medicine like everyone else, son,' he said. 'You'll never respect yourself if you don't do right by your country.'

Mum made me promise to attend church whenever I could, showing her concern for my lack of spiritual commitment. I knew she worried about my finding the right girl to 'settle down with'. As a teenager, I had been very shy when around girls, probably because I had no sisters to grow up with.

Thankfully, the pimples that had plagued me with a lack of confidence and had delayed my maturity were now gone, but my inexperience with the opposite sex still showed whenever I was around them.

Although we never spoke of my going, I did think about it. What would army life be like? Would I get on with the other blokes? Would I go to Vietnam? Be wounded? Killed? I tried to push these thoughts out of my mind, because I knew I would go and there was little point in wasting time worrying about it. It was time to put aside my old life and push on to a new one.

When he saw me off this morning, Dad shook my hand and said goodbye, and I could see he wanted to hug me, but he wasn't going to. He believed that men did not do that sort of thing. I wanted to hug him too, but I felt awkward about that as well. Finally, he said, 'You'll be all right, son. It'll make a man out of you.'

They got into the car and Mum started to cry, so Dad drove off without any delay. I waved goodbye to Mum, who was leaning out the car window with her hand held to her mouth.

I sighed and looked around the dining room. Everyone was moving towards the train, so I hurried to finish my tea. A man at a nearby table stood up with a jerk, tipping the table and everything on it towards his companion, who saw it coming and tried to get up but got caught in his chair. As he went back and the table came down, he reached out to his side for support, grabbing at a woman to his left. He got a hand full of hair which came off in his hand. There was a loud crash as table, chair and man hit the floor.

Everyone's attention was attracted. The poor woman, who had lost her wig, tried to cover the sight of her natural hair flattened to her scalp with bobby pins. A rising wail issued from her open mouth, almost gentle and soft at first but reaching high pitch in a remarkably short time.

The man on the floor jumped back to his feet, brushing a large wet spot in his groin, put there by the spilled dregs of his cup of tea. 'Jeez,' he said. 'Sorry, love, but I'm a clumsy bastard sometimes.'

He placed the wig back on her head wrong way round, so that she looked through long strands of hair covering her eyes like a shaggy dog. The man started to laugh. Parting the hair of her wig, the woman looked down at the man's wet groin and joined in his laughter. 'Am I really that funny?' she asked.

*

The next day I arrived at Enoggera Military Camp where I joined a group of other conscripts and enlisted men who were waiting for transfer to a training camp. It was at Enoggera that I first met Nick Murray and Toby Smith. They were both enlisted men and were older than the rest of us conscripts.

Nick was tall, the tallest in our squad, lean as a hungry beast, a Russell Drysdale figure, tanned as leather, plain clothed, alert. His face was strong, wide and square-jawed as a tiger. He would have made a great fullback in a rugby team. There was sandy hair with just a hint of the larrikin in his pale blue eyes. He was older than the rest of us and a veteran of the Korean War, although he never spoke about it. When Toby asked him about it, he simply brushed it off by telling him that he would find out for himself soon enough. But the thing I remember most about Nick was his disarming smile. One smile told you this man was incapable of deceit, yet his eyes held you with the intensity of their power.

Toby, on the other hand, was twenty-eight years old but looked and acted like he was just out of high school. He had volunteered for army life to escape the boredom of civilian life, or so he said – I couldn't imagine Toby being bored. He was short, wide-eyed and always laughing. People naturally liked Toby because he made them laugh; he made them feel that they weren't as careless or thoughtless or clumsy as he was, and so people naturally laughed at Toby and Toby didn't mind because he usually laughed back.

While at Enoggera, our group was led by a soon-to-be retired sergeant responsible for landscaping the area around some newly erected three-storey brick and tiled barracks. Rock walls were his speciality, so we spent our time breaking boulders, mixing mortar and bringing the two together on a carefully graded slope.

It was here that I learnt my first lesson about the army: never volunteer for anything. The sergeant asked if anyone could play a musical instrument. Toby and I raised our hands and were given sledgehammers to break large rocks. The army used sledgehammers, the sergeant explained, to beat out a rhythm on the rocks. We all laughed. Then the others were divided up on long-handled shovels, a cement mixer and the wall itself.

Toby and I had been breaking rocks for a while without much success when our sergeant finally came over to us.

'Havin' trouble?' he asked.

'Yes. We're not loafing, though. It's just that these rocks are so hard to break,' I replied.

'Freeman, isn't it?'

'Yes, Sergeant, Jason Freeman.'

'Yeah, well, Freeman, ya gotta listen to 'em talk.'

I looked at him in silence. The old sergeant smiled.

'When ya strike the rock, listen for the sound it makes. You'll know when ya find its weak spot because it'll make a different sound. Keep strikin' it there and it'll open up fer ya. That's what I mean when I say they talk. The rock itself will tell ya where ter split it and stop chipping' at the edges. These tiny bits are useless.'

He looked at my heaving chest and wet forehead. I knew what he was thinking, *Fifteen minutes of real work and this boy is already exhausted*, but he didn't say anything.

'Strike here,' he said, pointing with his boot to a spot just right of centre.

I took a big swing and brought the sledgehammer down hard.

'No, that's no good,' he said. 'That was just a testin' swing. Ya only need half that force, and anyway, that spot was no good, so ya wasted all that effort.'

I didn't know a damn thing about breaking rocks, and it showed.

'Try here this time,' he said, pointing to a spot left of centre.

Again, I swung the sledgehammer, this time with half the force.

'That's good,' he said, 'That's a good swing and I think its talkin' ter ya. Did ya hear the difference?'

'Ah ...' I hesitated.

He looked up and smiled. 'That's all right, lad,' he said, 'Ya will before ya leave here. Hit the same place again, only this time a bit harder.'

I swung harder, and the hammer came down with a heavy crack. This time, I did hear a splitting sound coming from within the rock. I swung again, with still more force. The rock made a tearing sound. Another swing as hard as I could, and it split in two.

I was satisfied. I looked at old Sarge, and he was smiling.

'Good work, lad,' he said. 'Now split the two halves again. Only this time, take ya time about it. Don't only think about splittin' one rock. Think about a whole day of splittin' rocks. Ya hafta pace yerself, lad. Don't rush at it so much or ya won't get through the day.'

He was right. It was hard work breaking rocks in a warm autumn day, but it felt good when that rock finally split in two. I knew I had it licked, and I wanted to see it open up.

'Hey, Sarge. This rock says it's gettin' a headache and fer me ta piss off,' Toby shouted.

The sergeant turned and smiled. 'It wants ter know if ya could kinda keep its pieces together on the wall. Says it don't like the idea of havin' its privates on display all over the place.'

I started to laugh, and the sergeant placed his hands on his hips. 'Keep swingin' young feller, an' don't take no lip from that rock,' he advised.

Toby slipped and fell from the rock, landing on his backside in the dust. 'See! See! I told ya that rock don't like me, Sarge,' he said.

The old sergeant laughed and shook his head, then he turned away, waving his hand. 'Get back ter work, ya silly bastard,' he said, heading off towards the others.

After three hours we stopped work and sat in the shade of a large gum tree. Some hot tea and freshly baked scones were provided by the kitchen staff. The sergeant sat with his back to the tree trunk and the rest of us sat around him, propping ourselves up on our elbows or with knees bent and hands clasped in front. Nick sat next to the sergeant who explained to him that he wanted us to rotate our jobs so that no one would get bored with what he was doing.

My body felt good from the work I had done. I lay back, looking up into the deep blue sky while watching a few loose clouds drift idly by. After a while, we went back to work.

*

On one occasion we left the camp and went into Brisbane for a night out. After a while, I broke from the group, promising to catch up with them later. 'We won't be hard to find,' Nick said. 'Just search the pubs.' He seemed determined to catch up on a weeks' drinking in one night.

I went in search of a church to make good my promise to Mum and found one in Ann Street, which offered a high ceiling and a cool, sheltered interior. The back pew was as far as I would venture before sitting down. At first, I sat on the edge of the huge wooden pew, then gradually settled back into it. Even so, I felt awkward, as if I were a stranger or that I didn't belong, but I told myself the door had been open and people were welcome to enter any church.

A large organ dominated the front view with its arrangement of thick and thin brass pipes reaching towards the ceiling. In this setting, I thought Bach would be most appropriate. I closed my eyes and imagined Bach's 'Toccata and Fugue in D minor' being performed by some half-demented, lost soul whose body jerked and thrashed with the rhythm of the piece. I laughed, then tried Handel's 'Hallelujah' sung by a choir of angelic beauties clothed in long, flowing, pure-white robes. Again, the image seemed extreme.

Perhaps my imagination was too intense; perhaps something softer was needed. Why was I here? I asked myself. Was it solely that I had promised Mum? Or was there something more personal? Could this church give me solace now that my world had changed so dramatically? My mind moved to a more comforting hymn. Something sung by a small, soprano boys' choir would be good. I had it now – 'Abide with me', sung softly and gently by a small choir accompanied with a mature, sensitive organist. *Yes, that was it*, I thought. As my imagination continued with this image, I could hear my favourite words from this hymn echo within my mind: 'When other helpers fail and comforts flee, Help of the helpless, oh, abide with me.' The hymn slowly faded from my mind but, before it ended, I heard the final line: 'In life, in death, O Lord, abide with me.'

I looked around and noticed how airy yet intimate the room appeared. The high ceiling and arched balcony running around the walls gave it a sense of openness while the small stained-glass windows and marble tables added a sense of tradition and devotion. There was a feeling of something larger than life in this building but, at the same time, it was a grandeur of human dimensions. It was an uplifting, not a diminishing, grandeur. This building could offer comfort in times of distress, joy in times of elation. All buildings should be like this, I concluded, built for people, not aggrandisement.

Then I noticed the marble plaques celebrating the good deeds of past church members. *Why do people do that?* I wondered. *Why do some people want to elevate themselves above others?* How incongruent it seemed here, where people come to worship a loving Father and celebrate their belief in the moral equality of all. Religious piety directed towards self-gain is obscene, I told myself. These people see good deeds as a bank account where they do good deeds in order to build up their account rather than offer genuine help to the needy.

An immature attitude that encourages people to pray for the granting of favours, even in some cases offering to strike a bargain with God, if He will only give them what they desire. At this moment in my life, all I wanted was the courage to face the failures and setbacks I knew it would deliver. I knew I could not ask God to give me that. Courage was something I had to cultivate for myself. I could, however, ask God to help me in my endeavour to find courage within myself.

I became uncomfortable, shifting my weight in the now cold, hard pew and moving to its edge once again. Why does my visiting a church always end like this? Why does it always leave me feeling like I don't belong? Like I belong on the fringes rather than a central part of the church community? Perhaps one day, it will all make better sense. This thought offered me some comfort, but my restlessness wouldn't leave me, so I stood up and hurried away to find the others.

I caught up with them at a corner pub. It had a clean, functional bar with shining black-and-white tiles running across the floor and halfway up the walls. The bar was U-shaped with the open end leading to a doorway into the next room. The bar top was coated with an olive-green vinyl and the top half of the walls were painted in the same colour. The ceiling was a standard white with long fluorescent lighting. A glass mirror ran from the ceiling to the top of an island bench inside the bar. It was littered with glasses of every shape and spirits of every kind so that the reflected images gave the impression of an abundance of liquor and shining crystal.

Behind the bar itself, and in front of two enormous, black-handled, gold-tipped taps, stood a barmaid in a black nylon blouse. Her arms were folded and her brow knotted. She wore no bra and the nipples on her large breasts stood out against the sheer nylon. Nick and the others stood to the left of the beer taps. They were laughing and talking among themselves, and Toby couldn't take his eyes off the barmaid.

I moved to the far end closest to Nick. 'Sit down and put ya money on the bar,' he said. I did as I was told, placing a five dollar note in front of me. 'Where ya been?'

'Oh! Just walking around, really.'

'Nothin' to see around here, mate.'

The waitress appeared and asked if I was drinking alone or with the others. I told her I was with the others, so she poured a glass of beer for everyone and took the five dollars from in front of me. She returned with my change and then disappeared again. I turned to talk with Nick, but he was listening to one of the blokes in our group tell him about a girl he had met who was a great French kisser. Nick replied, 'Good. Find a Frenchman and tell him all about it.' We all laughed at Nick's dry wit. After that, I tried to follow the conversation but eventually lost interest, choosing instead to concentrate on my drinking.

Nick was always the first to finish his beer, emphatically placing his empty glass on the bar. This was a sign for the others to finish their drinks and for the barmaid to bring the next round. I timed the space between drinks and discovered that Nick finished his glass every ten to fifteen minutes. Since it was a little after eight-thirty and all the pubs closed at ten, I figured we would drink about another ten beers. I had only had two beers, so I decided to break my boredom and have some fun.

The next round I finished before Nick in twelve minutes and left the empty glass on the bar. I was to the side of Nick, so he didn't notice my empty glass until he placed his on the bar.

His eyes went from my empty glass to me. Feigning innocence, I smiled back at him.

The next round Nick completed in ten minutes, and I came in after him. The round after that, I finished in eight minutes. This time there was no hiding what I had done, and this time Nick smiled back at me. The next round we both finished in eight minutes.

'Jesus, this is too much for me,' said someone in the group. 'Count me out unless you want me spewing all over the place.'

'Yeah! Slow down, you two. Is the place on fire or something?'

Nick smiled at me. 'Ask the kid,' he said.

'I wasn't trying to be smart, Nick. I was just bored. That's all.'

'Well, I'm game if you are, mate.'

'What do you mean?'

'What I mean is, do ya wanna drinking match?'

'What's that?'

'That's where we find out who can drink the most in the shortest time.'

'How do you do that?'

'Simple. We match each other, drink for drink, until one of us doesn't want anymore.'

'Hang on a minute, Nick,' said one of the others. 'You already have a good hour's drinking on Jason.'

Nick turned on him. 'Don't tell me things I already know. I figure the lad has never been in a drinking match before.' Nick looked at me, waiting for my answer.

'No, no, I haven't.'

'Well, that makes us just about even, I'd say. Right! Who's in and who's out?'

Most of the group took their glasses and stood back from the bar, shaking their heads and muttering to themselves.

Toby, his attention momentarily distracted from the barmaid's breasts, moved up to Nick. 'Yeah!' he said, placing his full glass of beer beside Nick's. 'Reckon I'll have a bash at this.'

It was decided that we would call the match the 'Enoggera Challenge', and the three of us chipped in for a bottle of Scotch to go to the winner. Then, the drinking got underway. At first, we were smiling, but this was soon to change. Nick raised his glass and skulled his beer. Toby and I followed.

'What's goin' on here?' The barmaid asked. She smiled when she was told about the drinking match. I guess it broke her boredom and at least kept Toby's eyes somewhere else.

'Right,' said Nick. 'Let's make this interesting, love. Bring out the schooners.'

I soon learnt that we had been drinking pots which contained only 10 oz (285 ml) of beer, while a schooner contained 15 oz (425 ml), making it harder to skull. The big beers were placed in front of us.

'Who's paying for this?' asked the barmaid.

'The first to throw up,' the three of us chorused and laughed.

Nick raised his glass only once; Toby and I raised ours twice. My stomach was feeling full but I had not lost my taste for the beer. The tips of my fingers and toes were going numb, and my lips and ears were starting to tingle. Much more of this, I thought, and I might lose my balance. Toby had lost his smile and looked uncomfortable at the next round.

Again, Nick raised his glass only once, I raised mine twice, but Toby made a rush for the toilet midway through his second attempt. It was down to Nick and me when the next round arrived. This time I watched what Nick did.

First, he looked at the beer and seemed to set his mind on it. I guessed he imagined drinking all of it in one attempt.

Next, he took a deep breath and held it. Then, he raised his glass slowly to his lips and took slow, deliberate and large gulps of beer. Finally, he returned the empty glass to the bar while expelling the air from his lungs. I thought about this and reasoned that the expelled air would make more room for the beer in his belly and help keep it down. I did what he had done and finished my beer in one attempt.

Nick looked surprised and ordered another two schooners. We both raised our glasses only once. Nick lost his smile and looked annoyed.

My face was numb, and my mind was beginning to lose concentration. I had trouble focusing on what I was doing. I had to think hard just to get the glass to my mouth, but another schooner went down. When I put the empty glass down, it fell over. I missed the foot rail beside the bar and stumbled. The others cheered and laughed at me, and Nick's smile returned.

Nick drank another schooner. I looked hard at mine and tried to concentrate. I reached out for it but spilt some beer when I tried to pick it up. The others all cheered. 'Chugga, chugga, chugga …' they called out as the glass reached my lips. I thought I had put my head back, but I found myself lying on the floor, the beer spilt all over me, the empty glass clattering across the tiles towards the corner.

'Sh …' I heard myself saying. 'Wa' happ' …?'

'It's all right, lad,' Nick said, helping me to my feet. 'Ya just lost. That's all. Don't worry about it. Ya did good, lad. Ya did good. Ya can hold ye liquor. That's fer sure. You can hold ya liquor better 'an most. Ya need practice, that's all ya need, lad, practice. Ya'll get plenty of that in the army all right. Don't worry about that. Plenty of practice in the army.'

That was the most any of us had heard Nick say at one time.

Everyone stood in silence looking at him.

'What ya all lookin' at? What's wrong?' Nick said.

No one answered. They muttered, shifted their weight and looked at their shoes.

'Come on, fellers. Let's go someplace else. Whaddya say, someplace else, eh?'

Again they muttered. Someone said something about work tomorrow and the others agreed.

'Piss off, then. Go on, piss off, ya lousy bastards. Me an' the lad got places to go, haven't we, lad? Places to go,' Nick said, placing his arm around my shoulders.

I was standing beside Nick, but the room wouldn't stand still with me. 'Yeh,' I said. 'Places t' go.'

We broke up. Nick mumbled something about drinking mates not being what they used to be, then led me, with his arm still around my shoulders, out of the pub.

The rest of the evening became a blurred jumble of dreamlike events. Afterwards, I vaguely remember Nick pushing someone aside who had taken exception at our state of intoxication, a ride in the back of a taxi that left me swaying like a wobbly wheel on a pushbike and, finally, sitting in the front yard of a shabby house in some back alley, drinking the Scotch with Nick.

'Nick,' said a woman, dressed in a nighty and cotton bathrobe. 'Nick, it's good to see ya, love. Where ya been? Ooooh, who's the good looker with ya? Ann'll love him. Come in, love. Come in.'

It was all said without waiting for an answer. She stood, holding open the door to her house, and waved us in with her free hand. Next, I was sitting naked on the edge of a bed, and a strange young woman was smiling at me and taking off her brassiere. This excited me. I had never seen a woman's naked breasts before; the barmaid's, of course, but that was different. I was fascinated with the fullness of these breasts, their curved symmetry and their bare nipples. Curiously, she took pleasure in my interest. She inhaled deeply, thrusting her breasts forward and cupping them underneath with her hands. Then, she moved forward and placed one of her breasts on my lips. I opened my mouth and she pushed it in. I gently sucked on her nipple, while she placed her hand behind my head and stroked it. I sucked harder.

'Oh, baby, baby,' she whispered.

Next, she stood back while sliding her hands down over her hips and stepping out of her panties. My surprise must have pleased her because she giggled and smiled cheerfully. Then, she lay flat on the bed beside me. I turned to face her.

'Come on, handsome, show me what ya got,' she beamed.

I sat up and tried to join her but sank slowly to the bed and finally passed out face down beside her with my arm draped across her midriff.

I woke the next morning with Nick standing over me, shaking my shoulder. I opened my eyes, but the light stabbed at my brain. My head ached terribly. My stomach felt like a giant wave about to break on the hot dry sand of my mouth. My tongue felt like it had been jammed into a mouth half its size. I looked at the empty space beside me on the bed.

'Go away,' I slurred, rolling over and stretching out. 'I want to sleep some more.'

'Come on, Jason,' urged Nick. 'Ya can't bludge on ya mates because of ya drinking.'

I didn't care for his logic. 'Leave me alone,' I said.

Nick threw back the bed covers and pulled me into a sitting position. My head screamed.

'Ooh,' was all I could feebly manage.

'Come on, Jason. On ya feet! Let's go, lad.'

I stood up and Nick led me to the shower. He turned the cold water on hard and pushed me into it. The stinging jets of cold water shocked me into consciousness; then, the water began to take the heat from my body. I put my head under the jets, and it tickled my scalp, clearing my head. I opened my mouth and let the coolness drench my dry mouth.

'Don't drink any water,' Nick warned.

I didn't argue. I just drank. The water felt good going down, but when it hit my stomach, it made me want to retch. I had water going down and the contents of my stomach wanting to come up. I choked, coughed and spluttered, ending up with a burning throat and a smarting nasal passage.

'Silly bastard,' was all Nick said before disappearing.

I went back to dress in the strange room I had slept in. Outside, there was a drizzle which gave a dampness to the old wooden house I was in. I tried to clear my mind, but a feeling of detachment and unpleasantness overcame me. I tried to remember what had happened the night before. Then the drinking and the girl came to mind, and I wanted to shout out but didn't. A sudden wave of shame and self-loathing passed over me. *What an idiot I made of myself last night*, I thought. I had always thought that people who got drunk were weak-willed, and people who made a spectacle of themselves were undeserving even of pity. But now I knew differently, and the amazing thing was that it had all been so easy! Outwardly, I was physically sick; inwardly, something was not right. It was as though I had spotted a stain on my clothes that needed removing. I was disappointed with myself, but I told myself, it wasn't important. After all, it was only a one-night binge. It wasn't as though I was an alcoholic. Still, I wanted to remove the stain, but I didn't know how. I wondered if my feelings now would be enough to stop me drinking in future. Probably not, I told myself.

I looked around the sorry mess of the room I was in. Carelessness caused this, I thought, carelessness created from the despair of poverty. There was something about poverty I hated. It was not just the squalor and the ghastly stench of old clothes and human waste, but the inevitability of it. Those living in it accept it; those outside it hate it with the rich fearing that one day it will overtake them. I wasn't rich but that's why I hated poverty, because of its stark reality, a stark reality that I secretly feared would one day consume me. This dingy room, for instance, was oppressive. Its walls of faded, peeling wallpaper, cracked glass windows and chipped wooden frames depressed me. The rank smell of soiled linen and sickly perspiration revolted me. The poor were a careless, tired people, I told myself, and I hated them for it. There may have been a time when there was something noble about poverty. Heaven knows Steele Rudd and Henry Lawson thought so; but, for me, poverty was the ugliest thing in the world, and if it wouldn't go away, I could only hope that I'd never be a part of it.

'Here,' Nick said, passing me a cold bottle of Coke after letting himself in. 'This is the only thing ya can drink first thing in the morning. But take it slow and let the gas out'a ya gut slowly.' He was right. The carbonated liquid tingled and refreshed my mouth, and the belching did help to settle my stomach. 'Now for some tucker,' he said.

We went to breakfast in a dirty old kitchen with table and chairs to match. The smell of greasy cooking had my stomach protesting immediately. Nick got himself fried eggs and bacon, two pieces of toast and a cup of hot, black tea. I only managed a half serving of scrambled eggs. Next, he mixed his eggs into a gooey mess, then added Worcestershire sauce. I turned away. *He's doing this deliberately*, I thought. But he went on eating and drinking his tea as though the previous night's drinking bout was long gone.

'You must have a cast-iron gut,' I said. Nick looked up at me innocently. 'How can you eat that muck? Doesn't anything turn your stomach?' I asked, pushing my plate away.

Nick smiled. 'The only thing that'll turn me stomach is a pair of warm breasts on me back,' he said, pushing my plate back. 'Now eat that. Ya have ter get something into ya stomach.'

Nick never mentioned that night to the others and, although they questioned me, I never did either. From that day, we always held each other in high regard but I never came closer to Nick than at that time. Toby did, but between Nick and me there was a mutual respect that closer friendship would have broken.

We stayed a few more days at Enoggera, then moved to Kapooka Recruit Training Centre outside Wagga Wagga in New South Wales.

CHAPTER 2
Training

'Get off those buses and get your luggage. Move! Move! Move!' a short, threatening corporal shouted at us.

The train ride from Brisbane had been long and sleepless, and the bus from the railroad station had found every pothole.

'Welcome to the army,' someone said.

'Every day's an adventure,' someone else replied.

The corporal arranged us into three ranks; then a huge sergeant in starched greens and spit-polished boots spoke to us in a confident, authoritative tone.

'As of now, you are members of Two Platoon, A Company, Royal Training Battalion, Kapooka. Your time here can be done in one of two ways: the easy way or the hard way. The easy way is when you do exactly what I tell you to do, immediately I tell you to do it. The hard way is when you don't do what I tell you, and I have to discipline you until you do. Now, I know everyone here is of reasonable intelligence, otherwise the army wouldn't let you be here, so you'll do it the easy way. If you don't, you'd have to be a smartarse who deserves to have the shit beaten out of him.' He paused. 'Do I make myself clear?' he asked, menacingly.

We gave a muffled response, so the corporal took over.

'The sergeant asked you a question, people. Do you

understand?' he said stiffly with an upward inflection.

'Yes, sir,' a few more replied.

'Dumb! Don't you people know anything? This is Sergeant Jones. Him you call Sergeant. I am Corporal Williams. Me you call Corporal. Later you will meet Lieutenant Rogers. Him you will call sir. Now let's try it again. Do you understand?'

In our confusion, some of us replied 'Yes, Sergeant' and some 'Yes, Corporal.'

'Dumb! Dumb! Dumb!' The corporal's face was turning red and his lips were drawn tight across his teeth. 'The Sergeant is addressing you. Not me. Now get it right. Do you understand?'

'Yes, Sergeant!' we all shouted.

'That's better, recruits,' the sergeant went on. 'A recruit is the lowest form of life in the army. You are civilians no more, but you are not yet soldiers. In fact, you are nothing and you will remain nothing until we make something out of the miserable nothing that you are. What are you?'

'Nothing, Sergeant!'

We were warming to this game. The sergeant smiled, then went on.

'If you are good enough you will become privates. Not just any sort of private, however, but a private in the Australian army. The greatest fighting force in the world. A finely tuned and efficient killing machine. When you leave here, you will be part of that machine. You will love your weapon. You will be loyal to your army mates. You will become part of the Anzac tradition. What will you become a part of?'

'The Anzac tradition, Sergeant!' we shouted.

'I can't hear you.'

'*The Anzac tradition, Sergeant!*'

'I still can't hear you.'

'THE ANZAC TRADITION, Sergeant!' we screamed.

'Good. Good. Take over, Corporal.'

The sergeant disappeared and the corporal took us to a series of supply stores where we went round and round, being issued with equipment and uniforms. None of these fitted, so we tried to exchange among ourselves, which proved impossible because the regular sizes were all taken and only the large ones were left. From then on, most of us walked around dressed like Charlie Chaplin look-a-likes.

Next, we were led to our barracks, old metal igloos dating back to the last war. They had corrugated iron roofs rolled into a semicircle with wooden ends and floors. There was a door and two windows with wooden crosses at either end. Inside, naked lights hung from the ceiling and grey metal beds with thin foam mattresses lined each side along with grey, metal lockers, leaving a narrow passage connecting the doors at either end.

This small hut became the home of sixteen besieged recruits for the next fifteen weeks. During this time, I was amazed at how fastidious the army was about minor detail. The hut had to be swept, dusted and polished in that order. The sweeping raised dust that had to be removed; the dusting removed the gleam that had to be replaced.

Each of us was allotted a tiny area in the shape of a square for which he was responsible. To the left was our grey metal bed, all made the same way, with regulation hospital square bashed corners, and the sheets at the head folded down to exactly one bayonet length. If a coin was dropped on our bed, it was supposed to bounce. Under the bed was our footwear, all arranged in exactly the same order, and with spit-polished toes pointing out.

To the right of the bed was our grey, steel locker arranged

at right angles to the bedhead, with a small rectangular piece of carpet as a mat in front of it. Inside, the locker was precisely the same arrangement as all other lockers, with all our personal items in the same places. I remember that a particular point was made about the razor blade being left out of the razor for hygiene reasons; apparently the temptation for a suicide was not in the army's scheme of things ... but I digress. All our undergarments and socks had to be folded and arranged in our cupboards in the exactly the same way. The hanging space to the right had our clothes, which again were arranged in the same order, with the hangers pointing in and our shirts all facing the same way. Under the clothes were our kit bags, in which were stored our dirty clothes, which were washed and ironed in exactly the same way every Sunday. The fact that we would all want the same machines at the same time did not seem to worry those in command. The personal belongings we had come with were all stored in a separate hut, to be returned to us when we left recruit training, either by graduation, mental or physical inability to complete the training or dishonourable discharge.

Failure for anyone in our barracks to meet these requirements would result in collective punishment, the entire barracks being put under punishment, which usually meant no dry canteen privilege. This left the wrongdoer feeling like a pariah.

We spent hours every day sweeping, dusting, polishing, folding and arranging, always with the threat of denied privileges hanging over us. I was astonished how important the positioning of a pair of socks could become when a night's relaxation at the unit canteen was riding on its precise location.

The unit canteen was dry – that is, it did not serve alcohol

– but this did not stop it becoming the main distraction for a camp full of bewildered recruits. Inside was a smoke-filled, cramped atmosphere punctuated with loud, assertive language. Most stood with their feet apart, thumbs tucked behind their belts, and took long deep gulps from a large bottle of Coke held high above their tilted heads. They poked fingers, cut with an open hand or clenched their fists as they spoke.

I walked out into the cold, evening air and made for a fire burning in a small drum on the top of a grassy knoll. Our commanding officer had had these installed. They were 44-gallon (205 litre) drums that had been cut in half and had a grill installed inside them, so that the ash and charcoal could fall through to the bottom. There was also a firebox next to the drum that had fresh firewood in it, so we could continue feeding the fire whenever it died down. He also had wooden blocks set up around the fireplaces for us to sit on. My mind went back to the times when I was in the Boy Scouts, and we used to sit around a campfire and share stories. I pulled the wooden block closer to the fire and sat, overlooking the naked lights of the camp.

The empty, dark space beyond the camp beckoned me, and suddenly I felt alone and lost. For the first time since I left home, I really missed it. I longed for my old room and the comfort of caring parents and cheerful friends, but these thoughts only made my longing stronger. Somehow, I would get over this, I told myself, but right now I simply wanted to be back home. I looked at the stars in the clear night sky and thought how insignificant my affliction suddenly appeared. Was there a place for anyone in all this? I wondered.

Billions of years held the secret of this most ancient of lands. How many others had sat here before me, pondering the significance of this frighteningly beautiful sight? How many stories had been told to rationalise such indifference? Or was it benign, like Jacob wrestling with God's messenger? What stories, I wondered, did the Aboriginal elders tell their young about this land of endless dreams? Did they too delight in the lesser light of the Southern Cross as we do today? Or does it take a culture, schooled in the sacrifice of Christ, to recognise such a prize in a collection too numerous to count?

My mind drifted to the current brutal struggle Australia's Aboriginals were experiencing in their attempt to bridge the gap between their violent tribal past and our modern Australian civilisation, and I recalled the same horrific struggle my Celtic ancestors had to endure to arrive at our current place in Australian society, leaving behind the hunger and sorrow of their troubled past in exchange for the hope of a new start in a land of liberty and promise. To protect their newfound freedom, my grandfather had fought in the trenches of France to protect Australia's liberty from Europe's autocratic monarchs, and my father had stood defiantly against Japan's military dictators. Now it was my turn. My country had called on me to defend its liberty from communist dictators.

'What are you doing out here, mate?'

It was Nick and Toby. I was surprised to see them, thinking they would prefer the atmosphere inside to out here.

'Nothing. It was just too crowded inside.'

'Know what you mean,' Nick replied.

We lapsed into silence, drinking slowly, enjoying the warmth of the fire.

'Army life isn't so bad,' I said, cheerfully. 'The secret is to be obedient. Just do what you're told and keep yourself out of trouble.'

Nick and Toby looked glum. 'Sounds like you're doing time in a prison,' Nick finally said.

'I guess there are similarities,' I answered. 'Both are single sex institutions, both demand obedience and both confine you.'

'Yeah, but we're not locked up at night,' Toby said.

'True. But to survive here you have to be obedient just as you would in a prison.'

'That's for sure,' Toby went on. 'Hey, Nick, do you reckon that David Hughes will survive camp life?'

David Hughes was a young-looking, intelligent Nasho from our hut. He had arrived later than everyone else, and it was rumoured he came from a wealthy, privileged background in Melbourne.

'Hard to say with that sort,' Nick replied 'Some of 'em are tough and some are soft. One thing's for sure, though – we'll know in a couple of weeks if he's going to make it or not.' He paused for a moment then remarked, 'This Coke is too sweet and tastes like shit. It's only good for a hangover.'

We lapsed into silence again, each of us retiring to his own private world, far from the confines of present circumstances.

*

From then on, camp life became one continuous experiment in communal living, with the army trying to strip away everyone's individual identity and replace it with their own version of team loyalty. Incidents and conversations abounded, which in isolation were meaningless, yet, when combined, formed the nucleus of a powerful philosophy based on team survival.

Our day started at five o'clock in the morning when we

woke from a deep sleep, with either Sergeant Jones picking up the end of one of our beds and letting it crash to the floor or Corporal Williams standing in the centre of our hut shouting, 'Wake-ee, wake-ee. Hands off cocks and on to socks!'

Either way, we sat bolt upright in our beds, staring blankly to our front while they stomped outside, slamming the door behind them. The whole time I was there, I waited in vain for that door to come off its hinges.

Whichever our rude awakening, we all collapsed back into the warmth of our beds, lingering for the last possible moment of stolen pleasure before emerging into the cold, misty morning.

Shorts, singlets and sandshoes were all we wore on the five o'clock run every morning.

'Left, left,' the corporal shouted.

'Left, right, left,' we all shouted back in time, with the rhythm of our feet hitting the hard, dusty road.

'Left, left.'

'Left, right left.'

'Left, left.'

'Left, right, left.'

All step to the beat, I thought.

'Left, left.'

'Left, right, left.'

Arms in, hands on chest.

'Left, left.'

'Left, right, left.'

Eyes front, chests held out.

'Left, left.'

'Left, right, left.'

All feet move in time.

'Left, left.'

'Left, right, left.'

All move as if one.

'Left, left.'

'Left, right, left.'

Don't stop, keep jogging.

'Left, left.'

'Left, right, left.'

Fifty minds. Hold the beat.

'Left, left.'

'Left, right, left.'

'Left, left.'

'Left, right, left.'

When we weren't jogging, we were drilling by numbers. An order would be shouted at us, and we would have to count out loud, 'One ... two, three ... one.'

For example, to present arms, we would swing our rifles from our shoulders and place them in front of us on the count of 'one', then pause to the count of 'two, three', then on the next count of 'one', place our right foot behind our left and our right hand behind our rifle.

The corporal would shout, 'Present arms!'

And we would shout back, 'One!' and swing our rifles to the front.

'Two, three!' and stand still.

'One!' and place our right foot behind our left and our right hand behind our rifle.

This counting and shouting went on endlessly, hour after hour, day after day, week after week.

Sometimes we did other exercises like rope climbing. We all had to do the rope climbing in the same way. You reached up with your arms, pulled your feet up until your feet were just below your bottom, then you locked your feet onto the rope. After that, you pulled with your arms and pushed with your legs until your arms were in front of you. Then you reached out once again and repeated the exercise until you reached the top. Once at the top, you had to slide back down without burning your hands.

'This is no bloody good,' Toby said as we tumbled into our hut after a hard day's exercising, drilling, marching and rope climbing. 'What's the record for desertion? I'm too late, I suppose. The smart ones left long ago. Jeez, just think of it., twelve more weeks of this bloody nonsense! Oh, well, someone's got to do it, so it may as well be us dumb bastards, eh?' he laughed.

'We've got a long way ter go here, Toby,' Nick said dryly, 'an' it won't help if ya constantly remind us.'

'Ya right, Nick,' Toby replied, hitting the side of his head with the butt of his hand. 'I'm a stupid bastard sometimes. Tell ya what, Nick, whenever I do something stupid, just kick me up the arse. That's where me brains are.'

We all laughed, then Nick reached out his arm and wrapped it around Toby's neck, pulling his head down and twitching his nose. 'Ya all right, Toby,' he said. 'Ya a good mate.'

They both went back to cleaning and arranging their spaces for the lieutenant's inspection later that evening.

'Hey! Look at this,' Toby shouted, laughing and holding up his long woollen underpants. 'Ya know what you do with these?' he asked, pulling the pants over his head. 'No, doesn't fit here.'

'Don't know why,' Nick said. 'Ya a bit of a dickhead, sometimes.' We all laughed again.

'No. Tell ya what, Nick. I'll get dressed up in this fer the lieutenant's inspection.'

'Don't be bloody silly. You'll only cause trouble fer yourself, Toby. Remember, this is the army, not civilian street. Ya can't walk away from ya troubles here, ya know, mate.'

'No, Nick. They're a bunch o' fools who need makin' fun of.'

Toby seemed to get an idea. He changed into his winter underwear and wrapped his thick army belt and scabbarded bayonet around his waist. Placing one hand on his hip and the other limp wristed in front of him, he swaggered up and down the barrack calling out in an effeminate tone.

'Now, dearies, don't be naughty boys here at camp. Remember, it's the hard way (thrusting his hips forward) or the easy way (bending right over with his palms on the floor and looking behind). But, really, ya know (swaggering again), I'd just love to punch ya in the mouth and squeeze ya nuts (right hand now imitating the squeeze). Oh, and don't forget, dearies, to line up ya socks and undies just exactly like we told ya now (both hands now, fingers down bouncing back and forth in front of him). We wouldn't want any nasty surprises in ya lockers now, would we?'

With this said, he did a cartwheel down the centre of the hut followed by a backflip. Landing on his feet, he shouted, 'One … two, three … one', then flung his arms wide apart.

The hut exploded into laughter. Everyone stopped what they were doing to look at Toby, who was delighted with their attention. He looked around for a new idea to embellish his act. The others waited eagerly.

'No, no … wait a minute. I've got it. I've got it now,' he finally said.

Racing back to his locker, he put on his boots and gaiters

and slouch hat and picked up his rifle. Then he went into a drill routine, marking time, ordering arms and other things we had learnt in the last couple of weeks, while shouting out, 'One … two, three … one.'

The whole barracks roared with laughter and others came in from outside to see what was going on. Toby was fully primed now and not even Nick's warning to give it away could stop him. He finished his routine with a classic pose. His left foot went forward with his leg bent at the knee, his rifle was shouldered on his right side and with his left thumb, he pulled his singlet across, exposing his left nipple. With an earnest look and slight shake of the head, he shouted in a high-pitched tone, 'Son of Anzac!'

At that exact moment, Lieutenant Rogers and Corporal Williams entered the barracks. Instead of the expected laughter, Toby was greeted with absolute silence. He followed everyone's gaze to the lieutenant and immediately came to attention without a trace of mirth on his face. The sight of Toby in his winter underwear, standing at attention, awaiting inspection, had everyone choking back laughter. The lieutenant walked up and stood directly in front of him.

'There's one in every platoon,' he said, looking down on Toby and pausing for effect. 'The platoon goose!'

On hearing this, Toby took one step backward and presented arms. Everyone in the barracks burst into laughter except Lieutenant Rogers and Corporal Williams. A smirk crossed the lieutenant's face.

'A short time in this camp can seem like a lifetime,' he said softly, 'even to an idiot.'

Without another word, they left. From then on, Toby was singled out by Corporal Williams to perform extra push-ups, extra running or extra duty. 'Recruit idiot,' he would say when addressing Toby, 'give me fifty more push-ups.'

'I can't do fifty more, Corporal.'

'Yes, you can, recruit idiot. I'll explain it to you, recruit idiot. How many can you do, recruit idiot?'

'About twenty, Corporal.'

'Good, recruit idiot. You can do two sets of twenty and then one set of ten for good measure, recruit idiot. You can do that, can't you, recruit idiot?'

'Yes, Corporal.'

'Good, recruit idiot. Get started.'

When we returned from our morning run, he would say to Toby, 'Don't stop running, recruit idiot. The rest of the platoon may have finished, but you're not finished, recruit idiot. You're special. Don't you remember how special you are, recruit idiot? Running on the spot now, recruit idiot. Lift those knees higher! Higher, you dumb bastard! Can't you understand simple English, recruit idiot? I said higher.'

This would continue until Toby could barely lift his knees.

'Recruit idiot, the kitchen staff need a hand with the washing up and I told them how delighted you would be to help out. Get to the kitchen now, recruit idiot. They're expecting you.'

Toby would stand, stripped to the waist, sweat running from his body, bent over an enormous sink of hot, soapy water, scraping and scouring away the burnt remnants from a mountain of pots and pans.

Amazingly, Toby's punishment gradually ended when Lieutenant Rogers overheard David Hughes say that Rogers was a fool for allowing this sort of treatment to continue. From then on, Corporal Williams shifted his ire from Toby to David.

Gradually, we heard less and less of 'recruit idiot' and more and more of 'recruit smartarse'.

*

'Have ya ever had it with someone ya didn't like, Nick?'

'Toby, I've had it with someone nobody liked.'

The three of us laughed and moved our blocks closer to the fire drum. Nick had rigged a rod across the top of the fire and hung a billy from it. When the water boiled, he dropped a handful of tea leaves into it, tapped the side with a stick, took it off the rod and swung it three times. Then he placed it on the ground and let it stand for a while. Finally, he poured the hot tea and added a teaspoon of honey and squeezed lemon juice into our mugs. Nick had scrounged and bargained with the canteen and maintenance crews to acquire all these extras. We wrapped our hands around the mugs, drawing the warmth into our cold fingers, blew across the top and sipped the brew, savouring its distinct, smoky flavour.

'So, looks don't count with ya?' Toby went on.

'Well, ya don't admire the mantelpiece while ya pokin' the fire, do ya?' Nick replied.

'It's just that ya gotta get in the mood. How do ya do that with ugly?'

'Ugly's in the eye of the beholder. Look, when ya see ugly, everybody else sees the same thing. That means the poor girl wants ter be touched an' nobody'll do it fer her. Play it right, an' I guarantee you'll enjoy yourself. Besides if ya see ugly, just close ya eyes an' imagine beautiful.'

'Why, Toby? What is ugly to you?' David Hughes asked.

He had been standing back, but within earshot, and now

he walked forward into our midst. Toby smiled and beckoned him to join us. He was still grateful at the corporal's ire having passed onto David.

'Well, ya know, plain, unattractive, no woman shape.' Toby traced an hourglass shape with his hands. 'That sort of thing,' he said, picking up his mug and taking a deep gulp of tea.

'But that has more to do with fashion than beauty, Toby.'

'What do ya mean? Beauty may be fashionable, mate, but ugly is just plain ugly.'

'Nonsense, Toby. The classic concept of beauty, still prevalent with some today, is full rounded buttocks, a gentle roll of fat on the stomach and long legs with thick thighs.'

'Yeah, an' who wants that today?'

'Well, fashion is moving in a different direction today. Jean Shrimpton has seen to that.'

'Who? What are ya talkin' about?'

David picked up the billy and nodded to Nick, who nodded back. Then, he poured himself a mug of tea and placed it on the ground beside him.

'You know,' he said. 'The member's enclosure at Flemington, Melbourne Cup Day, 1965. I was there, and I couldn't believe the fuss they made about her. Apparently, she had the nerve to attend the cup in a miniskirt. Ever since then, legs are in and tits and bums are out. Prue Acton has made millions selling simple, straight, short shifts to mature women who want to look like schoolgirls. It's amazing, I know, but Holeproof have created a whole fashion out of pantyhose because of it. Garters and stockings are out, pantyhose is in.'

We all went quiet, retreating to the shelter of our own thoughts, unsure of David's easy and confident expression.

'So, you see,' he continued, 'curves are out and skinny is

in. If this fashion continues, our women will become little girls and the full, curvaceous figures of ancient Greece and Renaissance Italy will become merely a historical curiosity. That's what fashion does, Toby. It defines beauty for each of us.'

He paused for a moment, then continued. 'There's more to women today than just fashion, though. Consider the pill. For the first time in history, women don't have to worry about getting pregnant when having sex. This could lead to a sexual revolution. Women can now look on sex solely as a source of pleasure without having to worry about having children. Who knows where this could lead? One thing is certain, though – it will have an impact on the population growth rate of our country.'

We were silent, sipping our tea and staring into the fire drum. I contemplated what I had just heard. David seemed to have a greater knowledge of these things than the rest of us, and I admired the confidence this gave him.

'But there's more to women than mere looks and sex. Isn't there?' I offered, breaking the silence.

'What do you mean, Jason? Personality? That sort of thing?' David asked.

'I'm not sure. Something like that, but more a question of feeling, really. You know. You have to feel right about someone before you can enter into a relationship, or is that going to disappear too? In the future, are we just going to seek out temporary sex partners and not bother about love and that sort of thing?'

'Yeah. That's what I mean,' Toby interrupted. 'If she's beautiful, you'll feel good about it, and I like the idea of temporary sex without commitment,' he said, a smile crossing his face.

'I don't think that's what Jason means,' David ventured. 'That may be a part of it, but it's not all of it.'

'Well, with all ya money, ya could be choosy, couldn't ya?' Toby said. 'Women would throw 'emselves at ya. Wouldn't they?'

'Not the ones who have money of their own. Some women guard their reputation and want security and a family, Toby. They are not interested in settling for less.'

'Yeah. I suppose that's right. Does that mean ya only go for the rich ones, or do you just want sex with those who are willing to give it to ya?'

'For me, different women serve different purposes, but I do have to be careful. About women, I mean.'

'Women!' sneered Nick. 'What do you blokes know about women? What does any bloke know about women? I believed in 'em once but not anymore. Now I never sleep with anyone I wouldn't share with me mates.'

'What?' I questioned. 'I couldn't accept that.'

'Listen, Jason, women are the source of man's misery. They get ya in an' then they screw you up. First, it's a house. Then it's all the things that go with it. Then ya mates have ter go, and before ya know it, all ya got is her and what she wants, and ya whole life is gone.' He raised his hands and shot his fingers into the air. 'Phtt.'

'Yes. But that's what life's all about, isn't it?' I asked with genuine concern. 'Finding the right woman and starting a family?'

'Yours maybe, but not mine. Not anymore. I was married once, an' tried all those things. I fell in love, gave her all the things she wanted, but then I came home an' found her in bed with me best mate. It wasn't right. I gave so much, an' I trusted her. It hurt like hell, but I came out of it. So now I only take from women what I'm willin' to share, an' if I don't want ter share it, I don't want it at all. That way there's no hurt, an' I keep me own life and me own mates.'

His eyes narrowed and his jaw set. Sniffing strongly, he turned his head away and stared at the fire drum. No more words were spoken after that. Only the wood crackled as the flames licked at its sides and the red heat within spat and glowed.

*

We stood at ease, three ranks of men with feet apart, some rubbing their hands together, others with them tucked into their armpits, since we weren't allowed the warmth of our pockets. When I am cold, it's the extremities that feel it first: fingers and toes, nose, ears and lips. That's what I remember most about recruit training – the cold. I was always cold, trying to keep warm without success, except when I sat near the fire drum outside the canteen. Otherwise, it didn't seem to matter what I did; I was always cold.

I wore woollen underwear and socks, but it didn't help. The army issued me with a woollen greatcoat, but I was only permitted to wear it on guard duty. Other than that, I was expected to wear jungle greens and cotton fatigues with a brown woollen jumper. I'm sure this was adequate for winter in the tropics, but not for winter in outback New South Wales. I was cold. The cold seemed to penetrate deep into my body. I stamped my feet, blew warm air from my lungs into my cupped hands, vigorously rubbed my arms, but nothing seemed to work. Whatever I did, the cold stayed with me.

I stood looking at Sergeant Jones while he instructed us on the merits of our newly issued rifle, the self-loading rifle (SLR). He clasped the end of the SLR's barrel with his huge hand and raised it until his arm and the rifle extended in the same straight line parallel to the ground. His grip locked and he began his instruction holding steadfastly this position.

Surely, he can't maintain this position, I thought. *It isn't humanly possible for him to keep his arm straight under such strain.*

'This is an SLR,' he said. 'The SLR is the best rifle in the world. That is why the Australian army has chosen it for you. It is a 7.62 calibre, gas-operated, self-loading rifle. That means you cock this weapon once only for your first shot. Thereafter, the weapon cocks itself automatically. All you have to do is aim the barrel and squeeze the trigger. Everything else is done for you by this beautiful weapon.'

He spoke slowly and his arm did not waver. When he finished, he lowered the SLR slowly, placing its butt immediately in front of him.

'Because this weapon does so much for you,' he continued, 'you will learn to love and respect it. One day, it will save your life, and that is more than any woman will ever do for you. In return, you will love your rifle more than you would love any woman. In the army, your weapon is your first love. To show your weapon how much you love it, tonight you will sleep with it.' Some of us chuckled. Without a hint of mirth, Sergeant Jones continued. 'And you will continue to sleep with your rifle until you learn to care properly for it. Proper care involves keeping it clean and working perfectly.'

At this point, Corporal Smith flicked open a ground sheet, laying it squarely in front of Sergeant Jones.

'Gather around this ground sheet,' Jones ordered. 'To keep your weapon clean and working perfectly, you must be familiar with its separate parts.'

In a matter of seconds, he stripped the rifle into its individual parts and laid them out on the groundsheet. Then he re-assembled the rifle again, slowly this time, explaining as he went what the parts were, how they worked and how we should clean them. Next, we lined up and tried to repeat with our own rifles what had appeared so simple for Sergeant Jones.

Nick and Toby had no trouble doing what they had been shown, but David and I floundered. Corporal Smith tried to show us but soon lost interest, passing the task on to Nick and Toby.

'If you don't learn it quickly,' he said as he left, 'you will spend a lot of time sleeping with it.'

After a while, David and I fell into a comfortable routine for stripping and assembling our rifles, becoming more familiar with our weapons and confident in our newly learnt skill.

We were then taught some drills to carry out if our rifle stopped firing. Sergeant Jones called the drills IA One and IA Two, which stood for 'immediate action one' and 'immediate action two'. If our rifle stopped firing, we carried out IA One, and if it stopped a second time, we carried out IA Two. Sergeant Jones explained that, in battle, our lives depended on how quickly we could perform IA One and IA Two.

At this point the whole exercise seemed remote and technical to me. It simply did not register that this was for real. Although it was necessary to learn this life-preserving skill, for some reason it never occurred to me that at some time in the future my own life, and the lives of my mates, really might depend on my being able to carry out these simple actions.

How absurd, I thought, *that a life, a living, breathing, feeling, caring, unique life full of joy, hope and love, could actually depend for its continued existence on the ability to carry out a simple technical routine. What if I did learn this skill as second nature, so that I could carry it out smoothly and efficiently under the pressure and stress of battle? What then? Did it not also mean that another life, just as joyous, just as hopeful, just as loving would end? How absurd! If I did not learn these skills, my life would end, but if I did learn them, someone else would die. Either way, humanity is the loser, isn't it?*

This thought stayed with me the rest of the day. I couldn't shake it. I laughed out loud and shook my head a couple of times, but it wouldn't leave me.

'What's up?' David asked.

'Nothing,' I replied.

That night at the canteen, stretching my legs towards the fire drum, I explained my thoughts to the three of them. To my surprise, they greeted the question in silence, showing reluctance to be drawn into conversation.

'Why the silence? What's wrong? Haven't you thought about it before?' I asked.

'Jason,' said Toby, 'you think too much about these things. It's no good for ya, son. When it comes ta war, it's a simple case of survival. Kill or be killed. When it comes ta squeezin' that trigger, remember the other bastard's not gunna sit around worrin' about you. If ya get the drop on 'em, blow 'em away.'

The way he said it, I believed he looked forward to doing it. I was more than surprised – I was shocked. I thought I knew Toby. He seemed a regular bloke, but on this issue, he was insensitive. When he spoke of blowing someone away, all I could see was someone clutching his stomach, writhing and screaming in pain. I wondered what Toby saw. What would he do if he saw what I saw? Would he want to offer care and attention as I would? What would be the army's IA in such a case?

Then it struck me. The army didn't have one. In all our training, we never discussed such a situation. I guess they figured we'd just do what comes naturally. But what comes naturally would differ according to who was there, wouldn't it? That hardly seemed right. Why doesn't the army have an IA for dealing with injured enemy soldiers? I wondered.

'That's an awful way of putting it, Toby,' I finally said.

'That may be true,' David interjected, 'but, essentially, Toby is right.'

Again, I was shocked. I had expected some understanding, some sensitivity from David, but here he was about to justify what I considered an essentially barbaric attitude. I decided to appeal to his religious belief.

'Doesn't the bible say somewhere that thou shalt not kill?' I asked.

'Yes, but you must maintain perspective and put things into context when talking about the bible. What you have quoted is one of the ten commandments given to Moses to make a mighty nation out of a large group of Jewish refugees. It was a law designed to civilise an essentially barbaric tribe of liberated slaves and goat herders.'

'But that's what I'm saying. Isn't killing barbaric? As civilised people, shouldn't we avoid it?'

'Jewish rabbis believe that the King James translation of their Torah into the Old Testament mistook "murder" for "kill",' David went on. 'That certainly would make a difference in our understanding of the sixth commandment, would it not? After all, the Jews killed animals as a sacrifice to God by His commandment, so "thou shalt not kill" makes little sense if you believe in God's consistency. Regardless, what you do not seem to appreciate is that it is all a question of circumstance and timing. The bible is also full of examples of the Jews warring against rival tribes. In fact, the quote that best summarises this issue is in Ecclesiastes, chapter 3.'

It was clear that David had thought long about this. Perhaps he had even taken advice from priests because he now quoted from the bible:

> *To everything there is a season, and a time to every*
> *purpose under heaven:*
> *A time to be born, and a time to die; a time to plant, and a*
> *time to pluck up that which is planted.*
> *A time to kill, and a time to heal; a time to break down,*
> *and a time to build up.*

It goes on like this for a while but ends with:

> *A time to love, and a time to hate, a time of war, and a*
> *time of peace.*

'So, you see, according to the bible, killing really is a question of circumstance. Kill or heal, love or hate, war or peace, are questions of timing, not a question of right or wrong. Which is what you are trying to make it.'

'Fine. Let's assume for the moment that I agree with you about war being a question of timing rather than morality. Who determines when it is a time of war or a time of peace? Can I decide that for myself?'

'Yes, and no. In a democracy such as ours it is the responsibility of our elected representatives in parliament.'

'And what if they get it wrong?'

'Then it is up to the people, you and me, to tell them they got it wrong in the next election.'

'And in the meantime?'

'In the meantime, it is a time of war.'

'Yeah,' said Toby. 'We gotta stop those commie bastards before they get here. Remember Hitler and Stalin. We'll have to stop 'em sooner or later.'

'That was true with Hitler in Europe – he did have ambition to conquer Europe – but that's not Asia now, and Stalin is long dead,' David replied.

'What about the Chinese?' Toby asserted.

'What about them? Do you really think the Chinese want to conquer Australia?' David asked.

'Yeah, I do,' Toby said. 'Don't the commies want to rule the world? That means all countries, don't it? They're in Vietnam now, but if that falls, they'll want the rest of us next.'

'Well, if you buy that, I suppose you'll buy anything, and I've got a bridge in Sydney I'd like to sell you.' David said. We all laughed. 'The fact is that the war in Vietnam is really a civil war between the North and the South. Both governments are really dictatorships in all but name and, since we live in a democracy, their war has nothing to do with us. I don't accept the argument about communism versus liberty. You'd have to have a pretty vivid imagination to believe that Australia's security is threatened by what happens in Vietnam.'

'So, it is not a time of war. A time for killing,' I said.

'I didn't say that, Jason,' David replied quickly. 'Our elected government says it is.'

'Look,' said Nick, cutting his right hand through the air. 'I'm not smart like you blokes, so I don't follow what ya sayin', but what I do know is the last time I looked, my country was at war and it was hurtin'. One thing's for sure,' he continued, using his index finger as a baton, 'in war, you only have winners and losers. There's no prize for second place, and I don't intend to sit around an' watch my country and my mates go down the gurgler. Fuck the Vietnamese; it's got nothin' ter do with 'em. It's Australia an' our mates this war's about.'

We lapsed into silence. I could see David had more to say, but was reluctant about continuing after Nick's outburst.

'If you feel that way, David, why didn't you resist your call-up?' I asked, avoiding Nick by looking directly at David.

'That's a good question, and I agonised over it for a long time. My friends at uni all encouraged me to resist, especially after I got my call-up notice. They said I had a duty to the others not to go. Also, I could easily have deferred until after I'd finished uni. Chances are the war in Vietnam would have been over by then. Mother wanted me to wait as well.'

'Why didn't you?' I asked.

'It all seemed too convenient. For me, Vietnam became a deeply moral dilemma. To enter the army meant I might have to fight in a war I did not believe in, but not to honour the call-up meant I would have to break my country's laws. There was no convenient solution to this problem, and I came to believe this was one question that would shape my whole life. It was something I had to confront squarely and reason through logically and rationally, and when my decision came, the rest of my life would be affected by it.'

'So, what did you decide?' I asked urgently. David had our attention again. We all wanted to know how it came out. Even Nick.

'Well. I took advice from my friends at uni, and they mainly urged me to resist the authorities. However, I suspected they really wanted me to fight their fight for them. Some of them were terrified about the prospect of two years in the army and the possibility of going to Vietnam. I was determined their fears would not cloud my judgement.'

He stopped at this point and took a deep gulp of tea, then continued.

'Next, I went to my professors at uni and got pretty much the same response as I had from my friends, except for one professor of philosophy, who believed my dilemma was essentially philosophical.

'Nothing on earth is new,' he urged me, 'so look to the classics for your answer.'

He suggested Plato's book, *The Last Days of Socrates*. I read it and discovered that Socrates faced a dilemma similar to mine. You see, he had been condemned to death by the state of Athens for leading astray the minds of Athens' youth. Not wanting to see him die, some of Socrates' friends offered him a sure escape, but the escape carried with it the shame of banishment from the state that Socrates dearly loved. Socrates reasoned that he could not now turn against the state that had succoured and nourished him and protected him throughout his life, and for which he had fought in a war to protect. Because he had fought for and truly loved his state, he decided he had the right to do everything in his power to change the laws of his state, but that he did not have the right to break those laws. Ultimately, Socrates sacrificed his life for this principle. In the final analysis, the state triumphed over Socrates, but its triumph rested on his own principle. Without Socrates' decision to honour the laws of his state, it could not have triumphed. Ironic, isn't it? The state triumphed because of the individual's action.'

David stopped and looked at us. We stared back blankly.

'That is why I'm here today,' he offered, 'and if I die in Vietnam, it will be because of the principles I choose to live by and not because of what I am forced to do by this state. I will make every effort to change what I consider bad laws created by my state; that is why I speak out against the war in Vietnam, but I also choose to honour and obey the laws of the country I love, the country I claim as my own.'

'Good on ya, mate,' Nick said, reaching out and tapping David's shoulder.

I couldn't help but wonder why David never mentioned what his father had advised, but something else troubled me more.

'Is a principle worth dying for?' I asked.

'Yes, it is,' David answered strongly. 'We all must live by principles. Even to choose not to die for a principle is a principle in itself. It's not a very good principle, because it can lead to weak character and, in extreme cases, even cowardice. Eventually, we become what we are by the principles we choose to live by. Those who stand by their principles are the stronger for it. I've always thought the others were weak somehow, willing to surrender their principles for this reason or that.'

'But death seems so permanent,' I said lamely, the conviction ebbing from my argument. 'It seems like a high price to pay for a principle.'

'Only if you see death as an end, but life can go on after death. Socrates believed it did, so too did Jesus Christ. Their promise of a better life after death made them strong and principled in this life. Their promise can also make us strong.'

'But aren't you afraid to die? I asked, determined now to be better understood. 'I know that I am.'

'Those who fear death,' David continued, 'usually suffer

from uncertainty. They want to be certain about life and death and are uncomfortable with things beyond their reasoning. But some things in life cannot be understood without experiencing them. Death is like that, war perhaps and maybe even life itself. Whatever death is we will never truly know it until we experience it.'

'I live in fear of death,' I said, unwilling to yield to David's calm acceptance of it. 'I try not to think about it, because I don't have as much faith in a better afterlife as you obviously do. For me, death could be an absolute end, the beginning of nothing, yet that seems so pointless, doesn't it? Unless you believe the purpose of life is life itself. That is, we might die, but life itself goes on. But then I think this too is pointless. After all, didn't the dinosaurs become extinct? Many lifeforms have become extinct over time. God, I hate death! I hate the thought of rotting in a grave. I only hope that when I am caught in its pitiless grip, I won't die the death of a coward.'

'What's the big deal about death anyway?' Toby asked. 'See, the way I figure it is, we've all got ter die someday, so we gotta get what we can outta life while we're here. Fer me, thirty years of hard livin's better'n sixty years of boredom. Live fast, play hard an' go down fightin'. That's what I say.'

We reached an impasse at this point; nobody wanting to push on, yet I still searched for something more.

'What do you think, Nick?' I asked. 'What's death all about?'

'Death?' he said slowly, searching for words. 'Death is a dingo. Sleek an' shy an' always hungry. It slinks in the shadows, waiting to strike. It likes to stalk the weak an' frail an' the sick, but sometimes it'll pounce on the strong and fit. It plays the coward, only taking the vulnerable, usually hunting alone but sometimes in packs. It stays hidden, but if ya listen real hard, ya can hear it growl. Sometimes ya can even hear a pack of 'em howl before they pounce, an' when they do, the carnage they create is terrifyin'.' His eyes became strong and intense, like he was remembering something from his past. 'When ya see it,' he went on, 'ya want ter reach out an' touch it. Ter look it in the eye. But what it is is somethin' wild an' untouchable. Most times mysterious, sometimes ugly, but always strange an' out of reach. If ya get too close ter it, ya'll never be the same.'

'What do you mean?' I asked urgently.

'Ya always want ter know more, Jason,' Nick said flatly. 'Sometimes ya hafta accept what is, because there is no more.'

'The beauty of death lies in the questions themselves,' David offered. 'Death is beyond us, and that is why we fear it or we mock it, but that won't make it go away. So, it keeps coming back to haunt us, and that haunting gives rise to its mystery. We constantly wonder, but we can never truly know. But don't you see, the seeking to know is itself the source of our hope, and when we accept that, we can accept the pain and suffering, the joy and happiness of life and the loss of it.'

We drifted into silence after that, but the fear of death lingered with me, and I still worried how I would react when confronted with it. I was also determined to search my life and reason with my thoughts and ideas to discover principles to live my life by. Like David had said, principles make us strong, giving us a reason to live a courageous, fulfilling life. Such a life, I reasoned, could be mine if I searched hard enough for it, and a deep yearning filled me to live a principled life.

Just then, the commanding officer walked up to our small gathering.

'I heard you men had taken the trouble to set yourselves up around the fire. Mind if I join you for a while?'

'Sure, sir. You're welcome,' we all chimed in.

The commanding officer handed Nick a mug, who filled it, adding the honey and lemon juice. The CO took a long sip and added a smile. 'This is really good,' he said.

'Better'n that lousy Coke from the canteen,' Nick replied.

'Yes. Well, I can't do much about that, I'm afraid. The men seem to like it, and they need the energy they get from the sugar. The local supplier is delighted, though. He has to keep up with the demand.'

The CO smiled. We all laughed, then went silent for a time, each of us trying to think what to say. Then we asked the CO if he knew what corps we would be assigned to.

'Well, that has not been decided yet, but even if I knew, I wouldn't be able to tell you. It wouldn't be fair to the others.' We nodded in agreement. 'Still, I can tell you how we decide that. You see, recruit training is designed to help you fit into the army. Some of you come to us with a pretty low level of fitness, so we have to make you fit for what lies ahead. We also have to get you to accept working as a team rather than as an individual, and we have to familiarise you with the weapons you will be using. Your future survival depends on that.'

Again, we nodded. 'We also need to carry out IQ tests and personality tests to ensure that you are correctly matched with the job you will be expected to perform. So, it all depends on how you perform in these things. In the end, it is really up to you, as to where you will be assigned. Oh, yes, one other thing – we really can't just assign you to the corps of your choice, because you might not be matched with your choice. A lot of people make personal decisions based on glamour or perceived reward, and not on what they are best suited for.'

'As well as all that,' he continued, 'we also have to take into consideration the demands from the corps themselves. They tell us how many of you they want. We get the results of all the tests and the requests from the corps, and then we match you up with those corps we think best suit you, but if that corps is filled, we have to move on the next best. In the army, we believe that you will be happiest if you are matched with something you have the potential to be really good at.'

David spoke up. He told our CO about the bullying he and Toby had received from their lieutenant and platoon corporal.

'I see,' the CO replied. 'As a rule, I don't interfere with how the junior officers run their platoons, but I will look into it.'

With that said, the CO rose and wished us well. Then he said goodnight and left for some other groups of recruits.

A few days later Corporal Smith dropped all reference to recruit idiot or recruit smartarse and addressed us all simply as recruit. His unfriendly approach, however, continued.

*

Not long after that, I went to the orderly room and asked the duty sergeant if I could see the CO. He asked me what I wanted to see him about. I told the sergeant that I wanted to know why we were fighting in the Vietnam War.

He smiled at me. 'Didn't you attend the lecture on that?' he asked. I told him that I did, but that I was still confused, so he said, 'Just a minute' and walked to the CO's office. When he returned, he told me that the CO would see me in three days' time.

Three days later, I stood in front of the CO's desk. He told me to sit down and pointed to a chair directly in front of him. 'So, you want to know why we are fighting in the Vietnam

War?' he asked.

'Yes, sir. I know soldiers should not question their orders, and if I am told to go I will, of course. But it would be nice to know why.'

'You're friends with David Hughes, aren't you?'

'Yes, sir.'

'Yes. Well, I believe he is telling a lot of you that we should not be in Vietnam. Am I right?'

'Yes, sir. He has told me that we shouldn't be fighting in Vietnam, but he is willing to go, sir. He is a good bloke and very intelligent. That's why I came to you. I'm still a bit confused and would like to better understand what the army's reason is for us to be there.'

'Why do you think we are fighting a war in Vietnam?'

'I don't really know much about it, sir. When I was called up for national service, I just answered my country's call. I hadn't really thought much about it before that, other than that we have to fight the communists. Since the lecture and what David has told me, I'm not sure what to believe. I'm also a little embarrassed that I don't know more about it.'

'I want you to listen to this,' he said, removing a tape recorder from his draw. He placed it on his desk and pressed the play button.

It was President Kennedy giving his inaugural address to the American nation. I remembered having seen some news clips of him on TV and some photos of him in the newspapers. He looked so handsome and confident, and his wife and family seemed so supportive of him. He appeared to have good family values. Listening to him now, I was impressed by his smooth Bostonian accent and his oratory skills. Even from just hearing him, I could sense his charisma. Some evil force had snatched his life from his family and us all, but his words, full of conviction and principle, reached out to me from beyond the grave.

He spoke about how we should do whatever is necessary to uphold liberty throughout the world. Not to force liberty on others, but to support those who had chosen it. I was greatly moved by his words. He had a very clear way of expressing himself, and his confident tone highlighted the level of commitment that he had towards the ideas he was expressing. I believed he was a principled person. My mind cleared and my heart opened. Liberty – that was a principle I could live my life by, the right to choose for myself how I lived my life and not be forced by some dictator how to live it.

The CO pressed the stop button and smiled at me. 'Does that help you understand?' he asked.

'Yes, sir. But why South Vietnam? David said it's just another dictatorship, and that we should not get involved.'

'Do dictatorships have elections?'

'No, sir.'

'Well, South Vietnam does. Doesn't that make it a democracy?'

'I guess. But don't the communists have elections too?'

'Yes. But only the candidate endorsed by the Communist Party can stand for election. In communist countries, only one communist candidate can stand for election. In truly democratic countries there are multiple candidates, with differing ideas, who stand for election.'

'I see. And South Vietnam has multiple candidates, does it?'

'Yes. That's the difference.'

He waited for me to say something else, but I was at a loss for words. 'You don't seem too convinced. Let me explain further.

This is more complicated, but I think you will understand.'

He explained the difference between appeasement and peace through strength. How the democracies of the world had all tried to appease Hitler and the Japanese before WWII by allowing them to conquer countries that were not theirs, and how that had not stopped them. How, in the end, it had only made things worse. How what we were doing in Vietnam was making the communists understand that we would never surrender our freedom or the freedom of others to their dictatorship.

Next, he explained the policy of forward defence that the Australian government had adopted for the defence of Australia since the end of WWII. He explained that America and Australia had continued to trade with Japan during the 1930s and had supplied them with the commodities necessary to build their military machine, even after they had invaded Korea and China. Eventually, the Americans imposed an oil embargo on Japan in an attempt to halt its military actions in China, which were atrocious. Japan then chose to go to war with America and all other European countries with colonial empires in Asia. Australia was also a target for Japan because of our natural resources. Consequently, we had almost been invaded by the Japanese during WWII, and so today the government had decided that it would be better to fight a threat to our security overseas rather than wait until it reached our own shore. The communists, he explained, were that threat today, because they, too, wanted to destroy our way of life and were active in all the Asian countries to our north.

He explained President Kennedy's domino theory, how, if Vietnam fell, the other south-east Asian countries would all follow and fall under communist control. He also told me about the ANZUS alliance, and how Australia had an obligation to support the US in this conflict, how we depended so heavily on the alliance for our own security, and how being in Vietnam would mean that we could depend on the Americans to come to our aid if we ever needed them.

When he finished, he asked me if I understood what he had told me, and if I still had any questions.

'Actually, sir, David says we have nothing to fear from the communists in Vietnam. That the war there is just a civil war, and that we should not be involved in a civil war.'

'Hmm ... Have you heard about the Comintern?'

'No, what's that?'

'It stands for Communist International. It was founded in 1919 following the Russian Revolution and advocates for world communism. In truth, the communists are not pluralistic. They do not tolerate the existence of any other political system in the world except communism. So you see, our government doesn't believe that the communists will be satisfied with just Vietnam. Once they take Vietnam, they will look for the next country to conquer.'

'I understand the army's reason for being in Vietnam a bit better now, sir. You have been very helpful. Thank you for taking the time to explain all this to me.'

'That's good. Recruit Freeman, isn't it?'

'Yes, sir.'

'A very interesting name, given our conversation.' He removed a piece of paper from a draw in his desk. 'This is an extract from President Kennedy's speech. I would like you to carry it with you. If you, or any of your mates, ever have doubts about the Vietnam War, just read these words. I'm sure they will help you and others understand.'

He handed me the piece of paper and then dismissed me.

As I left his office, I reflected on how his words had given me so much information that I had not known before, and how appreciative I was that he had taken the time to share it with me. My respect for his leadership had grown enormously.

*

The hills across the open fields outside the camp rose gently to a modest height. They were lightly shaded by scattered gum trees, and the occasional boulder stood out, breaking the continuous gradient to their summits. The gentle sunlight of a clear winter's morning warmed my face and shoulders. The crunch, crunch of heavy army boots rose from the stiff, dry road we marched on. I shifted my backpack and moved the handle of my rifle, trying to adjust comfortably into the pace of the others.

We were marching to the rifle range where we were to fire our rifles for the first time. There had been much discussion about this the night before. Rifles had been cleaned and lightly oiled, while talk of fore sights and rear sights continued into the night. That seemed a long way off now as we finally halted at the range.

In the distance, at the base of a hill, a solid concrete wall approximately seven feet high ran from one side of the hill to the other. Stretching away from this wall towards where we stood was a wide, clear field of short, cropped grass with mounds of earth rising from it at regular intervals. It was from these mounds that we took our positions to fire at the targets held up from behind the concrete wall. We grouped around Sergeant Jones and Corporal Smith while they instructed us on the proper use of the range.

'Under no circumstances,' Sergeant Jones explained, 'will a loaded rifle be pointed in any direction other than at the target. Failure to do so will result in a swift kick up the arse. Under no circumstance will a weapon's safety catch be taken off unless and until I give the command, "Safety off". Failure to do this will result in an even swifter kick up the arse. Finally, under no circumstances will a weapon be fired unless and until I give the command, "Fire". Failure to do this and I'll have your guts for garters.'

I understood that Sergeant Jones considered all these as serious breaches of military discipline. However, it was an unseasonably warm morning, heralding the early arrival of spring. The air was crisp and clear, enticing me into a relaxed fantasy about picnicking on the rifle range: the spreading of a blanket on the green, open field; the opening of a cane basket; the salty, dry taste of a ham and cheese croissant followed by the bitter, sweet tang of a light Riesling and the gentle caress of a fair maiden clothed in flowing white frills and sporting pretty, pink lace.

'Are you listening, Recruit?' Sergeant Jones thrust an accusing finger into my chest.

'Yes, Sergeant!' I shouted, jumping with a start, my mind snapping back to reality.

'Good. I wouldn't want you to miss anything.'

Sergeant Jones and Corporal Smith then went into a duet in which Sergeant Jones explained the positions we were to adopt at the ridges while Corporal Smith demonstrated them.

'The lying position,' explained Sergeant Jones, 'offers your enemy the smallest target of the three positions and is therefore used wherever possible. On hitting the ground, look for any natural cover and something to lean your left forearm on to support your rifle barrel. Sandbags have been provided for that purpose today, but naturally in a real situation, you would have to improvise. Remember, the steadier your barrel the straighter your shot.'

I was beginning to lose interest again, but Sergeant Jones' eyes kept coming back to mine and realigning my thoughts.

'Turn your feet out,' he continued, pointing at Corporal Smith's feet, 'so that the inside of your feet rest flat on the ground. And I mean flat. We wouldn't want your heels to be shot off, would we? Now snuggle into the ground like it was a beautiful blonde you'd just given your last pay for. Get right down close; work your hips into the ground so that you are comfortable and relaxed.'

I no longer needed Sergeant Jones' glare to focus my attention.

'Resting your right cheek snugly into your rifle butt, line up your front and rear sights with the target. Now, with your right hand, gently squeeze the trigger. Notice, I said squeeze the trigger, not pull it. Imagine you're fondling the big tits of that expensive blonde you just paid a fortune for and not jacking off alone in your bed.'

We all began to chuckle. Remarkably, Sergeant Jones smiled, taking the tension out of our anxiety.

'If you do it right,' he continued, 'you'll have the satisfaction of seeing your bullet penetrate the big black dot smack in the middle of your target.'

Sergeant Jones and Corporal Smith then demonstrated the standing and sitting positions and had us practise them before lining us up in three ranks for Lieutenant Rogers to address.

'Stand easy, men,' he began. 'Now then, I want you to understand the importance of your actions today. For the first time since arriving at camp, you will be using live ammunition. One slip, one accident could cost a life. So, keep alert and think about what you are doing.'

Just then, Toby farted loudly. Lieutenant Rogers stopped talking and everything went silent. At first, someone chuckled and tried to suppress it, but eventually he gave up and started to laugh. His laughter infected the rest of us, and soon we were all laughing. Lieutenant Rogers went red in the face, then stomped over to Toby.

'I suppose you think that was funny, Re ...' His voice trailed off as he recognised Toby.

'No, sir,' Toby replied seriously, trying desperately to make amends. 'I'm sorry, sir. I couldn't help it, sir. It must'a been the beans last night. I'm sorry, sir. It's just that I've been holdin' it in all morning an' with the Sergeant an' the Corporal an' you an' ... I'm sorry, sir. It won't happen again, sir.'

With each outpouring, we found it harder and harder to contain our laughter, convincing Lieutenant Rogers that Toby was deliberately trying to mock him. Finally, Lieutenant Rogers told Sergeant Jones to take over and stormed off behind us. He spent the rest of the day there, looking through his binoculars at the targets and writing on our scoresheets.

We fired at thirty and fifty yards, and the best shots had a shoot-off at a hundred yards. We adjusted our rear sights as we moved back in an attempt to group our shots. My natural shot was high and to the right. I figured this was because of the rifle's kick when it fired, so I tried to steady it more with my left hand, but this had no effect. Next, I deliberately aimed low and to the left, hoping to compensate. My shots then went low and to the left. It was hopeless. I just wasn't any good at shooting, so I went back to aiming at the centre. My shots went high and to the right again, but at least this time, I got some consistency in my grouping. At the end of the day I felt pleased with myself, but I noticed Lieutenant Rogers flick quickly past my score sheet.

Those with the highest scores were given a shoot-off at the hundred-yard mound. When the scores were in, Nick had been the best shot of the day. Toby was nearer the top than I was, but neither of us drew attention from the lieutenant. By this stage, most of us were tired or bored and we sat around talking and smoking while Lieutenant Rogers congratulated Nick. Those in charge of us looked pleased with their day's work. Lieutenant Rogers turned to Sergeant Jones and told him to march us back to the barracks, before getting into his Land Rover and driving off.

Later that week, we were at a shorter shooting range to fire the F1 light calibre, semi-automatic machine gun. The F1 was an upgraded model of the Owen gun with the same simple, gravity-fed, spring-loaded bolt action and the same reliability in wet conditions. Like the Owen gun, the F1 could be dropped in mud or drenched in a tropical downpour and still fire. Unlike the Owen gun, the F1 had no front pistol grip and a curved magazine which stopped it from jamming. Replacing the front pistol grip was a perforated metal plate which surrounded the barrel, allowing it to cool and giving the user greater aiming ability. Although the F1 and Owen guns fired the same 9 mm calibre rounds, the F1 didn't have the same hitting power as the Owen gun. Over thirty yards, it needed more than one hit to stop a determined enemy soldier. The F1 was usually fired in bursts of three rounds.

The inherent problem with both the Owen gun and the F1 was that they had a very limited range and were easily triggered. If they were dropped with the safety off, three rounds could be automatically fired. This was avoided by a small, curved metal plate which was pushed down behind the bolt, stopping it from retracting far enough for a round of ammunition to drop from the magazine into the firing chamber.

The routine we performed was to stand on a firing line with the F1 facing our targets, which were within twenty yards of our position. Sergeant Jones stood behind us shouting orders.

'Watch your front! Watch your front!' On this command we tightened our grip, leaning into a firing position.

'Safety off!' We pulled the metal safety up.

'Cock your weapon!' We slid the bolt back, allowing the first round to drop into the firing chamber.

'Fire at will!' We emptied our magazines into black, three-ply silhouettes of enemy soldiers.

The target in front of me disintegrated into a thousand splinters. The smell of cordite gripped my nose and filled my lungs, adrenalin pumped through my body, my mouth went dry and open, the F1 rocked lightly in my hands, my grip tightened, my whole body felt like it would float away ... and suddenly ... it was over. My magazine was empty, and the F1 had stopped firing.

I looked at the shattered remains of my once whole target, and a strange, satisfying sense of power surged within me. *God help me*, I thought, *that felt good.* I placed the F1 on the ground and stepped down from the firing line, wiping my palms on the sides of my trousers.

After shooting, I took my place behind the concrete wall and held a wooden target high above my head for someone else to fire at. Graffiti covered the wall in front of me. There was the usual 'so and so was here', and the figure of Foo peering over a brick wall, only this time bullets flew past his head. But the item that held my attention was a life-sized painting of a man and woman engaged in sexual intercourse. They were standing, or at least he was. She had her legs wrapped around him, head thrown back, mouth open wide and hair falling behind her. Her hands held the man's head down, burying it into her large breasts, while his fingers bit deeply into her large round buttocks. The moment of climatic urgency frozen in art. It was good. I wanted to reach out and touch it but was conscious of the other devouring eyes.

Above my head, the target disintegrated into tiny pieces, bullets thumping and tearing at its fabric. The deafening roar of gunfire filled my ears as bits and pieces of plywood fell all around me. I opened my eyes and craved the large, round buttocks and swollen, proud breasts in front of me.

*

A short time after this, we were told we had four days leave coming. Days before our leave came up, the camp tattled on in an air of expectant joy. Where are you going? Who are you going with? What are you going to do? David invited me to go with him to Melbourne while Nick and Toby decided to try their luck in Sydney. Kings Cross, they said, was calling them. When our buses arrived late in the afternoon to take us away, we were lined up and handed a condom by Sergeant Jones.

'Remember, lads,' he said, 'If she's under sixteen, its rape whether she agrees or not. If she's over sixteen, it's only rape if she's not willing. And whatever you do, don't come back to camp with the clap.'

65

CHAPTER 3

On leave

Was it the city itself, the buildings, the parks, the hotels? Was it the people I met, their independence, their opulence, their carnality? Or even the climate, its dampness, its patchy sunlight, its changing moods, that made my leave in Melbourne so memorable?

On the bus, David boasted he would show me his Melbourne. We would have a great time, he claimed. Among other things, he promised an introduction to the most beautiful and celebrated woman in all of Melbourne. She would even stand naked before me. We both laughed, settled comfortably into each other's company and talked endlessly until our arrival.

Melbourne at 5.30 am was cold and damp. Across the street, a horse pulling a red milk cart stamped its feet and snorted bursts of steam from its nostrils. It was a curious thing to see in a modern city, but it was more than just quaint, bestowing a sense of familiarity on the stranger. We walked the streets looking for a taxi. Some of the buildings were old, dating from the glory days of gold and boom. Others were new, rising in the style of commercial grandeur, all steel and glass and concrete, with cranes hanging overhead, their fingers pointing skyward where Melbourne's destiny seemed to lie. It caught me unaware, the blending of old and new into a tension that pulled at my pride and my sentiment – the old reluctant to surrender its grip on the city's heart, the new tearing at its fabric with steel fingers.

We found a taxi, and David directed the driver to Canterbury Road, Kew. David's home had the imposing presence that old money generates. Built in a grand style fashionable in the 1880s, it displayed a prominent tower complete with parapet and classical motifs. There were grouped, arched openings and bracketed eaves, two stories with a veranda running right around the building on both levels. The upper level also had a wrought-iron balustrade linking the vertical columns, which ran from the ground to the roofline, set off with a cast-iron bracket. The walls of the house were furnished in stucco. There was a large, semi-circular gravel driveway leading to a portico contained within the tower. The grounds were formal with open, lawned spaces, a large old oak tree and a few tall conifers. An attempt had been made to maintain a picturesque relationship between building and landscape, but in its suburban setting, the overall effect was somewhat cramped.

David took me to the kitchen where we had a light breakfast of coffee and toast with Vegemite and joked about the heavy breakfast served to us in the army. We were just finishing when David's father entered.

'David!' he said. 'I heard a noise. Why didn't you wake us?'

He walked over and extended his hand.

'I didn't want to disturb you, Dad,' David replied.

'Welcome home, David,' Mrs Hughes said, standing in the doorway, one hand clutching the top of her coat, the other arranging the loose strands of hair hanging in her face. She looked hard at David.

'Hello, Mother,' David said, averting his eyes from her unyielding gaze. 'This is Jason. Jason is a Queenslander I met at camp.' He turned to me as he spoke. 'I like him, so I asked him here. I hope you don't mind.' He smiled at me, turned back to his mother and continued, 'Sorry I didn't tell you about it, but I really didn't have time. The leave came up so fast, you see, and I couldn't get to a phone.'

I felt uncomfortable. Had David avoided telling his mother about me because she would have disapproved, or had he simply been careless? He was undoubtedly lying to his mother now, because we knew about the leave days in advance. In fact, we were all looking forward to it and were counting down the days to leave camp. Also, there was a phone in the dry canteen that everyone used and knew about. Whatever the reason, his mother was clearly annoyed.

'Yes, dear, never mind that now,' she smiled with a face that diplomats reserve for midnight callers. 'Come and give Mother a kiss.'

She offered her cheek while David walked stiffly to her side and lightly brushed her cheek with his lips.

'It's good to be home, Mother,' he said.

'Yes, dear. You must tell us all about camp and what those little soldiers do all day. I really can't begin to imagine how you put up with living with so many people,' she said, half closing her eyes.

'It's not really that bad, Mother.'

'But it is depressing, isn't it? Just thinking about it is bad enough. I really don't know what possessed you.'

'Esmay!' David's father interjected. 'Not now, please. The boy's just got home.'

'Yes, you're right, dear. I do go on sometimes,' Mrs Hughes replied, her hand resting on her neck with her head tilted back. 'Now you must get ready for the office, dear, and I have several appointments today,' she said, organising her hair once more. 'I suppose you will want to show Jason around Melbourne?' she said, looking at David.

'Yes, Mother. Don't worry about us. We have lots to do, and I've arranged to meet Sarah and her friend for lun ...' his voice trailed off, recognising his careless admission of contacting Sarah and not calling his mother.

'Oh,' Mrs Hughes replied coldly. 'I see.'

'I ... that is, we ...' David fumbled.

'For Pete's sake, Esmay,' David's father said. 'Give the boy a break. Don't worry about it, son. Young people have different priorities; we were all young once.'

David smiled at his father, relief flooding his face.

'We must get together sometime during your leave, though,' Mr Hughes went on. 'Make any arrangement with your mother, and I will try to be there. Right now, I do have to get ready for the office. It's good to see you, David. And you too, Jason. You look great, son.'

He smiled, squeezed David's shoulder and was about to leave when Mrs Hughes put her hand up to stop him.

'Just a minute, dear,' she said. 'Why don't we all meet at the Windsor for lunch today? And you and Jason can bring your girls along.'

'Sounds good to me,' Mr Hughes said hurriedly. 'But now I really have to go.'

He placed his hands on his wife's shoulders. Turning her sideways, he kissed her lightly on the cheek, and was through the doorway and onto the steps leading to the upstairs rooms before I noticed he was gone. David's mother turned slowly and followed.

We were alone again. I smiled at David, but noticed the sad, dejected look on his face. I wanted to reach out and comfort him, but I didn't know how. We stood in silence in the large empty dining room until David finally said, 'Come on. I'll show you to your room.'

*

Later that day, we walked the length of Collins Street, lined as it was with deciduous English oaks, passed the T&G building on the corner of Russell Street, traversed the entrance of the Russell Collins restaurant with its smells of hot roasts and home cooking and the hurried passage of ladies in fox furs, noticed the tall, pointed roof of Georges, crossed Elizabeth Street and stopped outside the Commonwealth Bank building near the south-eastern corner of Queen Street, which David explained had been known as 'The Exchange' in the 1880s because of the share trading which had taken place there.

Collins Street bore the impressive substance of commercial activity. The solid look of aging limestone and the yellow sandstone-clad buildings with their straight lines and curved arches inspired confidence. The people, dressed in heavy woollen coats and rich furs, walked this street with purpose and direction. It filled me with ambition, a yearning to belong, but at the same time a recognition that I never would.

'God, I love this place,' David said. 'I belong here, like the generations of Hughes before who have called this street theirs.'

At that moment, I envied David his identity. He knew with a certainty, that I never would have, who he was and what his life held in store for him. My envy soon melted, however, when David confessed that he had to succeed at making money, because it was the only measure in life that had given meaning to the existence of generations of Hughes. He told me his great-grandfather, Sean Hughes, had come to Victoria during the gold rush days of the 1860s but had not founded the family fortune on prospecting. Rather, he prospered from the sly grog shops and, later, the hotels and bordellos of the boom towns of Ballarat and Bendigo. His great-grandfather had died young, something to do with a scandal over a married woman, which had led to a confrontation with her husband.

David smiled and seemed proud of his great-grandfather's exploits. 'He was a ruffian and a philanderer,' he said and gave a laugh.

Before he died, however, Sean Hughes had bought cheap farmland around the outskirts of Melbourne, which later became the closely settled suburbs of Fairfield, Ivanhoe and Heidelberg, making a fortune for his son, David Hughes, the present David's grandfather.

It was this first David Hughes who had brought respectability to the Hughes' name by marrying the daughter of a member of the Victorian Legislative Council. The old member had been financially embarrassed by the land boom crash and had taken out a secret composition in 1892 to avoid a scandal. He had found the Hughes' wealth a godsend, and his connections enabled David Hughes to establish a brewing empire in Victoria. In the 1930s, David's father diversified into wine and spirit retailing and, since the 1950s, he had developed further commercial interests in the City of Melbourne and invested in the Melbourne Stock Exchange. Now that his turn was coming to manage the family fortune, David believed that minerals and energy would be Australia's future. Get in now, he urged me, before it is too late. I didn't have the heart to tell him that I didn't have any money to get in with.

Then he turned to me with eyes tired beyond his youthful years and explained, 'Wealth is a state of secure uncertainty. I am daily confronted with my own fear that I might lose my family's fortune. I am always saying to myself, "look at you, and yet you have so much". This is not to say that my family's money is not without benefit. It provides me with security, the security of being different from those without it. My wealth dictates my life, though; it has made me different from, yet fearful of, my fellow Australians. I cannot relax, I am overcautious and vulnerable. I could never be poor.'

Was money really David's problem, I wondered, or was it just his fear of failure? I suddenly realised why rich people always wanted more and never seemed able to enjoy what they had. Wealth provides no immunity from fear, greed or envy, I concluded.

'Ironic, isn't it?' David continued. 'I worry so much about money, yet I went to Xavier College, which is run by the Jesuits. They are very strict on discipline, so my intellectual and spiritual training was very long and very thorough. I was taught that what I learnt and what success came my way was not for me but to further my faith in Christ and my service to my fellow man. I was told to cast myself in the same mould as Ignatius Loyola and Saint Francis Xavier.'

'Who were they?' I asked, wondering why David felt the need to share so much of his personal background with me.

'Oh, sorry! Ignatius Loyola was the founder of the Society of Jesus, whose members are called Jesuits. He went back to school at the age of thirty-one and graduated from the University of Paris. His followers were all highly educated men who used their knowledge in the service of Christ. I was told that learning should not stand in the way of my faith, and to use Ignatius as an example of what I could achieve with my education.'

'And did you?' I asked.

'Of course not. I'm much too worldly for that, but I suppose it has left a mark somewhere in my character.'

'What about Francis what's-his-name?'

'Francis Xavier. He was a world-renowned Jesuit missionary of the sixteenth century. His mission took him throughout the East Indies, Japan and China. Again, the strong idea of service and sacrifice was held up for me to emulate.'

'Is that how you see yourself then? As a missionary?'

'Hell, no! I'm no saint. These days, the younger Jesuits are influenced as much by radical politics as they are by the Society's belief in spiritual good work.'

'Well, how do you see yourself then?'

'A rich young man with an annoying conscience, I suppose,' he chuckled without much conviction.

'What will you do when you get out of the army?'

'Finish my law degree at Monash and then go into Dad's business and make a fortune. It's all very simple and straightforward really,' he laughed.

'Sounds wonderful. You're a lucky fellow.'

'Yes. I guess I am really. Except sometimes it all seems a bit much,' he said seriously.

'What do you mean by "a bit much"?'

'Well, it's a bit hard to explain. Like all this religious nonsense about service and humanity, when all my family really does is serve its own interests. You know, it's our wealth we really serve. That's the most important thing to us, to make more money than the generation before. Sometimes, I think the whole of life is just one great big hoax, a stinking pile of hypocrisy. Know what I mean?'

'Not really,' I replied. 'I don't have a lot of money to worry about.'

'No, I know that,' he said earnestly. 'But what about other things in your life? Don't you see hypocrisy there?'

'Like what?'

'Like Vietnam, for instance. Would you go and fight there?'

'Yes. I guess so,' I said cautiously.

'Why? Do you believe the communists are out to get you?'

'Probably, but I don't know for sure. Anyway, isn't the South trying to keep its freedom?'

'I don't think so. Haven't you heard about the corruption of the South Vietnamese government?'

'Yes, but that's not the issue, really. After all, you can find corruption everywhere, can't you? North and South Vietnam, and even in Australia, if you look hard enough for it.'

'Perhaps, but there's your hypocrisy. Are we fighting to uphold the South's freedom or its corruption? Don't you think some Americans are making a lot of money out of the war?'

'How do you mean?'

'Well, all the companies in the military–industrial complex in America, don't you think they're making a lot of money from the war? Don't you think they might be paying kickbacks to the politicians to keep it going?'

'Gosh, I hope not. I suppose they could do that to get awarded contracts, but to do that to keep the war going would be a diabolical conspiracy. Surely, they wouldn't do that! Besides, their scientists work hard to produce superior equipment for us, including laser precision targeting to reduce civilian casualties in order for us to win the war. If they are doing that, they wouldn't want to keep the war going. Would they?'

'Yes. They do that, but that is not helping us to win this war, is it?'

'I guess not. We'll have to see why the war hasn't been won yet once we get there.'

'That's the point, though, isn't it? Are we fighting for South Vietnam's liberty or the corruption created by the war?'

'Well, if I'm asked, I'll be fighting for South Vietnam's freedom, and because my country says I have to. That's what you said back at camp. Wasn't it?'

'Yes, But in my case, I'll be trying to stop the war by speaking out against it. Whereas you're just going along with it,' he said matter-of-factly. We lapsed into silence then he turned to me and asked, 'Why don't you speak out against the war, like me?'

It was then I realised what all this was about. David wanted to convert me; he wanted me to oppose the war as he did.

'Well, for one thing, I'm only just beginning to understand the issues,' I replied.

'But we've spoken about it often enough.'

'That doesn't help. I've still got a lot to learn, and sometimes we have to experience something for ourselves before we really know what it's all about. Didn't you say that back at camp?'

'I was talking about war in general when I said that, not this war in particular. We should not be fighting in this war. Anyway, what are you going to do after the war? Provided you survive it, of course. What are you going to do then?'

'Well, I guess I'll make up my mind at that time, not now. I would like to start my own business someday. I'm still saving for it, but I'm a long way off that at the moment.'

'That's not good enough, Jason. You have to make a stand in life sometime, otherwise you'll just drift.'

We went silent for a moment, and I wondered what the people who passed by thought of us standing on a Melbourne footpath discussing the Vietnam War. Then David looked into my eyes.

'You might have to kill someone, you know,' he said strongly. 'Don't you think you should know why before you pull the trigger?'

'Yes, that worries me, but I'll just have to see what happens if that arises.'

'You can't just leave it at that. It's too important, surely. Even for you, Jason.'

We went silent again. Showing his frustration, David moved away from me but came back.

'You know what you are, Jason,' he said, pointing his finger. 'You're a witness. All you want to do is stand back and observe others.'

'What's wrong with that? Shouldn't young people do that? After all, we have so little experience of life,' I said quietly.

'But, Jason, you have to believe in something. You have to take a stand in life if you want to amount to anything.'

'Why? I'm not that passionate, and I'm too young to really know what I believe in. After all, you never truly know anything until you've done it, do you. Besides, isn't fighting for South Vietnam's freedom taking a stand?'

'Yes. But it's the wrong stand. That's why we have a brain,' he said, placing the tip of his forefinger on my forehead. 'To think things through before we act. A nice mess we'd be in if we all went around doing things just to get the experience.' He paused, then asked, 'Do you really think South Vietnam is free?'

'I don't know, and I don't want to go around doing whatever

I want. We can't break the law, can we? You said that yourself, remember, and I guess I'll find out if South Vietnam is free after I get there.'

'Look, just tell me,' he said desperately. 'Do you believe in the war or don't you?'

'I don't know, but I have thought about it. You got me thinking about the war, so I went to our CO back at camp and asked him about it. He told me about John F. Kennedy's words from his inaugural address to the American nation. Let me read them to you.'

I took the piece of paper my CO had given me out of my pocket and read from it:

> *Let every nation know whether it wishes us well or ill,*
> *that we shall pay any price, bear any burden, meet any*
> *hardship, support any friend, oppose any foe to ensure the*
> *survival and success of liberty.*

I paused for a moment to allow the beauty of Kennedy's words to take effect.

'What I believe is that great leaders have told us to support South Vietnam's liberty, and the people of Australia have told us the same thing. So, I guess it is now our duty to obey.'

David sighed deeply, and I read the disappointment in his face.

'We're different, you and I,' I said, trying to ease the situation. 'You want to think about things and believe in them. I want to gain knowledge, trust my country's leaders, follow its laws and make conclusions after I have some experience.'

'I worry about you, Jason,' David said, his face relaxing. 'I don't know whether you're clever or just too smart for your own good. One thing I know for sure is that I don't trust our leaders.'

I laughed and gently punched his shoulder. 'What now?' I asked.

'Now the most celebrated and beautiful woman in Melbourne will reveal her all,' he replied, charging off down Queen Street and left into Flinders Street. I eventually caught up with him when he stopped on the corner of Swanston Street. We stood on the footpath breathing deeply and admired Flinders Street Railway Station, a truly remarkable old building with a granite foundation, cement rendered sandstone detailing, a dome and arches with classical lines. I stood in awe of its beauty. Curiously, however, it was littered with commercial advertising boards. A Mercedes-Benz symbol stood on the rooftop, a Mitchell neon sign, looking skeletal in the daylight, hung on the side and a BP temperature sign, reading a pleasant 64 degrees F (18 degrees Celsius) for this time of the year, defaced the entrance.

'Is this it?' I asked.

'Don't be silly,' David replied, grabbing my elbow and leading me into Young and Jacksons pub. 'This way, young man. The toast of Melbourne awaits you.'

Inside, it was dark and cold. The room was long and narrow and the bar ran along the far side, almost from end to end. Having just opened, only a few customers had arrived. David directed my attention to the bottles behind the bar and led me to the beer taps.

'Jason,' he said light-heartedly, 'There comes a time in everyman's life, a rare moment when all the beauty of the universe crystallises into the smooth curves of a woman's naked body.'

As he spoke, his voice rose in confidence, and the few people at the bar turned to look at him.

'Such a moment,' he went on, 'brings with it rare feelings of delight and sensuous stirring.' He paused for effect. 'Such a moment,' his voice now ringing with glee, 'came to me when first I beheld the voluptuous, the beautiful, Chloe.'

He stood to one side and waved his hand towards a painting hanging at the end of the room. I was fascinated. Never before had I seen a painting of a naked woman hung in public. My fascination quickly turned to embarrassment, however, and I looked away.

The people at the bar laughed, enjoying David's lighthearted entertainment, and my reaction to the naked Chloe.

'No, no, no, my friend,' David cheered. 'This is no time for shyness or shame. This is a time of sweetness and light.' He walked over and stood by the painting. 'Notice the innocence in her expression,' he said, raising his hand and pointing at her face, 'the gentle curve of her shoulder,' his open hand tracing a curve, 'the voluptuous swelling of her breasts,' cupping his hands, 'the full, rounded curve of her buttock,' patting the air, 'and the hidden passion between her thighs.' His eyes rolled upward with delight, his hands joining in a 'V'.

I was stunned, at both David's eloquence and the naked Chloe. Those at the bar cheered.

'Ah, the province of the truly romantic,' David continued, in a mocking tone, 'Such beauty should not be the sole delight of the gods, but the joyous pleasure of all who dare to speak, to reach out, to touch the very essence of our existence. This, my friend, is life cast in the romantic's mould.'

He paused, looked at his watch, and then added hurriedly, 'Would we had time to wallow in the licentiousness of our present state, but we must away. Our ladies await.'

He took me by the arm and walked me towards the door. Applause rang from the bar. He paused, turned and took a deep bow, and then we disappeared through the sunlit doorway.

On our way to Queen Victoria Gardens, David explained that the two girls we were to meet, Sarah and Clarissa, were friends from his university days. Apparently, Sarah's father had run a successful firm of chartered accountants before he died suddenly of a heart attack, leaving Mrs Rothenberg a successful company and a generous insurance payout.

Since then, the eligible male population of Melbourne had courted Sarah's mother, but to date she had committed herself to none, choosing instead to revel in her newly acquired financial independence. This had left Sarah confused and embarrassed by her mother's behaviour, and, David confessed, it was Sarah's shy and retiring nature along with her traditional values, clearly inculcated by her father, that had first attracted him to her. Also, her family belonged to the rich upper-middle class of professionals, doctors, lawyers and accountants, upon whom the old money establishment depended, that made her acceptable in his social circle.

Clarissa, on the other hand, was naturally rebellious, he explained. Her father was a successful builder who had recently made a fortune from the building boom. It was this money that had given Clarissa's family a step up in the social circles of Melbourne but had also alienated her from her old friends. Apart from Sarah and him, Clarissa was never really accepted by her new circle of friends, who believed she belonged to the vulgar group of *nouveau riche*, and this had fuelled her rebellion.

The three of them had become active in the anti-Vietnam

movement at university, but, David concluded, Clarissa was the passionate devotee while Sarah was more interested in her artistic pursuits, warming to the anti-establishment sentiment of popular music and contemporary poetry.

Rising to their feet at our approach, Sarah and Clarissa smiled and moved nervously until David spoke.

'You look wonderful, Sarah,' he said, placing his hands on her hips. She raised her arms and linked her hands behind his neck.

'It's so good to see you,' she said, looking into his eyes.

As they kissed more in greeting than passion, I noticed Sarah was the smaller of the two girls. Her legs were short but shapely, and her long blonde hair fell almost to her waist. She wore a plain white cotton skirt with a cool, silk blouse sporting a large, crinkled collar. When they finished, she turned to me and smiled.

'I'm sorry. You must be Jason.' I nodded. 'Your full name is Jason Freeman. Is that right?'

'Yes.'

'Jason Freeman,' she said, turning to her friend, 'this is Clarissa Swanson. Clarissa, Jason. Clarissa is our friend from university.'

In contrast with Sarah's hair, Clarissa's was short but styled. It was teased at the front and cut close at the back. She wore a turquoise silk blouse with long sleeves that buttoned tight around her wrists and puffed out below the shoulders, a tight-fitting miniskirt and white, knee-high boots. She had an attractive, round face with full cheeks and a small upturned Irish nose. A wide mouth with generous lips set off her clean white teeth and strong chin.

'Hello, Clarissa,' I smiled.

'Hello yourself, soldier boy,' she replied cheekily.

I reached out my hand and she took it confidently. The four of us started walking down Alexandra Drive, relaxing in the country atmosphere of a shaded, tree-lined driveway. The drive was lined on each side with parked cars awaiting the return of a wedding party. A large white limousine with 'Just Married' written on the rear window and tin cans tied to the rear bumper caught David's eye. Reaching into his pocket, he broke from us and approached the limousine on the driver's side. He pulled out the condom given to him by Sergeant Jones, unravelled it and slipped it over the wireless aerial. He chuckled as we walked away.

'They'll spend the rest of their lives trying to figure out which of their friends did that,' he said cheerfully.

We walked to the Myer Music Bowl where Sarah told us how The Seekers had thrilled her with their performance there and how exciting it was to be a part of the enormous crowd. Standing in front of the bowl, dwarfed by the huge canopy and the wide, green expanse of manicured lawn, I tried to imagine it.

'You know, it was fabulous,' she said, her arms moving in a wide arc. Then she turned more serious. 'Actually, I liked the men's tenor harmony, which enabled Judith's perfect pitch soprano voice to stand out. She clearly is the lead singer in the group, but the boys are very accomplished musicians too. As a group, they all work so well together, don't you think?'

We all nodded in agreement and sat down. David and I stretched our legs out and leaned back on our elbows, while the girls crossed their ankles and sat upright.

'They were all there on the stage,' she went on. 'Guy Athol played guitar over there. He's so talented. And Judith Durham sang there. Her voice is pure perfection, you know what I mean? She's just so …' Sarah searched for the right word. 'So … exquisite,' she finally said, tilting her head back and looking up at the patchy sky. She raised her right hand to her head, forefinger pointing up along her cheek and thumb tucked under her chin. She crossed her left arm across her body and supported her right elbow with the back of her left hand. 'I think I liked "Morningtown Ride" the best,' she said cheerfully.

'What about "Georgie Girl"?' I asked. 'That's very popular now.'

'I know what you mean,' she replied, disentangling her arms. 'It's modern, isn't it? But I still like "Morningtown". It's got something, don't you think? It takes you back to your childhood and you're actually in that train, rocking and rolling home.'

'That's good,' I said. 'There are times I feel like that. Even now when I'm supposed to be grown up.'

She smiled at me. 'That's right,' she said. 'That's what I mean. It keeps us in touch with our childhood.'

Her clear blue eyes opened wide with her smile, and for a second, I saw deeply into the wide expanse of her innocence. Eventually, her eyes dropped away and we lapsed into silence.

'Yeah,' Clarissa said. 'But you should be independent, right?'

'Huh?' Sarah and I replied.

'You can't be a child forever, and you shouldn't depend on others to care for you. You have to look after yourself, right?' Clarissa's voice was high-pitched and nasal, yet it finished with a rounded sound.

'Yes,' said David. 'You're right, Clarissa. You do have to take charge of your life sooner or later. If you don't, the responsibility of adulthood will crush you.'

'Yes, I know that, David,' Sarah asserted, looking into his eyes. 'But the thing is, I don't care about the things adults find important. I don't think money and material stuff are that important in my life.'

'That's probably because you have it. But tell me, Sarah, what is important to you?' David asked.

'People,' she immediately replied. 'People are more important than material things. I know I have to have sufficient material thing to enjoy a good life, and I am lucky in that regard, but that doesn't mean I have to devote my life to it.'

'But many people live miserable lives without sufficient material things, and they are forced to devote themselves to acquiring them.'

'I don't think it's fair that you should say that, David,' Sarah replied seriously. 'You make it sound like it's a choice we have to make between money or people. Why can't we have both?'

'Because for some to have more, others have to have less,' David said matter-of-factly. 'And those with more make even more for those with less. Modern life is all about productivity and growth. Everybody must make more so everybody can have more. The fact is, we live in a world of rising expectations, which can only be met by raising productivity, and that starts with those with more investing in things that raise our productivity.'

'But if you don't want to have more, if you only want to have enough, can't you be happy and make people important in your life?'

'No, because what is enough for you is not enough for someone else, and then you don't think it's fair that someone else has more than you,' David asserted, his face lighting up. 'Eventually, you have to compete to get more, and then you're into the money game, the pursuit of self-interest where the winner gets more while the loser gets less. Unless you want to live the life of a hippie and envy the taxpayers who support your unproductive lifestyle.'

'I don't go as far as that,' Clarissa said, 'but I do agree with David that ultimately we do have to get what we want for ourselves. If we don't, we can never be truly independent. In this life, we do have to look after ourselves, because nobody else will.'

Outnumbered, Sarah went silent. She folded her arms and looked down at her knees; her shoulders heaved in a deep sigh. I felt sorry for her. At that moment, I wanted to say something to encourage her, but I didn't know what, so I just sat there looking at her. David stood up, brushing the grass from the back of his trousers.

'Let's go and see the war memorial,' he said.

As couples, we walked hand in hand to the bronze stature of a WWI soldier. Standing in hushed respect, I thought of the huge sacrifice and the loss of young life WWI had bought to our country.

'It seems so sad, really,' Sarah said, 'that so many had to die.'

'They didn't, you know,' Clarissa said.

'What?' I asked, somewhat shocked by her reply.

'Well, it was a European war really, wasn't it?' she said with conviction. My forehead furrowed. I concentrated, waiting for her to go on. 'Australia wasn't threatened, was it? Not really.'

'Well, why did so many go then?' I asked.

'I guess they didn't really understand,' Clarissa said flatly.

'Didn't they go to make the world safe for democracy? That's what President Wilson said, wasn't it? And after the war, all the major crowned heads of Europe fell and were replaced with liberal democracies. Liberty triumphed over autocracy. Didn't that make the world a safer place for Australia? And what about all the colonies around Australia? They would have fallen into Germany's hands if the Germans had won. The Pacific islands, Indonesia, Malaysia – all would have become German colonies. How was it not in Australia's interest to stop that from happening?'

'They also said it was "the war to end all wars".'

She smiled and put her arms around my waist and looked up into my eyes.

I nodded. 'Yes, they did. I guess they couldn't see that there would always be tyrants and dictators – call them fascists, Nazis or communists – who, not content with living their own lives, wanted to dictate how others must live theirs. How could they predict that liberal democracies would fall so easily to dictators?'

'I suppose you think that we're in Vietnam to protect freedom too,' she said.

'Yes,' I replied solemnly.

'Kiss me,' she said, reaching up and taking my face in her hands.

I bowed my head and kissed her lips, and she opened her mouth and searched for my tongue, thrusting her hips into my groin, moving them in a slow circular motion while moaning lightly. She wrapped her arms around me and squeezed me in a tight embrace, and I felt myself being aroused. Then she suddenly broke from me and stood back.

'There, soldier boy,' she smiled. 'There's more truth in that than you'll ever find in your bloody war. It's simple really – make love not war,' she remarked, a note of triumph echoing in her anti-war slogan.

'You're wasting your time, Clarissa,' David said. 'He's going to Vietnam, and he doesn't want to think about it.'

Clarissa's eyes searched my face. I wanted her to understand.

'I'm a soldier,' I said, earnestly. 'I can't help what I am, and soldiers have a duty to perform for their country when asked.'

She looked puzzled. 'You don't have to be a soldier, do you?'

'Yes. I do. As I said, it's my duty.'

'You're not trying to be a hero, are you, Jason?' David asked light-heartedly.

'Nothing like that. We've been through all this, David.' I pleaded. 'Can't we just drop it? Please.'

'Yeah. Sorry, mate,' David said. 'Anyway, Australia is not a country for heroes.'

'What do you mean, David?' Sarah asked.

'Australians have only had three national heroes,' he explained. 'One was a criminal in an iron suit, another was a cricketer with an unstoppable bat and the third was a racehorse with an oversized heart. The first they hanged, the second they knighted and the third they stuffed,' David mused. We all laughed.

'That's very good, David,' Sarah added, pressing her cheek against his chest. 'Who will be the hero of our generation?' she asked, looking up into his eyes.

David's forehead furrowed. 'Perhaps a male singer with a high-pitched voice and tight jeans. That's what everyone wants to be, isn't it?' his question more rhetorical than inquiring.

We left our bronzed soldier and walked along the shaded banks of the slow-moving Yarra. It had a curious mixture of native gums with high branches reaching out over the cool water, and European weeping willows with tired strands forming the water's edge. The morning passed unnoticed while we lay in the shade, watching the gentle ripples of the river as the small boats cut their paths up and down and passed under the arches of Princes Bridge. We had to leave and, as I climbed into the taxi that would take us to the Windsor for lunch with David's parents, I felt a sudden longing to be back at the water's edge.

*

The Windsor Hotel in Spring Street was an opulent setting for those who could afford it. Built originally as the Grand Coffee Palace in 1888, it boasted high towers topped with copper domes and walls of tiered arches and columns. Inside, the luncheon room was decorated with hanging pots, creeping vines and polished wooden floors. An abundance of vases crammed full of freshly cut flowers filled the room with a rich, fulsome fragrance. Women in long dresses and tailored coats and sharp sunglasses sat around tables covered in white linen. Miniskirts, pantihose and slacks may have revolutionised women's fashions outside but, in here, the establishment reclined in their high-backed Victorian chairs, sipped their gin slings and to hell with all that common vulgarity outside. David found his mother at a quiet table sheltered by a large square column of marble clad concrete. She looked unapprovingly at Clarissa's attire.

'Hello, Mother,' David said, nodding his head and pulling a chair out for Sarah. 'Where is Father?'

'He said to offer his apology. He has business to attend to.'

'This is a busy time for him.'

Mrs Hughes smiled, her narrow eyes never moving from his face, the gaze, lynx-like and concentrated, oblivious of anyone other than David. We settled ourselves around the table and I noticed the subdued light caught only one side of her face, highlighting the firm, straight line of her thin-lipped mouth, a dark notch in its corner joined by a stiff crease running from the corner of her nose.

'I'm sorry we're late, Mother ...' David began before he was silenced by his mother's uplifted hand.

'That's something I've learnt to anticipate, David,' she said coldly. The waiter arrived and took our orders. 'What are your plans for this evening?' Mrs Hughes asked as the waiter left.

'Jason and I are taking the girls out dancing.'

'One of those dark, smoky nightclubs, I suppose.'

'I suppose.'

'Your father and I are having dinner at home tonight ...'

'Sorry, Mother. Jason and I are eating at Sarah's place tonight.'

Sarah nodded her head in agreement. 'That's right, Mrs Hughes,' she said. 'Mother was so pleased when I asked ...' Her voice trailed off, as she noticed Mrs Hughes stiffen in her chair, shift her weight and sway her shoulders from side to side. Sarah's eyes dropped, and she busied herself with her napkin.

'Do you intend spending some of your leave at home, David?' Mrs Hughes asked flatly, unconcerned about chastising David in public.

'Oh,' Sarah whispered, her left hand moving nervously to her mouth.

'But, Mother,' David said slowly, smiling and waving his hand to one side. 'I saw you this morning and I'm having lunch with you now.'

'As a family, I mean, David,' she said, her voice dropping slightly.

'Dad's too busy. You know he won't be home tonight,' David said matter-of-factly.

'That's not true. He assured me this morning ...'

'That was this morning, Mother. Tonight, he'll be too busy.'

'I know you never saw enough of your father, David, but ...'

'I never saw him, Mother, because he was never home.' David took a deep breath, before pushing on with his verbal assault. 'He never wanted to be at home, did he, Mother? He was always more comfortable with his business colleagues and his friends at the club than he was with us. Why was that, Mother? Why was he never home with us?'

'You ungrateful little––' She quickly composed herself.

We were silent and Sarah looked as though she was about to cry. The waiter arrived, placed our food in front of us and left quietly.

'I gave my life to you and your father,' Mrs Hughes said firmly.

'You got your reward, Mother,' David continued, casting his aspersions. 'You got your house in Kew, your imported cars and your rich furs and jewellery, but you'll never get me. You'll never run my life any more than you run Father's. That's why he was never home, wasn't it, Mother? Because you never let him be himself. Because at home, you always tried to shame him into doing what you wanted.'

'That's not true! I––'

'It is true. It's the same with me. I know why you resisted my going into the army. Wanted me to get an exemption. You could no longer boast to your friends about your successful son, the university student, the bright young lawyer-to-be who would one day take over from his father. But what have you got now, Mother? A private in the Australian army about to fight in a war that nobody wants anymore. What a shame patriotism is out of fashion this year. Think of the social mileage you could have got out of that, Mother.'

Mrs Hughes looked stunned. David remained on the edge of his seat, eager to go on.

'I guess we're stuck with each other, you and me. But one thing I promise you, Mother, is that you'll never own me. You'll never smother my determination to live my own life any more than you did with Father.' David stared hard at his mother.

'No point in my staying,' Mrs Hughes said, rising to her feet and opening her handbag. 'Your father wanted you to have this,' she said, throwing a bundle of twenty-dollar notes on the table. She turned abruptly and walked away, leaving us in silence.

David's shoulders slumped forward and he stared, ashen faced, at the money in front of him. The muscles of his face dropped and his eyes moistened. We remained in silence until Sarah reached out her hand and caught David's arm.

'Oh, David,' she said. 'How awful.'

With her other hand, she took the side of his face and placed his head on her shoulder. 'Poor darling,' she continued, taking her hand from his arm and rubbing his back.

Clarissa stood up and excused herself saying she had to meet someone. When she had gone, David picked up his father's money and the three of us left for Sarah's place.

*

'Clarissa said she couldn't make it to the dance tonight,' Sarah said, returning from the phone to her seat at the dining table.

'Oh! Well, the three of us will still have a good time,' David offered.

'I'm not sure I'll be going,' I said.

'What? Don't be silly, Jason. We'll be fine,' David said.

'No. Three's a crowd,' I replied quickly. 'Besides, there's a movie I want to see.'

'Oh,' David said. 'What movie is that?'

I did not reply immediately. Instead, I looked at Sarah's mother sitting opposite me. She had to be well into her forties, but she looked a young thirty, with a face as fresh as a summer shower. She wore a light blue strapless shift revealing her glowing, olive-skinned shoulders. She was framed by lightly draped windows and the soft light from outside settled over her like a garment of sheer silk. I searched her wide, brown eyes, and an attractive smile filled me with desire.

'Yes,' she said slowly. 'I was hoping to see that new Peter O'Toole movie. What's it called, Sarah?'

'*Lawrence of Arabia.*'

'That's the one. Would you like to take me, Jason?'

'I'd love to, Mrs Rothenberg.' I said cheerfully.

'Rebecca will do, Jason. I always feel more comfortable on a first name basis. Don't you?'

'Yes. Yes. I do, Rebecca.'

The corners of her mouth lifted further, and two dimples appeared in her cheeks. The rest of the meal was spent in relative silence, broken periodically by polite questions and answers about army training and camp life. After David and Sarah had left, I offered to help with the washing up.

'I have a dishwasher,' she said. 'You bring the dishes and I'll stack.'

'Fine,' I said, carrying a pile of plates into her fully equipped kitchen.

I put the plates on the bench above the dishwasher and

rolled up my sleeves to the elbows. I returned to the dining room, then brought out the remaining crockery and cutlery and put it down beside the other plates.

She moved very close to me as she stacked the dishwasher, and her musk perfume surrounded me.

'It's awfully nice of you to do this, Jason,' she said, placing her hand lightly on my forearm.

'I ... I ... It's nothing, really.'

My ears burned and my heart beat rapidly. She smiled and stroked the hairs on my arm. I stood motionless wanting to do or say something, but not knowing what. She continued stroking my arm and laughed merrily.

'Come on then,' she said finally. 'If we don't hurry, we'll miss the start of the movie.'

*

'Peter O'Toole was great, don't you think, Jason?' Rebecca said, opening the door of her house on our return.

The movie had gone slowly for me. I kept wanting to do something with Rebecca – hold her hand or put my arm around her – but it all seemed so childish somehow, so I just sat there nervously shifting in my seat. When we were leaving the movie, I took her elbow in my hand. She turned and smiled at me and slipped her arm into mine. That had filled me with relief. Now I followed her lead as we entered her house.

'Yes,' I replied. 'Very dramatic. He was certainly the right actor for that part.'

'He has such beautiful blue eyes,' she continued. 'I thought I was going to melt at some of those close-ups.'

We entered her sunken living room. Placing her hand on

my arm for support, she removed her shoes, then walked me to a candy-striped sofa. I sat down and took off my shoes and socks, letting my naked toes sink deep into the shaggy pile carpet.

'What would you like to drink?' she asked, raising her eyebrows and allowing a smile to fall naturally across her face. I smiled back and told her I would have what she was having.

'Surely you don't want a sherry?' She laughed.

'Well, no. Do you have a beer?'

'Certainly,' she said, and disappeared into the adjoining room.

I looked around the living room for the first time. Soft, sheer curtains hung over sliding doors with access into a private courtyard. Formal armchairs, a polished timber coffee table with two chairs and a polished marble lampstand coordinated with the sofa to convey a sense of tradition.

Rebecca returned carrying a silver tray with an empty beer glass, a can of Fosters and her sherry. She waited until I poured before placing the tray on the table, taking her sherry and joining me on the sofa. I drank my first glass quickly and refilled while she sipped and watched me over the rim of her glass. Feeling a little more relaxed, I leaned back into the sofa, leaving my refilled glass on the tray.

'Let's have some music,' she said, rising from the sofa and moving towards the high fidelity Lowboy on the opposite side of the room. 'See if you can guess who this is,' she said, placing a record on the turntable.

She held the record cover behind her and moved slowly towards me. Her arms wrapped her dress tightly around the outline of her body. She moved graciously with a gentle sway of her hips, which accentuated the feminine curves of her mature figure. The music started to play. It was soft and sensuous at first, then moved gradually into the full sound of a complete orchestra. She stopped in front of me with her legs slightly apart and looked down at me.

'Come on,' she teased. 'Who is it?'

'That's easy,' I replied. 'It's Mantovani.'

I was smiling up at her, but I wanted to hold her in my arms.

'You're right,' she said, handing me the record cover. I took the cover, but my eyes never left hers. 'I'm going to freshen up,' she said. 'Won't be a minute.'

She disappeared and I was alone again. Romantic music filled the room. I closed my eyes, and my mind flashed up images of Rebecca. Her hair, her smile, her walk, her skin – all of her. I wondered what she would look like naked.

She returned wearing a sheer robe with a pure-white silk nightgown on underneath. 'Miss me?' she asked, holding out her hand. I nodded and took it. 'Dance with me,' she said, urging me to my feet.

She took my arms and placed them around her waist. Then she put her left hand behind my neck and rested her head on my shoulder. We swayed gently with the music, her body warm and soft against mine. For the second time that night, her perfume engulfed me. She kissed me lightly on the neck, and we continued to sway together, and hold each other that way.

Finally, she broke from me and led me by the hand to her bedroom. She stopped in the middle of the room and turned to face me, her robe dropping to the floor. Behind her, lace curtains moved gently from a breeze through bay windows. She gently removed the thin straps of her nightgown from her shoulders, and the white silk slipped from her body. She stood with her arms by her sides, her right knee bent slightly covering her left.

'Hold me,' she said softly. 'Hold me and kiss me and make love to me.'

I removed my clothes and embraced her fully. She rested her head on my chest, and though our bodies touched, she seemed lonely and far away, and I felt sorry for her. I took her face in my hands and kissed her lightly on the mouth. We moved slowly to the bed as a sudden gust of wind caught the lace curtain and carried it up to the ceiling.

Later, we lay on the silk sheets of her enormous bed, and she played with the hair on my chest.

'I think you're wonderful,' I said. 'I love how natural and relaxed you seem to be, and I envy you your confidence.'

She smiled happily; a string of rich, cheerful laughter filled the air.

'You are a dear thing. It's so nice of you to say such lovely things.'

'But I am truthful. I do think you are wonderful.'

'You are too kind, Jason,' she said, taking my hand and placing it on her breast.

'Come on,' she continued. 'Show me how confident you can be.'

My mouth reached for hers and we kissed once again, and once again I felt her longing for something other than what I had to offer.

She broke from me and left the room. When she returned, she held a thick, hand-rolled joint of marijuana in her fingers. She sat cross-legged on the bed and inhaled deeply, holding the smoke in her lungs for a while to get the full effect of its magic.

'Do you want some?' she asked, passing it to me. I took it and hesitated. 'Go on,' she said. It won't hurt, and we'll have such fun.'

'I've never done this before,' I said.

Then I did what she had done. I coughed, and we started to giggle and passed the marijuana joint between us until it was finished. I started to feel light-headed.

'Do you love me?' she asked.

'Yes,' I replied, my head spinning.

'Take me then,' she said, reaching out her arms towards me.

I took her face in my hands and kissed her roughly on the mouth. We started giggling again and I fell on top of her. I knew I was clumsy, but it didn't seem to matter. Nothing seemed to matter.

There was something about our nakedness and the unbridled abandon of that night that left me unsatisfied. I thought of Greek mythology and Norman Lindsay, the satyr-mouthed nudes, the lovely maiden forms of woodland nymphs, the wild eye of Pan as he played upon his pipes of reeds. I felt free and open and clean, which was why I thought Rebecca had brought me to her room, but what also went with the freedom was a sense of affectation and showiness. I sensed a deep sadness, a heartache that she did her best to hide from me. Throughout the night, I couldn't shake the feeling that we were trying too hard, that I was an actor playing out my role to the whim of some invisible director.

At night's end, I was happy to leave her bed for the mind-clearing shock of a cold shower and a brisk towelling down. I had experienced my first awakening with a woman. It had been exciting and different, but it had also been disjointed, like we were reaching out for something that had once been there but was there no more, and we had become lost in a dislocation of time.

It was time for breakfast but, in the kitchen, Sarah stood

waiting for us.

'Oh, Mother,' she said sadly. 'How could you do that with David's friend?'

'What difference does it make, Sarah?' Rebecca replied, 'If your little boyfriend doesn't understand that I live my own life, he'd better get to know it now. I have no intention of living my life according to social acceptability ever again. You know that,' she said flatly.

I was shocked by her reply. I stood silently looking at both of them, my hands falling loosely at my sides. Sarah's face went blank, the emotion draining from it. The corners of her mouth dropped, and she took a deep breath. I fought back a desire to reach out for her. Finally, she turned to me and asked in a broken rhythm. 'What ... will you ... say to David?'

I wanted to turn and run, but they both stood there looking at me, waiting on my reply.

'Your mother is a special lady, Sarah,' I said, 'I won't quickly forget our time together, and I won't cheapen her memory with barrack room bragging.'

Sarah smiled, but her eyes remained full of sorrow.

'It wouldn't matter to me if you did,' Rebecca said. 'I have no claim over you, Jason. As far as I am concerned, we both had the courage to take what we wanted last night, and now it's the morning after. We both knew you would be going back to the army, and whatever that brings you is your affair, and whatever my life brings me is my affair. If you boast to your friends, so what? Perhaps I'll boast to mine. After all, you are a handsome, fit, young man and we did spend a vigorous night together.'

'Mother, please!' Sarah shouted indignantly. There was nothing more Sarah or I could say. We both stood there looking in shock at Rebecca.

'Oh, come now, you two,' she said, taking us both by the arms and giving us a gentle shake. 'What you need is a good breakfast. Jason, you get the orange juice out of the fridge. Sarah, you get the toast and coffee, and I'll get the rest.'

*

Later, when our leave was over and we had boarded the bus to take us back to camp, I thought how lucky I had been to meet Rebecca Rothenberg and her daughter Sarah on my leave in Melbourne.

The bus ploughed through the night, its wheels humming their way back to camp. Inside, most of us were asleep, our noisy departure behind us. I looked out on the darkened country landscape punctuated by the bright headlights of recurring traffic.

'How did you go with Rebecca's mother?' David asked.

'Um ...' I replied.

'You don't get off that easily. Come on, tell me what happened.'

'We went to the movies, had a drink after, then went to bed.'

'Together?'

'You said that. I didn't.'

'Ah, so you did! I knew you did. I just knew it. Tell me, what was she like?'

'Why? Even if I did – and I'm not saying I did, mind – why is it important to you?'

'It's important because I'm curious. I've wondered for months what it would be like to bed Rebecca. If I ever got the chance, I don't know if I'd be able to resist, and you come along and score on the first night.'

'What?' I asked incredulously.

'Oh, now, Jason, don't go all puritanical on me. Don't tell me Rebecca's mother isn't a desirable woman.'

'Yes, but she's Sarah's mother. I thought you liked Sarah.'

'I do, and I'll probably marry her one day. But we're not married yet, are we?'

'I don't think I care for this conversation, David.'

'Why? Perhaps I need to explain myself better. You see, Sarah is loyal and dependable, the sort of qualities to look for in a wife, but not the sort of qualities that make for good sex. For that, you need someone like her mother.'

'That's awful, David. I think you're making a big mistake.'

'Nonsense. You've got to admit Sarah will make a wonderful wife.'

'Yes, but for the right man. You only want to use her.'

'Ah, so that's what it is. You think people who get married should love each other and commit to each other.'

'Yes.'

'And since I clearly don't love Sarah, I shouldn't marry her.'

'Right again.'

'But what if love itself is a nonsense? What if love is precisely the wrong reason to get married? After all, a lot of marriages fail because two people say "I love you".'

'Perhaps they say it, but they don't really mean it.'

'But how can one tell? How does the person hearing it know that they are loved? And how does the person saying it know that they mean it?'

'I don't know,' I replied. 'Maybe it's just something that happens naturally. Like, you just know it at the time that it happens.'

'And perhaps, my friend, you never will know, because love

exists only in the imagination of irrational, romantic people. Oh, I know, you think I'm wrong. Of course, love exists and you will fall in love just to prove me wrong.'

'No. I wasn't thinking that,' I replied. 'I was just wondering how you know this when you are so young? Clearly, you haven't experienced love, have you?'

'No, I haven't, but I have observed the power games people play when they use love as their bargaining chips.'

'What?'

David laughed. 'When you think of love, you think of kissing and hugging and the whisper of sweet words, don't you?'

'Yes, I suppose I do.'

'Well, I think of power,' he said emphatically. 'Every human relationship has a dominant partner and a submissive one, and the one who holds the love of the other in his hand has the upper hand.'

'That's awful, David. Why can't there be mutual respect and shared commitment between two people?'

'In friendship perhaps, but in love, never. You can never walk away from love without carrying it with you. To be truly in love involves abandoning part of your own identity for the sake of harmony, and it is from this personal sacrifice that power flows. To have someone tell you they love you is to have power over them.'

'And this is the power you seek over Sarah?'

'Yes, of course. She already submits to my will, and marriage will take us beyond that into the realm of personal sacrifice.'

'Personal sacrifice?'

'Yes. After we are married and she has children, she will willingly sacrifice the last vestige of her identity. Not only will she bend to my will but any personal desires she may have now will be abandoned for the needs of her family. Her children will become her life and I, as the provider for her children, will become her master.'

'How awful!' I said. 'It sounds like you want a slave, not a wife. Sarah won't submit. She'll see through you, and anyway, don't men also want children? Aren't men willing to sacrifice for their children?'

'No, she won't see through it. Not only Sarah but most women who marry and have children submit and have done so for thousands of years. As for men wanting children, the same argument applies. Those men who sacrifice for their children leave themselves open to the same sort of exploitation. Those men are dominated by their wives,' David said, smugly.

'I don't believe this. Marriage and love and family is more than power and domination; otherwise, it would never work. It would never have lasted through the ages.'

'You tell me then, what is it all about?' David asked.

'Well, it's more to do with feelings than reason. I see it more as an issue of cooperation between men and women, not one of domination and submission.'

David laughed.

'No,' I said. 'Let me finish. It's how we act, our actions and behaviour to one another. We do what we do not out of obedience and sacrifice but out of love and devotion. It is precisely this sense of service and devotion that is the real source of our happiness and, rather than leaving us in despair, it gives us fulfilment. Surely, when we say we are in love, we are not describing a power relationship but rather a state of being. We are in love because we feel something special for another human being, not because we want power over them. It is my belief that to be truly in love is to reach a state of happiness unattainable in any other human endeavour, a happiness that comes from the love we share with another, and that love is built upon trust and mutual respect, not dominance.'

'Jason, you really do leave yourself vulnerable. Nothing in this life can fulfil the expectations you describe. No woman on earth can give you what you want. I think you will become bitter and disillusioned in later life.'

We fell into silence after that, and I looked back out into the black night. Strange, I thought, how David's assessment of my ideas sounded like my assessment of his. I was sure David was wrong about Sarah, and anyway, the terrible relationship he described could not last, could it?

CHAPTER 4

The soldier and the protester

'Why did you break our date?' I asked.

'Because I liked you too much,' Clarissa replied.

'I don't understand. Wouldn't that make you want to see me?'

'No. I didn't want to get involved.'

'Why?'

'Because you're a soldier and you'll probably go to Vietnam,' she said, looking up at me.

'But I can't help that. It's my duty to defend my country. If I'm told to go, I will.'

'Yes, you can. You can refuse.' She paused for a moment, then looked down and sipped the wine from her glass.

'If I did that, I couldn't live with myself,' I replied, raising my beer and drinking deeply.

'But how could you live with yourself if you do go? It's a rotten war, and it's not necessary for us to be there,' she said, her voice trembling slightly.

'I don't see it that way,' I replied. 'All I see is that I'm a soldier, and soldiers have to fight in defence of their country.'

'You see? You see what I mean? You can't get past this nonsense about country and duty and honour. And, anyway, you won't be defending your country by going to Vietnam.

You'll just be killing Vietnamese.'

'Don't you think that's a little unfair? I have been told by my government and the people of Australia that I will be defending our country against communism, and I don't see it as nonsense. For me, it's very real and very natural. If I'm asked to go, I'll have to do my bit. Others are, so I can't let them down. Can't you see that?' I pleaded.

'What I see is stubborn, narrow-minded, old fashioned ...'

She ran out of words and just stood there, looking at me, waving her free arm. Finally, she dropped her arm to her side.

'That's why I don't want to get involved with you,' she said. 'You don't believe you should think for yourself.'

I smiled at her and a look of concern passed through her eyes.

'And yet ...' she said, stumbling for words.

'You're very attractive,' I said, stepping forward and reaching for her hand.

'Oh, no. No, you don't, buster. I'm not interested.'

She pushed my arm away and walked to the other end of the veranda where she took up a conversation with another group at David's party. I stood where she had left me and continued to drink. After a short time, she looked in my direction. I raised my can of beer and smiled, but she looked away, so I left her and went inside to the heart of the party.

Looking around the room, I noticed how small and crowded it was. People were pressed face to face, almost touching one another. The crowd spilled into other rooms and finally out into the cold night air. The room I was in had a heavy blanket of marijuana and nicotine-laced pungent smoke throughout, which made breathing uncomfortable. Glowing embers lit pale faces, and glasses full of alcohol bobbed up and down into open mouths full of smiling teeth. Stove pipe pants clung to hips and stretched tight around prominent bums. Only the women's wide hips distinguished them from the long-haired men. The heavy beat of The Rolling Stones played so loudly that it seemed to come from within my chest. Mick Jagger screamed at me that he "can't get no satisfaction". David couldn't be right about musicians being the heroes of our generation, could he? Surely, our generation wouldn't look up to Mick Jagger. His lyrics seemed to be about little more than sex for sex's sake. The music in here was too heavy and loud, and the smoke was stifling. I had to find a quieter place where I could find some peace of mind. I left the room in search of a back door.

My search led me into a laundry, which was in an awful mess. A tub full of ice, water and bottles of beer had spilled onto the floor. Broken glass, blood and beer swill filled the room. A vacuum cleaner, broom and dustpan lay scattered in the mess. I was about to leave when I heard moaning coming from within a closet. Thinking that someone might be hurt, I opened the door only to find a couple in hot embrace. Her back was against the wall and her chin rested on his shoulder. One leg hung over his hip and the other rose and fell from the floor. She half-opened a pair of sleepy eyes and a light smile crossed her lips. She looked as if she was tripping on something heavy. If she was, I could only hope that she had not mixed it with alcohol, a potentially deadly combination. Her tripping was unusual because marijuana was the preferred drug of the hippies and educated classes, while heroin was the drug associated with the working class. If she was from the working class, what was she doing here with these university-educated, middle-class elites? Whatever her situation, she appeared to be a willing participant. None of my business, I concluded, before closing the closet door and stepping outside, retreating from the madness within.

I found a quiet place in the backyard and sat down on the cool grass. Strange, I thought, how we had all gone separate ways after recruit training. Nick got posted into the infantry and ended up in Holsworthy, David did a truncated officer training course at Portsea, then went into intelligence and worked out of Canberra, while Toby and I did our training for the Royal Australian Army Medical Corps at the School of Army Health at Healesville. After our training, Toby and I were sent to a casualty clearing station (CCS) in Melbourne; Toby did ambulance work, however, while I did ward work. This meant we saw little of each other during the day, although we did share a barracks at night, so we occasionally enjoyed each other's company.

The use of helicopters for medical evacuation meant that the badly wounded could be taken straight to a hospital from the field, making our CCS redundant. Consequently, we were left unsure of our role in combat, so our leaders spent most of their time making up things for us to do to break the boredom. It was during one of these periods that David had phoned and invited me to this party.

This was not really my scene, however, and I was disappointed not to have spoken with David at all this night. Funny how people drift apart, I thought, lying back on the grass and staring up into the night sky. My mind went back to the nights at recruit training where friendship and good cheer had led four young men to a relaxed examination of life. Those were good times, I thought, as a light wisp of cloud crossed a full moon, and a shooting star fell from the softly lit sky. My eyes followed it down from the heavens until it disappeared behind Clarissa's head, where it flamed out. She stood at my feet, looking directly at me.

'If you want to take me home, I'm ready to leave now,' she said, walking away. I hurried behind her and caught up when she stopped at my car. I reasoned that she must have witnessed my arrival at David's party, and therefore knew which car was mine.

'Are you sure you want this?' she asked, turning to face me.

'Yes,' I replied. I reached out and took her hands in mine and rubbed my thumbs backward and forward across her knuckles. 'And you?' I asked. 'Do you also want this?'

'Yes,' she replied without hesitation. 'I feel like I'm running away from something by not being with you, and I don't like that. Do you know what I mean?'

'Um ...' I said, nodding my head.

'I don't want to run away from my feelings, but I also don't want my feelings to run my life,' she said with conviction.

'You're a lot like David,' I said. 'You want to think everything out and get it right before you act.'

'What's wrong with that?'

'I don't know that you can do that with life, because there are no right and wrong answers. Life is something that just happens. Like conception, it either happens or it doesn't. All we can do is learn to live with it.'

'You're behind the times. Women have contraception nowadays, so we only get pregnant when we want to.' She laughed.

'I meant you can't plan to have a baby and, bingo, you get one. Life is more complicated than that, and we have only limited control over what happens, so we should just let it be. Let it happen and learn to live with it.'

'I think my professors would say such carelessness leads to exploitation.'

'I'm not clever enough to know what that means, but I think I know when I'm being got at, and I'm not talking about that, either,' I said.

'Oh! But you must,' she replied. 'You can't avoid it. Age and experience will eventually run your innocence to ground.'

'To hell with that,' I said, letting go her hands and taking hold of her shoulders. I leaned forward and kissed her lightly on the lips.

'Can't we just enjoy ourselves and let life look after itself?' I pleaded.

'Um, perhaps,' she said, breaking from my hold.

'Come on,' she invited, turning and waiting for me to open the car door. 'Take me somewhere where we can be alone.'

Next morning, I watched as her moist eyes opened and her tongue traced a wet line across her upper lip. She looked at me and smiled softly, her tangled hair arousing in my mind fresh visions of the previous night. She would throw her head back and moan softly, and our excitement carried us to ever higher levels of physical pleasure. We pushed ourselves with an urgency beyond our earthbound needs. Harder and harder we drove ourselves; higher and higher went our emotional energy. 'Oh! God!' I cried out loud. But in that moment of climactic pleasure, I could not realise that this earth has no capacity for such unbridled passion. Even as I shuddered in my earthbound paradise, the worm of doubt was already gnawing into my pleasure and crippling it with earthly pride. *She's mine*, I told myself. *I want her always.*

Only later would I learn that my pleasure could not satisfy her, and my pride would never hold her. But for now, I leaned over her and ran my hand along her naked thigh and closed her eyes with gentle kisses.

*

I must admit from the start that we were well trained, probably better trained than any other Australian army before us. The army sent me to recruit training and corps training as a medical orderly. After that, I was posted to my unit where I engaged in further training and subject training for promotion to corporal. I went back to Healesville to complete further training to become a medical assistant, which allowed me to gain my corporal stripes. I also completed jungle training at Canungra and went on an exercise held in the Shoalwater military training area near Rockhampton. During unit training, we practised weapons training at the rifle range and held mock battle exercises as a functioning CCS. All in all, the training I received was second to none, and there were times in between training when the lighter side of army life emerged. Such were the times that I remember with a degree of fondness and mirth.

Regimental Sergeant Major Sheen was a soldier who knew the value of keeping his troops active. Since there was little for us to do at the CCS when we were between training sessions, RSM Sheen kept us busy by carrying out three inspection parades a week at which we all presented ourselves in clean, starched uniforms with regulation creases and spit-polished boots, which reflected our image in their glass-like toes, and brass that flashed brilliantly in the sunlight.

Sheen himself was a complete picture of 'spit and polish'. He changed his uniform twice daily so that he was always the sharpest and cleanest dressed in the unit. His batman (which was an unusual privilege for an RSM, but our commanding officer had granted his batman to RSM Sheen) was constantly busy starching and pressing and polishing. The standing joke of the unit was that whenever Sheen removed his hat, his batman would polish his bald head – it did give the appearance of having been polished.

In any event, every Monday, Wednesday and Friday morning, we all paraded for RSM Sheen, who cast his sharp eyes over our uniforms for the slightest infraction of our dress code. His ploy worked, because we lived in constant fear of what he would do if he found something wrong, so we polished and starched and went to his parades with fear in our hearts. Sheen's reign of terror kept us all in check – but then Private Jones arrived at camp.

Private Jones was a national serviceman who was transferred in late one Thursday night and was told to present himself on parade the next morning. When Jones saw our spotless uniforms, he commented that his was not up to scratch, but that RSM Sheen would understand that he had not had time to get his gear in order. We told him we didn't like his chances, but he just shrugged his shoulders and said, 'Oh, well.'

We marched onto parade with Jones at the end of the column directly behind me. On command, we did a left face and shuffled ourselves into position for inspection. RSM Sheen snapped his baton, which had a polished brass shell case at one end and a polished bullet head at the other, under his right armpit and marched to the head of the column. As he progressed along the columns of soldiers, he came to attention at each soldier, shot his head around ninety degrees and cast his penetrating eyes up and down. If, by mistake, a soldier's eyes engaged Sheen's, he screamed, 'Watch your front!' into his face and glared menacingly at him, enjoying the sight of the textbook soldiers his campaign of terror had created.

And then he came to Jones. His eyes lit up, his left hand flashed to his baton and, with a sharp flick of his wrist, he shot the bullet-tipped end into Jones' gut.

'There's a bag of shit at the end of this baton,' he shouted.

Without hesitation, Jones replied, 'Well, it's not at this end, sir.'

*

For weeks after our first night together, I could not get Clarissa out of my mind. I would spend all day thinking about the colour of her skin and the sparkle of her eyes. I would phone her at every opportunity just to hear the soft resonance of her voice. When we were together, I would gaze at her, and she would turn her head and engage my eyes, then bow her head and giggle with embarrassment. I always wanted to be near her, to hold her hand, stroke her hair or gently wrap my arms around her and kiss her softly on the neck. I was enchanted with the sweet smell of her presence and the soft touch of her body next to mine.

At first, she enjoyed my attention, and I think she was even flattered by the intensity of my feelings, but soon she began to take me for granted and came to expect my excessive behaviour as a natural part of my being with her. I was the infatuated fool in her life, and she took for granted the power that gave her over me. There came a time, however, when we had a difference of opinion, and I tried to explain my side of the issue. It was the first time I had stood my ground, and she came to understand that, although I loved her, I still had the freedom to think for myself.

One day, we got into a prolonged discussion about gender stereotypes. She explained to me that our male-dominated society conditioned men and women into playing gender-specific stereotypical roles. She said she had never realised before just how much men exploited and dominated women. She explained to me that she had read books by Simone de Beauvoir, Betty Friedan and Germaine Greer. These books, she said, showed her how tyrannical men had run society at women's expense, largely by locking women into marriage and motherhood and forcing them to be housewives. She now believed that women could no longer accept that and be truly free. No man would ever make a slave of her, she said. When she spoke about her parents and their relationship, she became very angry and upset, sometimes breaking into a rage, which drew the attention of other café patrons. I had to calm her down before she went too far and brought the café manager to our table.

I had read one of these books and had been disappointed. Its analysis seemed shallow and lacked sufficient scientific data to support its conclusions, relying instead on assertion and emotional accusation. It did, however, identify some institutional discrimination, like the lack of equal pay for work of equal value as well as the fact that single women, working for the public service, had to resign or be sacked once they married. I also concluded that David's appraisal of love and marriage sounded so much like their conclusions that I wondered if he had gleaned his ideas from their books.

Clarissa went on by asserting that she hated her father for all the suffering and hurt he had caused her mother and herself. But, when I questioned her about it, she became vague and evasive, mentioning only that he loved his work more than her and her mother, and that her mother loved her friends more than her, and that they both were playing roles determined by dominant males.

'You couldn't possibly understand,' she said. 'Being a male, you've had it easy. You couldn't understand, because you take your privilege for granted.'

I was offended by her accusation. 'How have I had it easy? And the only real privilege I received in my life was being born into the loving arms of parents who did the best they knew how in raising me. They realised that life is difficult, and that their child needed all the love and support they could give him to prepare him for those difficulties. Anything else I have achieved in my life has been through my own effort. I feel sorry for those who don't have loving parents, but that has nothing to do with being born a male or a female. Anyway, only men, like me, get conscripted to fight in wars, don't they? How is that a privilege? As far as the sexes' place in society is concerned, it's pretty clear that men are expendable while women are protected. Seems to me we should be concentrating more on becoming better parents, squabbling less over who gets what, or obsessing less over perceived power struggles within society. These are things we have to deal with for ourselves, and there are laws that protect us from harm. You say I don't understand what you are talking about, but I do. It's just that I don't accept your premise. For me, both men and women have to live hard lives. Their lives may be different, but they are both hard. Neither sex has it easy.'

'But you just admitted that you do have privilege. What about those you feel sorry for? Don't you think they deserve more than just your pity?'

'Yes. I do. But the government can only do so much. It can't force people to live ethically correct lives or be good parents. That they have to do for themselves. If some people are not prepared to make the effort to improve their circumstances or live better lives, I don't see what more society can do for them. Shouldn't we all be responsible for our own lives and the choices we make? And, anyway, you were not talking about that. You were talking about privilege based on sex, and I find it hard to accept your underlying premise, that our society is male dominated. There is a hierarchy, and men have a larger portion of the higher positions, but it is a hierarchy based on competence and merit, not sex. There is dominance within our social hierarchy, but it is apex dominated not male-dominated, and the apex is made of both males and females.'

'That's interesting, but incorrect. It *is* male dominated. For one thing, you get paid more. Men are paid more for the same work.'

'I agree that is wrong, if the work is the same. I believe that men and women should be paid the same for work of equal value. If women put in the same hours on the same job, they should be paid the same. Once this is achieved, would you be happy? Would you say that men and women were equal in our society?'

'Absolutely not! Are you crazy?' she began to raise her voice again. 'You admitted before that all the positions of power in our society are dominated by men. Why don't women have positions of power?'

'I didn't say all, I said most,' I replied quietly. 'Well, I guess that's just not as important for some women as it is for men. Anyway, let's consider those women who are in positions of power. If they were able to get to the top, how were men stopping them? I don't understand your point, and anyway, how do you propose to change what you see as male domination?'

'Don't you think women should be given more positions of power?'

'If they earn it, yes. But that doesn't mean men should be discriminated against just so more women get positions of power. Discrimination of any form is bad for society, because it takes an opportunity away from someone who is deserving of it and gives it to someone else who is not. Society is best served when individuals advance within it based on effort and merit, not because of their sex or any other discriminating factor.'

'But don't you see, we need to right the wrong that has existed for thousands of years. And, anyway, it's not discrimination, it's positive discrimination, or what we like to call affirmative action.'

'First of all, two wrongs don't make a right, and positive discrimination is an oxymoron. I can see why you want to call it affirmative action, though, because the term disguises what it truly is – blatant discrimination, something I thought you were against. Also, I thought you were arguing for equality of opportunity, not equality of outcome, which is what communist countries want. I thought liberal democracies were all about liberty and equal opportunity. Don't you ever spare a thought for the victims you would create by stealing from them the opportunity they have rightly earned through their own effort and merit? Besides, affirmative action expresses a belief that women can't compete equally with men, that women can't achieve equality on their own merit. So, affirmative action belittles women, as it displays a belief that women are not as competent as men, a fundamentally sexist belief.'

'Honestly, Jason, sometimes I can't believe your naïvety. Don't you understand that men dominate women and keep them at home, barefoot and pregnant in the kitchen? It's been that way for thousands of years. Look at the social conditioning that women go through. Girls play with dolls while boys play with trucks and guns. Girls are told that they have to have babies and stay at home to raise them. Boys are told that they have to earn a living and provide for their families. Of course, we have to discriminate in favour of women to overcome this unfair conditioning.'

'Are they really told to do this, or do they choose to do it? Maybe girls just like to play with dolls. Do you really think they are forced to? Don't you think that, for most women, their families are the most important thing in their lives? I support the right of women to choose, because it is good for society if the most capable and enterprising of its members are encouraged to participate in its growth and development, but you do not seem to value the contribution those women who choose to be wives and mothers make to society. Don't you think that the raising of healthy, capable members of society is valuable?'

I gathered my thoughts before continuing.

'I do not support the right of society to force a choice on women. That is social engineering, and it has produced bad results in the past; just look at the communist countries, for example. Do you intend forcing men and women to occupy jobs that they find boring, unfulfilling and for which they are unsuited, simply to build some idealistic society that only feminists want? Where does your social engineering end? And why would feminists want this? What is their motivation? Is it a sense of injustice or their own resentment and envy of successful men?'

'I can't believe you just said that. You really are a relic, Jason. You need to catch up with the times. Women will never go back to the world you espouse.'

'Why? Why am I a relic? And, anyway, does being a relic negate my opinion? Look, I know that my mother and father loved each other and cooperated with each other to produce a stable family environment for me. Nobody forced my mother to stay at home and give me the kind of home that she believed I needed. That was a decision she made for herself, and she was proud of it. She never felt ashamed or inferior at having made that decision, because my father didn't force her into it. And, anyway, my father made a huge sacrifice on our behalf. He was the sole provider for his family. That meant he had to work long, hard hours and give almost all of what he earned to his family. He was strong and dependable and loyal. He wasn't selfish, nor was he domineering. True, he was the authority figure in our family, but he did not dominate. Authority is not the same as domination. And men who want to dominate women are fools, for they trade genuine gratitude and respect from their women for submission, timidity and resignation.'

'So, women have to forever surrender to the authority of men. Is that what you are advocating?'

'Where is the surrender in making a free choice? And why does it have to be a battle? If you think women have no power in a traditional family, you are mistaken. I have seen my mother humble my father with just a look. So why can't women and men just cooperate with each other to get what they both want from life and provide a stable family environment for their children? Both women and men should be grateful for and respectful of the sacrifices each make for their families.'

'I give up, Jason. You just won't learn. You just keep holding on to these outdated ideas of love and sacrifice,' she shouted at me, and threw her arms into the air. Then she turned on me with a sharp look of defiance. 'What about when men physically abuse their wives?' she said, with thinly disguised anger. 'Doesn't that negate your idealistic, romantic views about marriage?'

'Not really, no. I admit that domestic violence is real, and it is also wrong and needs to be corrected, but there are already laws that address that issue. It is illegal in liberal societies for a man, or a woman for that matter, to physically abuse their spouse. Would a male-dominated society have such laws? And, anyway, just how prevalent is this in marriage? Isn't it the exception? Aren't the majority of marriages held together through cooperation, not physical abuse?'

'You're not trying to justify physical abuse in marriage, are you, Jason?'

'That's unfair, Clarissa. Does what I said sound like I was justifying it?'

She didn't answer me. She just shook her head. I didn't know whether she agreed that I was not justifying physical abuse in marriage, or just letting me know she didn't believe anything I had said. After that, we went quiet. I wanted a better resolution to our difference of opinion, but I didn't know what else to say, and I didn't accept her interpretation of the relationship between men and women any more than I accepted David's. Clearly, they felt the same about my interpretation.

*

One day in late summer, Clarissa invited me to meet her parents. Their house was in the country off the road to Lilydale.

We arrived in the late afternoon when a fading sun gave way to a cool, clear evening. As we drove through the gate to her father's property, she explained that he had built this house and that her mother worked in the fashion industry.

Their house was of contemporary design set atop a hill overlooking a valley below. The facade of the house was compact and disciplined, penetrated on the right by a double garage giving quick access to a short, straight walk into a sheltered recess flooded with light from translucent glass covering one whole side of the entry. Clarissa took me through a large, open living area and then through large, glass sliding doors out to the rear of the house, which was extended by a trellis protecting an even larger outdoor living space from the hot summer sun.

Her father sat in a reclining chair, sipping from a glass containing Scotch mixed with soda and ice. On the table beside him was a small bucket of ice and Black Label whiskey, and an empty bottle of soda water.

'Where is Mother?' Clarissa asked flatly.

He ignored her, continuing to drink from his glass. I don't think he was being rude; rather, our presence simply hadn't registered. She went around and faced her father. He saw her and rose slowly to his feet.

'Hello, darling,' he said. 'Mother's just gone in for a shower. She'll be out in a minute.'

Turning to me, he said, 'You must be, Jason. I'm pleased to meet you.'

I took his hand and smiled. He appeared a little shaky on his feet, but I was surprised he remained so articulate; he obviously had been drinking for some time. He was dressed as though he had been playing tennis. He wore a short-sleeved, open-necked sports shirt with white shorts and sandshoes. He sat back down and resumed sipping from his drink.

Clarissa and I sat with him in silence around the table. Eventually, Clarissa heaved a deep sigh and stood up.

'Would you like a drink, Jason?' She asked.

'Oh, good idea, darling,' her father replied. 'Bring another bottle from the cabinet behind the bar, and there's a bottle of soda water in the fridge.'

She returned with a bottle of Scotch and a bottle of soda for her father, a cold can of Fosters for me and a glass of Riesling for herself, all carried on a silver tray. Hearing the glass door slide, we looked up to see her mother walk onto the patio.

Mrs Swanson wore a black evening dress with glass beads attached, which made her figure shimmer as she walked towards us. Her hair was teased up and held in place with a golden comb. She wore a heavy gold necklace, and her arms were bare which made the large gold earrings, the thick gold wristwatch, the bangles and the gold rings with flashing inserted gemstones stand out all the more. When she got close to me, I could see she had been a very beautiful woman in her youth, but tonight her face was heavily made up.

'Oh, dar-ling,' she said to Clarissa. 'You're such a naughty girl. Fancy not telling me how handsome your young man is.'

She extended her hand. I didn't know whether to kiss it or shake it, so I just lightly touched her fingers and let my arm fall to my side. She immediately turned to Clarissa.

'Come and give Mother a kiss,' she said.

Clarissa went dutifully to her side and kissed her lightly on the cheek. Mr Swanson remained seated, poured himself another drink and swallowed it down.

'Dar-ling, I'm so sorry, but the Wallaces are in Melbourne

tonight and I really must take them to dinner. I know we had arranged to meet Jason tonight, but the Wallaces are very important clients, and you know how it is in the fashion business. I really am sorry, Jason. I hope you'll let me make it up to you on another occasion.'

I smiled. 'That's all right, Mrs Swanson. I understand, and don't worry, I'd feel worse if you stayed at home and your business suffered.'

'Oh, what a darling thing to say,' she said. 'Clarissa, I love this boy of yours. Not only is he good-looking but he has manners as well.' Almost in the same breath, she added, 'Got to go, terribly late.'

She left us, hurriedly searching her handbag. She passed through the doorway and disappeared from our sight without looking back. Clarissa and I sat back down.

'You have a lovely home, sir,' I offered.

'You think so?' he sneered.

'Yes. I do,' I replied.

'There's a big difference between a home and a house,' he scoffed.

'Oh, no,' Clarissa said bitterly. 'Is this going to be another of those painful "look what you've done to me" sessions?' Her father looked angrily at her. 'Don't be nice on my account, Father,' she continued. 'I want Jason to see the real Swansons and not the pretend ones you put on show for the rest of the world. After all, he'll find out soon enough for himself.'

'What do you want me to tell him, dear? That I'm a bastard? That I've exploited you and your mother all my life? That I don't allow you to be yourselves?'

'No, I thought you might start with Justine. That smart young girl who's half your age.'

'Typical,' he blurted out. 'You're just like your mother. Neither of you ever tried to understand.'

'What's to understand? You got tired of Mum, so you had it off with the first piece of skirt that came your way.'

'It wasn't like that. I told your mother I was sorry,' Mr Swanson said desperately.

'Of course you did,' Clarissa replied sarcastically. She stood up and walked towards the kitchen. 'I suppose I'll have to get dinner tonight,' she said over her shoulder.

'I've bought Chinese,' her father explained. 'All you have to do is heat it.'

I stood up to follow Clarissa, but she stopped me. 'No, Jason. You stay with Dad. It's best you get to know him for yourself.'

With Clarissa gone, we lapsed into silence and Mr Swanson continued drinking heavily. His hand started to shake, and his head and shoulders swayed.

'I'm sorr––'

'––Don't be. Clarissa's right. You should see us as we really are.' He sighed. 'It's just that it's all so sad.'

'What is, sir? What is sad?' I asked.

'Life,' he replied. 'My life. The stuff that dreams are made of, that nightmares seep into.'

'What do you mean?' I asked.

'How could you understand? You're so young and innocent. You have no idea what I'm talking about. Do you?'

'I would like to try, sir,' I said.

'We're beyond each other, you and I,' he muttered.

'I'd still like to try.'

'Oh, you are so young and keen. I was like that once, full of trust and vision and desire. But now I know life's simply not worth the effort. Don't you see?'

'No,' I urged. 'Please go on.'

'That's just it. It's not worth the effort. When you're young, you fight, you face the big deals, you cheat a little here and there – only a little, mind – but you know, you just know it'll be worth it one day. But that day never comes. The deals keep getting bigger and you keep wanting more. Graft and corruption are your constant companions. You can't escape it. You make friends with people you despise and get drawn into the orbit of their world, leaving your own further and further behind. And one day you look around and realise you hate yourself for what you have become, but you've got everything you ever dreamt of as a young man. You've got money and power and family. You've got it all. And, yet, the funny thing is, you're still not happy, because you have lost your dignity ... your integrity.'

He let out a deep sigh. Desperation crossed his face before he collected his thoughts and continued. 'But you are so far gone that you still want more, anything to make your sacrifice worthwhile, and so you start looking. There must be more, you tell yourself, and when you can't find it, you invent it. The clear, golden skin of a young woman takes you back to an age of innocence you want to relive. But that doesn't work either, and you're too far gone for redemption, and so you turn to this,' he said, holding up his glass of whisky. 'It slides down the back of your throat so effortlessly and helps you forget the deceit and the lies, the self-loathing and the lost trust.'

At this point, his eyes filled with tears, but he went on in a clear but slightly slurred voice. 'It helps you forget, don't you see? It helps you forget the tenderness of a soft touch in the dark of night, the delight of a carefree laugh in open sunshine, the flash of a passionate eye in the candlelight.'

Tears flowed freely down his cheeks. 'Oh God,' he cried. 'I

want it back. I want my life back. I want the golden days of a carefree summer. The woman who stood by her man, the little girl who loved her dad and the man who wanted only the best for the ladies in his life. But that's the big lie. It's all an illusion. Life gives you the vision, then it kicks you in the guts.' His chest heaved with the effort to go on. 'I can't find the strength anymore. It's not worth the effort. It's simply not worth the effort.'

I didn't know what to say. I sat there looking at Mr Swanson, who had covered his face with his hands and who shook violently under the impact of his sobbing. After a little while, he got control of himself, stood up and disappeared inside the house.

After that, Clarissa reappeared. 'Where's Dad?' She asked.

'He just went inside,' I replied.

She placed the dinner on the table and sat down beside me. In a little while, Mr Swanson returned. He had showered and changed into trousers and a sports coat. 'I'm goin' to the club,' he said, his words slurring into each other.

'Please yourself,' Clarissa shot back. 'But you're in no fit condition to drive, and what about your dinner?'

'My darling daughter,' Mr Swanson replied sarcastically. 'I have driven in conditions much worse than this, and I'll get dinner at the club.'

'Suit yourself,' Clarissa replied, waving her hand and shaking her head in final dismissal. After a while, we heard Mr Swanson drive his Jaguar out of the front gate and open the throttle down a long straight stretch of road. Clarissa looked at me and raised her eyebrows, a mocking smile highlighted the corners of her mouth.

The rest of the evening we spent playing Clarissa's

favourite records. She had just purchased a copy of the new Beatles album, *Sergeant Pepper's Lonely Hearts Club Band*, and was keen to share it with me. We listened to it right through.

'What did you think of it?' she asked me.

'Well, it certainly is different.'

'Come on, Jason, I need more than that. What do you mean by different? Do you like it?'

'Yes, I like it. It is a very creative piece of music. It seems to bring together a lot of different music styles, yet still keeps it all together in one smooth flowing piece with a distinctive Beatles beat. It is very popular, too, right?'

'Oh, yes, it is *the* album of the year.' She said it with such earnestness that I thought she believed it gave the album some sort of validity other than that The Beatles' music was popular. 'But what do you think about the message in the songs?' she eventually asked.

'What do you mean? It's a piece of music, right? It's supposed to entertain, and it does that well.'

'Oh, Jason, don't tell me you didn't get the message. This album speaks to our generation. It encapsulates our values, our feelings.'

'Are you sure? The Beatles are musicians, right? They are not philosophers or poets. They're just entertainers. How can you derive a deep understanding of your values from a three-minute song?'

'Oh no, you are wrong. The Beatles are a lot more than just entertainers. They speak to us. They touch us with their words, not just their music. Look, listen to this song again, and tell me what the words are saying.' She played 'Lucy in the Sky with Diamonds'. 'Well, do you see it now? What do the words tell you?'

'Actually, nothing. The words make no sense. It's just a jumbled-up mixture of images. The music is good, though. It's got a strong beat and an underlying melody.'

'Oh, Jason, sometimes you really disappoint me. Don't you see that "Lucy", "Sky" and "Diamonds" stands for LSD? The Beatles are describing an acid trip. That's what the images are all about.'

'Oh, okay, I get what you are saying now. But how does that speak to our generation? What values are they promoting? Do they want us all to take LSD? And if they do, count me out. If it does that to your mind, I can't imagine what damage it will do to your brain.'

'Well, it's true that LSD is a mind-altering drug, but it opens up our minds to new ideas and new possibilities. Even Timothy Leary, a Harvard professor, is urging us to take it. Do you get it now? We need to open up our minds, to consider new ideas, new values.'

'Well, I'm not impressed by Timothy Leary. Some university professors are way out there with their ideas. Leary? Leary? Wait a minute, isn't he that hippy professor? Didn't he advise young people to "turn on, tune in and drop out"?'

'Yes, that's him.'

'Well, why are you at university? Why haven't you dropped out?'

'I don't have to follow everything he says. I value a university education.'

'So, you don't want to destroy the establishment like Leary; you want to become a part of it. What I don't understand is that hippies depend on taxpayers to survive. If we all did what Leary suggests, there will be no taxpayers and no hippies, so he doesn't really want that at all. What he actually wants is to overthrow the establishment but doesn't give any practical advice about what to replace it with. I'm guessing he is a part of the counterculture who wants to overthrow capitalism but doesn't know what to replace it with.'

'I don't know about that. All I know is that I want a university degree, and I like the idea of opening my mind to new ideas, like feminism.'

'Actually, universities were created by the establishment. Without the establishment, there would be no universities. By getting a degree, you will become a part of the establishment, even if you promote new ideas like feminism.'

'That doesn't bother me as long as I can promote feminism and change our male-dominated culture.'

'Yes, I see that. But I want to return to The Beatles and their promoting of LSD. If LSD makes our minds behave like they describe, with meaningless images floating in and out of our minds, how does that open our minds to new ideas? You said feminism. What is the connection between meaningless images and feminism? And are there other values we need to consider? Do they explain that?'

'The connection is that we can see things differently by taking LSD. Let's go to another song. This one really speaks to me.' She played 'She's Leaving Home'. Then she became very excited. 'Isn't it great? It really explains my life. This is exactly how I feel.'

I really didn't know what to say. How could Clarissa reach that conclusion? The song was so shallow and one-dimensional. Surely, her life was more complicated than that.

'Well?' she demanded. 'Come on, Jason. Tell me I'm right. Tell me there is value in this song.'

'Umm ... Do you really want me to analyse this song? I might disappoint you with my observations.'

'Yes, of course. And I want you to be honest.'

'Well, first of all, this is a sad song about the acrimonious break-up of a daughter and her parents.'

'Why is it acrimonious?'

'The parents feel they have sacrificed their lives for an ungrateful, selfish daughter, and the daughter feels that her parents have provided her with all the material things in life but don't love her, or at least don't make her happy.'

'Yes, yes, you do understand. See, that's me. I have all the material things I need but I'm not happy.'

'And that is your parents' fault? Why do you think that your parents are responsible for your happiness? Surely, we are all responsible for our own happiness. How can anyone make someone else happy? I don't think that is even remotely possible, and anyone who believes that is bound to end up disappointed and unhappy.'

'Umm ... maybe. But being with you makes me happy, and your being with me makes you happy. Doesn't it?'

'Yes, but it is still you who is in charge of your own happiness. You are happy to be with me. I don't make you happy – you make yourself happy. And what would happen if we broke up? You would be unhappy, but you would find happiness somewhere else, right?'

'I guess so.'

'Also, it is impossible to fully understand the real issues behind this girl and her parents' relationship, because The Beatles don't provide us with enough information. What has caused this relationship breakdown?'

'Well, I'd say because she doesn't feel that her parents love her.'

'We don't know that. What is worse, The Beatles seem to be

placing all the responsibility on her parents. What are parents supposed to do – allow their children to do whatever they want in order to make them happy and win their affection? Do you think this is good advice for parents? Don't children need discipline and guidance as they mature?'

'I suppose, but their children should be happy, right?'

'Yes, when they derive their happiness from being respectful and learning from their parents, not when they demand their parents let them do whatever they want. Children need to bear some responsibility, too, you know.'

'Maybe. I'm not sure, but that sounds right.'

'Then there is the daughter herself. What do The Beatles advise her to do? Again, this is vague. Are they encouraging the daughter to leave home to improve her life? The "bye, bye" at their song's end suggests this. Don't you think that when the daughter leaves home, it will bring despair to her parents, and a sense of guilt for the daughter that will make it difficult for her to achieve lasting happiness? Do you think that is good advice for any young person?'

'Well, probably not, but she is only trying to make a fresh start, isn't she?'

'You said that this song really understands you, that it speaks to you.'

'Yes.'

'But this daughter doesn't even say goodbye to her parents. Instead, she sneaks out and leaves a note. If you were to take this advice and leave home under such circumstances, do you think you would find enduring happiness?'

'What do you mean?' she said. There was an implied accusation in her tone.

'Well, your problem with your parents could have something

to do with you. It could be your attitude to life. Maybe you want to see yourself as a victim, because that way you don't have to hold yourself responsible for your own unhappiness, and your parents are convenient scapegoats. Or maybe you are feeling neglected by your parents and are trying to draw attention towards yourself. I don't know your particular circumstances, so I can't draw any conclusions, but I think it would help if you told your parents how you feel about them and listen to their explanation about why they behave the way they do, rather than sneak out and leave a note.'

I knew this would upset her, but I wanted her to consider an alternative possibility.

'You really are something, Jason. That was a hurtful thing to say.'

'I'm just saying there might be other reasons for your unhappiness. It might not be all your parents' fault. Look, didn't you just say that The Beatles wanted us to open up our minds? Well, there are so many things to consider when contemplating life. Life is not simple. It's complicated.'

'So, you think it's my fault that I'm unhappy?'

I smiled at her, hoping to lighten up her mood, but she kept staring at me, waiting for me to respond. Her mouth was set hard, and her eyes narrowed.

'No, not entirely. Your parents have obviously hurt you, but isn't our mood determined by our own interpretation of the events in our life? How we respond to the events in our lives determines not only our moods, but also our very future. Ultimately, aren't we all responsible for our own lives? Look, you could respond to your anger about your father by recognising that he is just human and, as such, capable of mistakes and human frailty. You could be a little more understanding and forgiving; after all, your father is hardly the first man to be unfaithful with his wife. Such an attitude on your part could help you grow and gain some happiness.'

Her expression softened. 'Yes. I see what you are saying, but I still think my parents make me unhappy, particularly my father, with their hypocrisy and selfish pursuits, and I am not really a forgiving person. How can I become more forgiving?'

'Well, you could start by looking for things in your life that you are grateful for.'

'Like what?'

'Why not consider all the things that your parents have done for you. For giving you life, for example. That alone took a sacrifice on their part. Your mother had to go through a pregnancy and give birth to you, and your father had to support her through it all. When you were helpless as a baby, who was there to care for and protect you? And who guided you through your childhood and rebellious teenage years?'

'But I didn't ask them to do that. That they did for themselves. I was just another of their possessions, something they could show off to their parents and friends. I didn't ask to be born.'

'Do you really believe that? Do you think they never loved you, were never proud of you? That you were just another of their possessions? I don't think anyone's parents are motivated by that. Raising a child takes so much sacrifice on the part of parents. Seems to me the least we can do is recognise that and be grateful for our good fortune to be alive in a wondrous world and kept healthy in a secure home, provided for us by our parents. Yes, not everyone is that lucky, and our world is full of pain and suffering, but it also contains beauty and amazement. Why not try appreciating more those things that inspire and excite us and stop obsessing so much over the cruelty and injustice in our lives? That way, you might gain meaning in your life and be happy that you were born.'

'That's such a Pollyanna view of life, Jason. Those things are only the surface things. Life is more complicated than that.'

I didn't want to pursue this matter any further. I felt we had reached an impasse. And I didn't want to point out the inconsistency in her accusing me of shallow analysis when she was willing to accept The Beatles' simplistic message, contained in a three-minute song.

'What do you want to do now?' I asked.

She smiled deeply. A mischievous glint highlighted her eyes.

'Do you know what they say about our generation?' she asked.

'No, what do they say?'

'That we're all about sex, drugs and rock 'n' roll.'

I looked at her, wondering what would come next. She rose from her cross-legged position and said, 'Wait here. I'll be back in a moment.'

She returned carrying a marijuana joint. She had taken off her boots and pantyhose and walked with a slight swaying of her hips that I found very enticing. She sat back down and lit up. We passed the joint between us. I felt my body relax and my inhibitions begin to fade. We both started to giggle and touch each other. Then, she stood up and put on 'Lucy in the Sky with Diamonds' again. She stood in front of me and pulled up her miniskirt, revealing she had no panties on, and lay on her back. She raised her arms up to me and beckoned me with her hands. I removed my clothes and as I knelt down to join her on the floor, she opened her legs and a brazen smile crossed her face.

I fell into her warm embrace, abandoning myself to the pleasure of her sexual offering. Afterwards, I remember thinking how similar my feelings were to the ones I had experienced with Mrs Rothenberg. Clarissa's night of lighthearted abandon seemed to have been planned, set up, orchestrated and executed with perfection, which now left me unfulfilled. Sex for sex's sake, drugs for temporary escape and music with its endless repetition of shallow platitudes had left me empty. No wonder Mick Jagger, and all those who follow him, scream, "I can't get no satisfaction". Could it be because they are looking for satisfaction in all the wrong places? However, an event occurred that night that changed the dynamic of my relationship with Clarissa.

About 2 am, the telephone rang and Clarissa answered it. I could tell it was serious when she exclaimed, 'Oh!', with a sudden intake of breath. I walked over and joined her by the phone. She hung up and turned towards me.

'That was the hospital,' she said. 'Dad's been in an accident. He's dead.'

I reached for her hand.

'They said he was going way too fast, that his car left the road and hit a huge gum tree. They said he never had a chance. That he would have died instantly.'

She said it in a way that made me think she hadn't fully understood what she had said, like she was passing onto me something she had just heard on the news.

'What about your mother?' I asked.

'She's there. They've sedated her and put her to bed.'

'And you?' I asked. 'How do you feel?'

She threw her arms around me, buried her head in my chest and began shaking all over.

'Help me,' she whispered, clutching me. 'Help me, Jason. I need you.'

I wrapped my arms around her, and my heart filled with sympathy for her. *Strange*, I thought, *how different Clarissa is now from the strong, opinionated young woman of just a few short hours ago.* Suddenly, a strong desire to protect her from the grief and emotional turmoil I knew she would have to go through filled my very being.

*

Major Wright was a commanding officer who knew 'the book' and ran his unit accordingly. He had a book of standing orders hung from the unit noticeboard and a sign that read, 'Ignorance is not a proper defence.'

When not engaged in active service, Major Wright believed his men should be kept busy. Consequently, we were always exercising, training, running assault courses or firing off rounds at the unit rifle range. Every morning at camp muster, we would go on a two-mile run and exercise for half an hour, after which we hit the showers and took breakfast. Next came a parade, and then we were broken up into squads headed by corporals, who would take us to the various courses and activities arranged for that day. Those who did not have some specific training organised for them would be led to the quartermaster store and issued with gardening tools. They would be kept busy beautifying the grounds around the administration building, and, as the day wore on, they would gradually drift farther and farther away until they finally broke up and wandered into their barracks, where they played pontoon or five hundred for the remainder of the day.

Every so often, however, Major Wright would get a pang of conscience over a lack of involvement with his men and call a snap inspection. This meant that he and RSM Sheen would suddenly appear in the grounds and in the barracks, checking that everything was clean and tidy.

Consequently, a lookout was posted whenever a group was playing cards inside the barracks. He kept the administration building under constant surveillance and would shout a warning whenever Major Wright and RSM Sheen came out. If they moved towards the barracks, he would say, 'Heading this way', and the men would go into immediate action.

First came a lighting fast tidying of the room, then a collection of their garden tools and finally a busying of themselves outside the barracks. Major Wright and RSM Sheen would carry out their inspection and there would be smiles all round.

'Well done, Corporal. Carry on.'

'Yes, sir. Thank you, sir.'

Then it would be back into the barracks, cards out and the lookout reposted. Life with Major Wright was smooth, ordered and peaceful, the way life in the army was meant to be. How sad that one day it all came unstuck.

One hot day, the lookout dozed off, his head dropping slowly until it jerked up suddenly to see Major Wright and RSM Sheen almost upon him. He immediately jumped to his feet, scrambled down the stairs, saluted and shouted out.

'Good morning, sir. Warm day today, sir.'

The soldiers inside took their cue. Some dived out windows, some fell down the back stairs and one jumped into his locker, holding the door closed from inside.

Major Wright and RSM Sheen entered the barrack.

'This barrack is not up to the usual standard, RSM.'

'No, sir. Beds untidy, ash on the floor. I'll have words with Corporal Jones, sir.'

'Yes, do that, RSM. Now, look at this. These men know the security regulations, RSM, yet here is a locker with its lock hanging open. Why, anyone could just come along and ...'

Major Wright opened the locker to find one of his men staring blankly back at him.

'Afternoon, sir,' said the private, coming to attention and struggling to salute amid the hanging clothes.

*

After Mr Swanson's funeral, I saw as much of Clarissa as I could, believing she depended on me for comfort from the pain she suffered. During this time, I found it hard to accept she needed her independence and saw her instead as a vulnerable young woman. I always tried to make her laugh and was uncomfortable when she got sad. I didn't understand her need to grieve and regain her confidence.

On one occasion, we ran into her younger cousins at the beach. She played with them – holding hands and running, laughing and building sandcastles – and then sat down with me as they ran to their parents, jumping and kicking sand and screaming with delight when they were tickled and cuddled. Clarissa looked on, tears running down her cheeks. I put my arms around her while she pushed her face into my chest and I tightened my grip around her. I wanted to hold her in my arms forever and never let anyone touch her or hurt her again.

'You know, Jason,' she said, looking up at me. 'What you said to me the night my father died was right. I should have tried to understand him. We should have sat down together and tried to express how we felt about each other. He could have told me why he did the things he did, and I could have told him how much he had hurt me. But we never got that chance. It seems even in his death he cheated me.'

I wanted to urge Clarissa not to continue blaming her father for all the pain in her life, but I didn't want her to think that I was taking her father's position, which would break the close bond we had now forged. I knew it was going to destroy her future if she could not come to terms with the relationship she had had with her father, but I was too selfish to confront her about it.

Over time, Clarissa came out of the shock that had driven her to depend on me and, when she did, she began to fume at my possessiveness. My problem was that I never came to accept her recovery, and my protective behaviour eventually drove her from me. She would say she wanted to go out more or to be with other people more, and I would argue that we had each other. I was so captivated by her presence that, in the midst of my joy, I could not see how my possessiveness tormented her.

When we were apart, I imagined her university friends would call on her, and their long, greasy hair and rank breath would pollute the purity of our relationship. I would close my eyes and see the soft, slow turning of her indolent head, the beauty of her hypnotic face framed within the crumpled sheets of our pleasure, and I would cry the tears of a jealous man. Through my jealous eyes, I never saw that my true rival was myself and that my persistent demands on Clarissa's privacy, at first laughingly dismissed but later angrily snapped at, were the true source of our lost emotion and not the dark strangers I always imagined shared my pleasure.

*

I decided that I had to do something to calm my fears about Clarissa's friends and develop confidence in my own opinions. To counter my feelings of inadequacy, I went to a library and told the librarian that I was a soldier likely to be posted to Vietnam soon, and asked if she had any books that might help me understand the Vietnam War. I also told her that my girlfriend was at university and had a lot of university friends, and that I felt inadequate when discussing the issues with them.

She told me that the solution to my problem would require more than just a reading about the war, that it would require a reading into the differing philosophies behind the war. She said some of the reading would be difficult for me, but if I was determined enough and read what she would recommend with the aid of a good dictionary for an explanation of words I did not understand, she could suggest some reading material for me. I said I wanted to read whatever she would suggest.

She came back with a book by John Stewart Mill, titled *On Liberty*. She then suggested I buy myself a copy of *The Condensed Oxford English Dictionary*. She said that Mill's book explained the concept of liberty which underpinned the American position on the war and that, if I wanted to go further after that, to come back and she would offer me a book that would explain the communist position.

I left and did as she had suggested. I settled down in my bed back at the barracks and read Mill's book. I was thankful for the dictionary because I had to refer to it a lot at first, but as

I read, my vocabulary expanded and my references became fewer and fewer.

Essentially, what I discovered was that Mill was arguing the nature of liberty versus authority. He seemed to be very much in favour of liberty, because it allowed people freedom, which led to greater creativity and a more equal society. He believed people in a free society should be able to make life choices for themselves and exercise free speech without these things being restricted by some authority. He was very much against the monarchy and aristocracy of his time and in favour of democracy, which would give sovereignty to the people by way of elections, which in turn would place their representatives in parliament. It was parliament that would decide the laws by which people would live their lives and not some authority figure like a monarch.

This seemed to be correct. The free world had developed strong economies that provided its citizens with a high standard of living – certainly higher than any other system of government – and the advancement of its medical achievements was miraculous. Also, the emergence of science and technology in the free world had achieved astonishing things.

What went with this freedom, however, was the responsibility of the individual for the free choices that he or she makes. It should not be society's responsibility to help people from suffering the consequences of their own free choices. This seemed a bit harsh. Should society simply ignore the plight of drug-addicted individuals, for example, or should it take a more humane approach? This question remained unanswered in my mind. What Mill recommended was logical, but was it reasonable? This continued to puzzle me, but I had to move on.

Mill did warn that there should be limits placed on the individual's right to freedom. He believed in the practical application of the 'harm principle': that is, that individuals did not have the right to harm other individuals. The trouble comes, however, in how one defines 'harm'. I could see that if one were to expand the definition of harm, one would, by necessity, reduce the limits of liberty, and this would be counterproductive to what Mill believed were the benefits of liberty. For example, if one were to expand the definition of harm to include 'offence', then most rational discussion about any topic could be shut down simply on the grounds that it offended someone. The question for a society based on liberty, under such circumstances, then becomes: does someone's offence have the right to infringe upon the liberty of another? I felt sure Mill would reply, 'Absolutely not', because Mill did not conflate violence with speech. I could see that Mill was very particular about this. The only exception to complete freedom of expression, thought, conscience or feeling was if this led to *physical* harm for someone else, and he gave the example of 'incitement to violence' to highlight this. For Mill, then, the only restriction on an individual's liberty should be if that individual intended to physically harm someone else, and to determine this, I guess he was advocating that people use their common sense. In the end, though, this is not very helpful because what is practical or common sense for one person may not be for someone else.

This issue, I realised, had naturally led to much dispute and confrontation. Mill's model does, however, accommodate this, because it provides for the logical exchange of ideas and the emergence of a logical solution, provided, of course, that those in dispute accept a logical approach for the solution to their problems and not a referral to bigoted ideology, be that religious, cultural or political.

Mill also warned about the danger of the "tyranny of the majority". In other words, since the majority would always decide who the representatives would be, then whatever they believed in would become law. But he recognised that the majority was not always right, and that the majority could itself stifle creativity. To counter this, Mill suggested that people should have the right to peacefully and publicly assemble and dissent; that is, to be able to express their sentiment or opinion, particularly if it differs from the majority, freely and publicly, and without fear of harm being brought upon them. This assembly and dissent, however, did not include things like damage to either private or public property, or the deliberate slowing down or halting of people going about their commercial or private interests.

Mill also recognised that there were some individuals in a society who were not capable of handling liberty. Minors, for example, who had not yet developed the ability for logical or rational thought, would be unable to accept the consequences of their choices, and therefore, of necessity, should not be granted liberty. He did, however, believe that society had a responsibility to guide and educate its youth in gaining the ability for logical, rational thought and, therefore, the capability to acquire their liberty: hence, the need for public education.

I felt I had a fairly good, though elementary, grasp of what Mill was on about, so I returned to the library and gave the book back to the librarian.

'I think I have a better understanding of what the Americans are on about when they talk about freedom now,' I said.

'That's good. What have you discovered?' she asked.

I explained what I had read.

She listened quietly until I had finished my summary, then replied, 'You have done well. Congratulations.'

I smiled back, 'Thank you.'

'There is one thing that you seem to have trouble with.'

'Yes, that free choice in a liberal democracy comes with consequences. Mill says that individuals must take responsibility for their choices. The consequences that an individual suffers as a result of making bad choices is not the responsibility of society to correct or alleviate. That's up to the individual himself or herself to correct.'

'That's right. What are your ideas about that?'

'A bit harsh, I should think. After all, what about forgiveness and redemption? Doesn't that have a role to play in a Christian nation?'

'Umm ... aren't you overlooking something?'

'What's that?'

'Doesn't forgiveness first require contrition and repentance?'

'That's right. So, people who make bad choices must first recognise that their choices were wrong and seek to correct their actions before society steps in to help. Is that what you are saying.'

'Yes. Those who work with alcoholics and drug addicts will tell you that there is little they can do for those suffering from these ailments until they genuinely seek to change their lives. Any attempt to alleviate their suffering without their commitment to change only enables them to continue with their bad choice and complicate their problem further. Helping them when they won't help themselves only leads to greater suffering by enabling their bad choice. This also helps overcome another weakness in liberty: the atomisation of society. You see individuals are the atoms of society, the smallest parts of a society. If individuals went their own way, it would be impossible for a liberal society to function. However, making individuals responsible for their own choices, and not enabling them to continue living a life that they alone cannot sustain, makes bad choices impossible. If the individual is contrite and repentant for making bad choices in their lives, however, it means that a liberal society can continue functioning because the bad choices of individuals will be eliminated.'

'That's true. So, society does have a role to play if the circumstances are right.'

'I don't think Mill would agree, but I believe that would be a more empathetic way to tackle the problem of free choice gone astray. What do you think?'

'I agree. Thank you so much for your insight. You have given me much to think about.'

'You're welcome.' She smiled at me, her eyes reflecting the pleasure she derived from my curiosity and growing awareness. 'Well, I guess you are ready to look at the communist world view now,' she said.

She returned with a copy of Karl Marx's book, *The Communist Manifesto.*

'The writing in this book is less scholarly and more journalistic, so it is easier to read. Marx was not attempting to explain his ideas philosophically, but rather incite workers into revolution. I hope you find it interesting.'

'Thank you,' I replied.

Again, I went back to my barracks and had settled down for a good read when Toby entered and came over to my bed.

'What ya readin'?' he asked.

'*The Communist Manifesto.*'

'What? Are ya thinkin' of becomin' a communist or somethin'?'

'No, I just want to understand what they are on about. After all, we are at war with them, you know.'

'Suppose. Don't know why ya want ta go ta all that trouble, though. Doesn't matter what ya discover about communism, mate. If ya have ta go, you will, no matter what ya ideas are.'

'That's right. It's just that I want to be able to hold my own in a discussion with some of Clarissa's friends.'

'Now, that makes sense. Well, good luck with all that,' he said, and walked away towards his bed.

I settled back into my reading. I quickly discovered that Marx's main idea was based on "dialectic materialism". I looked up "dialectic" and found out that it was a philosophy first advanced by Hegel, a German philosopher. He believed that reasonable people, when discussing serious issues, would advance a "thesis", an "antithesis" and a "synthesis". It would go something like this. One person would advance a thesis (an established and accepted idea), another would advance an antithesis (a challenging idea to the accepted idea), and through their reasoning, they would come to agree on a synthesis (an idea that contained elements of both the thesis and antithesis), and this in turn would become the new thesis, which would start the whole process over again. Hegel believed this process explained the cultural and political evolution of Western civilisation.

What Marx (who was influenced by Hegel) believed was that the process of the dialectic could be applied to the material distribution of wealth. That is, that an established order (thesis) could be challenged by another order (antithesis) and a new order (synthesis) would emerge. He called this "dialectic materialism" and used the example of the Roman empire, based on a master–slave order, which was challenged by the slaves, whereby a new feudal order based on nobles and peasants emerged. This new order was, in turn, challenged by the peasants and what emerged was a capitalist order based on what he called a bourgeois–proletariat order, what we would call a system based on a capitalist–worker order. His conclusion, however, was that when the workers rose up in revolution against the capitalist class, a new classless order would emerge and, since there was no longer any exploitation in a classless society, the process of dialectic materialism would come to an end.

When thinking about this, I realised that dialectical materialism depended on an oppressor–oppressed view of society and oversimplified the historical evolution of Western civilisation. For example, the fall of the Roman empire occurred because the Romans faced numerous problems, only one of which was the revolt of the slaves. Two other major problems, for example, were inflation and tribalism. Still, Marx did advance a novel concept: class struggle as a historical force contributing to change.

The next concept that Marx advanced was the "accumulation of wealth" principle. He argued that since the capitalists exploited the workers and drew a profit from their labour, that profit would eventually lead to an accumulation of wealth in the hands of the capitalists. This, he argued, was bad for society since it would end with the working class being impoverished. In short, the capitalist markets would eventually collapse, owing to overproduction in terms of the working class being unable to afford the goods produced by the capitalists.

I thought about this and reasoned that the capitalist system did, in fact, go through periods of collapse that we called economic recessions or depressions. So, that seemed to fit the facts of history. Marx seemed to have discovered an economic principle. But then I realised those economic recessions and depressions did not last forever, so something had to have occurred to rectify this failing. I understood that economic depressions in themselves were a terrible failing for any society since they brought with them unacceptable high levels of unemployment and much human suffering and misery. I wasn't sure how the capitalist system self-corrected, but I knew that it did. I concluded that I would ask the librarian and see if there was some other book that I needed to read.

In the meantime, I read more of Marx and discovered that he did, in fact, offer ways to combat this accumulation of wealth problem. The three things he believed would combat the accumulation of wealth were progressive income tax and the abolition of inheritances and private property.

I could see that the capitalist system since Marx's time had, in fact, adopted the idea of progressive tax and a tax on inheritances. It did not, however, abolish inheritances altogether, and it had not adopted his idea about abolishing private property.

There were other ideas that Marx advanced. While it is true that others in the nineteenth century advocated for these same ideas, my main concern here was trying to understand what ideas Marx was advancing, so I kept my focus on Marx alone. For example, he called for the abolition of child labour, something I was glad that the capitalist system had adopted.

Another idea was the establishment of free public education. Again, the capitalist system had moved in this direction over the years. Another was the nationalisation of transportation and communication. This was something that the capitalist system had adopted in a mixed way. For example, the railways were owned and operated by the government in Australia, as was the Australian Broadcasting Commission, but the private sector was also involved in both these areas. Examples of this were the private airlines and transport sector and the private ownership of newspapers, radio and television stations. Yet another idea of Marx's was the establishment of a national (government-owned) bank and credit system. In Australia, the government did regulate these financial institutions, although it did not nationalise them – again, a sort of mixed approach. With this understanding of Marx, I returned to the librarian.

'Well, how did you go?' she asked.

'Umm ... somewhat mixed.'

'How so?'

I said that Marx's writing was indeed less scholarly than Mill's, but that it had raised some important questions in my mind.

'Go on.'

'Marx believed that the clash between the working class and the capitalist class would lead to a classless society.'

'Yes.'

'Well. I don't think it has. In the West, I think Hegel's dialectic model has held up, because Western capitalism has evolved into his synthesis. Capitalism now has a regulated economy, not the *laissez-faire* system of capitalism as it existed in the nineteenth century. It is a synthesis of both the old capitalist ideas and the ideas that Marx advanced as an antithesis to it.

As for the communist countries, they never seem to escape from dictatorships – hardly Marx's classless society.'

'I see your point. Do you see any more changes in the future?'

'Not really. I don't see the communist dictators ever giving up their control, and I don't see how capitalism can evolve much further and still maintain its liberty.'

'You don't think capitalism can change any further?'

'Well, only around the edges, like eliminating some forms of discrimination. You know, like women getting equal pay for work of equal value, and some other forms of discrimination like institutional racism. Any further than that, and it will collapse.'

'How so?'

'Do we abolish private property and inheritance? If we do that, it will remove all incentive for achievement, excellence and progress.'

'That could definitely happen. In fact, that has been what has happened in all the countries that have tried communism.'

'That's right. Marx said something like "from each according to his capacity to each according to his need".'

'Well, the term Marx actually uses is "ability", not "capacity", but your understanding of the concept is correct.'

'Oh, okay. But that means that anyone who makes, let's say, a million dollars will have to give that to the state and the state will distribute it according to the needs of the citizens.'

'Yes, correct.'

'Well, where is the incentive for the person to make the million dollars in the first place? There isn't any. So why would anyone set out to better one's position when the state will just take it away. I think people are more likely to just sit back, do the least they have to and allow the government to provide for all their needs. It seems to me that communism offers no encouragement for aspirational individuals.'

'You are right. That has been a distinct weakness in Marx's model.'

'I went further than you suggested and read about the history of the Russian and Chinese revolutions and the destructive aftermath that was wrought upon the people of those countries. The purges and deliberate famines under both Stalin and Mao, for example, which cost the lives of millions of innocent people, shows us how malicious they truly were.'

'I saw you come into the library last week, but you didn't come to see me, so I thought you must have been researching something. And what do you now think about communism?'

'That, during peacetime, communism has a pernicious effect in freedom-loving countries. It eats away at their liberty, national unity and self-reliance while encouraging envy, division and dependency. Once in power, its arrogant, paranoid leaders reveal their true malicious nature by keeping their people in constant fear of arrest, detention or worse, and without the possibility of just recourse. This leads me to believe that the communist system is really a reversion back to the master–slave order of the past rather than the classless order it professes to promote.'

'Oh, why do you think that?'

'Well, in a master–slave order, the slave owns nothing and is only given what the master decides the slave needs. How does that differ from communism, where the state owns everything and decides what others can have? And what is the "state" in a communist country anyway? Isn't it really a dictator backed up by a ruling elite?'

'I guess you have a point.'

'Why do communist countries always have dictatorships, anyway?'

'Well, Marx said that it was necessary for there to be a period of what he called the "dictatorship of the proletariat" immediately after the chaos of a revolution. This was needed to stabilise and organise society and allow the classless society to emerge. Eventually, the dictatorship was expected to remove itself.'

'Well, that isn't supported by historic evidence. The only time dictators ever relinquish their power is when the people rise up and take it from them. When has a dictator ever removed himself voluntarily, other than when the people demanded it.'

'You are right. There is no historical precedent for that.'

'Since he was calling for a dictatorship, after a violent revolution, there is another point that Marx overlooked.'

'Oh, and what was that?'

'The type of leader who would hold power in the dictatorship after a bloody revolution conducted against their own people. Surely, they would be violent, malicious, bigoted individuals who would not tolerate any dissent – hardly the right type of individuals who would bring about a classless society. Historically, this is what happened, right? Stalin and Mao both executed or exiled those who offered differing opinions about how to achieve a classless society, as well as those who did not want to live under the communist system of government. They tolerated no opposition to their own ideas. Also, both Stalin and Mao maintained their power through fear, propaganda and censorship – hardly the creative, free-thinking society Marx envisioned his dictatorship of the proletariat would produce.'

'Again, that's a keen insight. So, what are your conclusions about liberty and communism?'

'Well, I'm happy that the *laissez-faire* capitalism that existed in the nineteenth century has been changed by the insights that Marx offered us. I much prefer the regulated economy of modern-day capitalism to the depredations of the old one. On the other hand, I am appalled by the human suffering and misery that Marx's vision for a classless society has actually produced. The communist dictatorships it has created are a blight on humanity. Also, his vision of a classless society is impractical. Rather than producing a utopia it produces a bland, colourless society in which mediocrity flourishes, devoid of any individual greatness. Under the communist system, there is no incentive that encourages the struggle for self-fulfilment, no striving for excellence, no encouragement of creative genius as exists in a liberal democracy – only an insistence on mediocrity and blind obedience, which barely produces enough to feed itself. I, therefore, cannot support communism but I cannot support liberalism either if it produces the *laissez-faire* capitalist system of the nineteenth century. I guess I'm happy with the current regulated system we have in Australia today. So, I support the modern idea of a liberal democracy with a regulated economy, so long as the regulations do not impede the economy excessively.'

We drifted into a short silence. I collected my thoughts before I went on.

'One thing puzzles me about the capitalist system, however. Do you know why it self-corrects after an economic depression?' I asked.

'Umm ... this is difficult to answer because we are now drifting into the discipline of economics. Are you sure you want to go there? It can be complicated and hard to follow.'

'Well, yes. I'm curious now, and I would like to know.'

'Actually, one book always leads to another. I think you will find there are lots of books you need to read, and I hope you will in the future, because you clearly have the capacity for it, but for now I will try to explain a few simple economic principles for you, which you can follow up on with your own research. Two good economists to start with are Adam Smith and John Maynard Keynes.'

'Good. I'll keep them in mind. Please continue.'

'Well, Adam Smith advocated for free trade over the mercantilist system which existed in his time. More trade meant more wealth for everyone, and since markets depend on supply and demand to determine price, it was important that goods remained in plentiful supply and demand remained high. The problem arises, of course, when the markets are not free, when governments try to overregulate them, or individuals try to manipulate them. Both these activities produce false supply and demand outcomes for free markets, which in turn leads to economic recessions and depressions.'

'Umm ... there is a lot there. I can see I need to do more reading. Now that I know how economic depressions occur, how do we get out of them?'

'Some economists believe that if governments leave the markets alone, they will recover by themselves. They say the markets need a shake out now and then, which enables them to recover. This does, however, lead to a lot of suffering for all, especially the working and middle classes, and it can take some time for the market to recover.'

'Well, that's not good. Can something be done to alleviate the suffering of the people?'

'Ha, ha. You're not becoming a socialist, are you?'

'I don't know what that means, but something must be done, surely?'

'Actually, communists and socialists have the same goal: the equal distribution of a nation's wealth through the abolition of private property and inheritances, and state ownership and distribution of all property and income. The only difference between socialism and communism is that communists want to achieve these goals through violent revolution while socialists prefer evolution through government legislation.'

'I see. Well, they both will have trouble running national economies, because they both remove incentive from aspirational individualists. But don't you think rich, advanced countries should take some responsibility for the wellbeing of their citizens?'

'Yes, I do. You will be pleased to know that a new idea was advanced in liberal, capitalist societies during the Great Depression of the 1930s. Since then, we have seen the emergence of welfare, and the creation of government works and projects that provide work for the unemployed during times of economic downturn. The problem with this, of course, is where the money comes from to provide for this welfare and public works. In Australia, it can only come from one of three places: taxes, royalties or borrowing. If there is a world recession, the demand for minerals and energy declines, thereby reducing government income from royalties. If taxes become excessive to pay for these schemes, it removes the aspiration of individuals to grow the economy. If it comes from the government simply borrowing money and taking on unsustainable levels of debt or printing more money, it only leads to higher levels of inflation, which worsens the economic situation and further prolongs the depression. It can, in extreme cases, lead to the total collapse of a country's economy.'

She paused to see if I was keeping up with her explanation. I nodded my head, so she continued.

'The famous economist who first articulated these new ideas was John Maynard Keynes, whose advice to liberal governments during the depression years of the 1930s posed a solution for their economic depressions. His argument was that liberal nations should save money by implementing surplus budgets during times of economic growth, and then spend this accumulated surplus during times of economic downturn. Of course, a problem arises when liberal and socialist governments do not produce surplus budgets during periods of economic growth, so they don't have an accumulated surplus in times of economic downturn.

'Unfortunately, politicians ignore the need to produce a surplus and offer more and more reckless spending during times of economic growth, even to the extent where they produce deficit budgets during good times to get elected. This can lead to what critics refer to as the emergence of a national entitlement mentality. That is, some citizens in such countries come to believe that they are entitled to certain economic benefits simply because of what group they belong to. These groups emerge throughout a modern society, but the ones at both ends of the social spectrum do the most damage to a country's economy. That is, the top one per cent want more and more tax incentives or subsidies to encourage their investment, while those at the bottom believe that they are entitled to more and more welfare. There are some in the middle who also believe that they are entitled to more and more benefits on the grounds of their group identity. Those in the middle, who do not qualify for a group identity, are then expected to pay for all this increased spending through higher taxes, which saps their incentive for aspiration, leading to a drop in productivity, exacerbating the problems arising from the increasing wealth gap explained by Marx.

'Australia has been lucky so far because of our minerals and energy exports, which provide our government with income from royalties. If anything was to endanger this source of government revenue in future, however, our economy would be put at risk, particularly if this entitlement mentality continued. Obviously, this would lead to higher national debt, which would eventually lead to higher inflation, which, in turn, would lead to a weaker currency. More money in our economy, produced by unfunded government spending and productivity that has not increased, means higher prices until an economic recession emerges.'

A quizzical look crossed her face. 'Did you follow all that?' she asked. I nodded my head. 'Good. I'm afraid the only solution to this situation is a change in the mentality of Australian citizens, both rich and poor and the ones in the middle, who demand increased benefits from their group identity, who tend at election time to ask only one question: 'what's in for me?'

'Yes, I see now,' I remarked. 'It's unfortunate that some politicians respond to their citizens' demands in the way they do, but I guess the rest of us need to stop encouraging them by voting against any attempt to buy our vote. I guess more of us need to ask our politicians how much their promises will cost and where the money is coming from to fund them. All that you have pointed out, however, is more evidence of a regulated economy, isn't it?

'Yes., that's right.'

'So, in reality, capitalism and communism don't exist at all. What we have instead are regulated economies and dictatorships. It's just that capitalists' markets are regulated by elected politicians and communists' markets are controlled by unelected dictators. The result being that one is a welfare state and the other a dictatorship.'

'I think you are correct. You have been able to think this through nicely,' she said, smiling with admiration.

With that said, I thanked the librarian for all her help and wished her goodbye. She smiled back at me. 'It has been a pleasure. Please come back anytime you feel the need.'

I was about to leave when I remembered another question I had not asked. 'Oh, yes ... Before I go, I seem to remember that Marx said something about capitalism providing the communist countries with the means to bring about the downfall of capitalism. Do you know what he meant by this?'

'Ah, you see, Marx was writing in the nineteenth century when the European nations were building and maintaining their empires. He rightly saw that capitalism needed to discover new and ever larger markets to keep itself going. That is, a capitalist economy relies on economic growth to sustain itself; hence, the need for more and more colonies. It was the colonies that provided the new markets for the increasing number of goods that capitalism produced. The colonies also benefitted through the economic growth and trade expansion to their national economies.'

'I see. But how does that relate to capitalists giving the communists the means to destroy capitalism?'

'I'm coming to that. Marx believed that the capitalist countries would eventually run out of markets, and then turn to the communist countries for expansion into new markets and trade opportunities. In this way, the leaders of capitalism – that is the ruling elite, both political and commercial – in their relentless pursuit of growth and wealth accumulation would, according to Marx, provide communism with the wealth and technology it needed to defeat capitalism.'

'Well, that hasn't happened. And anyway, wouldn't the people in a democracy vote against that?'

'It hasn't happened yet, because capitalism hasn't run out of markets yet, and democracy does pose a check against the ruling elite. But who could say what will happen in the future? Remember, it's the media that keeps the people informed in a democracy, and if the media is in the hands of the ruling elite, who can say what would happen? There is propaganda in liberal democracies, too, you know.'

'Um ... so, this is still something that might happen in the future?'

'Maybe. What do you think?'

'It's possible. Marx was right about some things and wrong about others, and the ruling elite in capitalist countries do pursue growth and wealth accumulation relentlessly, so perhaps he was right. We'll have to wait and see.'

'Yes. We'll just have to wait and see.'

I remembered what I had read about the history of Russia after it had embraced communism.

'Oh, yes,' I added. 'After the communist revolution in Russia, Lenin introduced a New Economic Policy (NEP), which allowed the Russian economy to become more independent and less reliant on central planning. This resulted in more incentives for the people to become more productive. Consequently, productivity from agricultural farms and small businesses increased, and the Russian economy grew. When Stalin came to power, however, he declared that those who had profited from the NEP were counterrevolutionaries and confiscated all their grain and capital. Consequently, millions of Ukrainian kulaks died from starvation. Stalin traded this stolen grain and wealth on the international market and purchased machinery for his factories and tractors for his collective farms, so this shows that capitalists were willing to trade with the communists. Perhaps Marx was right.'

'Marxists and New Left historians,' she added, 'apologise for this vileness by pointing out that it enabled Russia to rapidly modernise. This highlights the sickness that afflicts Marxist thinking, which believes that the end result justifies the means used to achieve it. In this case, the death of millions of kulaks was justified by the rapid modernisation of the Russian economy. Such repulsive reasoning. I can only hope that our politicians will never embrace such vile values and turn their backs on the pain and suffering of millions of their citizens.'

The librarian slowly shook her head, her face marked with genuine sadness. I was surprised at the depth of her emotional response, but I understood objectivity seemed inappropriate when confronted with such malevolence. I thanked her once again for all she had done for me, then smiled and left.

*

I had reached a point in my understanding about the Vietnam War where I felt confident that I could hold an intelligent conversation with any of Clarissa's friends. Also, the heat had gone out of most of Clarissa's and my arguments and disagreements because she had observed my growing awareness of the problems facing modern Australia, so I agreed to go to one of her parties. Her face lit up, and she told me how happy she was, and how much she had missed the long conversations and the sense of involvement she got from being with her friends. Her words cut me deeply, but I smiled and pretended I was happy too.

The party had the usual mixture of long hair and loud music and pungent smoke and endless conversations about the Vietnam War. I hated these parties and had tried to avoid them, but now that Clarissa was reasserting the independence of her mind, I had to go along with it. The more she chattered and smiled and laughed, the more I withdrew into myself; the more she touched and embraced her friends, the angrier I became.

The research I had done in preparation for this party had given me a deeper understanding of the philosophical forces behind the Vietnam War and an abiding commitment to liberty. I was confident that I could argue the importance of liberty over communism, so I hoped to hold my own in a discussion with Clarissa's friends, but my first encounter at the party went nothing like I had planned.

'Clarissa tells me you're in the army.'

I turned to see a young man with long hair and a beard that belonged on a camel.

'Yes,' I replied, smiling and trying to look friendly.

'So, what's it like? You hate it, right?'

'No. It's all right,' I said, still smiling at him.

'What?' He sounded annoyed. 'You don't mean you actually enjoy that shit,' he hissed.

'I didn't say that,' I replied sharply, somewhat annoyed by his apparent intolerant attitude.

'Well, what did you say, man? Tell me. I'd like to know.'

'The army gives you training that you would not get anywhere else.'

'You mean training in how to kill, right? That's what you mean.'

'Actually, I was thinking more about things like self-discipline, team effort and task orientation.'

'Yea, but all that stuff only helps you become a better killer, right?'

I had to use all of my self-control to reply calmly, 'I guess that's part of it, but those skills help in other ways.'

I was beginning to get angry at his inability to appreciate what I was saying, and the bigotry he was clearly showing.

'How stupid. That's how you justify learning how to kill?'

I wanted to lash out and hit him, but I checked myself, knowing that it would upset Clarissa. I took a deep breath and counted to ten before replying.

'Actually, you are right. In war, soldiers kill each other, but it's usually because their country sends them to war, to protect the citizens of their country from a perceived danger.'

'But you're not just killing soldiers in Vietnam, are you? You also kill innocent civilians, don't you?'

Again, I hesitated before answering him. 'In all wars, that happens. It's something that can't be avoided. It's what is known as collateral damage. You don't really think that we kill civilians deliberately, do you?'

'Oh, yes, "collateral damage", such a useful euphemism for murder. You're such a dumb ass. You're really just a killer who won't admit it.'

He was getting excited. His eyes took on the look of a wild, fanatical zealot, and a smirk caught the corner of his mouth. It was difficult for me to remain objective in the face of such New

Left sophistry. *If this bloke had an original thought, it would be lonely*, I thought. Clearly, we were far from a meaningful, logical exchange of ideas as proposed by Mill.

'That's where you're wrong. The deaths that occur in war are not murder. People die in wars. That's just the nature of war!' I said forcefully.

'What a pathetic thing to say. When civilians die in war, it's murder!' He shouted, waving his arms around to emphasise his point.

'Look,' I said flatly. 'Why don't you take your narrow little mind and your bad mouth and go ruin someone else's night?'

'Oh!' He shouted with delight. 'Soldier boy is angry. I'd better watch out or he'll pull a gun on me. Did you bring your gun, soldier boy? Maybe you could have some real fun and kill someone. There's plenty of unarmed civilians here.'

He said it so loudly that people around us stopped what they were doing and looked at him. In response to his unwarranted personal attack, I turned my back on him to avoid doing something I would regret and tried to find someone else to start a different conversation with.

'Hey, soldier boy, I'm talking to you!' he shouted, and grabbed my shoulder in an attempt to turn me around. Instead, I spun around and, with a tightly clenched fist, punched him hard in the mouth.

I knew I had lost control and had simply hit out. I hit out at the New Left intellectuals and their narrow, ideological bigotry who treated me with contempt. I hit out at my frustration of having to be at this party. But, most of all, I hit out at who I believed was my rival for Clarissa's admiration.

He staggered backward and went down on one knee from the impact of my fist, blood welling in his mouth. My hand hurt so I shook it, then I rubbed the prominent middle knuckle that had been cut and had begun to bleed and was already swelling from its impact with one of his teeth. I took out my handkerchief and wrapped it around my knuckles. Those around us went quiet and looked reproachfully at me. One of them knelt down to help the young man to his feet.

'You bastard!' he shouted, through his thickened lip, then spat at me as I walked out. I sat in my car, hoping that Clarissa would soon follow.

'What a rotten thing to do,' she said, when she finally arrived. 'You may as well take me home,' she added getting into the car. 'I can't stay here. Not now.'

We drove to her place in silence, and when we arrived, I cut the engine and turned towards her. 'I'm sorry. I ...'

She turned to face me, and her angry stare hit me hard. 'Of course, you're bloody sorry. What else could you be? Happy?'

'I was provoked, and he grabbed me first,' I said defensively.

'That's no excuse, Jason. There is no excuse for violence,' she added, the contempt rising in her voice and face. 'Don't you understand that Derik was deliberately trying to get you to hit him?'

'Oh, you know that bloke?'

'Yes, of course. He is the most outspoken member of the anti-war movement. He's a member of the Trotsky Club at uni.'

'Wait ... Trotsky? Wasn't he a prominent member of the Communist Party during the Russian Revolution?'

'That's right. Trotsky had a falling out with Stalin after the Revolution and, after Lenin had died, they both competed for the leadership of Russia. Trotsky wanted to export communism internationally, while Stalin wanted to consolidate it in Russia first. So, the Trotsky Club supports the Comintern, the

Communist International.'

'So, Derik is a communist who wants to bring communism to Australia?'

'That's right. And you played right into his hands. Do you think he will tell everyone that he provoked you into hitting him? No. He will wear his thick lip as a badge of honour and tell everyone that an Australian soldier punched him when all he did was speak out against the Vietnam War. That Australian soldiers are just dumb, violent brutes who are behaving badly in Vietnam.'

'If you knew that, why didn't you come over and settle him down?'

'Because you seemed to be handling him so well. I was actually proud of the way you were handling the situation, but then you turned violent so quickly. Frankly, Jason, you shocked me. No, actually, your use of violence frightens me.'

'Yes, yes, you're right,' I added in a conciliatory tone. 'I know I lost control. I know I shouldn't ...'

'That won't help, Jason. Don't you army meatheads understand that you are losing the propaganda war on the streets of Melbourne? I think all of you have been watching too many John Wayne movies. You think that a showdown of violence in the end will vindicate your position, when all it will do is contribute to a loss of support for your cause.'

'I don't know what to say. I was wrong, and what I did was stup––'

'––But it's always like this, isn't it?' she replied sharply. 'When I'm with your friends, I embarrass you. When you're with mine, you embarrass me. We're just not suited, Jason. I guess we're just not meant to be.'

She moved around on the seat, unable to get settled.

'Please don't say that,' I pleaded. 'I'll do better. I just want—'

'—That's right! You want! It's always what you want or what you'll do. But the truth is that nothing ever changes. You go on doing what you've always done, thinking what you've always thought and telling me that you'll change. But you never do,' she shouted at me, her hands raised in the air as she leaned across at me.

'It's as hard for me to change as it is for you,' I said.

'Yes, but I'm not the one who's going to war, am I? I'm not the one who's going to be killing people,' a note of finality ringing in her tone.

I paused for a moment, trying to wait for calmness to return to our conversation.

'No, you're not. And honestly, I just can't see what's wrong with my doing that. All I am doing is answering my country's call to protect your liberty.'

'That's right. And you never will, because you don't understand that I don't want you to protect my liberty. What I want is for you to stop killing,' she replied angrily.

'But, Clarissa, we are trying to stop the communists from killing civilians in South Vietnam.'

'Really? By killing civilians yourselves?'

'We deliberately kill communists, not civilians. In this war, only the communists kill civilians deliberately.'

'You don't seem to understand that the result is the same. Innocent people are being killed by both sides. I think we'd better stop seeing each other,' she said, opening the car door and stepping out, 'so we can work out where we're going.'

I was surprised by Clarissa's outburst. How could anyone believe that liberty was not worth fighting for, because people died in the fight? Would she have to lose her liberty to the communists before realising how important it is, and how did she think her ancestors gained and maintained the liberty she now enjoyed? It took thousands of years of fighting to gain their liberty, and now we had to continue the fight against those who want to take it away from us. I reasoned that she must believe that we were not fighting for liberty in Vietnam, whereas I did. She must believe that the communists only wanted South Vietnam, that they would never threaten Australia.

Alternatively, she might want to relinquish her liberty altogether. She might believe that communism would liberate her from traditional values while relieving her of the responsibility that comes with that liberation, that communism would take care of her from cradle to grave. Was her feminist movement blending with communism? The feminists did see their struggle in terms of the oppressed–oppressor model, the same as the communists. Could she not see that traditional values would be replaced with the values of the communist dictator, not with those she could freely choose for herself? My mind was confused, unable to think this out clearly. Was I beginning to slip into an unjustified conspiracy theory? I could see it was useless to pursue this matter further.

'Please get back in the car,' I said desperately. 'You mean too much to me for it to end like this.'

'No,' she replied. 'I'm going.'

'I have to go away next week. Please don't leave it like this.'

'Where are you going?'

'Queensland. I have to do some jungle training for a few weeks.'

'Then it's really happening. You *are* going to Vietnam.'

'It looks that way,' I said.

She got back in the car, and we sat in silence. She looked straight ahead into the night.

'Is it as bad as they say?' she finally asked.

'I don't know.'

'Do you think you'll die?'

'I hope not. I don't think it's as bad as all that.'

'How do you know?' She continued looking straight ahead.

'I don't, really,' I said softly.

She turned and put her hand up to my mouth and I kissed her fingertips.

'Please don't come in,' she said, opening the car door and getting out again. 'I want to be alone tonight.'

'All right. Can I see you tomorrow?'

'No. Wait till you get back from Queensland,' she said, then added, 'Give me a call first.' She closed the door and walked away.

*

Unable to sleep in the barracks that night, I lay awake and went over and over again what had happened between Clarissa and me. I thought about the happiness we had brought each other and the mistakes we had made.

Then I heard Toby kick the end of his bed.

'Shit,' he said, and some girl giggled. 'Shh,' he said. 'Ya not supposed to be here.' Again she giggled. 'Get ya gear off, an' get into bed,' he whispered. The bed groaned and squeaked under the weight of their urgency. Then it stopped, and all went quiet.

Sometime later, the duty sergeant arrived and shook Toby awake. He shone a torch into Toby's eyes, and Toby put up his hand.

'What?' he asked.

'What's that woman doing in your bed, private?'

Toby looked at the young woman beside him, clutching the sheet modestly to her breasts.

'Yeah,' Toby replied. 'What are ya doin' in me bed?'

*

No sooner had Toby and I jumped from the trucks at Canungra Jungle Training Centre than we were running and jumping, sliding through mud, setting up ambushes and being ambushed, bumping into each other and into shrubs and rocks and creeks and leeches and vines and open fields of grass that cut through exposed skin like razor blades. Somewhere in all this was a sanity that said it was necessary if we were to survive Vietnam, if we wanted to come back, and somehow our minds took comfort in the idea that if we trained hard enough, if we did what we were told and got it all right, we would survive. We would become veterans, but what that idea took no account of, what our minds would not consider, were the tiny, dark-clad figures with raised rifles which kicked when we didn't see them and shot tiny pieces of lead into our bodies when we didn't hear them, which robbed us of the only life on earth we couldn't afford to lose. No, it wasn't individuals the army trained to survive; it was the army itself that was trained to survive. Nevertheless, we continued the charade, hoping it would somehow be our salvation.

We rose at 5 am to a crisp, clear morning and an aching body. First, we ran and exercised, then we showered and ate breakfast. This was followed by lectures and classes on weapons training, map reading, bushcraft and so on. Then came the obstacle course and training on patrolling and village manoeuvres. At night, our patrols around the camp perimeter were sometimes rewarded with raiding parties who lay in ambush for us and hours of analysis about what went wrong and what we should have done.

One day, when we were attending a map reading lecture, our sergeant told us that to locate a point on a map we would be given two numbers, that these numbers were the longitudinal and latitudinal markings on a map, and that we had to locate them in that order.

He turned to one soldier in our platoon and asked, 'Which number comes first, the latitude or the longitude?'

'Ah ...' was the soldier's reply.

'That's okay, son. I'll make it easy for you. Just remember when you want to take your girl to bed, she has to come across before you can go up. So, the first number is located on the map by reading across the map, while the second number is located by reading up the map.'

We all laughed at the sergeant's humour, but none of us ever forgot how to read the location numbers on a map following his explanation.

After two weeks of this, we became reasonably competent and began to work more as a team than when we had first arrived. The odds of team survival had certainly improved.

Survival was something that kept playing on my mind. I kept thinking about Clarissa and how we had parted. At night, I dreamt of making love to her and, during the day, thoughts of her with other men ran constantly through my mind. Why had I done it? Why had I allowed us to get like this? Images of us together again – smiling and laughing and walking – encouraged me to believe we would reunite. I longed to be with her, and hoped she was thinking of me in the same way I was thinking of her.

We were on the last manoeuvre of our training, a week out in the bush, searching mock villages, looking for enemy camps, ambushing and being ambushed. We walked all day in the hot sun and the steaming jungle, and the sweat ran from our bodies. The equipment we carried got heavier, and our packs and our rifles and ammunition weighed heavily on our backs and on our arms. Our straps cut into our shoulders, leaving muscles burning hot with an incessant ache. At evening, we would bivouac and establish a perimeter, only to break camp during the night and move to a new location. We were tired, we were restless, we were irascible, but still we went on, knowing that it would soon be over.

At one time, we got word that an enemy patrol was following a bush track directly in our path. Our platoon commander told us to establish an ambush, and I was directed to a spot behind a lone shrub. My cover was scant, leaving me exposed on either side, but my exhaustion left me careless. I went to ground, having been told to remain absolutely still until the ambush was triggered.

I hugged the earth, my feet turned out with my heels flat on the ground. At that moment, a yearning for Clarissa passed through me. I closed my eyes tightly, clamping down my eyelids, trying to shake her image from my mind and the ache from my loins. But still her presence stayed with me. I opened my eyes and saw a red meat ant on the back of my left hand. He raised his rear and bit deeply into my flesh. I brushed him aside only to discover a whole nest of meat ants at my side. My movement seemed to attract them. They swarmed out of their hole in the ground and ran towards me, disappearing into the cracks and crevices of my clothes. I brushed furiously.

Just then, I heard wild screaming and gun shots exploded everywhere. Looking up, I saw black-clad figures running towards me, so I raised my rifle to return fire, but it was too late: they had overrun our position.

Our instructor called us together.

'Who was the dickhead who moved?' he shouted.

I raised my hand gingerly, sporting a sheepish grin.

'You're an absolute prick,' he screamed at me. 'Your carelessness has killed this whole fuckin' platoon!'

'I was being eaten by ants,' I said lamely.

'And now ya six foot under bein' eaten by worms! You have to be aware of your surroundings at all times,' he said to the whole platoon. Turning his attention back to me, he continued. 'Didn't you see the ants' nest before you took up your position? Weren't you capable of understanding that lying down next to an ant's nest was not a very sensible thing to do? Can't you think for yourself? Do I really have to explain that to you?'

'I'm sorry, Sergeant. I'll do better next time.'

'There isn't a next time, son. This is it. Next stop, Vietnam. Hasn't that fact sunk in yet?'

I looked blankly at him. *My God, he's right*, I thought. When I make Vietnam, I'll have to leave everything behind, my thoughts, my feelings, my whole life, because to carry it with me would be dangerous. Then the realisation hit me that if I was in Vietnam now, I really would be dead. The carelessness of my action, the thoughts of Clarissa, all would have contributed to my death and the death of my platoon. I knew I had let them down, and I felt ashamed, frightened and alone.

That night in camp after I had showered and eaten dinner,

I stayed by myself and wrote a poem for Clarissa:

> *COME AGAIN*
> *You came*
> *With eyes that smiled of sweet refrain*
> *And jasmine filled the stillness of our nights*
> *Time took away your lightly salted skin*
> *And left you trembling far beyond my reach*
> *But where your soft response once made me sigh*
> *Springs hope your gentle eyes will turn to mine*
> *The smell, the taste, the touch remains*
> *Come again.*

I signed it, and thought of sending it straight away, but decided to give it to her myself.

*

The next few days passed quickly, and early one morning, after a sleepless train ride back to Melbourne, Toby and I shared a taxi back to our camp. On the way, I decided to surprise Clarissa by going straight to her house.

'Are you sure you want to do this?' Toby asked seriously.

'Yes.' I said, running my fingers gently over the neatly folded sheet containing my poem. 'We may have quarrelled but I want to change all that.'

'Um, I hope it works out fer ya, mate.'

I left the taxi outside her gate and, with bag in hand, raced to the house. Crossing the lawn, I saw the front door was ajar, and a light was still on inside. I headed straight for the bedroom.

Standing in the doorway, I looked down on the crumpled sheets and the two naked figures of Derik and her lying deep in an exhausted sleep. I don't know how long it took me to move, but it seemed a long time. Neither of them woke, so I turned quietly and left.

Her house had never seemed as large to me as it did that night when I pushed my way through the empty rooms and into the clear morning air of her front yard. I stood, caught between leaving and staying, but what I wanted most was gone now forever. I crushed the poem in my hand and threw it at the empty doorway.

'I thought this might happen. You two had little in common. The soldier and the protester.'

Toby laughed, trying to remove the tension from my face. He had waited, half expecting to see me come out of Clarissa's place. His attempt at humour had no effect on me, so the ride back to camp was a silent one. Later in the barracks, however, he looked out a window at the neatly manicured lawn and the whitewashed rocks lining the footpath and told me the strange story of his earlier marriage.

She was the first 'nice' girl he had ever known. There was a longing in Toby's description of her as though he felt she should have been unattainable for someone like him. Even when he spoke about her, he spoke in hushed tones, so unlike his usual boisterous manner.

At first, he explained, she had acted indifferently towards him, as though she cared little whether he wanted to see her or not. Something had made him persist, though. Maybe it was something in him and not her that had kept him wanting her, something that would not let him give up, or perhaps a belief that there could be more, perhaps laughter, romance and even nights alone. At last, he drew up his courage and kissed her. She stood with her eyes closed frozen like a Greek figurine. When finally she opened her eyes, she pressed herself against him and kissed him hard. His excitement raced ahead not only from her actions but from the fulfilment of a desire he had only previously shared with his dreams.

But he knew all along that something was wrong; girls like her were not normally interested in blokes like him. A few days later, she told him she loved him and wanted to marry him. Just days after that, owing to her insistence, they were married. Six months after their wedding, a baby was born, and she cried and cried and told him it was premature. He patted her head and told her it didn't matter, but deep inside he knew he felt cheated. He couldn't shake the nightmare of her lying with another man, and he couldn't escape the feeling she had set him up.

He became sullen and unapproachable. He took whatever he wanted from her, giving nothing in return. They quarrelled. At first, he avoided her, preferring instead to drink with his mates and come home drunk. Then he shamed her and then he broke her spirit. No longer was she the unattainable desire in lavender and lace who had enchanted him; now she was the object he took at will. He came to despise himself for forcing himself on her, for what he had done and for what he continued to do, but he couldn't stop himself.

But she stopped it. One night, he came home late to an empty house. She had left him and taken her child with her. Despite all that had passed between them, he was unable to raise enough interest to find them, preferring instead to stay alone in the big empty house with his mates and his beer and the occasional women who happened to stray his way.

'An' that's the way it's been ever since,' he said with no

remorse in his voice, 'because that's the way I like it. Oh sure, every now an' then, I think of what might've been if I'd acted different. But I didn't, so there's no sense dwellin' on it. When it comes ter women, Jason, keep it simple. Keep it simple an' nobody gets hurt.'

'What do you mean, keep it simple?'

'What Nick said at Kapooka. Ya got hurt because ya let a woman get too close ter ya.'

'But that's what life's about; isn't it?'

'Sure. If ya like it that way.'

'But you have to care about something, surely?'

'Yeah, ya care, but ya don't care about women.'

'What are you talking about – homosexuality?'

'Nah. That's just more of the same, I reckon. Look, what I'm on about is ya care, really care, for ya mates. Women ya take when the need or the opportunity arises, but ya mates is what ya really care about. Sex ya get in the sack, but friendship, mateship, that's what ya really care about, an' that ya get with ya mates, not with women.'

'I don't think that would be enough for me, Toby.'

'Sure it would. Look ya not goin' without, mate. Ya still get ter have it off now an' then. It's just that ya don't let it get ter ya. Ya know, ya don't let any woman get her claws into ya. So that way ya keep it simple and ya can't get hurt. Ya never have ter worry about a woman havin' it off with someone else, because ya never get that close, see. It works, mate, I tell ya, it works, an' the army's made fer it. Ya don't have ta worry about some woman comin' in an' complicatin' things. Know what I mean?'

He went on before I could answer him. 'Oh! An' one other thing, I've never had a mate – a real close mate, ya understand, not someone ya just met – I've never had someone like that ever let me down. Know why? Because it's simple, see. There's none of that love thing, no jealousy, no spite, no hate or anythin' like that to spoil it for ya. Ya just mates an' mates get drunk together an' sometimes, when they're lucky and a woman is willing, they even get to share the same woman, but they never take each other, see, so nobody gets hurt. Simple, keep it simple, an' nobody gets hurt.'

Nothing else passed between Toby and me that night, but I felt he was wrong. I kept thinking about Dad's advice. Never run away from life, he had said. Keep growing and reaching out for the next experience. Somehow, Toby's idea seemed to close that down. Sure, I wanted to have mates, but I also wanted more. The romantic in me wanted love and commitment and trust and mutual respect and perhaps even the responsibility of a family, but right now, when I thought about those things, I got a terrible ache inside me like a sickness that I couldn't cure. When I was younger, I would have gone to Mum and she would have had something to give me, but now I had to work it out for myself, and there just didn't seem to be anything I could do.

I was lucky in one respect: the army didn't give me much time to think about it, because my orders came through to report for duty pending my departure for Vietnam. I was given leave to return home and say goodbye to my family. At home, there were lengthy and concerned discussions with Dad about the war, and what my role in it would entail. Eventually, it was time to say our final goodbye. We went into the front yard of our home, and Mum gave me a hug. She pressed her head into my chest, and I wrapped my arms around her. She felt so small and helpless, and I could sense her vulnerability at having to send her only son off to war. She stepped back and took my hands in hers, and I could see the tears and desperation in her eyes.

'Please come back to us, Jason,' she said with a quiver in her voice.

'Don't worry, Mum. I'll be careful.'

I couldn't think what else to say. I could see she needed some kind of guarantee that I would return, so, when Dad took a photo of me, I took off my hat, and did my best to give Mum a reassuring look. I took off my hat, because I wanted Mum to know that I was still her son, and not just another soldier going off to war. I knew she would take the photo out many times during my absence, and I hoped that it would give her some solace.

CHAPTER 5

The war and more

The clean salt air filled my lungs and cleared my head as HMAS *Sydney* pushed its way through the sheltered waters of Sydney Harbour out into the open sea beyond. The flight deck of the old aircraft carrier had warped, such that planes could no longer land or take off on it, so she was now used to ferry soldiers and military equipment to Vietnam. Those who sailed on her referred to her affectionately as the Vung Tau ferry.

I looked back on the calm waters of the harbour and remembered how awkward I had felt climbing the gangway at Garden Island with my heavy kit bag while the people on the wharf had waved and cried, and how I had wanted to do something more than struggle up a gangway looking like I didn't know what I was doing.

One of the sailors showed us to our berth. In the navy, a berth is the place where you sleep. (The place where we ate was called the mess deck.) The sailor took a hammock from a wire cage and showed us how to string it. Then he showed us how to drop it and stow it back in the wire cage. He told us all hammocks had to be strung at night and stowed first thing in the morning. He warned us to remember which hammock was ours; otherwise, we would soon be sleeping in someone else's hammock.

It only took us two nights before everyone had lost his original hammock. One night, I ended up with one that had such a bad smell I couldn't bear to sleep in it. Try as hard as I did, I never got used to sleeping on my back, and in a hammock, there is no other way to sleep. It wasn't long before I was bunking down on a padded bench that ran along the side of the bulkhead (that's a wall). Sleeping was a problem for me; seasickness was another.

I was attached to the ship's sick bay when, two days out of Sydney, we skirted around a cyclone. The waves were so large the ship slid into their troughs. She would rise up one side of a wave, struggling and shuddering so badly I imagined she would break apart. She seemed to hover on the crest, and I said to myself, 'Here it comes, here it comes. Now we're going down.' Suddenly, she would tilt and slip and slide headlong down the other side while my stomach was still up on the crest of the last one. Then the whole procedure would start again. This went on for hours, and it wasn't long before I started handing out seasickness tablets to those who needed them.

The tablets themselves didn't work, but, when I gave them out, I was told by the ship's doctor to explain how it took scientists years to develop them and how much care and precision had gone into their research and testing. So, I stood close to my sick patients and looked into their eyes and said confidently, 'These tablets are really good, and they really do work. NASA developed them for their astronauts.' If I did it with enough conviction, it sometimes worked, but mostly they threw up the tablets in a couple of minutes and came back for more. When I gave them fresh tablets, I explained they had to hold them down if they were going to work. When the seasick tablets ran out, I started handing out aspirin tablets. I told the same story for the aspirin tablets as I had for the seasick tablets.

After a while, we came through the rough weather, the journey settling into a regular routine with isolated incidents breaking the monotony of an otherwise uneventful trip. There was the time we stopped at one of the islands on our way to Vietnam, and the islanders came out to barter with us. They were in canoes with their carvings and grass skirts and seashells and other island items laid out for our inspection. We bargained with them, looking down from the side of our large ship. They were interested only in packets of cigarettes, which we were able to purchase from the ship's store duty free.

I was interested in a necklace of carved boars' tusks hanging around the neck of an islander. I made a bid for it, but he shook his head, indicating he was not interested in selling. I waited until the bidding and selling had dropped off, and some of the buyers had left, then I repeated my offer, but he was still not interested.

Most of the islanders had turned and paddled back towards the shore, but the one with the necklace had not sold much merchandise, and I could see he was disappointed with his day's trading. I repeated my offer, but he shook his head and waved his hand, still indicating his desire to keep the necklace. I increased my offer. He hesitated, not wanting to part with the necklace, but also not wanting to refuse my offer. Before he could refuse, I increased my bid for the last time, a note of finality in my voice. He nodded his head, reaching up and removing the necklace from around his neck.

The necklace had red and white beads spacing the boars' tusks that were carved with strange, criss-crossed markings forming odd geometric patterns. I placed it around my neck and smiled with satisfaction.

'I didn't think ya was gunna get it,' Toby said cheerfully.

'No,' I replied. 'But I'm glad I did.'

'It's a real beaut.'

Then there was the time we crossed the equator, and the navy boys put on a show for us. They dressed up in colourful costumes of Neptune and his daughters, some of them capturing the feminine form and character, others merely trying for the comic effect. Those of us who were crossing the equator for the first time were dunked into large tubs of salt water and were made to do menial tasks for Neptune's daughters, like brush their hair and adjust their clothing. There was much laughing and good humour and, at the end of the activity, we newly initiated seafarers were given a certificate by Neptune himself, guaranteeing us safe passage.

As we drew nearer to Vietnam, our training intensified. Early morning physical training included exercising and running around the flight deck, which was spotted with lookouts on either side and at the stern. The navy had a 'man overboard' procedure ready in case someone fell from the ship. When the alarm sounded, two men on standby were to drop a rubber craft called a Gemini from the side of the ship, start an outboard motor and speed aft to make the pickup.

On our trip, they were never required to undertake a real life-saving procedure, but they did carry out many training runs, sometimes collecting real sailors who had volunteered to go overboard. The thought of going overboard, however, frightened me, because it all depended on the lookouts spotting you; no matter how hard you shouted, they would never hear you above the ship's noise. Also, I always imagined a race between the Gemini and whatever lurked beneath the waves to reach me first.

In the afternoons, we took target practice from the stern of the ship. Coloured balloons were dropped into the water and those assigned a colour would try to hit it before it disappeared.

The infantry were the only troops with rifles, because the army reasoned it was better for support troops, like me, to collect our weapons at our units in Vietnam. This minimised the possibility of accidental discharges on board ship. Consequently, I could only shoot when I borrowed Nick's rifle, which wasn't very often, but, when I did, I shot reasonably well. Toby, on the other hand, had been coached by Nick and shot so well the commanding officer arranged a transfer for him into Nick's unit as the company medic. Toby seemed pleased with the prospect of touring Vietnam with Nick.

One night, the captain patched through a radio broadcast by Hanoi Hanna over the ship's intercom. She claimed that all the Australian troops in Nui Dat had been wiped out by the victorious NVA and that those on board HMAS *Sydney* were heading for their deaths. When the broadcast ended, the captain came back on and said cheerfully, 'I thought you would like to hear the propaganda your enemy engages in, fellers.'

The intercom went silent, and we sat looking at it. We knew our troops had not been wiped out as Hanoi Hanna had claimed, so we laughed and joked about it, but the knowledge that the North Vietnamese had about our arrival worried me. Did someone back home notify them of our departure from Sydney?

We reached Vung Tau in the middle of the TET Offensive. Helicopters arrived and took the infantry to Nui Dat but the helicopters never returned, so those in charge decided the rest of us would go ashore by landing craft and be picked up by trucks to take us to our units. We packed into the landing craft as it pitched and tossed in the sea alongside HMAS *Sydney*. When the craft broke its line and moved away towards the shore, a spray, created by the bow pounding the waves, shot over the top and drenched those standing at the back. There followed a natural crowding towards the front which caused the pilot to shout at us, 'It's no good you all crowding forward. I won't be able to land on the shoreline if you do.'

Some of us moved back, but the craft was still heavy in the bow. Eventually, we struck bottom some metres from shore and the pilot dropped the front ramp. We had to wade ashore with our packs held high.

The trucks had not arrived, so we were told to sit on the beach and wait. Since the beach was covered in black rocks the size of tennis balls, most of us sat on our packs. Someone beside me, who was dripping wet, said sarcastically, 'Typical army. Hurry up and wait!'

'Were you at the back of the landing craft?' I asked.

'Yes. Not that it mattered much. I got drenched from wading ashore,' he replied.

'I don't think we'll have to wait long,' I said encouragingly.

Just then, a couple of isolated shots rang out down the road above us. This was followed by heavier firing and some exploding grenades. Two officers from our group raced off in the direction of the fighting and returned, waving their arms and shouting, 'Disperse! Disperse!'

'Not only am I as wet as a shag,' my sarcastic friend said, 'but I'm sitting here like one as well.' We both laughed. 'Oh well,' he continued, as we wandered off towards some cliffs to our right, 'if they come, we can always throw stones at them. This'll make a great story for our grandchildren – the day we stormed the beaches of Vung Tau with our kitbags.' We both laughed again.

Just then, our trucks arrived with M60 heavy machine guns mounted on their roofs and soldiers with flak jackets and steel helmets manning them.

Sitting in the back of an open truck on the way to camp, with my gear resting between my feet and no weapon in my hands, I felt exposed and vulnerable, but the most disturbing thing encountered that morning was the Vietnamese themselves. They went about their daily routine undisturbed, oblivious to our presence and the madness around them.

Vietnam, I learnt, is a country of cities, with crowds that throng and traffic that jostles. Vietnam is a country of farmers with cone hats and endless rice paddies. Vietnam is a country of remote highland rainforests with vegetation so thick it is twilight in the middle of the day. Vietnam is a country of open plains with grass so tall it could hide a herd of water buffalo, let alone a regiment of Viet Cong. But, for me, Vietnam became a country of coastal people where few lips smiled, where few relaxed in a carefree holiday atmosphere, where eyes reflected the suppressed fear of a people used to death and destruction. Vietnam is very hot. Nothing dazzles you.

My work at the field hospital started immediately. The medical assistant I replaced had left a week before I arrived, so they were already short-staffed, and the TET Offensive stretched the limited facilities of the field hospital.

The wounded were brought in by helicopter, then we carried them into a clearing room where surgeons sorted out their operational priorities. The wounded would then have their clothes cut from their bodies and their wounds cleaned, and any test ordered by the surgeons would be carried out. The most common of these were urine tests and X-rays; tourniquets were also removed and clean ones reapplied to arrest haemorrhage. Those with severe haemorrhage had saline or plasma drips applied or, when we were certain of their blood group and we had an adequate supply of it, blood was transferred.

In the operating theatre, surgery was performed competently by two small, professional teams. The most common operation was for gunshot wounds, but leg amputations became common later on, because our infantry kept stepping on American-made landmines, which had been laid by our own troops and dug up and reburied by our enemy.

In any event, when the remaining stump that once had been a leg was lifted up and the ragged talons of flesh hung lifelessly from its end, there was nothing to do but saw at the bone, slice through the flesh, stitch it all up neatly and hope the surgical drains and antibiotics would keep the stump from future operations.

Major operations, like amputations, would then go to an intensive care ward, which was the only air-conditioned ward and where a nursing staff, who enjoyed a low staff–patient ratio, kept a close, personal eye on their patients. In the early hours of the morning, when they would sob silently and whisper that they wanted to go home, the sister would go to them and hold their hands, listening and whispering to them about the possibilities of their future life without their limbs. When they were fit to travel, these patients were medevacked home on Hercules aircraft specially outfitted for the journey. On the other hand, minor operations, like non-life-threatening gunshot wounds, were sent to a surgical ward after operation to recover. Later, these patients were sent to a rest and convalescent centre (R&C) in Vung Tau to receive outpatient care before eventually returning to active duty. There was also a medical ward where all those who had picked up exotic diseases like malaria, dengue fever, hepatitis, gastro-enteritis and skin rashes that nobody seemed able to explain, were cared for.

The nature of my work was such that I had to detach my

emotions from what I was doing, or I would not survive. When the wounded arrived, I immediately switched on a machine inside me that concentrated on the work at hand. Bone and flesh simply became that, not living tissue. The surgeons knew incisions had to be clean and all metal pieces removed; emotion had no place in such an environment, and so I removed it just as the surgeons removed the metal pieces. But some things I couldn't remove, like the stifled sobbing of a young man who lay awake in the middle of the night unable to contemplate a life without his legs, or the stoic reply of another young man to a surgeon who told him he would lose his foot: 'Yeah,' the young man said, 'I had a look at it myself. It's bloody ratshit.'

*

The field hospital was built on sand dunes approximately half a kilometre from the beach on the southern stretch of the Vung Tau peninsula, which jutted out into the South China Sea. As a rule, the sea was calm and the waters warm, but, when the wind got up, the sea became choppy and dirty and the sand blew at will throughout the camp, because no attempt was made to stabilise the sand base, owing to the possibility of mortar attack. It was reasoned the sand would have a cushioning effect on the exploding mortar shells.

All the buildings in the hospital (both barracks and wards) were the same, with an open concrete floor, exposed timber framed walls and a galvanised roof. Large wooden slats hinged from the top opened out along both sides, and doorways at both ends allowed cross and through breezes to cool the inside. Around the outside was a metre-high wall of sandbags for protection against attack not only from the Viet Cong but also from the wind, which would tear away at the sand foundation of the concrete floor if the sandbags were not there.

The hospital wards were located at the northern end of a small valley between two large sand hills where our barracks were situated. The western hill housed officers and sisters while the eastern hill housed the other ranks (ORs) and non-commissioned officers (NCOs). In the small valley between the two sand hills stood a kitchen and dining hall and just beyond that was a canteen, which had a small pool table and a dart board. The administration building stood at the base of the western hill, and next to that was a bomb shelter dug into the side of the hill and reinforced with sandbags.

The hospital itself was surrounded by other army units. To the west were the engineers, to the south were the supply units, while the eastern approach, closest to the sea, was home to a transport unit. At the eastern perimeter, where the back gate stood, was a recreational centre, which billeted infantry units on a rotational basis. The infantry units were sent there for a rest from the combat operations they performed out of Nui Dat. They always complained we had it too good at Vung Tau and that we never knew what the war was really like. Conditions in Vung Tau were certainly better than what they experienced in Nui Dat and we never went out on patrol, so we did not experience firsthand the fire fights and the village searches we heard so much about.

In one way, I was grateful to be spared that. Working in the hospital, I witnessed the horror our boys went through, so I appreciated the truth of their words, but my knowledge also created in me a sense of debt, a belief that somehow I owed those young men for sparing me the pain and suffering they went through.

I had just come off a night shift, punctuated by the restless demands of my troubled patients, when Nick and Toby walked into my hut.

'Hey, Jason, what ya doin'?' Toby asked with a smile as wide as the Simpson Desert.

'Nothing. What are you two doing down here?'

'Got a thirty-six-hour leave at the Peter Badcoe Club,' Nick grinned.

'Some blokes get it easy,' I joked. 'It's good to see you both.'

'Yeah, you too, mate. Listen, Toby an' me are gunna hit Vungers. Want'a come?'

I nodded and changed into some fresh clothes, then we went to the orderly room where I explained to the duty sergeant my desire to show Vung Tau to my mates. He reminded me that I had to apply for leave at least twenty-four hours before it being granted.

'But these blokes only have a thirty-six-hour leave,' I pleaded.

The duty sergeant saw the desperation in my eyes and the disappointment registered on Nick and Toby's faces. Next, he handed me an application for leave form.

'Put yesterday's date on this,' he said, turning around and moving off to his desk. He came back and took the application form from me. 'Your leave has been granted, Corporal,' he said taking my application, and handing me my leave pass. 'Don't make a habit of this.'

'No, Sergeant, and thank you.'

Instead of heading immediately to Vung Tau, we went to the Peter Badcoe Club for lunch and drank beers next to a swimming pool while looking out on the clear water of the South China Sea as its waves broke on the beaches of Vung Tau. There was even a barbecue, so we had some grilled steak with our beer. It was surreal. Here we were in Vietnam fighting a war, but able to enjoy a distinctly Australian barbecue lunch together.

Later, in Vung Tau, we walked into the American-built Hotel Paradise, which had a bar and bordello. It was five stories high, rectangular in shape and built on a long, narrow block, giving it a squeezed-out effect. The top stories were enclosed with terraces with straight, grilled railings running the full width of the front and sides. The outside was rendered in a concrete finish and the gold and red flags of South Vietnam flew outside, providing the only colour relief to the whole building.

Inside was dark and cavernous. Atop a wide flight of carpeted stairs was an American bar, very different from Australian bars. It was poorly lit, with slinky, scantily clad, young Vietnamese women in abundance. We sat at a table near a bandstand where a group of Vietnamese musicians was having trouble keeping the timing to 'Hang on, Sloopy' because their drummer kept losing his beat. We had only just sat down when one of the girls broke from the bar and walked to our table.

'Buy me Saigon tea,' she said, and smiled without showing her teeth.

'Honey, I'll buy you anything as long as you sit on my knee,' replied Toby, tapping his right leg.

'Sure, baby. You, number one Joe.'

She sat on Toby's knee and put her arms around his neck. Number one meant that you were the best, number ten meant you were the worst. Number 'welve' (twelve) meant you were worse than the worst. Australians were generally called 'number welve, cheap Charlie'.

'That's what I love about this place,' Toby said, turning to us. 'Ya get right to the business without all the bullshit.'

A waiter took our order and returned with our drinks. The girl offered her glass for Toby to take the first sip.

'Jeez, that's strong!' he said.

'Not really,' I replied. 'These girls would probably drink ten to twenty glasses of that stuff every day. If it was for real, they'd be permanently sloshed.'

'Huh?'

'Look, to make a Saigon tea, the bartender fills the glass with Coke, dips his finger in whisky and rubs it around the lip of the glass. You get the first sip, so you get the strong whisky taste while the girl here gets a glass of Coke.'

'But why the charade?' asked Nick.

'Because the Yanks won't buy drinks for girls who aren't drinking, so the girls are forced to pretend. Like you said, Toby, there's no bullshit here.'

Nick grinned, then drank from his can of Budweiser.

'This Yank beer is bloody awful,' he said. 'Isn't there someplace we can get a VB or a Tooheys?'

'Only back at camp,' I replied.

Nick shrugged his shoulders and continued drinking. Toby and the girl moved gradually to the darkest corner of our table. He bought her a second Saigon tea, and she straddled his leg and rubbed herself hard up against him. Finally, he broke from her and moved sheepishly towards us while she pulled at his arm.

'She wants me ta go upstairs with her. What'd ya reckon, Nick?' He asked.

'Do what ya want, mate. But remember, every Yank in Vungers has been there first.'

'Yeah, I know. But she's got such great moves.'

We both laughed. Finally, Toby stood up.

'I can't stand it,' he said. 'If I don't go, I'll spend the rest of me life wonderin' what she would'a been like.'

We watched Toby and the girl disappear into the stairwell of the Hotel Paradise.

'Now there's a man who knows his own mind,' Nick said dryly.

When Toby returned, he grinned like a little boy caught misbehaving, then went on about how great it had been, how he had never experienced anything like it. Nick sat silently listening to everything he said.

Finally, he sighed and said earnestly, 'I'm happy for ya, Toby.'

Toby and I sat quietly looking at each other, then we burst out laughing.

'What?' Nick said. 'No, really, Toby, I am happy for ya.'

This made us laugh even louder. Eventually, Nick joined in.

'Bugger this,' he said, swallowing the last of his beer. 'Let's go somewhere an' get drunk.'

What followed was a bar crawl through the crowded streets of Vung Tau, where people were either dressed in the traditional Vietnamese dress, all black *ao dai* or in military jungle green uniforms. All the soldiers had short, cropped hair and all the females had straight jet-black hair hanging down below their shoulders. The buildings were dirty, the streets unclean with food scraps lying about and the butcher shops even hung raw meat outside, including the severed heads of pigs. When I stared at those heads, the dead eyes left me unsettled.

There were children everywhere who roamed the streets in groups. They would come up to you and beg, some approaching from the front and putting their hands on you and touching you as much as possible while shouting and begging. At the same time, the smaller ones would come at you from behind and pick your pockets. That's why we always kept our money in our button-down shirt pockets and only change in our pants pockets. If you were lucky enough to catch them at it, you took pity on them, because they were so small and so helpless and so destitute.

And so we went into one bar after another and drank the local *bar muoi bar* beer, a drink made with no attempt at alcohol consistency. Sometimes a bottle would be light, but mostly it was over-proof. Your head started to float and your lips went numb, and then you would start to talk a lot of nonsense, and some people would cry and some would sleep, but mostly they would fight. There was always a fight going on in a bar somewhere in Vung Tau whenever there were soldiers on leave getting drunk. The military police had their hands full, trying to keep order.

Then you would be back on the dirty streets again, where some little boy about twelve years of age would come up and offer you his sister for a couple of dollars. You would tell him no and he would insist she was a virgin and you would tell him to *de de mau*, which in Vietnamese is a rude way of telling him to get lost. Then he would offer you his younger brother and you would shake your head in disbelief and he would look at you in disgust as though there was something wrong with you and walk off, cursing and abusing you in Vietnamese.

Then you would notice the cheerful stalls in the street and the lightly coloured flags, the abundance of silk and colour, the bright blues and reds and the clean whites and the burnished golds, the stars and the tassels and the trinkets, and you would buy something and your eyes would well up because it reminded you of home, of your mother or your sister or your sweetheart or your wife, and you would think about the cleanliness and the brightness of home and wonder what that someone special was doing right now. Then you would take a long drink from your bottle and punch your mate in the arm and tell him what a dumb bastard he was and he would laugh and rough you up and tell you that it takes one to know one, and so you would both drink some more. And, finally, when you bounced around in the back of a crowded leave truck on your way back to camp, you laughed and sang and told dirty jokes, but you never spoke seriously about what you thought or felt because you knew, deep within your heart, that your mates were hurting too, and you didn't want to see what festered inside, waiting to ooze out if anyone pricked the surface. So, you would just get drunk and try to forget and, because Nick and Toby and I did this together, it made us mates. And mates were always there to help one another forget the pain.

*

The military had catchy phrases to describe the missions we were on. For example, when the Americans and Australians had first arrived in South Vietnam, the mission description was summarised with the term 'search and destroy', which made it clear what we were expected to do: search for the enemy and destroy them. This strategy was a simple one, but difficult to implement, because it was difficult to identify the Viet Cong from the villagers. The strategy was for us to kill as many communists as we could find until they gave up and no longer infiltrated South Vietnam. This strategy had limited success, because the North Vietnamese soon realised that we were forbidden to follow them across other countries' borders with South Vietnam, so, whenever we had the upper hand in any battle, which was the case in every single battle we fought against the communists, they simply ran for the border and entered protected territory. This left us constantly frustrated and unable to take the initiative. Nevertheless, our leaders continued with this strategy throughout most of the Vietnam War until President Nixon conducted an operation into Cambodia in an attempt to cut the Ho Chi Minh trail and took the war to North Vietnam in the form of concentrated bombing campaigns.

We also adopted another strategy called 'hearts and minds'. This strategy had us deliver projects that would help the local villages in an attempt to win their hearts and minds and turn their support towards us and away from the communists. This strategy also had limited success. For example, one project was to build wind-powered water pumps that would supply fresh water to the villages. However, the windmills required a gearbox that was full of oil. The local lads from the villages would steal the oil from the gearboxes for their motorcycles, so the gearboxes eventually seized up and the water pumps ceased to function. It became difficult for our engineers to replace the gearboxes, because of their limited supply, owing to the limited government funding for the project.

Another project was the one I was currently conducting with the patients that had arrived from one of the villages that Major Fox had visited. The project was successful when Major Fox and his team could treat the villagers locally, but when he had to send them to hospital he would send them down to us. We could not admit them into our hospital, and the Vung

Tau hospital did not have the funding nor the capacity to treat them. The Australian government refused to offer any funding for the local hospital, so this led to the local hospital being underfunded, understaffed and lacking the capacity to handle the increase in patient arrivals. There was one overall result for all our limited effort, however. These projects enabled our Defence Minister, Malcolm Fraser, to stand up in the Australian parliament and loudly proclaim what a wonderful success his new projects were having for the Vietnamese people.

A few days later, a group of Vietnamese sick arrived, and I had to take them into the local Vung Tau hospital. Among the villagers was a very young Vietnamese boy. He had been sent down by helicopter because his eyes were swollen and filled with pus from an infection that had left him blind. The boy was crying, upset at being alone and unable to see what was going on around him, so I took him by the hand and settled him on my knee in the front seat of the ambulance. The others got into the back of the ambulance. A young lieutenant closed the door of the ambulance and reminded me to leave these patients at the hospital and get out quickly, because the hospital staff wouldn't want to accept them and we could do nothing for them here.

I arrived at the hospital and led them straight to the admission desk. There was a woman sitting behind the desk and a young, female Vietnamese doctor bent over beside her.

'Four from Major Fox,' I said, laying the paperwork on the desk as I had been instructed. Then, I turned quickly to make my escape, but the boy clung tightly to my hand, so I had to forcefully knock his hand away. The young boy started wailing loudly, which briefly paused my exit. I was about to leave when the doctor said in clear English, 'Just a moment, please'. I turned and our eyes met. There was a depth there that told of a patience and understanding born from service and suffering. I couldn't disengage her eyes, so I stood, not wanting to leave but knowing that I shouldn't stay.

'No!' the admission clerk shouted, racing around the desk and grabbing my arm. 'No good. No can stay. No family,' she went on, shaking her head. 'You take, yes?' she continued. This time, her head nodded up and down.

I looked pleadingly at the doctor, who came around and knelt in front of the boy, taking his hand and speaking quietly to him in Vietnamese. He settled back down quickly.

'I can't,' I replied hopelessly.

The clerk said something in Vietnamese and the doctor answered her softly. The clerk went back and sat down behind her desk, shaking her head and mumbling to herself.

'I am sorry,' the doctor said, looking up at me. 'but we have so many to care for and so few to do it.'

'Yes,' I said, nodding my head. 'I've been told.'

'This boy has no family to care for him here at the hospital,' she continued. 'It will be difficult.'

'I'm sorry,' I said. 'But what can I do?'

'Nothing. Thank you for bringing him. We will do what we can.'

Looking down on her still kneeling in front of the boy, holding his hand and stroking it gently, I was struck by the contrast between my approach with the boy and hers. While I had befriended the boy for my own selfish ends, to get him to the hospital with the least amount of fuss possible, only to brutally betray him once we got here, hers was a genuine compassion and interest in the boy's welfare. The guilt over what I had done struck me with an impact that went straight to my heart.

'Wait,' I said, as she stood up and turned to leave. 'What if I come back to help you out when I can?'

'That is kind,' she said, looking at me quizzically. 'We would be very grateful for your assistance.'

She stood, facing me for a moment, a smile lighting up her face. I returned her smile, and a feeling of deep satisfaction passed through me.

'The lady here,' she continued, pointing at the admissions clerk, 'will direct you to the boy when you return.' Then she disappeared down a corridor, with the little boy holding tightly to her hand.

For the next week, when I was not on duty at my own hospital, I returned to the local hospital and cleaned the boy's eyes and changed his dressings. My commanding officer supported my effort to help out at the local hospital, because it was in line with the new 'hearts and minds' initiative and did not interfere with my work at the field hospital. The boy's eyes healed quickly.

One day I arrived and he was gone. I went to the admissions clerk.

'Where is the boy?' I asked.

'He go,' she said, shaking her head and waving her hand.

I was a little relieved. Coming here after my shifts at the field hospital had proved more of a strain on me than I had first expected, but my commanding officer had encouraged me to continue with it.

'And the doctor?' I asked.

She raised her eyebrows and her hands, tilted her head to one side and shrugged her shoulders.

'Can I see her?'

She smiled and shook her head. 'She no here,' she replied.

I was disappointed at not having seen the young Vietnamese doctor after our first meeting, so I returned to the field hospital where I continued my duties and never returned to the Vung Tau hospital.

*

A couple of weeks later, when I came off my shift, David was waiting for me. I smiled and shook his hand as he explained that he had been posted to an intelligence unit operating out of Saigon. He had some intelligence work to do in Vung Tau and told me that he didn't have much time, but that he had arranged my leave and dinner for us at the Grand Hotel that night. I thanked him and told him I could make it. He smiled and looked pleased.

'It's good to see you again, Jason,' he said, before turning to leave. 'Don't let me down,' he added as he walked away. 'We really need to talk.'

'Yes,' I said, watching him disappear through the doorway into the bright light outside. 'I'll be there.'

Later that night, I stood opposite the Grand Hotel and watched the sun setting behind it. It was one of those magical moments when the sunset seemed to soften a harsh setting. A helicopter banked right and slid sideways across a blood-soaked sky on the ocean side of Vung Tau peninsula. It landed on President Tieu's private helipad servicing his seaside villa, which had previously belonged to French colonialists. Vung Tau had been a favourite seaside resort of the French and, now they were gone, it had been taken over by the new military leaders.

The Grand Hotel was also a part of the French legacy. It was a fine example of French colonial architecture, a two-storey square building with arching windows and white stucco walls capped with a red, terracotta-tiled French style roofline. The exterior was a model of simplicity, displaying a Doric portico framed against the cubic mass of the wall. Despite its fresh paint, however, there was an air of haunting incongruity generated by its bleak surroundings.

Directly in front of me was a wide, tree-lined avenue with a narrow strip of bitumen running down its centre and dirt shoulders leading to the edge. Smoking lambrettas (a type of scooter with a passenger enclosed cabin), old taxis, dinted buses, military trucks and jeeps bustled for positions on the thin stretch of black ribbon. In their haste, they threw up large clouds of smoke and dust that settled on everything; the houses and trees nearest the avenue were a sickly grey colour contrasting with the dark green further away.

As I watched this cavalcade of noise and nuisance, an open horse-drawn carriage jolted slowly by. The carriage was old with chipped and flaking paint and a cracked leather bench seat had patches of protruding stuffing. It was drawn by a very old horse with a bad limp, its ribs clearly showing through its sagging hide. The driver leaned forward in his seat, flaying at the animal in a vain effort to compete with the faster traffic.

This scene reminded me of the claim of the communists – that the Americans were foreign colonialists who had replaced the French. Unfortunately, this was a claim too easily believed, but it failed to reveal the fact that the Americans were not making a single cent from South Vietnam. In fact, there were American programs that tried to develop the South Vietnamese economy, like the attempt to turn rice crops in the Mekong Delta into cash crops for the South Vietnamese farmers. The truth was that the Vietnam War was costing the

Americans millions of dollars a day, from which they got no return. Hardly an example of colonial exploitation.

I shook my head, then picked my way across the avenue, entered the Grand Hotel and was immediately surprised by its cool interior. A high ceiling and slow-moving, wide-bladed fans generated a cool refreshing breeze. There was a plaster ceiling with an inlaid leaf design on the cornice, complemented with an abundance of broad-leafed palms and shrubs in large earthenware pots. Polished mahogany walls and antique furniture completed a powerful effect; it was as though the new Vietnam did not exist. This belonged to an age of order and stability. Only the confidence and arrogance of the French, I mused, could have built such a place in Vung Tau. Then I thought of the American-built Hotel Paradise further down the avenue and the surrounding squalor of the city, and it left me in no doubt that both the French and Americans lacked an Asian perspective; both buildings had been built for a purpose which excluded the local people.

'May I help you, sir?'

I turned to see an Asian concierge dressed in what appeared an elaborate naval uniform, all white with an abundance of gold trim.

'Yes. Could you direct me to the restaurant?'

'Certainly, sir. Down the corridor,' he said, pointing the way with an opened hand, 'and it's the first door on your left.' He said it so perfectly I wondered how many times before he had helped lost foreigners.

The restaurant, too, was white. White walls broken only by an occasional dark painting, usually of a French rural scene, a white ceiling with the same inlaid leaf pattern cornicing as before and a black-and-white square-tiled floor which flowed outside into an open terrace capped with a trellis supported with white columns wrapped in ivy vines. A snippet of bougainvillea vine lay on each table, its brilliant purple sharpening the clear white linen and the lustre of the silverware.

I looked around and noticed David with the young Vietnamese doctor from the civilian hospital. They were sitting at a table near some wide French windows facing the avenue outside. As I approached them, David rose to greet me.

'Hello, Jason,' he said, then turned to his companion. 'This is Wu Sing. Wu Sing, Jason. I hope you don't mind, mate, but Wu Sing needed a break from her work, so I invited her to join us.'

'Not at all,' I replied, extending my hand to her. 'We've met before, but we haven't been formally introduced.'

She looked at me with a puzzled expression like she didn't know who I was but felt she should have known.

'In the reception area of your hospital,' I said.

She still looked puzzled.

'A few weeks ago. I brought in a child with infected eyes.'

Her eyes lit up. 'Ah, yes,' she said. 'Now I know. You were the one who couldn't leave the little boy.'

'That's right,' I said, sitting down.

'And now, Jason, do you have any trouble leaving children at my hospital, now that you return to nurse them?'

'I don't come to nurse at your hospital anymore, Wu Sing. I only did it for that one boy. I suppose that Vietnam has hardened me somewhat,' I said, annoyed that I had to tell her that my charity had its limits.

'I would be surprised if it had not,' she smiled.

'And that makes you happy?' I said defensively.

'Steady on, mate,' David interjected. 'Wu Sing didn't mean

anything by that. I'm sure she was only trying to make conversation. She's on our side, you know.'

'I'm sorry. I didn't mean any offence,' I said.

'No need to apologise, Jason. It's just that I was surprised by your compassion for those in serious need. I did not expect to find such a thing in a soldier.'

'But I'm not just a soldier, Wu Sing. I'm also a medic, and we are taught not just to fight but also to render aid where necessary,' I replied in a soft, conciliatory tone.

We drifted into a brief silence, and I marvelled at Wu Sing's mastery of English. She spoke it with a slight American accent, but she could certainly hold her own with David and me.

'What's this about you nursing a child?' David asked.

'Oh, nothing really. I dropped a child off at Wu Sing's hospital, and he had no family to nurse him, so I came to the hospital for a while to nurse him.'

'Well, that's highly commendable, Jason. My estimation of you has just risen even further,' David said.

We went quiet and I ran my fingers along the edge of the heavy linen tablecloth. An Asian waiter arrived dressed in black trousers, white shirt and a black bow tie, a white linen cloth hanging over his left arm. David gave our order in French, then handed the menu to the waiter before settling back in his chair.

'What did you mean when you said Wu Sing was on our side?' I asked.

'Wu Sing is French–Vietnamese,' he answered. 'Her mother was Vietnamese, and her father was a French officer. Her mother was killed by the Viet Minh in the Indochina War, and her father went back to his family in France. After that, she was raised as an orphan in a Catholic mission here in Vung Tau. That's where I met her.'

I looked at Wu Sing. Her head was bowed and she clasped her hands tightly together.

'I'm sorry, Wu Sing. It was wrong of me to misjudge you.' I reached out and put my hand on hers. 'Will you forgive me, please?' I asked.

She looked up and searched my face with her deep brown eyes, revealing a tormented sadness. I held her gaze.

'That's okay,' she finally said. 'You weren't to know, and Vietnam makes us all suspicious.'

I released her hand as the waiter brought our food. It was a plate of fresh fish and side salad with a liberal application of French dressing. A white wine helped lighten the heavy atmosphere that had settled over our table.

'I don't think it really matters anymore whose side we're on,' David said flippantly.

'Why?' I asked.

'Because we're going to lose and, whatever happens, the communists will rule Vietnam.'

'But how can you say that when we are winning? Didn't we just defeat them in the TET Offensive? Their plan to have the people of South Vietnam rise up never eventuated. The people showed that they don't want communism, didn't they?'

'None of that matters, Jason, because we can't stop the North's infiltration. You see, they're more determined than we are.'

'Why would we lose our determination to help the South Vietnamese, David? Didn't South Vietnam just have an election and witness a peaceful transfer of power from one leader to another? Isn't South Vietnam showing us that they want democracy and deserve our support? Why would we not be determined to help them?'

'Oh, that? They only swapped one military leader for another. Hardly a change of government, wouldn't you say?'

'Well, I don't know. In times of war, wouldn't people want strong, unified, military leadership? And, anyway, they did have a choice, and they did vote for President Thieu. Doesn't that show how much the people here want their freedom, want a democratic way of life?'

'But the South Vietnamese screen and filter out candidates for their election. You know that, right?'

'That is done to filter out candidates with communist connections. The South Vietnamese don't want their government to be white-anted by communists. I can understand their concern.'

'So, communists can't stand for election?'

'Not when South Vietnam is at war with them, no.'

'And what about Diem? Don't forget that he was assassinated in a bloody military coup. And the election that was supposed to be conducted over the whole of Vietnam, both North and South, and called for by the Geneva Convention, that was never held, how does that tie in with your fantasy about freedom and democracy?'

'Both Presidents Eisenhower and Diem believed that a fair and open election could not be held in communist North Vietnam in 1955. I think their reasoning was sound. Communist elections are never fair and open, and, anyway, Diem did hold an election in South Vietnam and won a handsome working majority in their parliament. As for the military coup in 1963, that was a terrible and unacceptable thing to happen. There is no excuse for that. However, South Vietnam has held elections since then, and the conspirators in that coup were not elected.'

'Look, Jason, I've already said, none of that matters, because we're fighting this war all wrong.'

'What do you mean?'

'We're into body counts, mate. That's what I wanted to see you about. We're not winning this war; we're just killing more of them than they are of us. Do you really think that will make them give up and go home?'

'Probably not. But do you really think we will?' I asked.

'Yes. I do. And when I go home, I'll do my best to see we do. I was hoping that by now you could see the futility of this war and join me.'

'And when you go, my people will fight on,' Wu Sing, who had been quiet until now, said softly.

'But, Wu Sing, it won't matter. The North Vietnamese and the Viet Cong are too strong for the South and they have a larger population. The Americans have taught you how to fight a modern war with aircraft and helicopter support for your troops. Once they are gone, you won't be able to sustain that type of warfare,' David said.

Wu Sing's face turned earnest. She placed her hands in her lap and looked directly at David.

'You come here and, if you survive your time with us, you go back home,' she said. 'But we cannot go, because this is our home. For you, Vietnam is a question of survival, and you and your people do not really care if we win or lose. That is not your concern, but it is our concern. The killing and the maiming goes on while you are here, and you, quite rightly, want it to stop. As we do. But the issue for us is not only that it stops, but why it stops. All you want is for the war to end. For you, the issue of our freedom does not matter, because you have your freedom, and nobody is trying to take it away from you.'

She paused, then went on. 'We know you will eventually say "enough is enough". For you, the reason for ending the killing will not be important and, on that day, we will know we have lost and all our sacrifice and all your sacrifice will have been for nothing. The army of occupation protecting our freedom will be replaced by an army of occupation subverting it.'

'Do you really think you are free now, Wu Sing?' David asked.

'Do you really think we will be free under communism?' she shot back.

'No, but the killing will have stopped, and that will make the difference for your people. The farmers of your country don't know the difference between the communists and us, but they certainly know the difference between war and peace.'

'I don't know if that is right, and neither do you. You are assuming things about our farmers without providing any evidence for your conclusion. Remember, the communists terrorise our farmers. They kill anyone who cooperates with the government and take their youth for service in the NVA and Viet Cong armies. That's why they are reluctant to cooperate with you. Anyway, I do know that most South Vietnamese people want freedom and democracy. As Jason said, the election of President Thieu and the outcome of the TET Offensive proves that. Remember, the communists called for a general uprising of the South Vietnamese people to throw your forces out, but they got support from neither our cities nor our villages, so you may claim that our farmers think like you, but the historical evidence does not support your conclusion. If only our freedom was reason enough for your people to really support our struggle ...'

She paused for a moment, took a short breath, looked David

in the eye, and then made her final statement. 'How little your protesters value the freedom of others, yet take for granted their own,' she sighed.

David clenched his teeth. The conversation had taken a turn he had not expected, and I could see the anger in his eyes, but he remained silent. He was a guest in Wu Sing's country; to cause a scene would violate his personal code of social etiquette.

He finished his meal hurriedly and in silence. Then, placing his serviette on the table, he rose and offered an apology for having to leave early. I knew he was lying but made no attempt to change his mind. He called the waiter and paid for our meal before leaving our table. I pushed my chair back to go after him.

'Let him go,' Wu Sing said. 'Like the rest of his people, he cares little for those he has been sent here to save.'

'You are mistaken,' I replied. 'He cares in his way the same as you care in yours. He just wants to end the suffering of this war.'

'As I do. But I want more than just an end of it, Jason.'

She paused here and closed her eyes. I think she was collecting her thoughts. She opened her eyes and went on.

'For me, freedom is like the difference between a colour movie and a black-and-white movie. With freedom, people live a rich, colourful life full of endless possibilities; without it, they live a drab, colourless existence where all their choices are made by someone else.'

'I agree. But, for David, that's not important, Wu Sing?'

'But it has to be, Jason. With peace must come hope or there will be no possibility of prosperity. I want the same for my people as you have in your country. If the communists win, there will be no hope, no prosperity, only occupation and concentration camps and more suffering. I don't want all this fighting and pain to be for nothing. Surely, we are entitled to the same freedom you enjoy after all we have been through.' She paused again, then added, 'It is not only the war we must win but also the peace.'

She didn't speak after this, but her eyes pleaded with me to offer her some hope. My mouth opened but no words came. Somehow, words seemed beyond my reach. Finally, all I could do was drop my gaze to the table, carrying in my mind the image of her pathetic face. I busied myself with my meal and, when I looked up later, a watercourse of silent tears glistened on her cheeks.

'I'm sorry the evening turned out so badly,' I eventually said. 'May I take you home?'

'You don't have to. I will be able to order a lambretta from here.'

'Please, I want to,' I offered.

'In that case, I would like you to. Yes.'

I ordered a taxi, and we sat quietly waiting for it to arrive while gazing indolently at the chaotic world beyond the French windows. A breeze picked up, played petulantly with the lace curtains and fought a desperate battle with a flickering candle on an empty table next to the window. The Beatles' song, 'Yesterday', echoed from a speaker in the corner of the room, Paul McCartney moving my emotions with his nostalgic appeal.

I rose and held Wu Sing's chair for her as she stood and moved from the table. She turned and smiled at me, then I held her elbow as we walked to the portico to wait for our cab. I looked over at Wu Sing who gazed on the muddled chaos that occupied the tree-lined avenue, a meditative, wistful look in her eyes. I wondered where her thoughts had taken her and suddenly wanted to put my arm around her and share her sorrow.

Later, we sat in the back of the open carriage I had seen before, whose driver whipped at his lame horse. I turned to Wu Sing and asked her to tell the driver to let his horse make its own time, and I'd pay him extra. She leaned forward and spoke to him in Vietnamese. Her warm-hearted voice brought a smile to his face, and he nodded his head and stayed his whip hand.

'This will take a long time,' Wu Sing said.

'Yes, but I will be more comfortable.'

'You are a surprising young man,' she said, smiling up at me. I returned her smile and leaned back into the seat next to her. Our shoulders touched, so I put my arm around her. 'Ah,' she said. 'This is more like the actions of your people.'

'Do you mind?' I asked.

'No,' she replied softly.

'Have you been hurt by our presence?' I asked.

At first, she did not reply; rather, she left my question hang there between us. With my free hand, I reached out and touched her hand.

'You are so sad and so beautiful,' I whispered. 'Do you think you could ever care for me?'

She became thoughtful as if wondering how she should reply to my question. 'Some years ago, I studied medicine in Saigon,' she said. 'I met a young American and fell in love. We walked together and lay in each other's arms. He kissed me and said he loved me and, foolishly, I gave myself to him.'

'But why "foolishly"? What happened?'

'He went back home to his fiancée in America, and I came

back here to work in the hospital. Now I am here, and he is gone.'

She said it so dispassionately a cold shudder passed through my body.

'I'm sorry,' I said, not knowing what else to say.

'Perhaps you are,' she replied, 'but now I must live with my memories and with this war.'

'What can I do?' I offered. 'How can I help you?'

'Be with me. Hold me as you now hold me.'

She looked up at me and her wide, brown eyes swallowed my heart. I took her face in my hands and kissed her gently on the lips. The carriage came to a stop, and she looked over my shoulder.

'This is where I live,' she said, taking my hands in hers and folding them in her lap, waiting for me to say goodnight.

'Will I see you again?' I asked.

'Yes, if you want to,' she replied. We sat in silence, looking at each other. 'When?' she finally asked.

'What?'

'When? When do you want to see me?'

'Oh!' I said. 'Tomorrow. I'll come to the hospital. Will that be all right?'

'Very good,' she replied, stepping from the carriage but keeping her hands in mine. When she stood beside the carriage, she stretched up on tiptoes and kissed me on the lips.

'Good night,' she said.

'Yes. See you tomorrow,' I replied.

She took her hands down, turned and walked through an open gateway that broke the straight line of a high concrete wall topped with tangled barbed wire surrounding her house. In a moment, she was gone and my night was empty once again.

The carriage moved slowly away, the clip-clop of the horse's shoes echoing down a street scarred by poverty but kept clean by a commitment to standards.

What a wonderful girl, I thought. *So much sorrow and yet so much compassion.*

All through the night and into the next day, I could think of nothing but seeing Wu Sing again. The effect she had on me was powerful. It was as though we were together, even though we were apart. I carried her with me wherever I went. She was in my mind and in my heart. Whenever I thought about her, a strange feeling deep within me welled up and eventually filled my whole being. My fingertips tingled with the anticipation of touching her and, when I shut tight my eyes, it sharpened the image my mind held of her.

Eventually, my shift ended, and I hurriedly showered and dressed into clean clothes and made my way to the transport section where the afternoon ambulance run took me to her hospital. My commanding officer had, once again, given me special permission to help out at the local hospital, but my real motivation was to see more of Wu Sing.

I searched the wards and corridors of the stark, well-aired hospital in vain, following directions from urgently pointing fingers and head gestures. It was difficult for me to communicate with the hospital staff. All I could say was, 'Wu Sing,' and they would grunt and point or nod their heads in the direction I should take. I would follow where they had pointed but end up lost again and having to ask someone else.

Finally, I came to a quiet room where Wu Sing sat at the bedside of a little girl whose body was badly burnt. The little girl had no clothes on, skin hung from her little body and the rawness of her flesh twitched and glistened in the soft light of the room. Wu Sing held her small hand and, when she moaned softly, Wu Sing stroked her thick, black hair and passed the inside of her hand gently down the side of her young face. The young girl's head moved slowly to the rhythm of Wu Sing's hand. Finally, Wu Sing paused, holding the girl's tired face in her palms. The girl's eyes flickered, she tried bravely to smile at Wu Sing, then the drugs took effect and she slipped silently into a deep sleep. Wu Sing bent over her and kissed her forehead.

I waited for a moment, then walked up behind Wu Sing and placed my hand on her shoulder. She turned and looked at me and placed her hand on mine.

'What happened?' I asked. 'Who did this?'

'She's asleep now,' she said, looking down at the young girl's body, 'and nothing can change what has happened. One of our pilots dropped a napalm bomb on a village that was occupied by the NVA. He had been told that the village had been cleared of civilians, but this little girl was still praying in the local church. In war, armies fight each other and sometimes civilians get caught in the wrong place at the wrong time. This was not a deliberate act against this child, so our judgement should be tempered with mercy, not just for this child but also those who did this. I'm sure the pilot's conscience causes him to suffer as well.' She turned her face towards me again and her eyes held mine. 'Guilt matters only for those who deal in revenge,' she whispered. 'Forgiveness is for those who truly love.'

Together, we treated the little girl's wounds by washing the burnt areas with a warm saline fluid. After that, we applied silver nitrate and wrapped her burnt areas in clean cotton bandages. Wu Sing explained that this was the best she could do to treat her wounds.

'We have no oxygen tent to enrich the oxygen content of her blood. This would hasten her recovery if we had it,' she explained. 'Later I will give her mineral baths.'

Wu Sing then applied a plasma drip to replenish the lost fluids of the young girl's body.

'That's all I can do for her at the moment. I'll ask the American hospital if they can take her. They have an oxygen tent,' Wu Sing said, turning and making her way to the door and hurrying off to another patient. I followed behind her, but my mind remained with the little girl and a wish that we could have done more for her.

What a horrible price the innocent were having to pay in this war.

*

What happened that day I heard from Toby. Over and over, I heard it until it burned itself so deeply into my mind I came to believe I really had been there. The day started, he told me, like any other he had experienced when out on operations. Nothing happened that morning that provided him with a forewarning or a premonition that this day was the one that would change his life forever. No dingos howled, nor did he experience any strange feelings other than that he had to do the things he did every morning to get ready to move out.

The dark lifted reluctantly from the jungle, and the slumber-inducing hum of insects, the stealthy movements of nocturnal animals and the occasional terrified scream of a defenceless animal caught in the jaws of its nocturnal predator gradually yielded to the muffled sounds of soldiers rising to their early morning chores. The hot, humid atmosphere began to make itself known as the cool of night gave way to the heat of a rising sun. In hushed tones, rumours passed among the troops about the coming day's activity. More sweat and insect bites and burning shoulders from heavy loads, sore feet and aching, almost numb legs in a hot, steamy, tropical climate.

'We're goin' in today for sure.'

'Into the Long Hai mountains?' Toby asked of the soldier he was treating during his morning company aid post sick parade.

Toby was lucky today, just a few minor cuts and muscular aches and pains, nothing serious like a snake bite or a torn ligament, which he would have had to pass on to the regimental aid post for evacuation to the field ambulance in Nui Dat. Only more serious injuries like gunshot wounds or amputations were evacuated from the battlefield to the field hospital in Vung Tau. Helicopter evacuation had made all this urgent medical care possible.

'Yeah, today fer sure.'

'But that's too far in these conditions. Back home, maybe, but not here.'

'Don't matter. The new boy wants it that way.'

'How do you know?'

'Someone overheard him talkin' to the colonel on the two-way. Says he'll have us there, no sweat.'

'That's bullshit. We'll be buggered if we make it, an' those little bastards 'll be waitin' for us.'

'Yeah. A force this size can't move without 'em knowin'. They're gunna send our company in ahead of the rest to clear the way and establish a perimeter. Reckon that'll allow the regiment to move faster.'

'Even so, the Viet Cong will know we're ahead of the rest. We'll be in trouble if we get caught in an ambush.'

'Yeah, poor us, eh?' The soldier gave a mocking smile.

Gradually, the regiment prepared itself to move out. The rumours proved correct: helicopters arrived to drop their supplies while A company moved out bound for the Long Hai mountains. When the rest of the regiment finally moved out, A company, which was ahead of the rest, formed the apex of an arrowhead formation while B and C companies covered the flanks and D company stayed back with the headquarters unit. First Platoon led the way for A company with Nick near the lead, while Toby, as the company medic, was further back, always ready to administer first aid.

They had many contacts that day, the Viet Cong obviously intent on slowing the regiment's progress. Only odd shots were fired, though, and by the time the rifle squads had completed their sweeps, the enemy was long gone.

About 2 pm, when it appeared the regiment would make its objective, the men having pushed themselves all day through the sticky atmosphere, they made heavy contact with the Viet Cong. Within the first few minutes of the exchange, First Platoon was cut off from the rest of the company. The point was down with a gunshot wound in the stomach, and Nick used rapid fire, trying to keep the advancing enemy from the wounded soldier. The rest of the platoon formed a protective line and returned fire on the advancing Viet Cong who, despite casualties, got closer and closer to the wounded Australian's position.

Without thinking, Nick stood and ran forward. The rest of the platoon, including the M60, continued to blast their deadly fire into the enemy's line, which hesitated and then withdrew slowly, returning fire as they went. Nick swung the wounded soldier into a fireman's carry on his shoulders and started to return to his line when he was hit suddenly in his right leg. At first, he tried to remain on his feet but his wounded leg started to shake, a little at first, but gradually leading to an uncontrollable wobble that spread throughout his whole body. He fell to his knees, throwing the wounded soldier in front of him. Bullets peppered Nick's back, tearing their way through his thin but muscular frame, and exploded out his chest in large bursts of blood and torn flesh. He looked skyward, then down at the wounded soldier with a sad, apologetic look of someone unable to fulfil a promise.

'Uh' was the only sound he made before collapsing on top of the young man he had given his life to save. They stayed like that until the company regrouped and counterattacked, the Viet Cong once again melting away in the face of a concerted military effort.

Nick and the wounded soldier had to be evacuated, so a dust-off helicopter was called up. After a quick pick-up and flight to Vung Tau, it landed on the helipad of 1st Field Hospital, and I was part of a two-man team that rushed out to collect the wounded and bring them into the pre-surgery prep room. Reaching the side of the helicopter, I looked down on Nick's motionless body. *Could it be Nick?* I thought. *Surely not. It was not possible that Nick had been killed. Was it?* Nevertheless, I could not escape the evidence in front of my eyes. I felt a terrible sadness deep within me rise up and leave me standing statuesque beside the helicopter. He looked so pitiful and lonely. Wherever he had gone, he was no longer with me, and I wanted him back. I wanted him to look up at me and smile, but that would never happen again. He was gone forever, and there was nothing I could do that would change that fact.

'Come on, Jason,' the other medic, who had come out with me to collect the wounded, shouted at me above the subdued roar of the helicopter's jet engine. 'We have to get this one in right now before it's too late.'

I nodded my head. Together, we took the wounded soldier in to be prepped for surgery. Then we returned to the helicopter and took Nick inside. A doctor examined Nick's body and pronounced him dead. He would now wait for transfer to the American 36 Evacuation Hospital where his body would be placed into a body bag and then a freezer drawer in their mortuary until it could be transported back home to Australia.

I stood looking down at Nick's dead body when the commanding officer approached me. 'The medic from the chopper has just been admitted to the hospital with a suspected case of gastritis,' he said, 'and we have just received an urgent call that a soldier has stepped on a land mine in the Long Hai mountains. I need you to go there with the chopper and collect him.'

'Yes, sir, I'll go right away,' I replied. I rushed to the helipad.

Back in the Long Hai mountains, the regiment had been nearing its destination when Toby had stood on an American-made landmine. It made a loud click, and Toby froze. He knew what that meant. This was a special type of mine that was intended to maim, not kill, because casualties placed a heavier burden than the dead on the Viet Cong and NVA forces. These mines had been laid by Australian troops to form a barrier between Dat Do, a village that supported the Viet Cong by providing them with supplies of rice and recruits, and the Long Hai mountains where the Viet Cong had their stronghold. Unfortunately for the Australians, the Viet Cong had learnt how to harvest these mines by digging them out of the ground and laying them in the path of their advancing enemy. This was one reason for carrying out a temporary ambush. It gave their comrades time to lay mines ahead of the advancing Australians.

The mines that the Australians had laid were intended to be secured at night, the time when the Viet Cong were active, by South Vietnamese troops and the placing of hand grenades under the mines. This did not work because the South Vietnamese army never had enough troops to adequately patrol the minefield, which was eleven kilometres long, and many of the hand grenades did not explode because they became damp in the moist Vietnamese soil. Some did, however, explode and the Viet Cong lost many soldiers as a result. Nevertheless, they persisted and harvested well over two thousand mines.

Toby stood perfectly still with his foot on the mine. The commanding officer and the regimental doctor came up and spoke with Toby.

'What do you want to do, son?' the commanding officer asked him. 'You know there is no way to defuse the mine, and the regiment has to bivouac before dark.'

'Well, what did the others do?'

'They simply jumped as quickly as they could to one side.'

'Did they survive?'

'Yes, they all survived, but they were seriously wounded.'

'I guess there's no choice, then.'

'No, son. I'm sorry but there is nothing else we can do, and it's no good calling in the engineers, because there's nothing they can do either. I'll clear the spot where you are, and you leap aside in your own time.'

Toby was left standing all alone as the others withdrew to

a safe distance and went to ground.

'Ready whenever you are, Private,' the commanding officer called out.

Toby didn't hesitate. He jumped to one side. There was an enormous explosion that deafened him. As he fell back to the ground, he became unconscious. The regimental doctor rushed up to Toby and applied tourniquets to what was left of both his legs.

*

I looked out the open side of a UH-1 Huey as we went in low over the treetops. Our helicopters had to travel low, because when they flew higher, they were vulnerable to RPG fire. The trees passed by me quickly and so close it seemed like I could reach out and touch them. I refocused my attention on the medical equipment inside, the intravenous drips and the plastic bags of plasma, the battle dressings, the tourniquets, the resuscitator, the defibrillator. There, fastened on its rack, was an F1 light machine gun. Strange, I thought, how in this war even medics were familiar with weapons of war, with the taking of life as well as the saving of it.

We crossed a river about half a kilometre from a clearing made for our landing, marked out by spiralling columns of yellow marker smoke. The pilot banked the helicopter sharply into the sky, slipped to the right and came around on the same line as before, descending tail down, into the clearing. Before landing the helicopter, the pilot did a one-hundred-and-eighty degree rotation, because we had to go out of the jungle clearing the same way we had come in.

The stretcher carrying Toby was placed immediately into

the helicopter. A soldier rushed to the front and indicated a raised thumb to the pilot. 'Shove off quick,' he shouted. 'This area's not secure.' The jet engine above me screamed and the blades chopped violently at the air. The tail lifted from the ground and we were airborne, the whole operation taking just seconds.

I knelt beside Toby with my left foot planted firmly on the floor and my weight resting on my right knee. I couldn't believe that it was Toby who had stood on the land mine. One of my friends had been seriously injured and another killed, both on the same day. It took me a few seconds to refocus my attention.

Toby had regained consciousness before we arrived but was in so much pain that he had started screaming and thrashing around. Morphine had been administrated and a large 'M' had been printed on his forehead, indicating that he had received a dose of morphine. The morphine had taken effect, and now that he sat propped up in the corner of the helicopter his head rolled about in semi-consciousness... Before I had time to examine him, however, it happened – a loud bang, which made the tail of the helicopter disappear and peppered the interior with zinging pieces of flying metal.

Everything went into slow motion. The pilot slumped over his controls while the helicopter went into an uncontrolled spin that became more and more violent. I reached out for a nylon strap hanging from the side wall, but, before I could clutch it, I was shot out the open side of the helicopter and spun lazily towards the river we had passed coming into the clearing. I was on the verge of passing out when I hit the water with a heavy smack that stung me awake.

Toby also was flung from the helicopter just before it crashed beside him, one blade thumping heavily into the riverbed. It howled and whined like an angry, wounded beast, lurched and shuddered and finally died, sinking slowly into the water and coming to rest on the bottom with half its underside above the water line.

Moving towards the wreck, I gathered Toby in my arms and entered it. I heard some frantic splashing from within the cockpit. Propping Toby in a corner, I turned my attention to the co-pilot. He was struggling under the water, his head only inches from the surface, eyes bulging in terror, tiny bubbles rising from his mouth. I looked around and spotted the resuscitator clipped to the wall. A plastic tube hung beside it, which I took down and unrolled. I moved forward to the co-pilot, placed my thumb over one end and pushed it into his mouth, while holding the other end above water. He blew out and started taking air through the tube. He gripped my shoulder with his free hand, and we stayed holding each other for a moment. Gradually, his confidence returned and he released his grip, patting my shoulder in gratitude. I gave him the other end of the plastic tube to hold.

The water was muddy, with visibility limited to only inches beneath the surface. I thought his shoulder must have been pinned by a piece of crushed metal, so I reached down and felt where a piece of aluminium stay had entered his shoulder just above the scapula, passed through the deltoid muscle and come out just beneath his clavicle. If I failed to free him, he might pass out and drown, and, if I left him too long, he would probably pass out from shock or loss of blood anyway.

I looked at the pilot who was still slumped over the controls above the waterline, so I pulled him back in his seat and examined him. I could not detect any pulse or breathing. There was a wound in his chest where his heart was located, so I assumed a piece of flying metal from the RPG explosion must have passed through his heart and killed him instantly.

I was thinking what to do next when I heard a splash and movement from someone entering the river and wading out towards the helicopter. Thinking it was one of our soldiers come to help, I stood up to see a black-clad Viet Cong moving towards me. He raised his rifle and the ping of his shot threw a small splash of water into the air near the helicopter. Fear gripped me and my legs went weak. I dropped down.

In a matter of seconds, frightful thoughts flashed through my mind. *Would I have to fire back?* I thought. *If I don't, he will surely come and kill me. What about Toby? I can't just leave him and make a dash for my life. And what about the co-pilot?*

Ping! Another bullet hit the water. Crack! A bullet smashed through the windshield, then I heard the urgency of the Viet Cong's feet slapping the shallow water as he began running towards me.

I grabbed the F1 from its rack, and my training took over. I heard Sergeant Jones behind me at the shooting range during recruit training: 'Watch your front! Watch your front!' He called out, his clear, confident tone ringing in my ears once again.

'Safety off!'

'Cock your weapon!'

'Fire at will!'

I stood and levelled the F1 over the rim of the helicopter. The Viet Cong was very close; determination marked his face. As I opened fire, I saw him look down at his rifle. My bullets thumped into his body and tore at his flesh. A look of hatred entered his eyes as he tried to keep coming, so I fired more bullets into him. Suddenly, he stopped, the hatred and determination leaving his face, replaced by shock, then by pain. He dropped his weapon and clenched at his chest. His eyes filled with the vacant stare of a condemned man. A hurt, innocent, childlike look crossed his face, which left me feeling sorry for him. I stopped firing. His knees buckled and he sank slowly into the water and floated away, his blood blending naturally with the silt-laden water. I stood watching his body as it bobbed away out of sight. He had died alone. Nobody mourned his passing. His family would never know what had become of him.

'What happened?' I heard myself ask out loud. *What have I done? Why is he dead? And why am I alive? Did he run out of bullets? Did his rifle jam? Is that why he looked down? Is that why I am alive, and he is dead?* These thoughts ran instantaneously through my mind.

I thought back to recruit training. How absurd, I had thought then, that a life should depend on such an accident of fate. How horrible it seemed now in the harsh light of its reality. I couldn't avoid it, though. He was dead and I had killed him. What I had done was instinctive, I told myself, and it was an act of self-preservation, nothing more. Kill or be killed, Toby had said, and he was right.

In that moment of terror before I squeezed the trigger, I knew that questions of right and wrong were immaterial. What the whole Vietnam War boiled down to in that moment was my primitive urge to survive, and, in that instant, I knew I would have gladly exchanged a hundred lives if it meant I could survive. How much of this war could be reduced to this simple level? I wondered.

'You all right, mate?' an Australian soldier asked. He had crossed the river without my knowing, and now looked down on me from above.

'Yes,' I replied, snapping back to my immediate situation.

'There's a man down here pinned beneath the water.'

On both sides of the river, several other Australian soldiers had formed a protective perimeter. Some more had accompanied the soldier who had spoken to me and had now formed a barrier around the broken chopper.

My mouth was dry, so I swallowed several times before turning to the co-pilot. He was still alive, but I could see him slipping into unconsciousness, so we put our hands behind his back and pushed with all our might. He came away from the aluminium stay, and I pulled him to the surface, his eyes opened wide from the pain. He had swallowed some water and was coughing. I pulled him into my side of the helicopter and held him face down so the water could drain out of his mouth and windpipe. He became limp and lost consciousness. I reached for the battle dressings and wrapped them over the bleeding holes in his chest and back. Together, we passed the co-pilot up to another Australian soldier leaning over the edge of the helicopter's floor.

The Australian soldier with me began freeing the pilot, so I turned to Toby, still propped up in the corner. He had lost consciousness again, his head resting forward on his chest.

'Let's get the hell out of here, Toby,' I said, lifting him under the arms and, with the help of the other soldier, raised him up to the soldiers waiting above.

'An LZ (landing zone) has been made on the sandy bank of the river over there,' one of the soldiers said.

I carried Toby in my arms towards the waiting chopper. Another soldier carried the dead pilot. I stopped where the Viet Cong had dropped his weapon.

'There's an AK47 down here somewhere,' I said, looking down at the water.

'Thanks, mate. We'll find it. You get Toby to the hospital,' was the reply. I nodded and left for the chopper.

Back at the hospital, as light was fading from the day, two medics rushed out and took the co-pilot and the dead pilot into the pre-surgery prep room. I followed them in with Toby still in my arms. The chopper's engine roared into life and its blades slashed angrily at the air as it lifted from the ground.

I placed Toby on a pre-op stretcher and stood staring down at him while the medics cut the uniform from his body. The commanding officer approached me and put his hand on my shoulder. Our eyes engaged.

'Go and take a hot shower,' he said. 'Take the rest of your shift and tomorrow off. Try and get some sleep.' He placed a sodium pentothal tablet in my hand. 'Take this when you are ready to sleep.'

I nodded, with a shallow drop of my head. 'Yes, sir,' I replied softly and left the room. I went back to my barracks, stripped off my uniform, placed a towel around my waist and walked to the shower block, which was unoccupied. I lowered the canvas bag with a shower rose at its bottom and filled it with warm water from the emersion heater. Next, I stood under the shower and let the warm water run over my head and down my body. My mind filled with images of moments I had shared with Nick and Toby: our time together building the rock wall at Enoggera, the night Nick and I had shared in Brisbane, sitting around the fire drum at Kapooka, the heart-to-heart Toby and I had shared the night Clarissa had betrayed me, getting drunk in Vung Tau. When the water ran out, I went to pick up my towel. I wasn't conscious of what I had been doing. All of what I had done since leaving the hospital pre-op room had been done without any conscious thought on my part. Suddenly, my legs went weak and I fell to my knees, while covering my eyes with my left hand.

*

Over the next few weeks, I saw as much of Wu Sing as I could, but we could only snatch a few moments here and there because of our heavy schedules and the demands we both felt towards the desperate need around us. Despite the brief moments of our meetings and the desperation and poverty of our surroundings, we touched each other in rare and unique ways. We had nothing and yet we had everything. We were desperate yet hopeful, surrounded by madness yet saw each other with clarity. Part of the fulfilment I felt with Wu Sing was the ability to accept what I could not change. It was not a resignation but truly an acceptance. When I was with Wu Sing, nothing else mattered; nothing else seemed important to me. The simple pleasure I derived from looking into her eyes, from walking arm in arm with her, from lying on her bed with my head in her lap, meant more to me than the squalor, the pain and the suffering that surrounded me daily. Even thoughts of Nick and Toby, although still strong in my mind, seemed manageable when I was with Wu Sing.

During the monsoon season, rain in Vietnam is a daily event. It came at five o'clock in the afternoon and was special for us both. When I was alone with Wu Sing, we would stand in it together. The drops would fall in thick, heavy clusters and soon we would be soaked and refreshed, the heat and sweat of our bodies washed away. We would open our mouths and arms to the heavenly cloudburst, and it would run from our bodies like streams down a mountain side.

One time, when we were alone in a heavy downpour, we removed our clothes and embraced. Wu Sing reached up with her tiny hands and pulled my face down to hers. She kissed my eyes closed and drank the water as it tumbled from my chin. I took her weight in my arms and she wrapped her diminutive legs around me. I kissed her neck and her mouth and told her that I loved her, and her trusting, brown eyes opened to the rain and told me that she loved me too. She had a beauty and mystery that inspired an appreciation of the intangibles in life that made it all the sweeter. In this way, she gave herself up to me with all the tender strength of her nature, and I came to understand that, even in poverty, it is possible to live a life full of purpose and meaning.

On this occasion, Wu Sing said to me, 'I can see you love me dearly and that you want freedom for my people and that your passion is noble. But the North Vietnamese also have this passion, and I wonder what will happen if you lose yours, if you finally decide the price of our freedom is too high? Will those whose lives you saw used as tokens in this huge gamble come back to haunt you? Will you really be able to close your eyes and forget? To say it doesn't matter anymore. I doubt it. But that will be the sorrow and the guilt you will carry in your soul and for that, my darling, I cannot give you absolution!'

At that moment, the rain ceased and a sunburst broke around us. She closed her eyes, and I saw the hot tears run down her cheeks, mingling with the wetness and the sunlight.

'I can only give you my love,' she sobbed, 'and pray that will be enough.'

'No,' I said. 'That won't happen. I won't let it happen.'

She pressed her tiny fingers gently to my lips.

'Shh,' she said. 'Words spoken in noble haste often come back to haunt us, especially to those with sensitivity in their soul.'

I looked down at the raised supplication of her arms and opened myself to her. She turned the side of her face to me and pressed her cheek into my chest.

'I *bookoo lov' oo, Uc dai loi* (I have great love for you, man from the south),' she said softly in the mixed vernacular of her people.

'Yes, yes. And I you,' I whispered into her ear in reply. Then I took her face in my hands and peered deep into her sad but loving eyes. 'Marry me, Wu Sing,' I said. 'Marry me and come to Australia with me.'

'But what of the hospital?' Wu Sing asked.

'What do you mean?'

'My work at the hospital. Who will do that?'

'Does it matter?' I pleaded.

'Without me, so many would suffer,' she said simply.

And so it happened that on a warm, calm afternoon, I found myself with Wu Sing at a Catholic mission near the seaside. The mission centred on a small church that nestled in a gentle fold between two hills. It had rock and concrete steps in three tiers leading up to a wide, double-door entrance under a flat concrete porch, supported at both ends with straight steel pipes that projected through the concrete. It had an A-frame roofline with a tall, thick spire to its right and a thin, white cross pointing skyward. Open concrete blocks provided ventilation, and the tower had a wooden louvred chamber, suggesting it doubled as a lookout. Inside the apex of the roofline was a statue of Christ with outstretched arms, inviting us to come to him. The fading light made it impossible to determine his expression, but to the left of us stood a statue of the Virgin Mary with arms bent at the elbows and open hands pointing skyward. A composed smile and understanding eyes highlighted her face while a serene expression accentuated her distinctly compassionate face.

The grounds were somewhat harsh. Being close to the seaside, the soil was sandy and stony and the vegetation clung tenaciously to the hillsides. Around the chapel, some eucalyptus trees and bougainvillea were scattered here and there in semi-ordered fashion. They had been planted by Australian soldiers in an effort to show they cared for the local people.

'Father, I want to marry Wu Sing and take her back home to Australia with me. She says she loves me but can't leave Vietnam,' I said desperately.

'Oh, Jason, I do love you,' she said to me, then turned to Father Ling and pleaded, 'but how can I leave when I am needed so much here? Father, please help me find the right answer.'

He said nothing, waiting for one of us to continue.

'Think of the danger, Wu Sing,' I said. 'It's bad enough with me just seeing you now and then, but if we married and stayed here, what chance would we have?'

'On the other hand, you are asking me to give up my world, a world that needs my skills so desperately, that bleeds daily and yields a little more each day to the forces of change.'

'Yes. I know, Wu Sing, but things change,' I said, looking at a sliver of reflected sunlight shimmering on the tranquil sea. 'I love you, Wu Sing.' I turned back to face her. 'I love you, and I'm afraid for you. I can't stay with you, and I can't leave without you. What am I to do?'

The three of us stood in silence. Eventually, Father Ling turned to Wu Sing.

'How do you know that God wants you to stay here, my child?' he asked.

'I feel the desperate need for me here, Father. But I also love Jason dearly,' she said, turning to me with eyes that pleaded for understanding. 'I can't imagine a life without you, Jason. I never knew I could love someone with such intensity,' she said with soft conviction.

'Yes, yes, it is the same for me, Wu Sing,' I replied, reaching for her hand.

Her smile lit up her whole face and I felt like holding her and never letting her go. Then she turned back to Father Ling.

'I'm so confused, Father. Why is the world like this? Why can't we all just live in peace, and live the lives we want?

'That is a mystery whose answer is known only to God, my child. Perhaps the truth will be revealed to us at some time in the future, but not now.' He paused for a moment's reflection then asked, 'Tell me, Wu Sing, if you feel this way about your people's need for you here in Vietnam, why do you encourage this young man?'

Her eyes softened as she answered, 'It's true, Father. I love Jason with all my heart. I hurt badly when I think of not being with him, and my will to remain here dims daily. Father, can I leave without deserting my people?'

'And what of the life that could be yours in Australia, Wu Sing?' he asked. 'Aren't you deserting that by staying here?'

'Am I, Father?'

'I don't know what you want from me. I cannot divine the will of God, and I cannot foretell your future. It is for each of us to search our hearts and live accordingly.

'And what of you, Father?' Wu Sing asked. 'Where did your search lead you?'

'Is that fair, Wu Sing? I am a priest, while you have been touched deeply by this world.'

'Tell me, Father.'

'If you believe in a universe that has design and order, as I do, then it logically follows that there must be some purpose to our being here, and only God, the creator of order and purpose, can reveal those truths to you.'

'But what is the truth?' I asked.

'Surely, this is the purpose of our existence, to discover it for ourselves, for no matter what others may say or do, our belief does not become truth until we accept it for ourselves.'

'But if each of us discovers our own truth, won't that lead to many truths, some of which may contradict one another?' I persisted.

'It appears that is what is happening in today's world. Our world is clearly confused and uncertain about its values and seems to lack moral clarity, a belief in any one thing. For me, the bible is my source of truth, and I derive my values from it.' Father Ling paused and looked up, as though he was seeking inspiration. 'It all depends on the honesty of your heart and the source of your revelation. Without purity in both, the revealed truth will be contaminated.'

'Then you are saying that I should search my heart with pure intent. But, Father, I have been doing this,' Wu Sing said despairingly.

'Then it is your impatience that is the source of your agony, my child, for God will not desert you. In time, you will know what God's will is.' We went silent again. Then Father Ling looked up and asked, 'Are you sexually active with Jason, Wu Sing?'

She looked down at her feet and replied softly. 'Yes, Father.

I know I shouldn't, but neither Jason nor I can contain our love for each other.'

'If you are asking for my advice, then I would say the first thing you should consider is marriage in the church, because you are currently living in a state of sin that could jeopardise your immortal souls.' He turned to me and continued, 'and if Wu Sing conceives, it will further complicate your position. That brings us to you, Jason. Are you willing to accept the church?'

'Yes, Father. For Wu Sing, I would accept anything.'

'Be careful, my son, You should accept the church because you find Christ in it, not Wu Sing.'

More procrastination, I thought, without really hearing Father Ling's advice. In my impatience, I wanted a resolution to our endless search, but all I could see was more discussion, more endless pleading.

*

Not long after that, I took Toby to his medevac plane at Vung Tau airport. He was leaving Vietnam for an Australian hospital. David arrived too. He was on one of his trips from Saigon, and the three of us tried to go back to the way it was before, but we couldn't, not with Nick gone and Toby like he was.

'This stinking war,' David said, looking down at Toby's missing legs. 'It's got to end.'

'Oh, yeah, smartarse. And how's that gunna happen?' Toby asked.

'When we get back, we've got to protest. The government will listen if enough of us join in.'

'Oh! An' what if I don't wanta? Ya know what we found

in some of the Viet Cong camps we captured? Large tins of rice with messages of support for the glorious, liberation forces of the Viet Cong and the NVA. Know who sent them? Ya righteous protesters back home. They were proud enough to tell everyone in the message they sent printed on the tins.'

'That's not all protesters, Toby. Only the more radical.'

'Ya mean the communist ones, right? Great company ya want me to keep. There must be plenty of 'em if they can organise and raise all that food, and then get it to the Viet Cong. No, David, I'll never join ya protesters because I believe they're nothing but a bunch of traitors.'

David went silent for a moment. 'What about you and Nick? Do you think that's right? With Nick dead, and you like that?'

'Don't bring Nick into this! Those little bastards did this to me, an' those little bastards'll pay.'

'But, Toby, it's not just soldiers who are dying in this war. Women and children also are dying here – every day,' David pleaded.

'What der ya know?' Toby spat. 'Ya never put ya arse on the line, did ya? The only thing ya ever squeezed a trigger at was a bloody target. Ya never watched a live body drop, an' then prayed like mad that someone didn't make a mistake. Jesus, don't ya know those bastards use women and kids against us? How do ya think it feels ter roll over a body an' find it's a young woman or a young boy? Well, I'll tell ya. It hurts at first. It sorta gnaws in ya guts. But ya really want ter know the horror of it all? The really scary part is that ya get used to it. Yeh. After a while, it don't matter, because it's just another gook an' they're all gooks in this stinking place.'

Toby paused for a moment, looking up to the sky. 'This place really is a festering scab on the face of the earth,' he said, returning his stare towards David. 'Everything about it is rotten. Even the dead rot quicker here. Ya know why? Because it's a pox-ridden country full of pox-ridden people. That's why. So help me, I hate this place. It took me, mate, it took me legs and it took me future from me. I'll never be the same. I just want those little bastards ter pay, an' don't give me anymore of that peace crap until they have.'

We went silent for a while after that.

I talked to Toby about his flight back and explained he would probably be taken to Heidelberg Repat Hospital, and that I would come and see him there sometime when I got back.

The medics came and wheeled Toby away. As they pushed him up the ramp of the Hercules aeroplane that would take him home, we waved and smiled and shouted for him to take care of himself. He smiled and shook his head as he disappeared into the body of the aircraft.

David and I turned to leave. 'Toby never was very smart,' was all he said.

*

About this time, Wu Sing was sent to a Catholic mission in Binh Ba, a small Vietnamese village in the Duc Thanh district, north of Vung Tau. She was to stay there for a few weeks and see to the medical needs of the local people, then return to Vung Tau. Father Ling had baptised me into the Catholic faith and we planned to be married shortly after she returned.

Early one morning, a combined force of NVA soldiers and local Viet Cong guerillas occupied Binh Ba where Wu Sing was staying. The communists were hoping to show the locals that they could move anywhere without interference from Australian or Republic of Vietnam regular or local forces.

However, a tank and an armoured recovery vehicle passed through Binh Ba while they were there and, to display their fearlessness of the Australians, the communists fired on the tank with a rocket-propelled grenade. The Australian task force reacted swiftly and, in the ensuing battle, Binh Ba was entered by Australian forces with tanks and intense house-to-house fighting followed. NVA and Viet Cong soldiers still in the village were cleared with tank and machine gunfire and Australian soldiers fought enemy soldiers face to face inside the local houses. Eventually, the NVA and Viet Cong withdrew, using civilians as a human shield, leaving behind much death and destruction in Binh Ba.

During the battle which lasted two days, one of our medics was wounded when an RPG round struck a tree behind where he was sheltering. The shrapnel rained down on his back and he was medevacked to our field hospital. Ever since I had heard about the battle taking place in Binh Ba, I had been worried about Wu Sing, so I volunteered to be flown to Binh Ba to help sort out the medical emergency.

I don't remember much of what happened that day. It was hot and there was smoke and dust and flies, and helicopters kept landing and taking away the dead and wounded. For the critical cases, we started by first triaging our soldiers, administering drugs, bandages and drips and sorting out their evacuation priority. When we had available space on our choppers, seriously wounded civilians were sent to our hospital for transfer to the civilian hospital in Vung Tau. Civilians with minor injuries were sent to their local hospital for first aid treatment, so I wondered how Wu Sing was handling the sudden influx of patients in her medical centre.

Towards the evening, when the flood of patients had dwindled to a trickle and I was on a break, Father Ling, who had accompanied Wu Sing to the Catholic mission, approached me with a serious look on his face.

'I have some bad news, Jason,' he said, waiting for me to grasp the seriousness of what he was about to tell me. 'Wu Sing is dead.'

'Wu Sing is dead?'

'Yes. I'm sorry. Would you like to sit down?'

'No. Where is she?'

'In the church,' he said, nodding in its direction.

'Can I see her, please?'

'Yes, of course,' he said, taking me by the arm and gently leading me to a small church in the middle of the village.

Entering the church, I could see Wu Sing lying on a table in the centre of the room. Father Ling released my arm and stood beside me. Wu Sing's face was clear and calm, but the colour had faded from her skin. Her expression was blank, like that of a sleeping child. A blood-soaked sheet covered her body to her shoulders, and some local people stood around her, their eyes still red from weeping. I noticed her arm had slipped from the table and lay suspended in midair outside the cover of the sheet, so I moved up to her side and took her hand in mine. I raised her hand to my lips and felt the dead weight of her arm. I kissed the palm of her hand, then placed it against my cheek, but all I could feel was the cold of her absence.

I broke down. My shoulders shook and heaved with the intensity of my sobbing. I raised my head and stared at the ceiling. I continued to sob, as my head moved from side to side. 'No,' I moaned. 'Oh, Wu Sing ... How? ... Why?'

I looked back down, and my attention fell on the bloodstained sheet. Confusion filled my mind as I carefully laid her arm on the table next to her still, lifeless body. I couldn't hold the thought that Wu Sing was gone from my life forever. Father Ling moved up beside me, placed his arm around my shoulders and held me in a firm but warm embrace. I turned my head and our eyes met. I could see the deep concern that filled his eyes.

I looked down at Wu Sing's broken body and wondered what I was doing when the darkness closed in around her. Was I caring for another's wounds? Was I still in Vung Tau at that moment, laughing, perhaps joking with someone? Our life together ended in that moment. I wondered how many others started a new life together in that same moment.

What would I do now, now that Wu Sing was dead? I couldn't hold that thought in my mind. I kept thinking that it wasn't true, that this whole thing was a mistake. Surely that was it. Wu Sing wasn't really dead – but there she was in front of me. She looked so still, so lifeless. There was no mistake. Wu Sing was dead, and I would have to accept that, and go on without her. She would never speak again, never smile again, never touch ... My love for her still lingered, but she was gone forever. How could this be? Surely Wu Sing was not dead. She would come back to me somehow. Maybe I was just dreaming. That's it. I'll wake up and she'll be here with me again, smiling up at me like she always does. But she *was* dead, and the proof of her death lay in front of me.

Later, at her funeral in Vung Tau, many questions disturbed my peace of mind. Both David and Clarissa had warned me that what I expected from a loving relationship was naïve, too romantic and unattainable. Had the love that Wu Sing and I shared been like that, so innocent that it belonged to an age whose pages had faded yellow with the passage of time? Had we become enchanted by a fairy tale vision that resided in an age of carriages and candles and crystal chandeliers rather than our own time of change and uncertainty? Whatever our love had been, one thing was certain: it was inevitable that today's world with all its misery and malevolence would run the sweet innocence of its truth to ground and rip out its hope-filled heart.

Nevertheless, Wu Sing had shown me the splendour of love found in the touch of her hand, the care in her voice and the passion in her eyes. From her, I had learnt that love is more than a power game or a moment's pleasure; that it is the intangibles, the invisible things in life, that are essential to satisfying the yearning within us all that calls out for fulfilment in the quiet, lonely moments of our lives. We came to know that splendour was something in the heart and, in that moment, our passion melted into each other, making us one. But now Wu Sing was dead, and I had to live alone with the memory of a love that haunted me.

After I had gone through the funeral and the other mourners had left, I knelt by her grave with one hand on the earth and the other covering my eyes. Even Father Ling had recognised I needed time alone at Wu Sing's gravesite and had withdrawn. It was then that it struck me the hardest. Wu Sing was dead, I would never see her again, and she would forever remain here buried beneath the earth.

*

I lost time after that. Days drifted into days without connecting. Everything around me seemed empty. Buildings appeared hollow, without substance. I couldn't relate with people. They, too, seemed empty somehow, ghost-like. When they spoke, their words seemed to echo in my mind without associating. I couldn't seem to grasp the significance of what they said. I was lost – there was no substance, no reality to my existence.

Around this time, I began having sleepless nights. Visions of the young Vietnamese man I had killed came to me in my sleep, his innocent face, his pleading eyes. Wu Sing was also there. She reached for me, but her blood-soaked body receded and disappeared into the mist that was my dream. I would wake up sweating with my heart racing and find it hard to get back to sleep. I became so tired during my working hours that I found it difficult to stay awake. My eyelids would drop, my head would slowly sink to my chest, and, for a moment, I would drift into sleep, only to jump back suddenly into consciousness while shaking my head. This pattern would repeat itself during my shift, but, when I returned to my bed, sleep remained elusive.

The helicopters kept bringing in the wounded, the downdraft from the chopper blades pushing against us as we rushed out to get the wounded, the jet engine making a subdued whine. Later, when it took off, it would make an aggressive chopping noise, with its engines screaming, but for a while it was a subdued beast, almost sympathising with us as we unloaded its pitiful cargo. Or was it really grinning in mock foreshadowing of the slicing and sawing and stitching about to start on the broken, young bodies we rushed to the anxious looking surgeons?

'Clean this one, Private. I'll take him first. Take a look at this one, Corporal. Is the operating room ready for surgery, Sister?'

Amazing how efficient the army became at a time like this. Notice the 'Private' and 'Corporal' business. That's so we couldn't get too familiar. That's so we concentrated on the job at hand and not the actual results of what our actions produced.

I was looking down on a young man somewhere in his late teens or early twenties. His heart was beating and he was breathing. I opened his eyelids and his pupils were extremely dilated. Why? How could this be when he was unconscious? He didn't seem to have too much damage, only a small hole and a trickle of blood on his right cheek. I slid my hand under the back of his head. *Sweet Jesus*! My hand was full of red, grey goo. Oh, help! I was going to be sick. I grabbed for a bowl and dry-retched into it.

'What's the matter with you, Corporal? Can you snap out of it? We need you here,' the Chief Surgeon urged me. Then he noticed I was not responding. 'Do you need to take a break?'

The commanding officer came over and looked at me. He was a father figure to us all. In his quiet times, he would smoke a pipe while his chief surgeon smoked a cigar. Together, they sat and talked quietly about how they could improve the efficiency of the hospital. Our commanding officer was someone we could trust and confide in. Only trouble was, he couldn't stop the wounded coming in and I didn't know how much more of this I could take. I looked up at him and he could see the hopeless pleading in my eyes.

'I think you need a break from this, Corporal. Go to my office and wait for me there. I'll see you when I'm finished here.'

The commanding officer's office was smothered in the reality of the war. The walls were covered in charts and graphs, the classical dichotomy portrayed in stark visible reality. I looked at the graphs and began to laugh uncontrollably.

You take two variables and plot them on a two-dimensional plane and, wonder of wonders, you have a line. A line! Now that's something you can really get emotional about. That's something to really arouse your passion.

You see, a line on a graph can go up or down or straight across. Straight across is nothing; it's going nowhere. I mean, straight across represents no change, situation stable, no progression. We're going nowhere on a straight line. What we really need is an up–down or a down–up line.

Now if an up–down or a down–up line goes up when it should go up, or down when it should go down, we've got elation, happiness, joy. There's a smile on everyone's face and pride in everyone's hearts. Everyone can see our commanding officer is a success, he's doing a great job. We all celebrate in his success. Look at the line – it goes in the direction we want it to. Our commanding officer is the best. We are the best.

On the other hand, the up–down or down–up line could go down when it should go up, or up when it should go down. The result of such a catastrophe is, naturally enough, failure, but even so, it does arouse one's passion. One does feel for the little line moving in the wrong direction. Now these feelings can be dejection, humiliation or frustration, or they can be commitment and determination to right the wrong. The up–down or down–up line moving in the wrong direction can be a challenge or it can be a crushing defeat. If a challenge, it can spur us on to do better, to meet the enemy head on, to overcome.

And if the up–down or the down–up line is moving in the wrong direction but suddenly changes direction and moves in the right direction – oh! Happiness of happiness, joy of joys, life is worth living, life is beautiful. Our faith in what we are trying to achieve is restored. The line is once again moving in the right direction.

On the other hand, if an up–down or down–up line moving in the wrong direction continues on its merry way, despite our every effort, one has a crushing defeat. Oh, well, we did our best, didn't we? We can always blow our brains out, can't we? I suppose that's why the commanding officer sent the boy with no brains to the American 36 Evacuation Hospital to die. That way our up–down or down–up line will move in the direction we all want it to go.

I was taken off my duties in the hospital and put on some paperwork in the admissions and discharge department. But that didn't work either. I made mistakes and those around me grew frustrated, so the commanding officer sent me to the R&C in Vung Tau for a week.

During my stay there, I went to see Father Ling at his convent. 'How could this happen, Father?' I asked. 'How could this happen when Wu Sing and I had so much to live for?'

'I have no answers for you, Jason. This is something you just have to accept,' he replied.

'But they hurt her ... they killed her ...' I choked on my words.

'It won't help to dwell on this, Jason.'

'But how could God let this happen?'

'This war is not God's doing. This is something man does to himself. Wu Sing was executed by the Viet Cong who, whenever they get the chance, execute those who cooperate with the government. In this way, they discourage any positive feelings that the villages might harbour for the government, and it also keeps the villages in fear of supporting the government. Since this is the case, you can hardly blame God for the actions of the ungodly. I know how evil this is, but God gives us free agency, so man has determined how this war will be fought, not God.'

'Is that true? Do you think we should stop fighting? Stop the evil being perpetrated on the villages? But wouldn't that mean that the worst among us would triumph? Do you think communism should triumph? Is liberty not worth fighting for? I thought it was, but if I wasn't here, if none of us was here, the war would not have gone on and Wu Sing would be alive today.'

'Perhaps. But remember, God calls us all home to His presence when our time is up. Besides, I believe there would still be fighting. There always has been. It's just that you got involved and not someone else.'

'But I thought I was fighting for your freedom. Wu Sing believed I was fighting for hers. She wanted so much for her people to be free, and now she is dead. How could that be?'

He looked at me with compassion, but no words came.

'I won't take the blame for her death, Father,' I shouted, turning from his gaze. 'I just don't understand how God could have let someone as compassionate and caring as Wu Sing die. She still had so much to give this world. What good did her death achieve?'

'It is dangerous for you to speak like this, Jason. If you turn your back on God now, you will never be at peace again. You must accept what you cannot change. God will not desert you in your hour of need and will not challenge you with things you cannot endure. Look to how you can grow from what you experience; don't be crushed by it. Your thoughts are of this world. Wu Sing was of this world. To find peace, you must go beyond the worldly, and only Christ and the church can do that for you.'

'All that you and your church can do for me, Father,' I said, sarcastically, 'is fill me with guilt for the rest of my life.'

'The church won't do that to you, Jason. That you do to yourself. The church teaches that we are all entitled to redemption, regardless of what crimes we commit,' he replied. Then added, 'I want you to know that I was able to perform the last rites for Wu Sing before she died. She was held for some time as a prisoner before they executed her, and I was able to administer to her during this time.'

'Oh,' I responded, sarcastically, 'am I supposed to be grateful?'

'I thought you would be comforted by the thought that you may not have endangered Wu Sing's immortal soul.' Father Ling replied, trying to console me. 'It is now up to God's grace. Don't you see, you have not put her possible salvation at risk. Isn't that thought of some comfort for you?'

But I wasn't listening. I turned my back on him and his church and walked away, carrying my guilt with me.

*

It was at this time that I started wearing the necklace of boars' tusks I had bought from the island trader on my way to Vietnam. I wore it around my neck under my singlet with my dog tags. Nobody knew I had it on, but the feeling of it close to my skin gave me a sense of primitive power. At night as I lay in bed, I would run my finger over the tusks and hear the gentle clatter of the ivory and dream of an existence removed from the rattle of gunfire.

After I returned to the hospital, I completed my duties competently and efficiently, but I had lost all connection with what I was doing. I gave penicillin injections, distributed medication, changed dressings and took blood pressure readings and temperature, pulse and respiration readings. When the wounded came in, I took them from the helicopter and carried out all the tests and treatments for them before they went into surgery, but none of this made any connection with me. Before, I had had a deep sense of commitment about what I was doing. Now, these were just tasks I performed, and the numbness inside me continued without abatement.

The rest of my time in Vietnam became a blur of flickering events. Newcomers arrived, old timers left, the war went on and I drank at the bars in town whenever I could get leave. I remember on those occasions sitting in smoke-filled rooms and the sound of rock and roll music bouncing around in my head. Everywhere I went, Eric Burden and The Animals screamed, 'We Gotta Get Outta This Place', or The McCoys urged me to 'Hang on, Sloopy', or Peter, Paul and Mary reminded me of what was to come: 'I'm Leaving on a Jet Plane'. I felt cold, wet liquid tumbling down my throat and filling my belly, and the harshness of a hot, sweaty, oppressive atmosphere everywhere I went.

At one time during my disorientated state of mind, David arrived and told me how sorry he was about Wu Sing. Father Ling had told him all about it. Then he asked me to take him to the Hollywood Barber Shop. He had heard all about it and wanted to experience it for himself before he went back home to Sarah.

The Hollywood Barber Shop in Vung Tau was a front for a brothel. Once inside, you had a haircut, shave, nail manicure and free head and neck massage. Then, if you wanted more of the pleasures that the establishment could offer, you were taken to the rear of the building for a sauna and a cold shower where all the grease and accumulated grime was sweated and washed from your body. Then, you were offered a full body massage before, finally, sitting in the heart of the Barber Shop, a dimly lit room with heavy drapes and cushions, you drank what you liked and chose from an array of willing, young Vietnamese women.

David and I had experienced all the outer trapping of the Barber Shop together and arrived at the inner sanctum. David tried to get me to choose one of the women but I refused.

'Come on, Jason,' he said, 'the quickest way to forget one woman is in the arms of another.' He said it with such confidence I was sure he spoke from experience.

'No, I'm fine. Enjoy yourself, though. I'll wait for you here and have a beer.'

'Suit yourself, but don't sit around with a long face when there's so much pleasure to be had here.'

I sat down with my beer and waited for David to return from his time with the young woman he had chosen, hoping something would help me connect with my surroundings. Opposite me were two young women who were laughing and giggling together. They would giggle and put a hand to their mouths to hide their mirth and then laugh some more and reach out and touch each other on the hand or on the shoulder. *How curious*, I thought, *that these women could retain their childlike innocence and innate happiness despite the nature of their circumstance.*

I continued drinking quietly by myself. A large, black American soldier entered the room. The girls went very quiet and one of them stood up and walked over to him. The other one quickly came over and sat by me.

'Buy me Saigon tea,' she pleaded. 'Black man number ten,

beaucoup conga.'

The black American looked over at us and smiled. I smiled back. I could see she was terrified by the thought of having to be with a black American, mainly because they had a reputation for having a large penis. I nodded my head, and she took my money and returned with her drink.

The American took the woman who had gone to him and disappeared. The young woman who was with me sighed and relaxed into her chair.

'You like me, Joe?' she asked, placing her hand on the inside of my thigh.

'Yes. I like, but not now,' I replied, taking her hand from my thigh and holding it in mine.

She frowned. 'You like boy?'

'No, no. I don't like boy. Stay with me, okay?'

'Okay, Joe.'

We sat quietly, holding hands, while she sipped her drink. I leaned back in my chair and closed my eyes. I remembered Wu Sing – her smile, the way she had held my hand – and I felt myself falling into a deep sadness, like falling down a deep, dark, empty mine shaft. The girl put her hand on my cheek and leaned across me.

'You okay, Joe?' she asked.

'Yes,' I replied, sadly. 'Joe okay.'

A look of concern passed over her face. 'You come me, Joe,' she said standing up and pulling me to my feet. 'I make good. You see, Joe. I make good.'

I followed her into one of the cubicles, where she took off her clothes and started to undress me. I stood and watched her, my hands hanging loose at my side. When she had undressed me, she placed my arms around her and smiled up at me, as she moved her hips from side to side and played with my necklace of boar tusks.

After a while, she stopped and said, 'No good, Joe. You lie down, okay?'

I did as I was told, and she used her mouth and her tongue to arouse my passion. Finally, she sat on top of me and gently rocked backward and forward, her head nodding in rhythm with her body and her hands resting gently on my chest. My desire for sexual gratification increased and I sat up. Placing my arms around her, I turned and laid her on the bed. She raised her legs above my hips and, as my urgency peaked, she gave me a noncommittal smile and took the boars' tusks on my necklace in her mouth and held them in her teeth and played with them with her tongue. I collapsed on top of her, and she briefly stroked my back as she continued sucking on my necklace. Suddenly, she pushed on my chest, and rolled out from under me. The abruptness of our separation left me feeling empty again, the brief feeling of connection gone.

'You number one time, Joe,' she uttered casually. Later, when I paid her, she smiled and said again, 'You number one time, Joe. Come back. See me long time, okay, Joe?'

I smiled and nodded my head. When we got back to the lounge, David was not in the room. I wondered where he had gone, when the woman he had been with came up to me.

'Friend say, go PX, meet there.'

When I turned to leave, the black American caught up with me and we left together.

'How's ya doin', man?' Without waiting for an answer, he went on. 'That Lana. She a fine one, that girl. Know what I mean, man? One fine girl. Why, she the best in the whole damn' place. That's what I'm talkin' about.'

'Well, I can't say. That was my first time.'

'Oh, try her, man. She good.'

As we walked on together, he described in detail the techniques Lana had used on him. They sounded similar to those used by my girl in our solitary session.

Suddenly, he said, 'Say man, I'm goin' the Y ta see a brother perform. He new. Got that rhythm and blues goin' just fine. Hear what I sayin'? Mighty fine R&B. Say, man, you dig R&B?'

'Yes, I do. I enjoy Percy Sledge's and Sam Cook's music a lot, so I'd like to come with you, but I've got to meet up with a friend at the PX.'

'Oh, too bad, man. Well, this where I hav' ta leave ya. Be seein' ya.'

'Yes. See you.'

He peeled off and left me to continue alone, disappointed at having missed out on some good R&B music. Sam Cook's 'Bring It On Home to Me' and Percy Sledge's 'When a Man Loves a Woman' and 'What Am I Living For' were songs I was sure could revive my sagging spirit. There's something about R&B that drags the pain right out of you.

My thoughts returned to thinking about what had happened to me in the Hollywood Barber Shop. Would I return to the girl who had provided me with a brief moment of pleasure and a fleeting sense of connection? Probably not, because it had left me craving even more for what I had lost with Wu Sing. Wu Sing and I had given each other something special. I had seen it in her eyes, her smile, and had felt it in her warm embrace, her lingering kiss. She had made me feel special, like I had a purpose in life. The girl from the Barber Shop had provided me with something more basic, something akin to primordial instinct. The two things stood in such stark contrast with each other that it left me feeling something was not quite right, like something was missing.

I caught up with David in the PX. The PX was where Australian servicemen could buy luxury goods at tax-free prices. Australian servicemen were mainly interested in electrical goods and watches, but Americans at their PX could even buy the latest model cars and have them waiting at the airport when they got home. David was concentrating on the watches. He smiled and punched me gently on the shoulder.

'You're a sly dog. Now that you've broken the ice, you'll be able to move on and meet someone else. Don't make a habit of girls like those at the Barber Shop, though. It's expensive and will keep you broke.'

We both smiled and lapsed into silence. Then David said, 'I want something as a memento of my time in Vietnam.'

I nodded and looked down at the watches. David continued examining them until his interest centred on a large silver one.

'This one looks the best,' he said. 'It's a pilot's watch. It tells the time in two places at the same time. It has a lot of rare gemstones to keep it balanced, and I'm sure it will become a collector's item in the future. Why don't we both get one?'

Tells time in two places, I wondered. *Is that where I was? In two places at the same time?*

I agreed to buy the watch. Then David said that he had to catch a flight back to Saigon within the hour and couldn't go back to the hospital with me, so we said goodbye and David left with a bounce in his step.

*

Somewhere in all this, I got lost. Days drifted into weeks and eventually I found myself on a plane heading back home for Australia. We arrived at Richmond Airforce Base and were told to change into civilian clothes before heading back to our units. Something was not right about our homecoming, and we were beginning to understand the depth of resentment many Australians felt towards us.

Two days later, I stood in front of a major at Enoggera who was about to discharge me. He was looking down at some paperwork in front of him. He kept me waiting but, eventually, he looked up at me.

'Freeman, is it?'

'Yes, sir.'

He looked down at my discharge papers. 'You don't need anything, do you, Freeman?' he asked, without raising his head.

'No, sir.'

'Good man,' he said, then signed my papers and dismissed me.

On my way back to the barracks, where I was to change into my civilian clothes before making my way home, I stopped by the rock wall we had built. It seemed like a lifetime ago that Nick, Toby and I had shared our friendship for the first time while working on the construction of this wall. Such a happy time for us that had been. I ran my hand over the rocks we had broken and cemented into the wall, then bowed my head as tears welled in my eyes.

CHAPTER 6
Learning to live with it

A few days later, I arrived home. I remember the embraces, the smiles, the tears and the earnest looks of concern, but something was missing. I couldn't fathom it – a hollowness that still surrounded me and an emptiness I couldn't fill, no matter what I did.

I went back to work, but I couldn't hold my job. It seemed silly to be doing the things I was doing. Those around me thought their work was important, but to me it seemed meaningless and boring, so I left, and drifted from job to job, my life becoming a meaningless repetition of senseless events. This had happened, now that will happen next, and it did. I seemed to be sleepwalking through a daily routine, and those around me seemed oblivious to the suffering of those paying so much for their liberty. Whenever I got into a discussion about the Vietnam War, I tried to explain the importance of liberty not being defeated by communism, but was told by people who had not been there that we had no right to be fighting in Vietnam, that the war was immoral and that I had participated in an immoral act, so I had learnt not to mention the Vietnam War, because it only led to heated arguments and lasting bitterness. Nothing gave me pleasure anymore, and the empty void inside me grew and grew, leaving me to operate on mere instinct. Sometime during this search for meaning in my life, I left home, hoping to find something I could hold on to.

At this time, I also became a functioning alcoholic. It was strange how I could drink so much yet remain reasonably competent. I drank whenever I had money or the opportunity presented itself. I drank during the week, but I had to be careful not to drink too much. Weekends were the best. I could get blind drunk and forget everything, yet still present myself for work on Mondays. It never ceased to amaze me how I could remain a functioning member of society without slipping into homelessness. At first, I drank beer, but I soon discovered that it took too long to get drunk on beer, and I got bloated from all the fluid and sugar I was putting into my body, so I graduated to spirits. I would choose the cheaper bottles of Johnny Walker Scotch and Bundaberg rum.

I came to realise that I had to drink alone in my room because of the stages I went through on my weekend binges. I went through the same routine. I would knock back a few quick shots before I started to develop a numbness in my lips and fingers. I knew then that I would soon be entering my second stage of drunkenness. This meant a deep sorrow would fill me from the inside, and I would start crying. That's why I had to drink alone in my room. Now I had to drink quickly to get through this second stage and into my third stage, which came on when the numbness filled me from the inside. It was so good to drink and not have to worry about the despair and sorrow that usually filled me. All the hollowness that filled my days would slowly drift away, and I would fall into a shallow slumber. I would keep drinking till eventually I would pass out, which was the best of all, because it meant being able to sleep without the dreams that haunted my usual nighttime routine.

My biggest problem, however, was to remain interested in what I was doing, and I never found a solution to this. I would remain in one place until I got bored and restless. Gradually, the yearning for change would get so strong that I had to move on. I drifted from town to town, city to city, never settling, never resting, just constantly on the move.

At one time, I went to see Toby. He told me he could not adjust after he had returned from Vietnam, that he had gone through stages of depression and had contemplated suicide many times, how he had trouble with the grog and went into fits of rage, losing his temper, throwing things and smashing whatever he could get his hands on. He said he couldn't talk to anyone – they didn't understand him. They would pity him or despise him, but nobody respected him.

'God,' he shouted. 'Didn't I give enough of myself for this stinking country and its ungrateful people?'

All I could do was nod my head and put my hand on his shoulder. When he started to cry, I held him and wept with him.

'Jesus, Jason,' he sobbed into my ear. 'What're we gunna do, mate?'

I continued holding him and shook my head. 'Endure, Toby, and hope that things will get better. That's all we can do.'

We sat in silence. I had no answers for him, no hope for improvement in his life. I phoned him a few days later just to make sure he was coping better, but he spent most of our conversation shouting into the phone about how nobody understood anything about what was happening. His anger was visceral and profound. I found it difficult to understand much of what he said. It seemed disjointed and confused. At one point, he became quiet and started to cry. I wanted so much to help him, but he was far from my ability to reach him. I was at a loss as to what I should do, so I asked him how I could help, and he told me not to worry, that he was all right and just needed to let off some steam. He thanked me for my call and, once again, told me not to worry. After he had hung up, I was left feeling powerless and sad at having witnessed this change in Toby. He had gone from the cheeky, cheerful young man I had known before Vietnam to this estranged, dysfunctional person that I no longer recognised.

A few days after that, he took his own life, and at his funeral I remember wondering why Toby had committed suicide. Sure, he had told me that he had thought about it, but thinking about it and actually going through with it seemed a desperate act of hopelessness. He had told me not to worry, that he was all right, so how had he become so despondent that suicide seemed like a suitable option for him? I reasoned that he must have had nothing valuable left in his life to keep him struggling against the inconsolable pain and suffering he felt daily. Everything he had believed in had come crashing down after the war, and he had no one in his life he could turn to in his desperate hour of need, no one to keep him stable. This thought filled me with guilt, because I recognised that I had not been there for him when he had obviously needed me.

Back in the dark room I lived in, I sat alone, watching the flickering images of Vietnam's unfolding tragedy. I watched street marches grow into mass protests, unending sit-ins at universities and a rise in conscientious objection, draft resistance and petitions to the government. Wu Sing ... something seemed to nag me, something wouldn't go away. I fingered the boar tusks on my necklace and whispered, 'It can't have all been for nothing.'

If we lost in Vietnam, I reasoned, we would all lose, because we were all a part of that loss, and our mates who had died in Vietnam and all the suffering that had occurred in Vietnam would haunt us forever. If we lost, nothing would ever relieve the guilt we would feel towards those who now suffered and hurt. We would also feel the shame of having betrayed those whose liberty we had promised to protect but who would soon suffer under the yoke of communist tyranny. We would have to find a way to endure the lifelong guilt and shame that losing the war would so obviously inflict upon us.

The debt could never be paid by those of us who went and came back whole, because we would have lost, and our losing would have let down our mates who died there or came home broken. The debt we owed towards those we had been sent to save would also linger. Their suffering and hurt would forever be a part of us. The shame and guilt we carried would be within us all, and remission for that would be beyond the reach of physicians and psychiatrists trained to relieve pain and suffering in a hedonistic society that had lost its soul. A society whose soul had been displaced by the stroking of its psyche and a seemingly endless pursuit of elusive pleasure fulfilment that left its advocates increasingly feeling empty and unfulfilled, while their lives brimmed with an addictive desire for material and sexual gratification coupled with a demand for guilt avoidance. What our society sought was remission without contrition. What, then, was left for those of us who were driven by conscience yet had to somehow survive while living in a culture that had lost its integrity.

What could we do in a society that had lost its moral compass, whose northern star had faded to the extent that it was no longer visible? What could we do when it was our moral character that carried the burden of our shame and guilt? I guess the answer is that we would suffer, but our real horror lay in the realisation that our suffering would not bring moral strength or enlightenment, only moral decay and despair. In the meantime, I could always keep knocking back my shots of Scotch or rum, take long, hot showers, run my fingers over my boar tusk necklace and weep, while descending deeper and deeper into the inescapable pit of blackness that engulfed me, for those no longer with me, for those whom I had let down so badly.

About this time, I sold the watch I had bought in Vietnam and, with the money, I went to see a psychiatrist. He listened to me, then told me that I first needed to stop drinking so much. He gave me the number for the local Alcoholics Anonymous (AA) chapter and recommended that I give them a call. He also told me that I was probably suffering from what psychiatrists were beginning to call PTSD, but that he would need to see a lot more of me before he could make that diagnosis. He prescribed some medication for me that he said would help me sleep and help with my depression.

I did call AA and they gave me the address and time for their next meeting, which I attended. They were very helpful, and I tried to give up the alcohol. I had some success for a time, but I kept relapsing. I didn't seem to be able to kick alcohol altogether. I kept going back to it, because I longed for the comfort it gave me and the temporary escape it provided from the suffering I felt inside.

Eventually, I had to give up my sessions with the psychiatrist and the medication he prescribed, because it was too expensive for my income. Whenever I stopped drinking, however, I was able to save some money, and this funded my moving, whenever I got the urge to move on to another location.

At one time, Dad came and asked if I was going to go back home with him. I just looked at him and said, 'No.' He tried to convince me that I needed to go back with him, that he didn't want to see me like this anymore. I thanked him for his concern but assured him that I was fine. I just needed some more time to be alone to sort out my life. I promised him I would return home when I was ready, but that right now I needed more time alone.

He turned away, unable to bring himself to say what had to be said. I had become a hopeless case, incapable of caring, incapable of needing anything except the basic necessities of life. I saw the pain I had brought to him, and I was sure Mum felt the same way, and it tore at me. They had given me a loving home, where love and joy had once filled its spacious rooms, replaced now with bitterness and sorrow. I couldn't return, but my absence only brought more sorrow and despair for them.

It was a terrible time for me, a time where nothing seemed substantial, where every action, every thought, seemed to bring more pain. I kept telling myself that it was useless to keep reliving the events of my past and letting it determine my mood today. Nothing I did could ever change anything, but I couldn't stop the pain that overwhelmed me daily, and the deep, dark depression I kept falling into would never leave me. I felt like the water of a river constantly running into rapids only to tumble over a waterfall, and falling ... falling ... falling into a pool of midnight blackness that was my depression, whose rock bottom continued to elude me. I had lost any ability to control my mood swings. More than once, I pleaded for the eternal agony to stop, but any thoughts of suicide were blocked by the terrible suffering I knew that would bring to my parents, parents who loved me and had only ever wanted the best for me. No, I could never bring that upon them. Also, a tenuous, primitive fight for survival had been sparked in me when I'd taken the life of another to ensure my own survival, which now lived on in the necklace I had hanging around my neck.

And so I continued to move from town to town, job to job, pub to pub. Not looking, not caring, just moving. In a crowded bar, I sat alone and drank; in an empty room, I sat alone and drank; and everywhere I went, the ubiquitous television flickered its mocking images of a cause long soured by the death and destruction of its reality with, somewhere in the background, an ever-lengthening line of protesters shouting:

'Ho! Ho! Ho Chi Minh! 1, 2, 3, 4. We don't want your bloody war!'

I came to despise the anti-war movement. Not for their view of war but because they made a mockery of our sacrifice and the cause of freedom. Of course, peace is preferable to war, but was the survival of liberty and the defeat of communism not worth fighting for?

Their analysis of the Vietnam War was also one-sided. They never tried to understand the veterans' point of view. I hated them for the role they forced Vietnam veterans to play, which at best amounted to the fool and at worst an uncaring killer. But most of all, I hated them for the shattered memories of those we left behind – young men who, in other circumstances, would have been remembered with hushed respect, now thought of, if at all, as the embarrassing refuse of a foolish enterprise.

In 1967, Donovan had released a song titled 'Universal Soldier'. The song's lyrics made it clear that the 'universal soldier' was to blame for all the killing in wars. That it was the fault of the solder, because if he refused to fight all wars would end.

Ever since its release, those words had troubled me and, after my Vietnam experience, they had cut deep into my conscience. Was I really to blame? Was I the reason Wu Sing had died? If that were true, how could I go through the rest of my life with that on my conscience? Protesters had called us baby killers and murderers. How many people in Australia believed that, I wondered. Did they believe we were universal soldiers and not Australian soldiers fighting to protect their liberty? I reasoned that the growing support for the protest movement was evidence of what an increasing number of Australians were coming to believe about us. This was so different from what we thought about ourselves.

We thought we were fighting for a noble cause – freedom for the people of South Vietnam, and the protection of Australia's liberty – and, when we first went in, the rest of Australia thought the same way. In fact, they had encouraged us to go, but as time went on, the Australian people changed their minds, and we were left carrying the can. Australians are hypocrites, I told myself. They send their young men and women into mortal danger yet are unwilling to stand by them later. I felt the persistent sting of betrayal.

In 1970, Jane Fonda, a beautiful, successful Hollywood actress, daughter of the Hollywood icon Henry Fonda, announced in a speech she gave at Duke University, 'I am a socialist, I think we should strive towards a socialist society – all the way to communism. If you understood what communism was, you would hope and pray on your knees, that we would someday become communist.'

Then, in 1972, when the Paris Peace talks were in progress, she conducted a two-week tour of North Vietnam. During her visit, she was photographed sitting in an anti-aircraft gun, peering down its sighting mechanism while wearing a North Vietnamese helmet. She also visited with six American prisoners of war outside the 'Hanoi Hilton', a notorious prison where torture and brutality regularly took place, a place where the North Vietnamese claimed that their treatment of the POWs was 'humane and lenient'. This photograph gave credence to their claims. She never toured the inside of the facility to see for herself the inhumane conditions that the POWs were suffering under, enabling her to later claim plausible deniability as to her knowledge of the conditions. As well as this, she conducted radio broadcasts where she condemned America's bombing of North Vietnam as being indiscriminate and causing the death of innocent civilians. For these acts, Vietnam veterans nicknamed her 'Hanoi Jane'.

What shocked many Vietnam veterans, however, was not only these traitorous acts but that she was the daughter of Henry Fonda, who had been an active supporter of America's efforts during WWII, which included the deliberate and indiscriminate bombing of enemy cities, inclusive of incendiary and atomic bombing and the deaths of countless civilians. This was while our military leaders were trying to limit our bombing to military targets only, and our scientists were working furiously to develop precision targeting for our military ordnance through the use of laser guided targeting.

The whole Hanoi Jane incident gave credibility and support to the communist-led protest movement, while crushing the morale of Vietnam veterans. Jane Fonda's actions only encouraged the North Vietnamese to believe they could outlast America's commitment to the war, and in doing so, prolonged the war itself. Her actions, along with those of the protesters, led to the continued suffering of the Vietnamese people by prolonging the war. No official action was ever taken against Jane Fonda.

*

Richard Nixon held the American presidency from 1969 to 1974. During his re-election campaign, he promised to bring an end to the Vietnam War though a policy of 'peace with honour'. He achieved a peace accord in 1973 with both North and South Vietnam through a threefold strategy. First, he negotiated a detente with China and Russia, which he hoped would isolate North Vietnam. Second, he carried out heavy bombing of North Vietnamese military targets, like missile sites, army barracks, warehouses, radio stations, railroads, power plants and airfields. Civilian and POW sites were to be avoided. The use of precision laser targeting bombing kept civilian casualties to a minimum. However, a civilian airfield and shopping centre were wrongly identified as military targets and accidentally hit. A total of 1600 civilians were believed to have been killed during these raids. Third, in May 1972, Haiphong harbour was mined, thereby stemming Russian aid to North Vietnam. As for the South Vietnamese, Nixon made commitments of military aid and a promise to recommence bombing if North Vietnam ever invaded South Vietnam.

With the success of these bombing raids in achieving peace, many veterans wondered why such a strategy had not been adopted years earlier. Why had so many young Allied soldiers been thrown into the meatgrinder that was the ten-year-long Vietnam War, when an eleven-day bombing campaign had achieved the peace accord that had eluded us for so long? Why had our leaders allowed us to be butchered by the communists in South Vietnam, and damned by the communists and their followers in America and Australia on returning home, when decisive action could have ended it so quickly? Was David right all those years ago? Did the military–industrial complex in America want the war to last as long as possible? I didn't want to believe that such a conspiracy theory was possible, because the military–industrial complex had kept us in a position of technical superiority.

No, that was not possible. What I think happened was that we were led by incompetent leaders, who did not want to appear to be bullying a small country like North Vietnam. They probably had the Korean War in mind that had ended with a division of North and South Korea. But there were essential differences between the wars. The Korean War was a conventional war while the Vietnam War was a guerrilla war. The Americans had United Nations support in the Korean War but only limited allied support for Vietnam. That's why Kennedy only wanted to commit military advisers while Johnson only escalated the war slowly. It wasn't until Nixon took control that America grasped the initiative and took the war to the North in a serious way. Nixon wasn't afraid to make the hard decisions that leaders have to make during war time.

As my dislike for those at home deepened, my admiration for the Vietnamese grew. The South, betrayed and frightened, valiantly fought on, knowing all along their cause was already lost. It was sad in 1973 to see the last Australian troops withdraw from the field of battle, in war a sign that has always been accepted as having been defeated. While it was true that Vietnam now had a peace treaty, the Viet Cong were still active in the Phuoc Tuy province, which had been Australia's main field of operation. We had failed to rid our province of the Viet

Cong, so now it would be up to the South Vietnamese troops to control them. Strange, I thought, how we had never lost a single battle against the communists but had ended up losing the war.

When I heard on the news that the US Congress had halted their military aid to South Vietnam, which violated the terms of the Paris Peace Accord signed by the US, I realised that everything that David had said to Wu Sing and me back in the Grand Hotel in Vung Tau had come true. Without that aid, the South Vietnamese Army would be unable to continue fighting the type of war that the US had trained them to fight. Once their ammunition and weapons began to run out, they would lose the war. As well as this, Congress tied the hands of President Ford, making it illegal for him to commit any American military action in South Vietnam without congressional approval.

I watched President Ford beg Congress to keep its word to the South Vietnamese people. It was all to no avail. The majority in Congress had made up its mind to betray its ally. I couldn't understand the logic behind their action. They must have known that to cut off military aid to South Vietnam would mean the defeat of liberty in that country and the triumph of communism. I realised that some members of Congress had marched in protest of the war and had wanted the war to end, but the Paris Peace Accord had already bought an end to America's hostilities in Vietnam. America and its allies had withdrawn their combat troops from the South, and all that the South Vietnam government had asked for, and the US had agreed to, was that the American government continue to resupply them with military aid on a replacement basis only. They had to depend on the American government for this aid, because they had no way of manufacturing it for themselves, and North Vietnam continued to enjoy the full military support of Russia. Clearly, it was only a matter of time before North Vietnam would build a superior military force to that of South Vietnam.

I know some in Congress had a moral objection to the war, but the fact was that America had committed itself to the conflict in Vietnam. In fact, when the original vote had been taken in Congress to support South Vietnam, only one member had voted against America's commitment. Now all their actions did was to ensure a communist victory. I wondered, were they now prepared to accept responsibility for the consequences of their actions that would inevitably follow, or would they simply pass off their responsibility on the grounds of their moral objection?

Furthermore, how could America justify its continued military support for Western Europe, Japan and South Korea and cut it to South Vietnam? There was no consistency in their decision, no sense to their vote, other than the fact that the communists would win. All the misery that would entail hinged on their decision. How far the US government had drifted from the determined words that President Kennedy had so forcefully and elegantly declared just a decade before. Despite this, however, the South Vietnamese people resisted the inevitable, and continued to fight on.

The North, triumphant and resolute, having endured ten years of defeat in battle, defiantly sent their sons and daughters into the conflict. On the battlefield, their soldiers had thrown everything they had at us, matching our courage with theirs and our commitment with theirs. It is true that they capitulated with the signing of the Paris Peace Accord in which they had recognised the presidency of Nguyen Van Thieu, agreed to a ceasefire throughout Vietnam and allowed the US to continue supplying military aid to South Vietnam on a replacement basis. For North Vietnam, however, the peace accord was simply a means to an end, not an end in itself. Even when they signed it, they intended to break it at their time of choosing, which revealed the diplomatic tactics of communists.

Since then, there had been many incidents of communist violence in South Vietnam that had violated the Paris Peace Accord, but these incidents were easily handled by the South Vietnamese army. Following America's and its allies' ultimate betrayal of the people of South Vietnam, however, the NVA decided to test Congress's resolve by launching a major attack on Phuoc Long province, a lightly defended province near the Cambodian border in the north of South Vietnam. The NVA had rebuilt its army with a flood of military supplies from Russia to the point that they were now a superior military force to that of South Vietnam.

The South Vietnam army resisted and fought bravely, but they were outmatched, eventually overpowered and forced to give up their position. The South's counterattack failed and, when their troops began to withdraw, it caused a rout. Since Congress had not responded to North Vietnam's aggression, the communists saw an opportunity to push their advantage, and so in violation of the terms of the peace treaty they had signed just two years before, they began their open invasion of South Vietnam. In the end, the North deserved to win, because their leaders were the more resolute, willing to do whatever was needed to win, their people never wavered and their Russian support never faltered. On the other hand, with the exception of the South Vietnamese people's unrelenting desire to live a free life, we lacked all these qualities.

When the communists swept down from the north and descended upon the people of the South, the citizens of South Vietnam did what citizens had done for thousands of years: they became refugees in their own country. I was horrified by the visions of South Vietnamese citizens trying desperately to escape the fast-moving invasion threatening to overwhelm them.

The roads leading to Saigon became clogged with displaced people, clutching their babies in their arms, their crying children trying to keep up and not get lost in the confusion. Disheartened people clung to the skids of helicopters, only to fall to their deaths, while ships teeming with terrified refugees pulled away from the docks as others were still trying to board. All this highlighted a desperate scramble of millions to reach the perceived safety of Saigon. This was reminiscent of the French refugees' desperate rush to reach Paris before the blitzkrieg attack of Nazi thugs could overtake them at the start of WWII.

In a final desperate act of defiance, the people of South Vietnam voted for their liberty with their feet, and all their former allies were willing to do was look on in shame and horror at the unfolding catastrophe. Clearly, what was happening in South Vietnam was not the image of a liberated people welcoming their liberators, but rather the actions of a frightened citizenry trying desperately to escape the clutches of an unwelcomed invading military force.

In a desperate attempt to garnish American air support for his troops, President Thieu produced a letter signed by President Nixon guaranteeing American air support should North Vietnam invade South Vietnam in the future. Thieu had insisted on this before he had signed the Paris Peace

Accord. At the time, it had seemed like a guarantee of safety. Now, because of the Watergate scandal, it was not worth the paper it was written on. Sadly, for President Thieu and the South Vietnamese people, Nixon was gone, and the American Congress dishonoured their former president's promise.

Later, when it was obvious to all that Saigon, too, would fall, there was the spectacle of a mad rush to reach the American 7th fleet sitting off the coast in the South China Sea. Thousands of South Vietnamese citizens rushed to the American Embassy in a forlorn hope that the Americans would rescue them, only to find the gates to the embassy locked and guarded by marines to keep them out.

Those within the embassy who did escape boarded helicopters and headed out to the waiting aircraft carriers, but there were just too many incoming helicopters and too little space to handle them, so those helicopters that were not being used for embassy evacuation, or had already landed and unloaded their human cargo, were simply pushed overboard to make way for others to land.

Still other helicopters packed tight with escaping South Vietnamese crashed into the sea, because they couldn't get permission to land on the decks of the American aircraft carriers. Their life-threatening actions demonstrating a desperate hope that the Americans would save them according to the laws of the sea.

With scant provisions, overcrowded ships made emergency departures into the emptiness of the South China Sea, destinations unknown, the people on board hoping for some miracle to save them. Even now, the South Vietnamese were willing to risk death to gain their freedom and escape the tyranny of communism.

I wept for the South Vietnamese 18th Division that resisted the advancing NVA just east of Saigon. They destroyed three North Vietnamese Divisions in their heroic stand and were nearly wiped out. Their desperate resistance ended only when their ammunition ran out, which showed how unwilling they were to surrender their freedom to the communists. Their action, which delayed North Vietnam's entry into Saigon by two weeks, allowed the American Ambassador valuable time to evacuate himself and his staff from the American Embassy. How ironic that in the end it was the South Vietnamese who sacrificed themselves so that Americans could escape to their freedom. Such a noble sacrifice, befitting of the Greek tradition displayed in the Battle of Thermopylae.

I was despondent as I watched the Russian-made tanks, crewed by North Vietnamese soldiers, rumble into the deserted streets of Saigon. This turn of events galled me, because I knew that with a real commitment to the war, we could have done that to Hanoi many years before. American-made tanks, operated by South Vietnamese crews, could have taken Hanoi at any time in the past, especially if they had been supported with a bombing campaign like that conducted under the two Linebacker operations. A perfect time for that, however, would have been immediately after the crushing defeat suffered by the communists after the TET Offensive. If only our strategy had been to reunite Vietnam under the banner of liberty rather than to simply hold onto South Vietnam, perhaps the outcome might have been different. I guessed that our leaders must have feared a widening of the war, and therefore were unwilling to undertake such a winning strategy. However, sticking with the strategy of 'body counts' after the TET Offensive, as David had said, was never going to work, so why were they so willing to sacrifice so many lives in the pursuit of what they must have realised was an unattainable goal? Nixon had adopted a different strategy and had achieved a peace accord, but Congress had scuttled his achievement.

The final image of the Vietnam War was the staged scene of Russian-made tanks, crewed by North Vietnamese soldiers, crashing through the gates of the American Embassy in Saigon. The Western media had been invited to witness this action by the communists, who had agreed to its filming. Thus ended the narrative that the Western media had been promoting about the Vietnam War for years on the television screens located in the homes of America and its allies. Around the world, a cheer went up from the communists and those who had supported them, while modern-day libertarians looked on in shock and disbelief.

Then there was the loss of all the military hardware left behind that fell into the hands of the communists. Hundreds of artillery pieces as well as mortars, tanks, armoured personal carriers, anti-tank weapons, helicopters and fighter planes were captured. As well as this, there were the military bases themselves that were overrun by the communists. Da Nang airbase and the naval base at Cam Ranh Bay were the two biggest prizes, into which the Russians stationed their backfire bombers that had a range that could reach Australia, and their naval ships, particularly their nuclear submarines, which now had direct access into the South China Sea and the Pacific Ocean beyond.

After all this came the added horrors of slave labour camps disguised as 're-education' camps for those arrested and not executed. Finding people to arrest was a task made easier for the communists by documents left behind by the Americans, especially the CIA, as a result of their indecent haste to escape South Vietnam.

Adding to this horror were the two million people who sought escape from South Vietnam after it fell to the communists, including the almost eight hundred thousand boat people putting to sea in rickety, unseaworthy boats, risking death from the elements and the rape and possible abduction of women and children at the hands of sea pirates. Such were the risks they were willing to take in their desperate efforts to escape the nightmare communist rule that had overtaken their country.

Then followed the obscenity that was the killing fields of Cambodia conducted by the inhuman communist Pol Pot regime, where millions of Cambodian citizens were murdered in concentration camps run by their communist masters. The communists forcibly relocated the urban population of Cambodia to the countryside in the belief that the 'intellectuals' from the cities would be re-educated and create a communist, agrarian utopia.

These events did not fit the Western media's communist propaganda narrative about the Vietnam War, so they were not pursued with the same vigour that the media had given to America and its allies during the war.

All this tortured my thinking. How was it possible that we had stood by and allowed all this to happen? Where was Congress' moral objection to war now? Where were the protesters who had protested the Vietnam War on moral grounds now? In the final analysis, they never accepted any responsibility for all the inhuman acts that the communists in Indochina committed after the fall of South Vietnam. Instead, they passed it all off on the war itself. For them, it was a war that no longer existed that had created this new tidal wave of human suffering and misery, and not the actions of the communists themselves. The real immorality of America and its allies was not so much the Vietnam War but the broken promises they had made to the people of South Vietnam and their neighbours, and the malevolent suffering those pitiful people endured under their new communist masters.

This thinking only led me into deeper despair than I already felt. I was appalled by my country's betrayal of South Vietnam and disgusted with myself for having followed such incompetent and irresolute leaders.

*

At one time, my moving around brought me back to Melbourne. I had been on the wagon for a few months, so I had saved quite a bit of money. I wrote a letter back home and told them where I was staying, and not to worry about me.

One Saturday, I phoned David's home and Sarah answered. David and she had married, she said. He had already left for work, but she gave me his number and suggested I go and see him, that he would be pleased to see me. Then she suggested we have lunch together at the Windsor. I told her I would prefer a picnic lunch on the banks of the Yarra where we had originally met. She laughed happily and said what a lovely idea.

Sometime later, I entered David's office. His secretary looked up and greeted me with a warm smile. She had shoulder-length blonde hair with a kick at the end and a fringe that ran all the way across her forehead, deep blue eyes and a generous mouth that flashed long, clean white teeth. Her makeup was lightly applied, effectively highlighting the attractive features of her face.

'Can I help you?' she asked.

'Yes. My name is Jason Freeman. I have an appointment to see David this morning.'

'Yes, Mr Freeman. Mr Hughes is expecting you. Just a minute.' She picked up the telephone on her desk and asked David if he was ready to receive me.

'Mr Hughes said you can go in now,' she said, rising from her chair and walking to the door to open it for me. I noticed she had a slim, shapely figure. She was dressed in a tight-fitting business suit. The skirt was a little too short, revealing her long, shapely legs, which shimmered from the light tan pantyhose she was wearing. She opened the door and addressed David, who seemed almost too pleased to see her.

'Mr Freeman to see you, David,' she said, smiling broadly.

'Yes, Ann, thank you. Come in, Jason.'

As I entered his office, I was struck by the view from the wall to my left. It was made of sun-reflecting plate glass and offered an amazing view of the Melbourne CBD, the Yarra River and the park beyond, all places David and I had walked what now seemed like a lifetime ago, when he described Melbourne to me as 'his' city. Immediately in front of the wall of glass was a lounge and coffee table, where I assumed informal meetings would take place with his management team and the representatives of the companies he did business with.

An image suddenly sprang into my mind of David standing in front of the plate glass window, legs wide apart, elbows bent and two fists firmly planted on his hips, as he surveyed the city he and his ancestors had 'conquered'. I remembered having read some articles in the newspapers about David becoming a corporate raider. Some reports were positive, stating that he had taken over companies doing poorly and fixed them up by firing some excess staff and improving productivity. Then there were some negative reports about him having bought companies merely to strip them of their assets, fire the majority of staff and simply dump what remained of the company for a profit.

My gaze came back to David, who sat behind an enormous desk, with an 'in' tray to his left, an 'out' tray to his right and a 'pending' tray in the centre. Immediately in front of him was a pile of papers he was currently working on. On the wall behind him were photo portraits of his male ancestors. A stern-looking great-grandfather, a formally attired grandfather and his father dressed in a modern business suit with a serious business-like expression were the images of what I gathered were David's inspiration.

He stood up, came around his desk to face me and offered his hand in friendship. He told me he was very busy at the moment and could only spare me a few minutes, as Ann closed the door behind her leaving us alone. I could tell he was uncomfortable with my presence.

I noticed he was dressed in a dark blue suit, white shirt and red tie. He had removed his coat, rolled up his sleeves to his elbows and loosened his tie. This made me feel a little more comfortable, because I was wearing blue jeans and a short-sleeved, colourful shirt open at the neck. It was after all a sunny, early summer Saturday morning and I had been expecting to go on a picnic with him later that day.

He indicated with an extended hand for me to sit with him on the lounge. I sat on a chair on one side of the coffee table and he on the other. He asked if I would like a coffee, and I replied that I had just finished a cup of tea. He went on to say he had married Sarah and that they had two children, both boys, and I told him Sarah had already told me. He said Clarissa had married and divorced, that she had a drug problem and that her mother was in a hospital somewhere. Something to do with her liver, he added. He also said that Clarissa had become very active in the women's movement.

'Oh, I'm sorry to hear about her misfortune. She was always interested in women's liberation, so it's logical that she would seek fulfilment through its promotion rather than more traditional avenues. I hope she can find happiness in the new values she espouses, but I have my doubts,' I replied.

I told David about Toby, and he said he hadn't heard about it. It was then that I realised how none of us were ever really a part of David's world. Our worlds had simply collided because of Vietnam.

We slipped into an awkward silence, before David finally spoke up. 'Well, how are things with you?'

I shrugged my shoulders. 'Okay,' I said, looking down at his pilot's watch.

He noticed that I was staring at his watch. 'Vietnam wasn't all bad, eh?' he said, leaning forward and tapping me on the upper part of my arm. Then he noticed I didn't have my watch. 'What happened to yours?' he asked.

'I sold it,' I replied, matter-of-factly. I didn't tell him that I had sold it to buy some sessions with a psychiatrist.

'Are you working?' David asked, with some concern in his voice.

'No.'

'I can get you a job,' he said. 'A friend owes me a favour. It's not much, understand, but it's a job.'

'That's all right, David. I make out all right on my own.'

'Oh,' he whispered. Then, leaned back in his chair and placed his hands behind his head, 'What do you want then, Jason?'

'I don't know. I'd like to get myself together, and I thought seeing you might help me do that.'

'What do you mean? I don't understand what you mean by "get yourself together".'

'I don't know, David. Something's wrong and I can't fix it. It's hard to explain. Don't you feel it?'

'No,' he answered. 'I'm happy with my life. I'm doing the things I always wanted to do. Everything's fine.'

'Um ...'

'Jason, can I be frank?'

'Yes, of course.'

'At heart, you are a good person, Jason. It's just that you were misled by unscrupulous politicians with jingoistic slogans.'

'Oh, is that right? And what about the shouting of slogans at protest rallies? What was that, a rational examination of the facts?' I replied, trying to be impartial but feeling myself slip into annoyance. 'Or were they following the jingoistic slogans of the communist leadership in Russia.?

'I suppose there was political sloganeering on both sides, but you wanted it too easy. You wanted someone else to make the decisions and solve the problems for you. You always wanted to be left alone to live your life without ever having to trouble yourself about the important issues.'

'Do you really think so?' I asked.

He didn't answer me. He just nodded his head, so after a short pause I went on.

'I suppose you have a point,' I replied in a conciliatory tone.

'As I remember it, I did say that I wanted to live life and worry about the why later. As far as the important issue of the war was concerned, however, I seem to remember that we were sent in to do a job that the overwhelming majority of people in Australia at the time wanted us to do. It wasn't just the politicians who encouraged us. For me, it was the patriotic thing to do and a noble thing to support the freedom of the South Vietnamese people and the liberty of the Australian people, not something I was just going to let happen to me. I didn't simply respond to jingoistic slogans. I studied it a lot and thought it out for myself. I believed in the just cause of the war, in the defence of liberty.'

'But your thinking wasn't clear, was it? You got it all wrong, didn't you. South Vietnam was never a liberal democracy. It was simply a corrupt military dictatorship.'

'I don't think the South Vietnam government had a monopoly on corruption, and they did hold elections.'

'Which only produced more military dictators. Why won't you accept that you were wrong?'

'Was I? Didn't the communists win after we left? Didn't the South Vietnamese people lose their liberty?'

'You still don't get it do you, mate,' he said bitterly, standing up and pacing up and down. 'You'll never learn. The people and government of Australia changed their minds about the war, because the protesters pointed out the stupidity of it.'

'And the protesters' views became important because of the media coverage they got, and the Australian public eventually accepted the communist narrative of the war,' I replied, feeling hurt. 'And we got caught in the middle.'

'Have you forgotten about My Lai? How can you justify that? After that, the protests gained a lot more support.'

'My Lai was an abomination, and those responsible for it were war criminals, just like those responsible for the massacres conducted by the NVA and the Viet Cong were also war criminals. Have you forgotten about Hue? Why didn't the protesters ever mention the 2,800 civilians massacred by the communists in Hue? Remember the mass graves we uncovered after the communist occupation of Hue during the TET Offensive? My Lai was inexcusable, but it was not on the same scale as Hue. And what about the thousands of innocent South Vietnamese civilians the communists killed in pursuit of their war against the South? Why didn't the protesters ever condemn the communists for that in the same way they condemned us?'

'So, two wrongs make a right?'

'I didn't say that. What I am saying is there was no balance, no fair-minded approach in either the protesters' outrage or the media's coverage of it. It was all one-sided and their analysis was shallow. They used My Lai to condemn us, but not Hue to condemn the communists. They condemned us for the loss of civilian lives but not the communists for exactly the same thing – just like you have done now. You were quick to mention My Lai but not Hue. Besides, Australian troops never committed any massacres in Vietnam. Like all ideas that are not exposed to opposing views, they solidified into prejudice and bigotry.'

'But isn't that what you did, Jason? Didn't you harden your ideas against the protesters without listening to their ideas?'

'I did listen to their ideas. I am willing to admit that My Lai was an abomination, and that our strategy in waging the war was wrong. What I am not willing to admit, however, is that our allowing communism to triumph over liberty will not have serious future consequences for our own liberty. The pernicious effect of communism will be felt in Australia for many years to come.'

He sat back down and stared directly into my eyes. 'Where are you going with this, Jason? I don't understand why you want to go over all this. The war is over, after all.'

I wanted to stop, but I had lost control of my ability to let it go.

'The protesters were lucky, weren't they, David? They made all the right moves, said all the right things and prevailed as morally superior to us. They made it seem like they wanted peace while we wanted war, which was never true. We wanted peace too, but not at any price. We were not willing to sacrifice liberty to communism.'

I hesitated to continue, knowing my next comment would be offensive, but believing it had to be said.

'You were a part of that lie, too, David. You joined them in condemning those of us who supported the war without admitting that we wanted peace too. The only trouble was that by making yourself look good, you made the rest of us – those you served with – look bad.'

'What? That's crazy! Are you paranoid or something?'

He shouted, his eyes continuing to engage mine. I was a little shocked by David's emotional outburst and his assessment of me, but I realised I had accused him of betraying us.

'Probably,' I eventually said. 'The protesters and those who supported them made me that way. While we were fighting, some Australians were offering aid and comfort to our enemy without consequence or censure. Even our own government, who had sent us there in the first place, betrayed us. Remember Jim Cairns and the 70,000 who joined him in his Vietnam moratorium protest rally on the streets of Melbourne? Why wouldn't some of us become paranoid? Who could we trust?'

'The bulk of protesters were never part of giving aid to the communists. I was never part of that. I don't feel any guilt about the Vietnam War, and it was the war that made you blokes look bad, not me, nor Jim Cairns for that matter.'

'But you did associate with them, didn't you, David? By doing that, their cause became your cause too. But you'll never recognise that because you're entrenched in that high moral ground of yours. You can't afford to give an inch, because then you'd have to admit that you deserted us and the people of South Vietnam, and it's too comfortable where you are now, isn't it?'

He looked up at me again, but this time his eyes revealed his anger. He stiffened his posture and replied strenuously, 'You said you came to me looking for help, but you obviously can't let go of your entrenched notions about the nobility of fighting for the freedom of South Vietnam – such a stupid position to hold. You still don't realise that the Vietnam War was a civil war, not some drummed-up notion about freedom and democracy. You have to let go of your obsession. You just have to move on and forget. Don't you understand, that the war is over now.'

For the first time there was a hint of anger in his tone. I knew I had gone too far with my personal attack, but I wasn't about to let it go. I shifted my position, pulling myself closer to David, while rubbing the palms of my hands on my jeans.

'Calling the Vietnam War a civil war does not negate the political dimensions of the conflict. The Roman civil war was a struggle between imperial and republican forces over the political future of Rome, the American Civil War was a struggle between republican Union forces and Confederate forces over the political future of America, and the Vietnam War was a struggle between communist forces and republican forces over the political future of Vietnam. All civil wars are fought over the political future of the people involved. You may call the Vietnam War a civil war, but it was still a conflict over the political future of the country, a struggle between liberty and communism.'

'But that's the whole point!' he shouted. 'We were never fighting for the political future of Vietnam, only the communists were fighting for that. What we were fighting for was to hold the line against communist expansion, and that meant keeping Vietnam divided. Not only were we fighting against the forces of communism but also the sentiments of Vietnam's national identity. The longing of the Vietnamese people for a united Vietnam.' He stopped and looked at me, waiting for his words to take effect. 'Our strategy of body counts was never going to work.'

'I agree with you that our strategy was flawed,' I replied, trying to pacify the situation. 'You are right about that, but that only means that we should have changed it. Nixon did that, but Congress scuttled his victory. And you are right about us wanting to keep Vietnam divided. Maybe we should have attempted to reunite Vietnam by bringing democracy to all of Vietnam.'

'Really, Jason? Do you actually think the Americans were ever willing to do that? You do realise that would have involved us in a much wider war, one involving not just North Vietnam with Russian support but also China as well. Remember how the Chinese intervened in Korea once we had taken North Korea. Do you think our political leaders were ever willing to risk triggering a war like that? Perhaps even a nuclear holocaust? Clearly, they were never willing to risk such an expansion of the war, and that's why we should never have got involved in the first place. You can't bluff your way to victory in a war.'

There was a pause in our discussion, while I regained my composure, then offered a measured response. 'And that's why it will be difficult, if not impossible, to win future wars fought in defence of our liberty with our current strategy. We impose politically generated rules of engagement on our military, which means it will always get bogged down and erode the will of our people to fight and the resolve of our politicians to continue with an unpopular war. Also, I think you are overlooking how the North Vietnamese were able to halt the Chinese advance into North Vietnam in 1979, and the Chinese did not use their nuclear weapons against Vietnam. If the Vietnamese were able to do that, why would we not have been able to do the same with our superior firepower?'

'But, Jason, what you are suggesting is a receipt for escalation. All that would have achieved would have been a much larger conflict, involving millions more engaged in another world war, not to mention the danger of triggering a nuclear war.'

'Yes, yes, I can see that and I agree with you. That would be a possibility, and our leaders were never willing to take that risk. However, I need to point out that the Vietnam War ended when North Vietnam invaded South Vietnam, so the communists were never worried about widening the war. Nor were they worried about triggering a nuclear holocaust. That shows the depth of their commitment compared with ours and, unless we are willing to match the depth of their commitment with our own, we will eventually lose our liberty, and I would hope none of us would want that.'

David was speechless, a look of incredulity covered his face. 'Didn't you hear anything that I just said?' he replied bitterly while shaking his head.

I wasn't making any headway, so I had to offer something more. 'After the Paris Peace Accord was signed by both North and South Vietnam,' I offered, 'we only had to keep supplying the South with replacement arms and equipment. We were no longer fighting there, so we could have held the line without widening the war.'

David became irate. 'Not only is your thinking impractical it is also dangerous, because we all knew that the peace accord was never going to work. The Russians were building a greater military force in the North than what the South was maintaining. It was only a matter of time before the North invaded the South.'

'That's what I don't understand, David, how casually the protesters accepted North Vietnam's lack of good faith in signing the peace accord. The protesters had been determined to achieve peace, but were not angry at North Vietnam for breaking the peace accord. Why? Why didn't they condemn the communists for breaking the peace accord they had all worked so hard to achieve? Why didn't *you* speak up for the people of South Vietnam by supporting the peace accord? Seems to me their agenda was never really about peace at all. What they actually wanted all along was a communist victory over liberty.'

We lapsed into silence. David seemed unable, or unwilling, to answer my question, so I continued, 'Wouldn't a bombing campaign against the invasion have stopped the North?'

'Well, that would have got us back into the conflict again. Remember, we were trying to end the war, not prolong it.' David rolled his eyes, reflecting his growing exasperation.

'I don't think that would have re-engaged us in the war. It would have been just a bombing campaign, after all, and it would have demonstrated that we were still determined to protect South Vietnam's liberty. Remember the Americans still had the 7th Fleet in the South China Sea and the B-52 bombers at U-Tapao Airfield in Thailand and Andersen Air Force base in Guam. They could have ended the North's invasion in a matter of days, like the Israelis did in the Six-Day War against the invading Arab armies in 1967, then let the South Vietnamese army regroup and drive the remnants of the invading force out of their country.'

I paused for a moment, trying to gather my thoughts, while waiting for David's reply.

He sat in silence, then shook his head. 'But it would have prolonged the war, Jason, and more people would have died.'

'So, the bloody aftermath of the Vietnam War conducted by the communists against the people of South-east Asia was worth ending the war for, was it? Don't you have any remorse for what happened in Vietnam and Cambodia after we left? Don't you feel any guilt for their suffering? And please don't try to tell me that the war against communism has finished. Do you think that will stop now, now that communism has triumphed over liberty? At some time in the future, we will be called upon to defend our liberty against the evil of communist dictatorship. Only next time, it will be closer to home.'

'What happened after the war was a consequence of the war itself. The communists did what they did because of the war.'

'That's a cop-out, David, and you know it! We are all responsible for the actions we take, and the communists are responsible for the misery inflicted on the South Vietnamese and Cambodian people. Besides, executions, purges and human suffering always follow a communist victory. Even a cursory acquaintance with history tells you that.'

David shook his head and pursed his lips, a look of incredulity crossing his face. I was determined to offer some argument that did not involve the sacrifice of liberty to communism, while at the same time placating David's anger.

'What about the domino theory that President Kennedy believed in? He believed in peace through strength, his "pay any price, bear any burden" speech encouraged our generation to take up the fight for liberty against communism, and his passionate appeal for freedom and peace was the driving force behind our involvement, that and our government's belief in the forward defence policy. Wasn't that why we were fighting the communists in Vietnam? Didn't we want to confront communism before it arrived on our doorstep?'

David gave me a cold stare; he had reached the end of his patience with me. He waved his hand in dismissal of my argument, clicked his tongue and replied, 'The domino theory was a load of nonsense. Look, Jason, I don't intend to sit here and re-litigate the Vietnam War with you. Frankly, it's a waste of my time and, if you were serious about getting on with your life, it would be a waste of your time too.'

He stood up and walked back to his desk. I followed and stood in front of it with my arms hanging limp by my side. I stared at the corner of the room where the floor met two walls. My argument had run out. I had nothing left to say. I had become an embarrassment to everyone, even myself. All the virtues and values I had tried to live by had crumbled in the face of David's rejection of my argument. His views had triumphed, while mine had died with the fall of Saigon.

I lifted my head and looked at him. He sat there, waiting

for me to say something, but I couldn't stop my mind from racing on. I couldn't accept that my continued thinking about the Vietnam War was a waste of time. Something still seemed wrong about the way it had ended. It was no good pretending that it didn't happen or that it didn't matter. It had happened, and we did not know what consequences it might have for Australia's future security. I lifted my head further and stared at the ceiling, hoping to gather some inspiration.

I knew I was being difficult, but I would hold out for the things I truly believed in. In my heart, I believed that liberty and democracy were infinitely better than communism and the dictatorship that accompanied it, and that we should stand by and support those who were willing to fight for their freedom. But I also recognised that we should not make promises to people that we could not keep, and that we needed to recognise how fragile our own liberty was without American support.

It was clear to me that Americans were no longer willing to accept President Kennedy's patriotic appeal to protect liberty at any cost. The casualties and material costs had proved too great. Their support had limits, and that made it necessary for those countries who supported liberty to take this into account. The idea that America would go to war in every country where liberty was under challenge was now not only unreasonable but no longer viable.

However, if America, and by extension its allies, were forced to go to war in the future, we had to know what victory looked like before we committed, and accept that the war would have to entail a clear military mission that was achievable in a reasonably short period by carrying out whatever methods were needed to defeat communism. It needed to be understood by all those involved that once our mission was accomplished, our commitment would end. We could not engage in nation building ever again. Providing civil aid to a country during times of peace is one thing; engaging in nation building during times of war is something entirely different – it doesn't work. It proved too costly both in terms of blood and resources and we did not have the resolve to see it through. Once our military mission is complete, the people whose liberty we defend must be willing to accept their responsibility to defend their own liberty.

At the same time, it is no longer good enough for us to change our minds during the conflict and simply throw up our hands and say, 'Oh well, we did our best,' and walk away, because the consequences of doing that are too horrendous for those we leave behind, and our loss of credibility too detrimental for our own future. Clearly, we needed to be more circumspect about going to war against communism, but also cognisant of the communist desire for, and commitment to, world domination.

If our commitment to liberty were weakened in the future, would the communists be able to align themselves with the political and economic elite of liberal democracies and bring about another major challenge to our liberty, like Karl Marx had predicted? Such a catastrophe would make defending our liberty exceptionally difficult, particularly if we continued to hold a moral objection to resisting communist expansion until it threatened our way of life and our borders. I knew that David had been willing to sacrifice the liberty of millions of South Vietnamese, so I wondered what he would be willing to have others sacrifice in the future, and what accommodation he would be willing to make with the communists if he could watch his millions grow into billions. Perhaps Marx was right; perhaps capitalist greed would sow the seeds of its own destruction.

I saw clearly that what was needed was a recommitment to the values and principles of liberty underpinning liberal democracy and a rejection of communist ideology. I couldn't help but recall Thomas Jefferson's famous warning to the American people following their success in the American War of Independence – "the price of liberty is eternal vigilance" – and I wondered if, in the future, we would be eternally vigilant in our defence of liberty.

With these conclusions in mind, I refocused my attention on David. He sat in front of me. A look of bored, uninterested impatience clearly displayed on his face. I realised there was no sense in continuing this discussion with him, as he and those who thought like him had triumphed and they would never change their minds now. What was worse, however, was that they would forever dismiss me as a warmonger and, whenever I raised the threat to Australian society of creeping, pernicious communism, they would mockingly reply, 'Careful, Jason, there's a red under your bed'. I had experienced this all before and had learnt to remain silent. I had not expected to feel this way after my visit with David.

'Sarah's got a picnic lunch for us. She'll be waiting,' I said finally, trying to change the subject, because, like David, I had concluded that it was a waste of time for us to continue, as neither of us would ever find common ground. I had thought David would understand what I was going through, but he had no concept of my internal struggle. From David's point of view, I was a loser and, in his highly competitive world, losers are never right or even worthy of understanding or respect.

'I know,' he said, a note of finality in his voice, 'I'd like to come, but I really can't get away. You go, though. Sarah is looking forward to seeing you again. Tell her I'm sorry and I'll make it up to her another time.'

'Thanks for seeing me,' I replied, as he picked up the piece of paper he had been working on when I had arrived. He obviously didn't hear me, for his mind had already refocused on the urgent issues at hand. For a brief moment, I envied him his dedication to the life he had created for himself, but then I realised that his success had been built upon a relentless pursuit of wealth accumulation and an overwhelming fear of failure. To make more money was the sole driving force behind his life's primary goal. I wondered what other life achievements he had been willing to sacrifice for this objective.

*

Sarah stood as I approached. She put out her hands and smiled, and I took her hands in mine and smiled back.

'It's good to see you, Jason,' she said, offering her cheek to me.

I kissed it lightly. We separated and I noticed she was dressed in a brightly coloured blouse and clean white slacks. Her face was as attractive as I had remembered, only now it had acquired a maturity borne from her motherhood.

'You look lovely.'

'Thank you. Couldn't David make it?'

'No. He's sorry, but he'll make it up to you another time,' I replied.

'Yes,' she answered, and a faraway look came into her eyes. I felt she wanted to say something else, so I waited for her to go on. She refocused her attention on me.

'David is a good provider, Jason,' she uttered, and paused briefly before adding, 'I am grateful for that and respect the sacrifice he makes for our family.'

We sat down on the picnic blanket she had brought, and she served lunch, smiling and laughing gaily while making light conversation. Something about her made me relax and I laid back on my elbows. She had maintained that fresh innocence of her youth, yet the years had given her a confidence and understanding unspoiled by the disenchanted views of our generation.

We ate in silence, then she turned and asked, 'How have you been, Jason?'

'Oh, you know ...' I replied.

'It must be hard for you. For all of you who went to Vietnam, I suspect,' she continued.

'Yes.'

'Don't you want to talk about it? I know David never talks to me about it,' she asked.

'Not really. It's just that I don't know what to say. What do you want to know?'

'What you're feeling,' she said.

'Vietnam's a part of my life now,' I said. 'The war ended in '75 when Saigon fell, but the war inside me won't go away.'

'What do you mean?'

'It's hard to say. When I talk about it, I get the feeling that I'm using Vietnam as a cop-out, and that people don't actually want to know what I'm going through. All they really want to do is correct my thinking. That's why I don't talk about it much.'

'I don't think you're copping out, and I won't try to correct your thinking, whatever that is. I'd just like to know, that's all,' she said earnestly.

'There's really not much I want to say about Vietnam, Sarah. After all, the war's over and we all have to live with the consequences. It's better if we don't talk about it.'

I realised that if I told her my thoughts and feelings about Vietnam, it might unsettle her marriage since David's view was so different from mine.

'Oh, all right, Jason. Vietnam was a silly time for us all. What do you want to talk about?'

'You and your family. You have two children now. I suppose they keep you very busy.'

'Oh, yes. I have little time for myself. I'm usually doing something with the house, or something with the children.'

David's words echoed back to me from the past: 'every human relationship has a dominant partner and a submissive one'. I looked at Sarah and said nothing. *David had achieved everything he had wanted from life*, I thought. For me, it was more a thought of fact rather than one of envy. Knowing how little I had achieved in my life left me happy for someone who had filled his life with the things he desired most.

Sarah looked up into the clear, blue sky and took a deep breath. I don't know whether she was deciding to share with me the usual face she exposed to everyone or trying to decide how best to reveal what she truly thought. She lowered her gaze, and our eyes engaged. I concentrated on what she went on to tell me. She started telling me all about her children, their diet and health, their challenges and aspirations, their personalities and potential, their supportive peer group. Her eyes lit up, and her expression became earnest and concerned. She smiled and spoke with such an intricate knowledge of their every need that I was left astonished by the depth of her understanding, compassion and commitment.

Clearly, Sarah was raising two healthy, intelligent, well-adjusted children, who could look forward to a bright, successful future as a result of the prudent lifestyle that their parents had chosen for themselves. *How lucky Sarah's children are to have such a dedicated and loving mother, and a hardworking, capable father in their lives*, I thought. *They truly are privileged.* Theirs was a privilege based not on discrimination but rather the values and principles their parents chose to live their lives by. I remembered what Mill had said about one's liberty: the right to freely choose comes with consequences for which individuals must hold themselves personally responsible. It is not society's place to right the wrongs of individual free choice.

The more I thought about it the more I had to admit that Sarah was happy and contented. Undoubtedly, she was doing the things in her life she felt were important, and this had given her a dignity that eluded me. She clearly saw those things she valued most in her life and had dedicated herself to them. Her dedication was closer to the natural order of things than mine ever was. Looking back, it seemed to me that the more I had engaged in the intellectual pursuit of understanding life, the further I had ventured down the rabbit hole of politics. This had given me an enlightened view of the importance of liberty in my life, but it had distanced me from my more natural, common sense wisdom. Combining an intellectual and common sense approach might have given me a better balance to and understanding of other possible fulfilments in my life, like taking on the rewarding responsibility of a family, as Sarah and David had done. They both had followed their intuition, and this now had bought love and contentment into their lives. This was something I had striven for but had never achieved. Perhaps if Wu Sing had survived ... No, I couldn't follow that train of thought. It only led to more suffering and depression.

This left me wondering who was exploiting whom in Sarah's relationship with David, or maybe there was no exploitation in their relationship at all. Maybe Sarah just cooperated with David to get the things she valued most from life, while David did the same. Then I pondered how much of David's domination would have lost its edge owing to Sarah's caring and compassionate nature. It surely must have had some impact on him. I couldn't see how David's conclusions all those years ago, about one partner being dominant, could have held up in his marriage. But, then again, would David come to believe that Sarah was just like his mother, having sacrificed herself for the benefits of his money and social standing? Would he turn away from Sarah in future and look for comfort somewhere else?

A magpie descended and stood looking at me. I looked back at it, and it hopped closer to me and gave me a light chirp. I broke off a piece of my sandwich and threw it at him. He snatched it and swallowed it, then gave out a hearty, melodious tune. I smiled and threw him another piece, then other birds descended to make up a small gathering.

'You will attract a lot more birds if you keep that up,' Sarah warned me.

'That's okay. Did you bring enough?'

'Oh, yes. I brought enough for three, so there is a lot left over.' She took out more sandwiches and began separating the fillings from the bread.

'I think they will eat the tomato slices, and the magpies will eat the meat fillings,' I pointed out.

'How silly of me,' she said, placing the fillings beside the empty slices of bread.

I started to feed the gathering, which attracted more birds, both large and small. Sarah started to feed them and laughed in delight at the happy scene we had created. Then the larger birds started to chase the smaller birds from the gathering. Sarah frowned and sighed deeply. She stopped feeding them and stared in disappointment at the newly emerging unfair scene.

'Throw larger pieces closer in where the large birds are and throw smaller pieces further out to the smaller birds, and don't throw a piece at a time. Get a handful and scatter them around when you throw,' I advised.

She did as I had told her. 'That worked well, Jason,' she said, a smile returning to her face. Then she paused and sighed again. 'Society's a lot like that, isn't it? The larger, more powerful get all the big pieces while the smaller, weaker ones get the smaller portions.'

'Yes, but in a liberal democratic society there is social mobility. The smaller can become bigger through competence, ambition and hard work. It's a mistake to believe that the same people occupy the same positions in a liberal society throughout their lives. Only those who don't want to compete or are incapable of competing are stuck in the same level throughout their lives.'

'That's interesting. Go on.'

'Well, in times past, civilisations survived on strength and power alone, so the biggest and strongest members were the more powerful. In recent times, however, becoming a member of the hierarchy of modern civilisations is based more upon competency, ambition and hard work than size and strength.'

'I guess that's right. Clarissa's parents started with little but became rich and powerful and took more of the big pieces.'

'Yes, that's right. They did.' I waited for Sarah to continue because she seemed to have more to say.

'But what about those who inherit their wealth? What about David who inherited his wealth and my father who inherited his family business? What about people like that?'

'They won't keep it for long if they don't exercise competency, ambition and work hard to keep it, like David, and I guess your father was the same. Remember, a liberal society is in a constant state of social flux with members constantly rising and falling.'

'Well, that's certainly true with regards to David. He works hard, and he certainly is competent and ambitious. My father was like that as well, maybe not as driven as David, but the same, nonetheless. My mother, on the other hand, inherited her wealth from Dad after he died, and she has lost much of it.'

We fell into silence and continued feeding the birds. Sarah looked up at me again and frowned in contemplation.

'But, Jason, what about those who can't or don't have the capacity to compete? Do they have a place too, or do we just ignore them because they don't contribute as much?

'That's the real shortfall of a modern liberal society – what to do with people who fall outside the parameters of its competence hierarchy. After all, it's not much good giving equal opportunity to people who are unequal.'

'Well,' Sarah insisted, 'What do you suggest we do about them?'

'Umm ... let me see. I guess those who are intellectually challenged should not be expected to compete with who are not. Logically, then, modern liberal societies should assist those who fall into this category. That doesn't mean they should become totally dependent on society. I'm sure there are some things they could contribute but not enough to make themselves self-reliant, so they should be assisted. Otherwise, they would fall into poverty and homelessness, and that is something that a wealthy, empathetic society should strive to alleviate. Do you agree?'

'That's good, Jason. I believe that too. And the disabled, they can't become self-reliant.'

'That's right. Anyone who is physically challenged falls into this category. We can't expect people with disabilities to compete the same with those who are not. Then there are others who happen to go through a crisis in their lives and find themselves unable to compete. Some need temporary assistance while others more long-term support, like when someone is temporarily unemployed, goes through a divorce, suffers a debilitating accident or experiences a mental breakdown. Then there are those who retire after a lifetime of hard work and find themselves unable to sustain themselves. They obviously cannot compete on the same level as the young and fit, so they will need assistance as well.'

I paused for a brief moment while thinking about what I had said.

'These are the people who need society's assistance. Anyone else, however, can, and should, compete within the hierarchy. All anyone needs in a modern society is a skill for which someone else is prepared to pay, and a modern society should help its members acquire such skills. That's what universities and technical colleges are designed to provide, so it's important that they should be available to all those who qualify for entrance, and society should help everyone to qualify. Beyond that, it is up to the individuals living in a liberal democracy to provide for themselves.'

'Yes, all that makes sense. I think Australia would be a better country if it adopted those ideas. What about discrimination, though? Should something be done about that too?'

'Surely that is taken care of by the existence of equal opportunity. All members of society who can compete should be granted equal opportunity to acquire positions within the hierarchy based solely on effort and merit. Other than that, I don't think society has a role to rig the game in favour of any individual over another. In my opinion, government welfare should be based on individual need, not group identity like sex, race or gender. Otherwise, taxpayers will be forced to give welfare to some individuals who do not need it.'

I looked into Sarah's eyes, and they were aglow with understanding, so I went on.

'Any attempt to adjust the scales for one person over another will erode the society's competitiveness, because people will be put into jobs for which they are not as qualified or as competent to perform as someone else. It clearly would create a less competitive society with resentment and recrimination between the individuals within it, as all forms of discrimination does. If society wants an individual to achieve a higher position in its hierarchy, then help him or her become more competitive and achieve it through his or her own individual effort, but don't give a reward where it is not deserved.'

'That's good, Jason. You have given me much to think about.'

We sat quietly, drifting into a comfortable silence while contemplating the ideas that had passed between us. We also ran out of food for the birds, so they eventually flew off in search of better opportunity elsewhere, much like competitive, competent individuals would do if they lived in in an uncompetitive society that discriminated in favour of the less competent over the more competent.

I laid back on the blanket Sarah had bought for the picnic and smelt the rich aroma of freshly cut lawn. A cool breeze came up from the river, cooling the shade of the large evergreen tree we shared. My belly was full of the nutritious food Sarah had provided for me. I sighed with delight in the luxury of my circumstances while enjoying the lyrical call of distant birds. A sense of quiet gratitude filled my being.

We drifted into small talk until it was time for Sarah to collect her children from her mother and return home to prepare the evening meal.

'Mother has changed so much, Jason,' she said. 'Since she has lost much of her wealth and good looks, men are not that interested in her anymore. She has shed her modern views about sexual promiscuity and adopted the more traditional views that Father had. She has become interested in her grandsons and teaches them the value of hard work and family. That's why I trust her with my children.'

'I see. That's good for you and your children, then.'

'Yes. Mother helps me in many ways now. I am grateful for everything she does for me.'

We rose, and she packed the picnic basket while I folded the blanket, then we walked to her car. As she was getting into her car, she stopped and said, 'Oh! Jason, I almost forgot.' She opened her bag and took out a crumpled piece of paper that had been ironed flat. 'Clarissa asked me to give you this.'

I looked down on the poem I had written for her in the unsullied days of younger times.

'She wrote her address and phone number on the back,'

Sarah continued. 'She said you can call her, or go and see her, anytime you want. I hope you don't mind, but I read the poem you wrote. It's very good.'

'Thank you, but I wrote that a long time ago. Clarissa and I have a shared history that ended badly. In times of strong disagreement, the disappointment we felt towards each other would resurface. No, the time for Clarissa and me has passed. It could never be the same. You can't sustain a relationship that's built upon last goodbyes; the emotional cost is just too high.'

'Oh. Well, why don't you just see her as a friend? She did tell me that she would like to see you.'

'As a friend?' I queried, a smile highlighting the corners of my mouth. 'Maybe, maybe we could be friends.'

'Remember, Jason.' Sarah said, getting into her car. 'David and I are your friends too, as well as Clarissa.'

*

When I returned to the boarding house in Kew where I was renting a room, Dad was there waiting to greet me. *Funny how everything happens at once*, I thought. *You go for weeks, even months, and nothing happens, then in one day so much happens.*

'Hello, Dad,' I said. 'What are you doing here?'

'I came to see you, Jason. Your mother and I are very concerned for your safety.'

'Where is Mum?' I asked.

'She didn't come down, but both your mother and I want you back home with us. Can we go somewhere private to talk?'

'Sure. Come up to my room.'

On entering my room, I sat on the bedside and motioned for Dad to sit in the chair near it.

'What's this all about, Dad?'

'Well, it's your letters for one thing. They don't sound like you, and they are getting fewer and fewer. And there's all this news about how many of you boys from the Vietnam War are suicidal. I'm not going home without you, Jason. I want you well, son, well and back home with me and your mother.'

'I'm all right, Dad. Really.'

'No, you're not, Jason. I know when you are all right, and this behaviour is not right for you. Tell me, son, tell me what's troubling you. Is it the war? Are you having trouble putting it behind you?'

'Yes, Dad. I am having trouble putting the war behind me,' I said sarcastically.

'I thought as much,' he said, untroubled by my sarcasm. 'I felt much the same when I came home ...'

I don't know why it broke at that time. Perhaps it was the soft, caring tone in Dad's voice, or the fact David had bought the anger inside me about Vietnam to the surface. Whatever the reason, I had to let it out, and I hoped that, whatever I said, Dad would be understanding.

'Oh, is that right, Dad? Tell me how hard it was for you to come home. Tell me all about how you had to hide from everyone that you were a returned serviceman. How you had to endure so many Australians calling you a baby killer who burnt down villagers' huts?'

I stopped and looked up at the ceiling, before continuing.

'So many back home believed all we did in Vietnam was ride around in helicopters and listen to rock 'n' roll music. Some even had the notion that we deliberately killed innocent civilians and children. So, go on, Dad, why don't you tell me? Tell me how silly I am for feeling this way. Tell me how hard it was for you to rejoin a society that welcomed you home as a victorious hero who had saved them from invasion.'

I shook with anger and wanted to shout at Dad about the pain I felt, but I couldn't. I couldn't put it into words; words escaped me. So, I just sat there, looking helpless.

Dad stood up and came over to me. He pulled me to my feet, and laid my head against his chest, holding me like that, stroking my hair until I stopped shaking.

I was surprised that he had done that because he had never hugged me before. It felt a little awkward at first, but then a surge of gratitude swept through me and I wanted to stay in his embrace for as long as I could.

Then he said, 'I'm sorry, son, sorry for what you are going through. Please let me help you. I do know what war can do to you, but you are right to tell me that I don't know about the suffering you boys are going through at home. It's true that we never experienced that.' We sat back down on the bed together, then he continued. 'Now that you have started opening up to me, please continue, son. I'm listening.'

'All right, Dad. Since you asked, I find it very difficult to relate to people and things. You know, like there's something sour inside me.'

He nodded his head, a look of concern in his eyes. It was his concern that made me go on.

'I keep having these nightmares, Dad,' I said, wrapping my arms around myself. 'I can't stop them ... they're awful ... about the young man I killed and Nick and Toby and Wu Sing ... it's ... it's just awful.' I began rocking back and forth.

'Tell me about them, Jason. It might help,' he said, putting his hand on my shoulder.

'I don't know, Dad. It's so hard for me to talk about it. I think you'll think I'm weak, not capable of facing up to life.'

'I would never think that, son. I want to know what you are suffering from. Please tell me about your dreams. It might help me understand.'

I stopped rocking, closed my eyes and nodded. After opening my eyes, I clasped my hands between my knees and began.

'First, the young man I killed haunts me – the innocence of his dying face as it slowly sinks into the muddy water. Then there's Nick. He stands before me, his arms stretched forward. He's beckoning me to him. His face has lost its colour, and his eyes are glazed over. I want to go to him, but I can't. I'm stuck in the one spot ... frozen ... unable to move ... I'm sorry, Dad. I shouldn't burden you with all this.'

He stood up in front of me again and put both his hands on my shoulders. 'Go on,' he said. 'Let it out, Jason. It's all right. I want to know.'

I nodded my head. 'Nick fades and Toby takes his place. Toby used to laugh so much ... and then the suicide ... I couldn't help him ... How could I stop him? Now he wants to come to me, but we're both frozen in our places. He smiles but then his face twists up, he opens his mouth and maggots crawl out.'

I stopped talking and looked at Dad. My eyes pleaded for understanding, as concern crossed his face.

'Tell me about Wu Sing,' he said. 'I want to know it all, son. Now that you have started, let it all out.'

'My beautiful Wu Sing. Wu Sing ... so sad ... We were going to be married ... I loved her so much, but the war killed her ... the war I was a part of. In my dream, I see her lying on the ground with bullet holes in her ... blood everywhere. She's crying and trying to crawl towards me, but she never reaches me ... she's crawling but she stays in the same place … and I can't move to her … and she keeps calling my name. Whichever dream I have, they all end the same way. I wake up, and I'm shaking and wet with sweat, and my heart is racing.'

I choked on my words and looked away, tears welling in my eyes.

'Oh, Jason, I'm so sorry,' he said, placing his hands under my elbows and helping me to my feet again. He took my head and placed it on his shoulder, stroking my hair and rocking me gently in his arms. I put my arms around him and sobbed.

'You need help, Jason. You must see a psychiatrist,' he said.

'I've already tried that, but they're too expensive and I can't afford the drugs they prescribe. Somehow, I have to learn to live with it, but it's always there with me. I can't run from it. I can't hide from it. Wherever I go, it's there with me.'

He lifted my head with his hands and looked into my eyes. 'Somewhere in all that is the source of your pain and the source of your cure,' he said. 'You've got to find out what that Vietnamese soldier and Nick and Toby and Wu Sing want.'

'Is it them, Dad, or my own guilt? I can't come to terms with having killed another human being, and I know that I let so many others down – all of them – and I can't let them go. I feel so guilty about everything. It consumes me, Dad. No matter where I go or what I do, it's always there.'

Dad let go, and we stood apart, but our eyes continued to engage.

'How did you let them down, Jason?'

'I don't know. I just did, and they haunt me.'

'I don't know what to say, Jason. How can I help you?' he asked.

'I don't know, Dad. I can't even help myself.'

'Jason, I want you to know that I respect what all you blokes who went to Vietnam did for us, and I hope you can forgive me too.'

'Forgive you?' I asked, puzzled by his request.

'Yes. For not understanding what you were going through. I should have been there for you before this. Please forgive me. I thought you just needed time to adjust back into civilian street, but clearly your problems run much deeper than that.'

I looked at him in amazement. For the first time since returning from Vietnam, I felt someone understood. An immense feeling of relief followed by gratitude flowed through me. I don't know why but an image of Dad and me sitting in the backyard and him telling me about the palm tree leapt into my mind.

'You once told me that I needed to keep reaching out in life. Not to be afraid of taking on something new or different,' I said. 'Well, I think that's what I stopped doing, Dad. I shut myself off from my friends and my loved ones, and I stopped growing.'

'You can't shut out the whole world, Jason,' Dad explained. 'You've got to keep growing and reaching out for new and different things. There's a whole world of people out there, and they can all be reached in their own unique way, and every one of them can touch you in a special way. Don't give up on them, Jason. They can be your friends.'

A lifetime ago in the backyard of my youth, my father had first spoken those words to me, and I had recognised the wisdom in them, but I had not recognised the essence of their truth until now. My eyes had witnessed the suffering and physical abuse of this world, and my feelings were assaulted by the cruelty of personal loss and, in my pain and hurt, I had turned my back on humanity.

I watched the curtains in my room move gently to the cool afternoon breeze coming up from Port Phillip Bay and felt I was close to something of immense importance, as if I were dreaming. Something warm and beautiful was very close and, if I just reached out, I would be able to touch it.

'I need time to think, Dad. I want to take a drive and be alone with my thoughts,' I said. 'Do you mind if I leave now? Come back on Monday, and I'll go home with you.'

'Remember, Jason,' he said. 'Your mother and I are here for you. We love you and want you home with us. Please don't do anything harmful to yourself. Do I have your word on that?'

'Yes, Dad,' I said with conviction. 'Don't worry. I will come back home with you.'

*

That night, I drove south, going over in my mind everything that Dad had said to me that evening, how I would try to re-establish a life for myself. Further and further south I drove, leaving behind the towering steel and glass monuments glorifying modern Melbourne, past the turn-off to the Mornington Peninsula, into a more natural setting that beckoned me further on. Eventually, I stopped at Foster and booked into a motel, but I couldn't sleep that night. I kept thinking that something important was about to break, something I had been searching for during all these years of isolation and suffering.

Before sunrise, I got back into my car and drove down to Wilsons Promontory. When I stopped the car, I got out and walked the eastern side of the promontory. With the range behind me, I could see the sun breaking out at sea. I climbed to a high vantage point near the mouth of Tidal River and stood alone, overlooking the waters of Bass Strait as they broke upon the golden shoreline. I had gone as far as one could go on the Australian mainland. I could go no further. I thought about the waters breaking on the shores of Vung Tau peninsula. Ah, yes, Vietnam. The country that had impacted my life in so many profound ways. The Vietnam that had ended my closest friendships in the most brutal of ways, granted me the love of my life only to snatch it away so cruelly and made me a witness to the horror of war, the killing, the maiming and the destruction. I watched the waters of Tidal River returning home to the sea and wondered whether Wu Sing and Nick and Toby had returned home now that they had emptied into the unknown void. *Oh, God, where are you? Help me, Father, find the courage to endure, please.*

A summer storm broke out at sea and moved rapidly towards me. Suddenly, a sunburst broke through in patches behind the huge cloud that was the storm, illuminating the heavens above and lighting a sheet of shimmering silver where the raindrops beat a path towards me. It came dancing across the water's surface like a thousand wild horses at full gallop, thundering and beating at the water as it came. I shivered in anticipation of this great vision before me as it moved steadily in my direction. It was one of those revealing moments in life when time and vision crystallise into a truth beyond question, beyond the nuances of our earthly orb. I stretched out my hand in a vain attempt to touch its beauty. Ideas tumbled into my head in such profusion it was difficult to grasp them and give meaning to them.

It is the strength of spirit that really matters in this life. The desire, when you rise in the morning, to release the energy of your life force into the uncertainty of a new day, to show courage in the face of adversity and to endure the suffering you cannot avoid. This is the stuff of life, and it has nothing to do with money or synthetic morality but everything to do with what's inside you, and you either search for it in this life or you live without it.

Instantly, the vexations that had troubled my conscience lifted and a sensation of calm and peace descended upon me and surrounded me. I fell willingly into its warm embrace. Wu Sing came to me, not in a physical sense, but I felt her presence. She reached out to me and gently laid her hand on the side of my face as she had done so many times before. When she spoke softly to me, again not in a physical sense but rather through ideas formed lovingly in my mind, I felt the soothing sweetness of her presence rush through me once again.

'I am part of your yesterdays,' she seemed to say, 'and nothing will ever change the intensity of our shared moments, but yesterday is all that we can ever have, and all our yesterdays can never change the course of your today. Yesterday we shared, but today is yours alone to live, so with you, and you alone, lies the power of the present – the power to dream, to love, to believe – if only you have the courage and the strength to reach out for it.'

I took a deep breath, afraid of her leaving once again. *Please, Wu Sing, don't leave me. Please stay with me.*

In my mind, she smiled and continued. 'The time we shared was ours and ours alone, and we stumbled through life while trying to create order out of the chaos that surrounded us daily. But, always remember, the greatest gift you had to give was the very same love you rightly claimed from me, and now that I am gone, that gift lives on. Do not despair, my love, for you possess within you the strength of our shared love to carry you through the certain beauty of each new day. Fill each day with the hope of your heart, not the despair of your sorrow.'

Then the rain broke upon me, its huge drops soaking me in seconds and washing the heat and sweat from my body, as it had done for Wu Sing and me in what seemed like only yesterday. But this time, it also took away my pain and suffering and left my soul refreshed. The rain washed me clean.

'Oh, Wu Sing,' I whispered. 'I'm sorry ... so sorry.'

In my apology was the torment of conflicting ideas. I didn't know whether I was sorry for my country's betrayal or for my presence in a war that had taken her life. Either way, it had been Wu Sing and her people who had paid the price, for our certainty turned first to doubt then ultimately to betrayal. For the first time, I was sure she understood my torment and my suffering.

'The redemption you seek, my love, is not mine to give. That you have to find for yourself, and it cannot be found in what you do, or even in what you think,' she seemed to say. 'It goes much deeper than that. Look into your heart and the shared moments of our joy and the love that we freely gave each other and realise that we were privileged to have had those moments in our lives. If you let that be enough, contentment will follow.'

I took the necklace of boars' tusks from my neck and held it in my hand. Its primitive power had enabled me to tap the last dregs of my courage to face what fate had thrown my way. At times, my hold on life had been weak but it had never broken, and the necklace had helped me muster the tiny remnants of remaining hope, primitive though they were, that would not let me give up. Now I understood the real beauty of life was its ability to adapt, to struggle and persist despite all our misfortune. I held tightly to the necklace, knowing Wu Sing would leave me once again.

'And one day soon,' she said joyfully, 'when you are gone, it will be another's turn to stand and watch the summer rain approach across the water, to hear the beating of raindrops on a shining surface, to smell the fresh, cool odour of a sweet cloudburst and to wonder at the joy of life and the sorrow of its departure. But you, my love, have found contentment in the wonder of it all and the truth within your own moment of time. Let that be enough. Love is never lost to the world; it is only the moments of time that pass unheeded and uncared for.'

I looked down at the necklace in my hand and thought of throwing it away, now that I didn't need it, but, remembering its importance in my life, I decided to hold onto it. I would no longer need to wear it, but I couldn't bring myself to part with it.

As quickly as the rain had burst upon me, it was gone, and with it went Wu Sing. It hurt to let her go, but now, finally, I was reconciled with our parting and able to embark on a journey of true redemption, a redemption made possible by my acceptance of the immense, ubiquitous power of God, who moves my universe while gifting me solace when in His presence.

*

And so it was that I came to understand that my generation had started with so much promise. We had been the best educated, best provided for generation that Australia had seen. We were born at a time when Australians enjoyed the highest percentage of home ownership and the most equitable distribution of the nation's wealth, yet we had been blighted by our failure in the Vietnam War, the shattering changes to the foundational values of our culture and a mad rush for accumulated wealth. In time, however, I came to be genuinely grateful for the blessings I enjoyed in my life, for the unconditional love and dedication bestowed upon me by loving parents, for the freedom afforded me by a country devoted to the values and principles of liberty, democracy and a regulated market economy and for the inherent ability I had to shape my own destiny.

From this sense of gratitude, I came once again to enjoy the pleasures of love and trust in my life. To love again the country of my youth. The captivating expanse of a wide, blue midday sky and a night sky full of countless stars. The beauty of an unending, wide beach with rhythmic waves breaking on its gleaming sands. The unbridled power of a surging river in dashing flood, the whispering gurgle of a sluggish creek or the quiet serenity of a peaceful billabong. The faint rustle of a gentle breeze as it plays with the scattered foliage of an evergreen Australian bush. The melodic calls of a tribe of magpies, or the jubilant laughter of a riot of kookaburras. The cracking lightning and booming thunder of an approaching thunderstorm. The cool, refreshing relief of rhythmic, summer rain as it falls on a hot, metal roof. The magnificent beauty of Australian cities, and the amazing technology and skill that not only built them but also keeps them running, as well as the crowded bustle of a generous, fair-minded people who inhabit them. These people I came once again to trust. Before, all this had been something out there, but now it was mine and my ownership made of me a slave. It would forever be my home, my own backyard, in which peace and trust and joy could always be found.

Today, a lot of people tell me how it was when young

Australians went overseas to bleed and die, and how it was when other young Australians took to the streets in protest, and a lot of people are wrong. What happened cannot be changed, and talk of what might have been or should have been is the preserve of those who face the haunting reality of a past constantly challenged by the shifting winds of an unstable present. The only certainty in life is this precise moment in time. Our past is gone, yet lingers in the darkened corners of our minds and our future continues to unfold in ways we can never predict.

AUTHOR'S FINAL WORDS

I have written three books in the hope that I might highlight some of the struggles and sacrifices that the present generation's ancestors made in creating this great nation of theirs. My reasoning is that all nations have a collective consciousness that carries them into their future. This collective consciousness, shaped by a shared understanding of their nation's history and destiny, will enable contemporary Australians to unite and take up the challenge laid down by those who went before them.

We can see what the successes and failures of our ancestors were by a rational, unbiased study of their history and the actions they took to defend what they valued most. We can also discover what they wanted to preserve by the writings they left behind for us. My three books, I hope, will help the present generation better understand what previous generations of Australians were prepared to sacrifice for the survival of their liberty.

As for what they wrote, the two great images that remain in sharp focus for me are what Banjo Paterson referred to as 'the vision splendid' in his poem 'Clancy of the Overflow' and what the former Australian Prime Minister, Ben Chifley, called 'the light on the hill' (derived from Matthew chapter 5 verse 14) in his 1949 Australian Labor Party conference speech. This vision and this light encourage each succeeding generation of Australians to love the unique beauty of this great country and to build, through hard work, self-reliance and prudent living, a more prosperous and fairer nation based on individual liberty, equal justice and equality of opportunity (with empathy for those who cannot compete) for all.

My conclusion is that today's generation should continue the struggle for these goals by using the same approach that their ancestors drew upon to build this great nation in the first place: namely, a rejection of ideological bigotry and an insistence on intelligent discussion based on reason, logic and critical thinking combined with the application of commonsense wisdom to decision making. They should also remember that previous generations showed gratitude and admiration for the great sacrifices and achievements of their ancestors and a love and appreciation of the unique beauty of their country. This is what united them and kept them striving for a better tomorrow, and it can be the same inspiration that will guide the present generation and unite them as they also, in their turn, strive for a better tomorrow.

OTHER BOOKS BY THIS AUTHOR

Broken Lives (Sid Harta, ISBN 9781925707663)
Kokoda Mist (Sid Harta, ISBN 9781922958099)

ABOUT THE AUTHOR

Kenneth Price is a retired Vietnam veteran. When he was seventeen, he enlisted into the Australian army and was trained as a medic. He was sent to Vietnam in 1968 and worked in a field ambulance and field hospital.

His grandfather served in the 9th Battalion in France from 1916 to 1918, and his father served in the Australian army during WWII. Kenneth's uncle also served as a bomber pilot in WWII and was shot down and killed in 1944.

After returning from Vietnam, Kenneth married and went to university where he graduated with Distinction in an Arts Degree, majoring in History and Literature. He also has a Bachelor of Education and a Masters (with Distinction) in Australian political history.

Kenneth spent fourteen years teaching History and English at Brisbane Grammar School and eight years as a lecturer in English in Singapore, where he helped his students obtain their O and A levels from Cambridge University.

Writing has always been his passion and, following retirement, he was inspired to research his family's military history. This led to writing his first book, *Broken Lives*, which covers some of the exploits of his grandfather's 9th Battalion.

Kenneth has six children and eleven grandchildren. He is currently married to his second wife and lives in Hervey Bay, Queensland.